TALK TALK

A NOVEL

T. Coraghessan Boyle

PENGUIN BOOKS

PENGUIN BOOKS

Published by the Penguin Group

Penguin Group (USA) Inc., 375 Hudson Street, New York, New York 10014, U.S.A. •
Penguin Group (Canada), 90 Eglinton Avenue East, Suite 700, Toronto, Ontario, Canada
M4P 2Y3 (a division of Pearson Penguin Canada Inc.) • Penguin Books Ltd, 80 Strand,
London WC2R 0RL, England • Penguin Ireland, 25 St Stephen's Green, Dublin 2, Ireland
(a division of Penguin Books Ltd) • Penguin Group (Australia), 250 Camberwell Road,
Camberwell, Victoria 3124, Australia (a division of Pearson Australia Group Pty Ltd) •
Penguin Books India Pvt Ltd, 11 Community Centre, Panchsheel Park, New Delhi – 110
017, India • Penguin Group (NZ), 67 Apollo Drive, Mairangi Bay, Auckland 1311, New
Zealand (a division of Pearson New Zealand Ltd.) • Penguin Books (South Africa) (Pty)
Ltd, 24 Sturdee Avenue, Rosebank, Johannesburg 2196, South Africa

Penguin Books Ltd, Registered Offices:
80 Strand, London WC2R 0RL, England

First published in the United States of America by Viking Penguin,
a member of Penguin Group (USA) Inc. 2006
Published in Penguin Books 2007

3 5 7 9 10 8 6 4 2

Grateful acknowledgment is made for permission to reprint an
excerpt from "From Love's First Fever to Her Plague" from *The Poems of Dylan Thomas*.
Copyright © by New Directions Publishing Corp.
Reprinted by permission of New Directions Publishing Corp.

PUBLISHER'S NOTE

This is a work of fiction. Names, characters, places, and incidents either are the product
of the author's imagination or are used fictitiously, and any resemblance to actual persons,
living or dead, business establishments, events, or locales is entirely coincidental.

THE LIBRARY OF CONGRESS HAS CATALOGED THE HARDCOVER EDITION AS FOLLOWS:
Boyle, T. Coraghessan.
Talk talk / T. Coraghessan Boyle.
p. cm.
ISBN 0-670-03770-2 (hc.)
ISBN 978-0-14-311219-8 (pbk.)
1. Deaf women—Fiction.   2. Identity theft—fiction.   I. Title
PS3552.O932T35 2006
813'.54—dc22   2005057470

Printed in the United States of America
Set in Minion • Designed by Francesca Belanger

Praise for *Talk Talk*

"T.C. Boyle's *Talk Talk* starts off fast and never lets go—and that's fun. . . . Boyle once again delivers an entertaining story with his usual laser commentary—about the way we identify ourselves and the role language plays."

— *USA Today*

"His most exciting novel yet . . . Boyle's new novel about identity theft is so perfectly aligned with the day's news that the FBI should search his house for stolen credit cards. *Talk Talk* grabs hold of the fragile structures that establish who we are and what we own and shakes them apart. . . . Boyle knows how to drill down through the surface of everyday life into our core anxieties, and he knows how to write constantly charging, heart-thumping chase scenes. . . . Boyle begins with the merely bureaucratic elements of identity, but soon he teases out the more profound ramifications of who we are and how we prove it. . . . The current perils of Internet security give *Talk Talk* a timely hook, but there's nothing ephemeral about the novel."

— *The Washington Post* (front page)

"By now Boyle possesses the unparalleled ability to create characters who can do far more than amuse. In fact, they're so absolutely human that they're annoying—in the way that humans are. . . . He's sweating not to make us sympathize with his creatures but to make us comprehend them. He lavishes his prodigious—and prodigiously humane— gifts on *how* they are, not *who* they are . . . it's not just the road but the scenery where the author marches out his chops. No character is too small to lavish with peculiar splendor."

— *Los Angeles Times* (front page)

"His least discursive, most tautly paced book to date, a tense thriller about a couple's ill-advised, cross-country pursuit of a twenty-first-century scourge: a dangerous identity thief. *Talk Talk* opens at full throttle and never slackens . . . a rage so intense that it overtakes reason runs through the book like a superhighway."

— *San Francisco Chronicle* (front page)

"Boyle takes the reader on a wild ride where sensation and thirst for justice overwhelm the need for likelihood . . . he never begs for a reader's sympathy on behalf of his protagonists . . . he depicts his characters in their pettiness and vexation, with their exonerating ambitions and addled schemes for fulfilling them . . . blessedly, Boyle never stoops to explaining his characters through the facile formulations of psychology. He allows them the dignity of being witnessed,

not decoded. They burn with primary passions . . . no one writes better about the wages of American sin. Or, if not wages exactly, sin purchased on credit, and that probably stolen."
—*The New York Times Book Review*

"The outrageously talented T.C. Boyle loves nothing more than demolishing a charlatan, and his fabulously entertaining fiction is packed with megalomaniacs, hypocrites, and overbearing nincompoops who make life hell for the intelligent and sensible mensch. When Boyle finds the delicate balance between his over-the-top satirical impulses and his startling sentimentality, no American novelist can touch him. . . . The novel flies along on the power of Boyle's propulsive and exquisitely perceptive prose." —*Entertainment Weekly*

"Funny, engaging, and suspenseful . . . using his gift for manic invention and freewheeling, hyperventilated prose, Mr. Boyle does an antic job of recounting the cat-and-mouse-and-cat game played by Dana and Peck, wittily dancing around his theme of identity and identity theft, even as he orchestrates a sense of foreboding and suspense . . . he manages here to mix clever narrative pyrotechnics with real character development." —*The New York Times*

"The normally extravagant T.C. Boyle tames himself in *Talk Talk* to deliver a chilling literary thriller. Or is it a horror story for our times? . . . Boyle has us in the fever grip of Peck's hostile takeover of Dana, the stealth attack of identity theft and the fear and fury it arouses." —*New York Daily News*

"Once again, Boyle examines a contemporary issue—identity theft—in very human terms with a very engaging story. . . . *Talk Talk* is a good read for summer or any season. On a deeper level, though, it's much more, an examination of identity that evolves from a fast-paced chase to something far more satisfying. It's a novel you'll be likely to talk about for a long time." —*St. Louis Post-Dispatch*

"From its fast and fluid pace, Boyle's new novel, *Talk Talk*, might seem like so much entertainment chatter, but embedded within it is a meditation on the nature of communication and identity. . . . His virtuosity at the quick-take description, and the slightly fevered feel of his prose, are on full display." —*Newsday*

"An identity-theft thriller that will appeal even to John Grisham readers . . . and for those who like a little literary meat in their summer page-turners, Boyle's knack for nuanced and intelligent characterization and language hasn't deserted him here . . . Although it's difficult to put *Talk Talk* down once the chase begins, few readers will be able to make it past the first chapters without frantically heading to the Internet to learn how to obtain their annual credit reports from those agencies the sage people who write financial columns are always hounding us to contact." —*Rocky Mountain News*

"Boyle brings a hard boil to a contemporary conundrum . . . he writes with great immediacy, his characters constantly in a state of motion, agitation and striving." —*New York Post*

"A dandy novel, complete with the timely subject of identity theft. . . . *Talk Talk* rarely falters, the sentences sharp and the characters well defined." —*The Atlanta Journal-Constitution*

"However unpatriotic this attitude is, identity thieves scare me more than terrorists. Reading T.C. Boyle's stirring new novel reinforces that anxiety . . . this novel is truly and movingly more about identity than about theft." —*The Miami Herald*

"In order to alleviate anxiety, I recommend readers run a quick credit check on themselves before they dig in. . . . Boyle successfully draws the reader in, so that we feel the tension of Dana's isolation in her silent world. . . . We sympathize with both the good guys and the bad guys. These worlds collide in unexpected ways and make this book a thriller, a page-turner formed by a master's hand. . . . Boyle writes with such authority it's a pleasure to bite your nails the whole way through." —*Pittsburgh Post-Gazette*

"*Talk Talk* makes the lurking danger of identity theft a dizzying reality. . . . A tricky novel of unlikely intimacies." —*O, The Oprah Magazine*

"This time Boyle delivers a fast-paced, edge-of-your seat thriller, applying his mastery of language and characterization to the compulsively readable mode of the commercial suspense novel. He proves that he can master his literary chops to maintain the tension as well as any old pro of the genre. . . . The great achievement of *Talk Talk* is the way the novel brings us into the moment-by-moment experience of its profoundly deaf central character. We feel and understand her every emotion and reaction." —*The Oregonian*

"If you are one of the 26.5 million veterans whose personal information was on that stolen laptop, stop reading right now. And under no circumstances should you buy *Talk Talk*, the latest novel by T.C. Boyle. The rest of us, though, will certainly enjoy the PEN/Faulkner Award winner's satirically clever take on that most modern of crimes, identity theft." —*The Christian Science Monitor*

PENGUIN BOOKS
ABOUT THE AUTHOR

T.C. Boyle is the author of the novels *The Inner Circle*, *Drop City* (a finalist for the National Book Award), *A Friend of the Earth*, *Riven Rock*, *The Tortilla Curtain*, *The Road to Wellville*, *East Is East*, *World's End* (winner of the PEN/Faulkner Award), *Budding Prospects*, *Water Music*, and eight collections of stories. In 1999, he was the recipient of the PEN/Malamud Award for Excellence in Short Fiction. His stories appear regularly in major American magazines, including *The New Yorker*, *GQ*, *Esquire*, *Harper's*, *McSweeney's*, and *Playboy*. He lives near Santa Barbara, California. T.C. Boyle's Web site is www.tcboyle.com.

For Russell Timothy Miller

and

in memory of Jack and Geraldine

Acknowledgments

I would like to thank Marie Alex, Jamieson Fry, Susan Abramson and Linda Funesti-Benton for their generous help and advice.

Author's Note

Except where indicated, it is not my intention to represent a literal translation of signed English, as a number of writers have done in the past, quite admirably, but rather to approximate what is being communicated by means of standard English dialogue.

We are our language, but our real language, our real identity, lies in inner speech, that ceaseless stream and generation of meaning that constitutes the inner mind.

—L. S. Vygotsky, *Thought and Language*

I learnt man's tongue, to twist the shapes of thoughts
Into the stony idiom of the brain,
. . .
I learnt the verbs of will, and had my secret;
The code of night tapped on my tongue;
What had been one was many sounding minded.

—Dylan Thomas,
"From love's first fever to her plague"

PART I

One

SHE WAS RUNNING LATE, always running late, a failing of hers, she knew it, but then she couldn't find her purse and once she did manage to locate it (underneath her blue corduroy jacket on the coat tree in the front hall), she couldn't find her keys. They should have been in her purse, but they weren't, and so she'd made a circuit of the apartment—two circuits, three—before she thought to look through the pockets of the jeans she'd worn the day before, but where were *they*? No time for toast. Forget the toast, forget food. She was out of orange juice. Out of butter and cream cheese. The newspaper on the front mat was just another obstacle. Piss-warm—was that an acceptable term? Yes—*piss-warm* coffee in a stained mug, a quick check of lipstick and hair in the rearview mirror, and then she was putting the car in gear and backing out onto the street.

She may have been peripherally aware of a van flitting by in the opposite direction, the piebald dog sniffing at a stain on the edge of the pavement, someone's lawn sprinkler holding the light in a shimmer of translucent beads, but the persistent beat of adrenaline—or nerves, or whatever it was—wouldn't allow her to focus. Plus, the sun was in her eyes, and where were her sunglasses? She thought she remembered seeing them on the bureau, in a snarl of jewelry—or was it the kitchen table, next to the bananas, and she'd considered taking a banana with her, fast food,

3

potassium, roughage, but then she figured she wouldn't because with Dr. Stroud it was better to have nothing at all in your stomach. Air. Air alone would sustain her.

To rush, to hurry, to fret: Old English and Latinate roots, the same sad connotative stab of meaning. She wasn't thinking clearly. She was stressed, stressed out, running late. And when she got to the four-way stop at the end of the block she felt momentarily blessed because there was no one there to stop for, yet even as she made a feint of slowing and shifted from neutral to second with a quick deft plunge of clutch and accelerator, she spotted the patrol car parked just up the street in the bruised shadow of an SUV.

There was a moment of suspended time, the cop frozen at the wheel of his car, she giving him a helpless exculpatory look, and then she was past him and cursing herself as she watched him pull a lazy U-turn behind her and activate the flashing lights. All at once she saw the world complete, the palms with their pineapple trunks and peeling skirts, the armored spines of the yucca plants climbing the hill, yellow rock, red rock, a gunmetal pickup slowing to gape at her where she'd pulled over on a tan strip of dirt, and below her, a descending expanse of tiled rooftops and the distant blue wallop of the Pacific, no hurry now, no hurry at all. She watched the cop—the patrolman—in her side mirror as he sliced open the door, hitched up his belt (they all did that, as if the belt with its Mace and handcuffs and the hard black-handled revolver were all the badge they needed) and walked stiffly to her car.

She had her license and registration ready and held them out to him in offering, in supplication, but he didn't take them, not yet. He was saying something, lips flapping as if he were chewing a wad of gristle, but what was it? It wasn't *License and registration,* but what else could it be? *Is that the sun in the sky? What's the square root of a hundred forty-four? Do you know why I pulled you over?* Yes. That was it. And she did know. She'd run a stop sign. Because she was in a hurry—a hurry to get to the dentist's, of all places—and she was running late.

"I know," she said, "I know, but . . . but I did shift down . . ."

He was young, this patrolman, no older than she, a coeval, a contemporary, somebody she might have danced alongside of—or with—at Velvet Jones or one of the other clubs on lower State. His eyes were too big for his head and they bulged out like a Boston terrier's—and what was that called? *Exophthalmia.* The word came to her and she felt a quick glow of satisfaction despite the circumstances. But the cop, the patrolman. There was a softness to his jaw, that when combined with the eyes—liquid and weepy—gave him an unfinished look, as if he weren't her age at all but an adolescent, a big-headed child all dressed up spick-and-span in his uniform and playing at authority. She saw his face change when she spoke, but she was used to that.

He said something then, and this time she read him correctly, handing him the laminated license and the thin wafer of the registration slip, and she couldn't help asking him what was the matter, though she knew her face would give her away. A question always flared her eyebrows as if she were being accusatory or angry, and she'd tried to work on that but with mixed success. He backed away from the car and said something further—probably that he was going to go back to his own vehicle and run a standard check on her license before writing out the standard ticket for running the standard stop sign—and this time she kept her mouth shut.

For the first few minutes she wasn't aware of the time passing. All she could think was what this was going to cost her, points on her license, the insurance—was it last year or the year before that she'd got her speeding ticket?—and that now she was definitely going to be late. For the dentist. All this for the dentist. And if she was late for the dentist and the procedure that was to take two hours minimum, as she'd been advised in writing to assure that there would be no misunderstanding, then she would be late for her class too and no one to cover for her. She thought of the problem of the telephone—she supposed she could use the dentist's receptionist as an intermediary, but what a hassle. *Hassle.* And what was the derivation of that? she wondered. She made a note to herself to look it up in her *Dictionary of American Slang* when she got home. But what was taking him so long? She had an urge to look over her shoulder, fix the glowing sun-blistered windshield with a withering stare, but she resisted the impulse and lowered her left shoulder to peer instead through the side mirror.

Nothing. There was a form there, the patrolman's form, a bulked-up shadow, head bent. She glanced at the clock on the dash. Ten minutes had passed since he'd left her. She wondered if he was a slow learner, dyslexic, the sort of person who would have trouble recollecting the particular statute of the motor vehicle code she stood in violation of, who would fumble with the nub of his pencil, pressing extra hard for the duplicate. A dope, a dummy, a half-wit. A *Neanderthal.* She tried out the word on her tongue, beating out the syllables—Ne-an-der-thal—and watched in the mirror as her lips pursed and drew back and pursed again.

She was thinking of her dentist, an inveterate talker, with eyebrows that seemed to crawl across his inverted face as he hung over her, oblivious to the fact that she couldn't respond except with grunts and deep-throated cries as the cotton wads throttled her tongue and the vacuum tube tugged at her lip, when the door of the police car caught the light as it swung open again and the patrolman emerged.

Right away she could see that something was wrong. His body language was different, radically different, the stiffness gone out of his legs, his shoulders hunched forward and his feet stalking the gravel with exaggerated care. She watched till his face loomed up in the mirror—his mouth drawn tight, his eyes narrowed and deflated—and then turned to face him.

That was when she had her first shock.

He was standing three paces back from the driver's door and he had his weapon drawn and pointed at her and he was saying something about her hands—barking, his face discomposed, furious—and he had to repeat himself, more furious each time, until she understood: *Put your hands where I can see them.*

At first, she'd been too scared to speak, numbly complying, stung by the elemental violence of the moment. He'd jerked her out of the car, the gun still on her, shoved her face into the hot metal and glass of her own vehicle and twisted her arms round behind her to clamp the cuffs over her wrists, the weight of him pressing into her until she felt him forcing her legs apart with the anvil of his knee. His hands were on her then, gripping her ankles first, sliding up her legs to her hips, her abdomen, her armpits, patting, probing. There was the sharp hormonal smell of him, of his contempt and outrage, his hot breath exploding in her ear with the fricatives and plosives of speech. He was brisk, brutal, sparing nothing. There might have been questions, orders, a meliorating softness in his tone, but she couldn't hear and she couldn't see his face—and her hands, her hands were caught like fish on a stringer.

Now, in the patrol car, in the cage of the backseat that was exactly like the cage they put stray dogs in, she felt the way they wanted you to feel: small, helpless, without hope or recourse. Her heart was hammering. She was on the verge of tears. People were staring at her, slowing their cars to get a good look, and there was nothing she could do but turn away in shame and horror and pray that one of her students didn't happen to be passing by—or anybody she knew, her neighbors, the landlord. She slouched down in the seat, dropped her head till her hair shook loose. She'd always wondered why the accused shielded their faces on the courthouse steps, why they tried so hard to hide their identities even when everyone in the world knew who they were, but now she understood, now she felt it for herself.

The color rose to her face—she was being *arrested*, and in public no less—and for a moment she was paralyzed. All she could think of was the shame of it, a shame that stung like some physical hurt, like the bite of an insect, a thousand insects seething all over her body—she could still feel the hot clamp of his hands on her ankles, her thighs. It was as if he'd burned her, scored her flesh with acid. She studied the back of the seat, the floormat, her right foot tapping and jittering with the uncontainable pulse of her nerves, and then all at once, as if a switch had been thrown in her brain, she felt the anger rising in her. Why should she feel shame? What had she done?

It was the cop. He was the one. He was responsible for all this. She lifted her eyes and there he was, the idiot, the pig, a pair of squared-off shoulders in the tight blue-black uniform, the back of his head as flat and rigid as a paddle strapped to his neck, and he was saying something into his radio, the microphone at his mouth even as the cruiser lurched out into the street and she felt herself flung helplessly forward against the seat restraint. Suddenly she was furious, ready to explode. What was wrong with him? What did he think, she was a drug dealer or something? A thief? A terrorist? She'd run a stop sign, for Christ's sake, that was all—a stop sign. *Jesus.*

Before she knew it, the words were out of her mouth. "Are you crazy?" she demanded, and she didn't care if her voice was too loud, if it was toneless and ugly and made people wince. She didn't care what she sounded like, not now, not here. "I said, are you crazy?"

But he wasn't hearing her, he didn't understand. "Listen," she said, "listen," leaning forward as far as the seat restraint would allow her, struggling to enunciate as carefully as she could, though she was choked and wrought up and the manacles were too tight and her heart was throbbing like a trapped bird trying to beat its way out of the nest, "there must be some mistake. Don't you know who I am?"

The world chopped by in a harsh savage glide, the car jolting beneath her. She strained to see his face reflected in the rearview mirror, to see if his lips were moving, to get a clue—the smallest hint, anything—as to what was happening to her. He must have read her her rights as he handcuffed her—*You have the right to remain silent* and all the rest of it, the obligatory phrases she'd seen on the TV screen a hundred times and more. But *why*? What had she done? And why did his eyes keep leaping from the road to the mirror and back again as if she couldn't be trusted even in the cage and the cuffs, as if he expected her to change shape, vomit bile, ooze and leak and smell? Why the hate? The bitterness? The intransigence?

It took her a moment, the blood burning in her veins, her face flushed with shame and anger and frustration, until she understood: it was a case of mistaken identity. Of course it was. Obviously. What else could it be? Someone who looked like her—some other slim graceful dark-eyed deaf woman of thirty-three who wasn't on her way to the dentist with a sheaf of papers she had to finish grading by the time her class met—had robbed a bank at gunpoint, shot up the neighborhood, hit a child and run. It was the only explanation, because she'd never violated the law in her life except in the most ordinary and innocuous ways, speeding on the freeway alongside a hundred other speeders, smoking the occasional joint when she was a teenager (she and Carrie Cheung and later Richie Cohen, cruising the neighborhood, high as—well, *kites*—but no one ever knew or cared, least of all the police), collecting the odd parking ticket or moving violation—all of which had been duly registered, paid for and expunged from her record. At least she thought they'd been. That parking ticket in Venice, sixty bucks and she was maybe two minutes late, the meter maid already writing out the summons even as she stood there pleading with her—but she'd taken care of that, hadn't she?

No, it was too much. The whole thing, the shock of it, the scare—and these people were going to pay, they were, she'd get an attorney, police brutality, incompetence, false arrest, the whole works. All right. All right, fine. If that was what they wanted, she'd give it to them. The car rocked beneath her. The cop held rigid, like a mannequin. She closed her eyes a moment, an old habit, and took herself out of the world.

They booked her, fingerprinted her, took away her pager and cell phone and her rings and her jade pendant and her purse, made her stand against a wall—cowed and miserable and with her shoulders slumped and her eyes vacant—for the lingering humiliation of the mug shot, and still nothing. No charges. No sense. The lips of the policemen flailed at her and she let her voice go till it must have grown wings and careened round the room with the dull gray walls and framed certificates and the flag that hung from a shining brass pole in limp validation of the whole corrupt and tottering system. She was beside herself. Hurt. Furious. Stung. "There must be some mistake," she insisted over and over again. "I'm Dana, Dana Halter. I teach at the San Roque School for the Deaf and I've never . . . I'm deaf, can't you see that? You've got the wrong person." She watched them shift and shrug as if she were some sort of freak of nature, a talking dolphin or a ventriloquist's dummy come to life, but they gave her nothing. To them she was just another criminal—another perp—one more worthless case to be locked away and ignored.

But they didn't lock her away, not yet. She was handcuffed to a bench that gave onto a hallway behind the front desk, and she didn't catch the explanation offered her—the cop, the booking officer, a man in his thirties who looked almost apologetic as he took her by the arm, had averted his face as he gently but firmly pushed her down and readjusted the cuffs—but it became clear when a bleached-out wisp of a man with a labile face and the faintest pale trace of a mustache came through the door and made his way to her, his hands already in motion. His name—he finger-spelled it for her—was Charles Iverson and he was an interpreter for the deaf. *I work at the San Roque School sometimes,* he signed. *I've seen you around.*

She didn't recognize him—or maybe she did. There was something familiar in the smallness and neatness of him, and she seemed to recollect the image of him in the hallway, his head down, moving with swift, sure strides. She forced a smile. "I'm glad you're here," she said aloud, lifting her cuffed hands in an attempt to sign simultaneously as she tended to do when she was agitated. "There's some huge mistake. All I did was run a four-way stop . . . and they, they"—she felt the injustice and the hurt of it building in her and struggled to control her face. And her voice. It must have jumped and planed off because people were staring—the booking officer, a secretary with an embellished figure and a hard plain face, two young Latinos stalled at the front desk in their canted baseball caps and voluminous shorts. *Put a lid on it,* that's what their body language told her.

Iverson took his time. His signing was rigid and inelegant but comprehensible for all that, and she focused her whole being on him as he explained the charges against her. *There are multiple outstanding warrants,* he began, *in Marin County, Tulare and L.A. Counties—and out of state too, in Nevada. Reno and Stateline.*

Warrants? What warrants?

He was wearing a sport coat over a T-shirt with the name of a basketball team emblazoned across the breast. His hair had been sprayed or gelled, but not very successfully—it curled up like the fluff of the chicks they'd kept under a heat lamp in elementary school, so blond it was nearly translucent. She watched him lift the lapel of his jacket and extract a folded sheet of paper from the inside pocket. He seemed to consider it a moment, weighing it like a knife, before dropping it to his lap and signing, *Failure to appear on a number of charges, different courts, different dates, over the past two years. Passing bad checks, auto theft, possession of a controlled substance, assault with a deadly weapon—the list goes on.* He held her eyes. His mouth was drawn tight, no sympathy there. It came to her that he believed the charges, believed that she'd led a double life, that she'd violated every decent standard and let the deaf community down, one more hearing prejudice confirmed. Yes, his eyes said, the deaf live by their own rules, inferior rules, compromised rules, they live off of us and on us. It was a look she'd seen all her life.

He handed her the sheet and there it all was, dates, places, the police department codes and the charges brought.

Incredibly, *her* name was there too, undeniably and indelibly, in caps, under Felony Complaint, Superior Court of this county or the other, and the warrant numbers marching down the margin of the page.

She looked up and it was as if he'd slapped her across the face. *I've never even been to Tulare County—I don't even know where it is. Or to Nevada either. It's crazy. It's wrong, a mistake, that's all. Tell them it's a mistake.*

The coldest look, the smallest Sign. *You get one phone call.*

Two

Bridger was at work, the morning obliterated by Starbucks and the twilit irreality of the long cool room at Digital Dynasty, seeing and hearing and breathing in the world within a world that was the screen before him. The scene—a single frame—was frozen there in a deep gloom of mahogany and copper tones, and he was working on a head replacement. His boss—Radko Goric, a thirty-eight-year-old entrepreneur wrapped in two-hundred-dollar designer shades, off-color Pierro Quarto jackets and clunky vinyl shoes out of the bargain bin—had underbid three other special effects companies for the contract on this picture, the last installment of a trilogy set on a distant and inimical planet where saurian warlords battled for dominance and human mercenaries shifted allegiance in observance of the tenets of an ancient warrior code. All well and good. He was a fan of the series—had seen the first two episodes six or seven times each, in fact, marveling at the detail, the sweep, the seamlessness of the effects—and he'd gone into the project with the best of intentions, a kind of euphoria even. But Rad (as he insisted on being called, and not Radko or Mr. Goric or Your Royal Highness) had given them zero leeway as far as the time frame was concerned. The film was due to premiere in less than a month and Bridger and his five co-workers were putting in twelve-hour days, seven days a week.

For a long while, he just stared at the screen, his chin propped on two pale fists that seemed to have gone bone-less on him. The world was there, right there in front of him, much more immediate and real than this cubicle, these walls, the ceiling, the painted cement floor, and he was inside it, drifting, dreaming, sleeping with his eyes open. He was beat. Dead. His fingers were limp, his backside blis-tered. He'd been wearing the same socks three days run-ning. And now he could feel an exhaustion headache building inside his skull like the turd-brown clouds that roiled Drex III, the planet he shaded and scored and pol-ished to the gleam of a dagger's edge with the assistance of his Discreet software and a finger-worn mouse. The coffee did nothing for him. It had been Banjo's turn to go for Star-bucks during coffee break, and he'd ordered a venti with a shot of espresso, and there it was, half-consumed, and all he felt was queasy. And sleepy, drowsy, narcoleptic. If only he could lay his head down, just for a minute . . .

But he had a message. From Deet-Deet. The icon popped up in the corner of his screen, and he opened it to find a cartoon image of a peg-legged pirate waving a cut-lass, onto which Deet-Deet had grafted an outsized cutout of Radko's head. The text read: *Har-har-har, me hearties! You'll all walk the plank if this project isn't in the bag by the thirtieth—and no snoozing on the job!*

This was the way they kept their sanity. The work was drudgery, piecework, paint and roto at twenty-five dollars and seventy-two cents an hour, before taxes, and while it had its moments of artistic satisfaction—like painting out the wires on the tiny flying bodies hurled into the scabrous skies by one nasty extraterrestrial explosion or another—essentially it was a grind. The head replacement shot Bridger had been working on all the previous day and into this soporific morning involved superimposing the three-dimensionally photographed face of the film's action hero, Kade (or *The* Kade, as he was now being billed), over the white helmet of a stuntman on a futuristic blade-sprouting chopper that shot up a ramp and off a cliff to skim one of Drex III's lakes of fire and propel its driver into the heart of the enemy camp, where he would proceed to hack and gouge and face-kick one hapless lizard warrior after another. It wasn't exactly what Bridger had imagined himself doing six years out of film school—he'd pictured a trajectory more like Fincher's or Spielberg's—but it was a living. A good living. And it was in the industry.

What he did now was superimpose The Kade's head over Radko's—he had The Kade winking and grinning, then grimacing (the look when the bike lands amongst the saurian legions with a sacroiliac-jarring thump) and finally winking again—and messaged his reply: *Scuttle the ship and bring me coffee, my kingdom for a cup, another cup.* He added a P.S., his favorite quotation from *Miss Lonelyhearts,* which he made a point of inserting wherever it applied: *Like a dead man, only friction could warm him or violence make him mobile.*

And then, from the physical distance of two cubicles over and the hurtling unbridgeable interstices of cyberspace, Plum chimed in, and then Lumpen, Pixel and Banjo, and everybody was awake again and the new day that was exactly like the preceding day and the day before that began to unfold.

He was painting out the vestigial white edges around The Kade's head and beginning to think about breakfast (bagel and cream cheese) or maybe lunch (bagel and cream cheese with lox, sprouts and mustard), when his cell began to vibrate. Radko didn't like to hear any buzzing or carillons during working hours because he didn't want his employees distracted by personal calls, just as he didn't want them surfing the Web, going to chat rooms or instant messaging, so Bridger always kept his cell phone on vibrate, and he always kept it in his right front pocket so that he could be instantly alerted to the odd crepitating motion of it and take his calls on the sly. "Hello?" he said, keeping his voice in the range of a propulsive whisper.

"Yes, hello. This is Charles Iverson with the San Roque Police Department. I'm an interpreter for the deaf and I have Dana Halter here."

"*Police?* What's the problem? Has there been an accident or something?"

"This is Dana," the voice said, as if it were the instrument of a medium channeling a spirit. "I need you to come down here and bail me out."

"For what? What did you do?"

"I don't know," the voice said, the man's voice, low-pitched and with a handful of gravel in it, "but I ran a stop sign and now they think I—"

There was a pause. The Kade stared back at him from the screen, grimacing, the left side of his head still encumbered with three-quarters of his white halo. Overhead, the barely functional fluorescent lights briefly brightened and then dimmed again, one tube or another eternally going bad. Plum—the only female among them—got up from her cubicle and padded down the hall in the direction of the bathroom.

Iverson's voice came back: "—they think I committed all these crimes, but"—a pause—"I didn't."

"Of course you didn't," he said, and he pictured Dana there in some anonymous police precinct, her face angled away from the phone and the man with the voice signing to her amidst the mug shots and wanted posters, and the picture wasn't right. "I thought you were supposed to be at the dentist's," he said. And then: "Crimes? What crimes?"

"I was," Iverson said. "But I ran a stop sign and the police arrested me." There was more—Bridger could hear Dana's voice in the background—but the interpreter was giving him the shorthand version. Without further elaboration he read off the list of charges as if he were a waiter reciting the specials of the day.

"But that's crazy," Bridger said. "You didn't, I mean, she didn't—"

"Time's up," Iverson said.

"Listen, I'll be right there. Ten minutes or less." Bridger glanced up as Plum slipped back into her cubicle, dropping his voice to the breath of a whisper. "What's the bail? I mean, what does it cost?"

"What? Speak up. I can't hear you."

Radko was coming down the hall now and Bridger leaned deeper into the cubicle to mask the phone. "The bail—how much?"

"It hasn't been set yet."

"All right," he said. "All right. I'll be right there. Love you."

There was a pause. "Love you too," Iverson said.

He'd never been to the San Roque Police Station and he had to look up the address in the phone book, and then, when he turned down the street indicated, he was startled to see it lined on both sides with idle patrol cars. It took him a while to find a parking spot, circling the block again and again till one of the cruisers finally pulled out and he cautiously signaled his intention and did an elaborate and constrained job of parallel parking between two black-and-whites. He was agitated. He was in a hurry. But this was hardly the time or place for a fender bender or even a bumper-kiss.

A puffing bloated woman who seemed to have a crust of dried blood rimming her eye sockets—or was that makeup?—was stumping up the steps ahead of him and he had the presence of mind to hold the door for her, which in turn gave him a moment to compose himself. His relations with the police over the course of his adult years had been minimal and strictly formal ("All right, out of the car") and he'd been arrested exactly twice in his life, once for shoplifting when he was fourteen and then, in college, for driving under the influence. He understood theoretically that the police were the servants and protectors of the public—that is, *his* servants and protectors—but for all that he couldn't help experiencing a sudden rapid uptick of alarm and a queasy sense of culpability whenever he saw a cop on the street. Even rent-a-cops gave him pause. No matter: he followed the bloated woman through the door.

Inside, a waist-high counter divided the public space (flags, both state and federal, fierce overhead lights, linoleum that gleamed as if in defiance of the bodily fluids and street filth that were regularly deposited on its surface) from the inner sanctum, where the police and detectives had their desks and a discreet hallway led presumably to the holding cells. Where Dana was. Even as he walked up to the counter, he shifted his eyes to the hallway, as if he might be able to catch a glimpse of her there, but of course he couldn't. She was already locked up in some pen with a bunch of prostitutes, drunks, violent offenders, and the thought of it made him go cold. They'd be all over her. It wasn't as if she couldn't handle herself—she was the most insistently independent woman he'd ever met—but she was naïve, too sympathetic for her own good, and as soon as they discovered she was deaf they'd have a wedge to use against her. He thought of the way street people would hit on her whenever he took her anywhere, as if she were their special emissary, as if her handicap—he had to check himself: her *difference*—reduced her somehow to their level. Or lower. Lower still.

But this was all a misunderstanding. Obviously. And he would have her out before they could get their hooks in her, no matter what it took. He waited his turn behind the fat woman, checking his watch reflexively every five seconds. Ten past eleven. Eleven past. Twelve. The fat woman was complaining about her neighbor's dog—she couldn't sleep, couldn't eat, couldn't think, because it barked so relentlessly, and she'd called the police, this very precinct, twenty-two times already and had a log of each phone call going back fifteen months to prove it. And were they going to do anything about it? Or did she have to stand here at this desk till she dropped dead? Because she would if that's what it took. She'd stand right here.

Radko hadn't been pleased when he begged off work. "It's Dana," Bridger had said, flagging him down on his way to the refrigerator. Bridger was already on his feet, already patting down his pockets for the car keys. "She's been arrested. It's an emergency."

The lights fluttered, darkened. Drex III glowed menacingly from the screen—there were twenty-seven days left till it was due to take its place in the firmament among the other interstellar spheres. Radko took a step back and squinted at him out of his heavy-lidded eyes. "Emergency?" he repeated. "For what? People they get thrown in jail every day."

"No," Bridger said, "you don't understand. She didn't do anything. It's a mistake. I need to, well—I know this sounds crazy but I need to go down there and bail her out. Right now."

Nothing. Radko compressed his lips and gave him a look Pixel had described in a sudden flare of inspiration as "Paranoia infests the frog."

20

"I mean, I can't leave her there. In a cell. Would you want to be stuck in a cell?"

Wrong question. "In my country," Radko intoned, "people they are born in cells, they give birth in cells, they die in cells."

"Is that good?" Bridger threw back at him. "Is that why you came here?"

But Radko just turned away from him, waving a hand in the air. "Pffft!" was all he had to add.

"I'm going," Bridger said, and he could see Plum leaning out of her carrel to savor the spectacle. "Just so you know—I don't have any choice."

Heavily, one hand on the door of the refrigerator, the other describing a quick arc as he swung round to point an admonitory finger, Radko rumbled, "One hour. One hour max. Just so *you* know."

The officer at the desk—balding on top, sideburns gone white, milky exasperated eyes glancing up over the reading glasses riding the bridge of his nose—reassured the fat woman in soft, placatory tones, but the fat woman wasn't there for reassurance; she was there for action. The more softly the policeman spoke, the more the woman's voice seemed to rise, till finally he turned away from her and gestured across the room. A moment later, a much younger officer—a ramrod Latino in a uniform that looked custom-fit—beckoned to her from a swinging door that led into the offices proper. The man at the desk said: "This is Officer Torres. He's going to help you. He's our dog expert. Isn't that right, Torres?"

The second man took the cue, not a hint of amusement on his face. "Oh, yeah," he said. "That's right. I'm the dog man."

And then the man at the desk turned to Bridger. "Yes?" he said.

Bridger shuffled his Nikes, focused on a spot just to the left of the cop's head and said, "I'm here for Dana. Dana Halter?"

Two hours later, he was still waiting. This was a Friday, a Friday afternoon now, and things seemed to be moving slowly, in a quiet retrograde tumble toward the weekend and the fomenting parade of drunks and brawlers who could go ahead and set the place on fire for all these putty-faced men and women cared, these desk-hounds and functionaries and sleepwalkers with the thousand-yard stares. They were going home at five o'clock to drink a beer and put their feet up and until then they were going to shuffle back and forth to the filing cabinets and peck at their computers in a zone where nobody, least of all Bridger, could reach them. He had managed to pry a few essential nuggets of information from the cop with the white sideburns— Yes, they'd brought her in; No, bail hadn't been set yet; No, he couldn't see her; No, he couldn't talk to her—and after that he'd stationed himself on a bench by the doorway with nothing to read and nothing to do but wait.

There were four other people waiting along with him: a very old man in a heavy suit who held himself so perfectly erect his jacket never made contact with the back of the bench; a Middle Eastern woman of indeterminate age, dressed in what might have been a caftan or a sacramental robe of some sort, and beside her, her ceaselessly leg-kicking son who looked to be five or so, but Bridger wasn't much acquainted with kids and the more he observed this one the less certain he was about that estimate—actually, the kid could have been anywhere from three to twelve; and, seated farthest from him, a girl in her late teens/early twenties who wasn't particularly attractive in either face or figure, but who began to take on a certain allure after two hours of surreptitious study. Beyond that, probably a hundred people had scuffed in and out of the place, most of them conferring in quiet deferential tones with the cop at the desk and then bowing their way back out the door. The fat woman had long since returned to her barking zone.

Bridger was profoundly bored. He had a difficult time sitting still under any circumstances, unless he was absorbed in a video game or letting his mind drift into the poisonous atmosphere of Drex III or some other digitized scenario, and he found himself fidgeting almost as much as the child (who had never ceased kicking his legs out and drawing them back again, as if the bench were an outsized swing and he was trying to lift them all up and away and out of this stupefying place). For long periods, Bridger stared into the middle distance, thinking nothing, thinking of bleakness and the void, and then, inevitably, his fears for Dana would materialize again, and he'd see her face, the sweet confusion of her mouth and the way she knitted her brows when she posed a question—*What time is it? Where did you say the omelet pan was? How many jiggers of triple sec?*—and his stomach would churn with anxiety. And hunger. Simple hunger. It occurred to him that he'd had neither the breakfast bagel nor the lunch—he'd had nothing but Starbucks, in fact—and he could feel the acidity creeping up his throat. What was wrong with these people? Couldn't they answer a simple question? Process a form? Dispense some information in a timely fashion?

He cautioned himself to stay calm, though that was difficult, given that he'd already called Radko six times and Radko had become increasingly impatient with each call in the sequence. "I'll work till midnight," Bridger promised, "I swear." Radko's voice, bottom-heavy and thick with the bludgeoning consonants of his transported English, came back at him in minor detonations of meaning: "You bed-der," he said. "You betcha. All through night, not just mid-night." But he was being selfish, he told himself. Imagine Dana, imagine what she was going through. He fought off the image of her locked up in a cell with half a dozen strangers, women who would mock her to her face, make demands, get physical with her. Dana would be all but help-less in that arena, the strange flat uninflected flutter of her voice that he found so compelling nothing but a provoca-tion to them, angry women, hard women, needy women. It was all a mistake. It had to be.

And then he was focusing on nothing, the cop at the desk, his fellow sufferers in Purgatory, the dreary walls and glowing floors all melding in a blur, and he was revisiting the first time he'd laid eyes on her, just over a year ago. It was at a club. He'd gone out after work with Deet-Deet, both of them frazzled, their eyes swollen and twitching as an aftereffect of fixating on their monitors from ten a.m. till past eight in the evening, the Visine they passed back and forth notwithstanding. First they'd gone for sushi and downed a couple of cold sakes each, and then, because they just had to unwind even though it was a Monday and the whole dreary week stretched out before them like a cinema-scape out of *Dune*, they decided to go clubbing and see what turned up. At the time, Deet-Deet had just broken up with his girlfriend and Bridger was unattached himself (go-ing on three fruitless months), and so, especially after two sakes, this had seemed like a plan.

They were waiting in line in front of Doge, ten-thirty at night, the mist coming in off the sea to insert itself in the al-leys and make the pavement shine under the headlights of the slow-rolling traffic, when Deet-Deet interrupted his monologue about the faults and excesses of his ex long enough to light a cigarette and Bridger took the opportunity to lift his head and check out their prospects. This particular club was open to the street so that the pulse of the music and the jumpy erratic flash of the strobe leaked out onto the sidewalk where the prospective patrons could get a look in advance and decide whether it was worth the five-dollar cover charge. Bridger observed the usual mass of bodies swaying under the assault of the music (or of the bass, which was about all you could hear), limbs flung out and retracted, people decapitated by a slash of the strobe even as their heads were restored in the next instant, knees lifted, butts thumping, the same scenario that had played out the night before and would play out the next night and the night after that. His eyes throbbed. The sake sucked the moisture from his brain. He was about to tell Deet-Deet he was having second thoughts about the club, about any club, because he could feel a headache coming on and it was only Monday and they had to keep sight of the fact that they were required to be in by ten to paint out the wires on the interminable martial arts movie they'd been working on for the past three weeks, when he spotted Dana.

She was poised at the edge of the dance floor, right up against one of the big standing speakers, lifting and dropping her feet—her bare feet—to the pulse of the bass and working her elbows as if she were doing aerobics or climbing the StairMaster. Or maybe, somewhere in her mind, she was square dancing, do-si-do and swing your partner. Her eyes were closed tight. Her knees jerked and her feet rose and fell. The red filter caught her hair and set it afire.

"So what do you think, anything worthwhile?" Deet-Deet was saying. Deet-Deet was five foot four and a half inches tall, he was twenty-five years old and he affected the Goth style, despite the fact that most of the SFX world had long since moved on to a modified geek/Indie look. His real name was Ian Fleischer, but at Digital Dynasty people went by their online aliases only, whether they liked it or not. Bridger himself was known as "Sharper" because when he'd first started as a dust-buster, when he was earnest and committed and excited about the work they were doing, he was always hounding the Scan-Record people for sharper plates to clean. "Because I don't know if I want to stay out too late," Deet-Deet added, by way of elucidation, "and that sake, I think, is really starting to hit me. What do you mix with that, anyway—beer? Beer, I guess, right? Stick to beer?"

Bridger wasn't listening. He was letting the lights trigger something inside him, allowing the music to seep in and transfigure his mood. The line moved forward—maybe ten people between him and the bouncer—and he moved with it. He had a new angle now—a new perspective from which to study this girl, this woman, heroically fighting her way against the music at the edge of the dance floor. Up came her knees, down went her fists, out swung her elbows. Her movements weren't jerky or spastic or out of sync with the beat—or not exactly. It was as if she were attuned to some deeper rhythm, a counter-rhythm, some hidden matrix beneath the surface of the music that no one else—not the dancers, the DJ or the musicians who'd laid down the tracks—was aware of. It fascinated him. She fascinated him.

"Sharper? You with me?" Deet-Deet was gaping up at him like a child lost at the fair. "I was saying, I don't know if I—you see anything worthwhile in there?" He raised himself up on his toes to get a better look. The music collapsed suddenly and then reassembled around the bass line of the next tune. "Her? Is that what you're looking at?"

They were almost at the door, twenty-five or thirty

people gathered behind them, the mist shining on everything now, on the streetlights, the palms, people's hair.

Deet-Deet tried one last time: "You want to go in? Think it's worth the five bucks tonight?"

It took him a moment, because he was distracted—or no, he was mesmerized. He'd been involved in two major relationships in his life, one in college and the one—with Melissa—that had died off three months ago with the sound of a tree falling in the woods when no one's there to hear it. Something tugged at him, the irresistible force, an intuition that sparked across the eroded pan of his consciousness like the flash of the strobe. "Oh, yeah," he said, "I'm going in."

Now, as he pulled himself up out of the haze of recollection to see that the woman with the child had vaporized and the cop with the white sideburns had been replaced by a female with drooping, possibly sympathetic eyes, he got to his feet. What time was it? Past four. Radko would have a fit. He'd had a fit. He was having a fit now. Bridger had missed an entire afternoon at work just when the team needed him most—and what had he accomplished aside from having a nice nap at the public's expense on a choice buttock-smoothed bench in the downtown San Roque Police Station? Nothing. Nothing at all. Dana was still locked up back there someplace and he was still here, clueless. He felt the irritation rise in him, a sudden spike of anger he could barely contain, and in order to calm himself he strode over to a display of pamphlets—*How to Protect Yourself on the Street; How to Burglar-Proof Your Home; Identity Theft: What Is It?*—and made a pretense of absorbing the sage information dispensed there. He gave it a moment, then casually turned to the desk.

"Hello," he said, and the woman lifted her eyes from the

form she was filling out. "My name's Bridger Martin and I've been waiting here since just past eleven—in the morning—and I was just wondering if you could maybe help me . . ."

She said nothing, because why bother? He was a petitioner, a special pleader, a creature of wants and needs and demands, no different from the thousands of others who'd stood here before him, and he would get to the point in his own way and in his own time, she knew that. The prospect seemed to bore her. The counter and the computers and the walls and the floors and the lights bored her too—Bridger bored her. Her fellow officers. Her shoes, her uniform: everything was a bore and a trial, ritualized, clichéd, without beginning or end. Her eyes told him that, and they weren't nearly as sympathetic as he'd thought, not up close, anyway. And her lips—her lips were tightly constricted, as if she were fighting some facial tic.

"It's my—my *girlfriend*. She's been arrested and we don't really know why. I took the whole afternoon off from work just to come down here and"—this was movie dialogue and the phrase stuck to the roof of his mouth—"bail her out, but nobody knows what the bail is or even what the charges are?" He made a question of it, a plea.

She surprised him. Her lips softened. The humanity—the fellow-feeling and sympathy—came back into her eyes. She was going to help. She was going to help, after all. "Name?" she queried.

"Dana," he said. "Dana Halter, H-a-l-t-e-r."

She was hitting the keys even as he superfluously spelled out the name and he watched her face as she studied the screen. She was pretty for a middle-aged woman, or almost pretty, now that the vise of her mouth had come unclamped. But he wanted to be charitable, wanted to be helped, babied, led by the hand—she was beautiful, wielder of the sword of justice, radiant with truth. At least for the few seconds it took to bring up the information. Then she lost her animation and became less than pretty all over again. Her eyes were hard suddenly, her mouth small and bitter. "We don't know what we've got here," she said tersely, "—the charges are still coming in. And because of the Nevada thing, it looks like the Feds are going to be interested."

"Nevada thing?"

"Interstate. Passing bad checks."

"Bad checks?" he echoed in disbelief. "She never—" he began, and then caught himself. "Listen," he said, "help me out here: what does it mean, because it's obviously all a mistake, mistaken identity or something explicable like that. I just want to know when I can get her out on bail? And where do I go?"

The faintest flicker of amusement lifted the corners of her mouth. "She's got no-bail holds in at least two counties because she walked in the past, which means I don't see anything happening till Monday—"

"Monday?" he echoed, and it was almost a yelp, he couldn't help himself.

A beat. Two. Then her lips were moving again: "At the earliest."

Three

THEY PUT HER IN A CELL that had been freshly scoured by some unseen presence, the caged lights glaring down from above, a residuum of drying mop strokes fanning out from the stainless-steel toilet set like a display model in the center of the room. The smell of the disinfectant, a chemical burn lingering on the clamped close air of the place, made her eyes water, and for the first few minutes she tried to breathe through her mouth only, but that just seemed to make it worse. She backed up against the gray cement wall with its hieroglyphs of furtive graffiti and rubbed at her eyes—and these were not tears, definitely not tears, because she wasn't intimidated and she wasn't scared or sorrowful in the least. She was—what was the word she wanted?— *frustrated*, that was all. Maddened. Outraged. Why wouldn't anyone listen to her? She could have written a deposition for them if somebody had thought to hand her a pen and a sheet of paper. And the interpreter, Iverson—he was all but useless, because in his eyes she was guilty until proven innocent, and that was wrong, just plain wrong. She needed somebody sympathetic. She needed a lawyer. An advocate. She needed Bridger.

He was here now—she could feel it. In this very building, in the front office with all those vacant policemen and hard-edged secretaries, straightening things out. He'd explain it all to them, he'd talk for her, do whatever it took to get her out—go to the bank, the bail bondsman, harangue the judge and the district attorney and anybody else whose ear he could bend. If he could just show them their mistake—it was some other Dana Halter they wanted; you'd have to be blind not to see that—they'd understand and come and release her. Any minute now. Any minute now the warder would shove through the heavy steel door at the end of the hallway and unlock the cell and lead her back into the light of day and they'd all bend over backward apologizing to her, the cop at the desk, the arresting officer, Iverson, with his punctilious mouth and accusatory eyes and his unforgivably sloppy signing . . .

In her agitation—in her fury and sickness at heart—she found that she was pacing round and round the toilet, which was the single amenity in that strictly and minimally functional space aside from the two bunks bolted to the walls, and she wasn't ready to sit down yet. She spoke to herself, told herself to calm down, and maybe she moved her lips, maybe she was speaking aloud, maybe she was. Not that it mattered. There was no one there to hear her, Friday morning an unlikely time to be arrested and locked away. The real criminals were in bed still, and the rest of them— the wife beaters, binge drinkers, motorcycle freaks—were at work, warming up for Friday night. TGIF. She remembered how in college she treasured Friday night above all, as the one time she could get really loose, looser than Saturday because Saturday gave onto Sunday and Sunday was diminished by the prospect of Monday and the whole round of classes and papers and tests starting up all over again. She would go out with her girlfriends on Fridays, drink a few beers, a shot of Cuervo, dance till the pulse of the music branched up from the soles of her feet and radiated through her body so she almost felt she could hear it just like anybody else. The release was what she craved, just that, because she'd had to work so hard to overcome her disability—and she still worked harder than anybody she knew, driving herself with an internal whip that kept all her childhood wounds open and grieving in the flesh, alive to the mockery of her classmates at school, the onus of being branded slow, one of the deaf and dumb. Dumb. They called *her* dumb when she was the equal of anybody in the hearing world, anybody out there beyond these walls. They were the idiots. The cops. The judges. The interpreters.

Friday night. She and Bridger were planning to go out for Thai and then to a movie he'd worked on, some kung fu extravaganza with actors flying around like Peter Pan on invisible wires. She'd been looking forward to it all through her long crazy work week, final papers coming in from her students, endless conferences and department meetings and hardly a moment to focus on her own writing, bills piling up and no time to sit down and balance her checkbook let alone mollify the gas and electric and American Express and Visa, and on top of it all the ceaseless fulminating throb of that molar on the bottom left—and she wondered if anybody had gotten word to Dr. Stroud?

But there was the toilet. Or the throne, as her mother used to call it. She couldn't help musing over the expression (was that jailhouse jargon, was that where the trope had come from?), and then she realized that she had to use it, the piss-warm coffee converted to urine—to *piss* itself—and she looked to the adjoining cell and the empty hallway and to the big steel door. Did they have cameras here? Was some dirty jailer or infantile cop watching a monitor in a musty back office and waiting for the moment when she would lift her skirt and perch on the stainless-steel seat? The thought of it made her burn all over again. She wouldn't give them the satisfaction—she'd rather reabsorb her own wastes, die of a burst bladder. She kept pacing round and round the throne, practicing thought control and comforting herself with the notion that she'd be out before she knew it, and then she'd use the ladies' room in the courthouse like any other innocent.

Time passed. How much, she couldn't say. There were no windows here and they'd taken her watch from her and in her world there were no church towers marking off the quarter hour or birds calling down the close of day. For her, it was as quiet at rush hour as it was for the hearing in the dead of night—or no: quieter, quieter by far. They heard crickets, didn't they? Ambient noise, the sound of the refrigerator starting up, the piping distant howl of a coyote on its prey, a car lost somewhere in the glutinous web of the night? They heard all that in books. They heard it on TV and in horror films. *Loud noise,* prompted the closed captioning. *Sound of glass shattering. A scream.* She didn't hear it. She heard nothing. She lived in a world apart, her own world, a better world, and silence was her refuge and her hard immutable shell and she spoke to herself from deep in the unyielding core of it. That was her essence, her true self, the voice no one could detect even if they wore the highest-decibel hearing aids or cochlear implants or marched thunderously through the world of the hearing. That they couldn't touch. Nobody could.

At some point, she stopped pacing. She was tired suddenly, overburdened, and she eased herself down on the edge of the bunk. For a long while she just sat there, her back slumped, one foot jiggling as she slipped the heel of her shoe off and on, off and on. It was all too much. Here she was, caged up like an animal, and for what? For stupidity. Incompetence. Some paper-shuffler's error. The thing that irritated her the most, more than the injustice and inanity of the whole business, more than Iverson and the cops and everybody else who supported this faltering twisted half-witted bureaucracy, was the waste of her time. Her student papers were in her car—which had no doubt been impounded at this point—and she'd have to skip dinner and the movie and any notion of spending the night at Bridger's, because now she'd have to stay up half the night correcting them. Which she could be doing right now, right here, in her enforced solitude. And her book. She'd vowed to herself—and to Bridger too—that she'd stick with it, a page a day, until it was done. What a joke. She'd been behind all month—it was more like a paragraph a day, if she was lucky—and she'd been looking forward to making up for it over the weekend, tapping away at her laptop while Bridger slept in, a cup of chai to grease the wheels, the morning unfolding in a sure steady flow of inspiration and the promise of summer break on the horizon.

Or now. What was wrong with now? Hadn't Jean Genet written *Our Lady of the Flowers* in prison? On scraps of toilet paper, no less? She wanted to get up and rattle the bars like Cagney or Edward G. Robinson in one of those old movies she revered and Bridger hated, rattle the bars and holler till they came running with a ballpoint pen and a spiral notebook. It was almost funny. And it would be riotous in the telling, her own personal reality show: "Use a Car and Go to Jail." Dr. Stroud would find it hilarious, wouldn't he, with two hours of dead time on his hands? And her students. And the headmaster, Dr. Koch—wouldn't he find it a scream, one of his teachers in the calaboose instead of the classroom?

Lots of laughs, oh, yeah. But she had to pee. It was an imperative now, no mere feeling of congestion or malaise or a vague gnawing urge—if she didn't use the toilet this very minute she was going to lose control, and how would Bridger feel taking her in his arms in front of all those cops and secretaries with a long dark stain trailing down the front of her skirt?

Her back was to the door when it opened, but she turned immediately, just as if she'd heard the slap of the approaching footsteps, the chime of the keys and the ratcheting groan of the iron hinges. All her life she'd been attuned to the slightest changes in the currents of the air, to rhythms and vibrations, to the vaguest scent or the faintest fleeting rumor of a touch the hearing wouldn't even begin to notice. She had to be, just to survive. And it was no parlor trick, as her hearing friends suspected, especially in grade school when her mother immersed her in the hearing world, mainstreamed her in a school where she was the only deaf child among eight hundred and more, the neighborhood kids creeping up the steps to her bedroom to stealthily push open the door and find her staring at them—no, it was elementary biology. When you were deprived of one sense, the neural pathways reconfigured themselves to boost the others, nature's synesthesia, and how many times had she adduced Ray Charles and Stevie Wonder as examples?

She looked up now to witness a moment of drama at the open door of the cell: two policewomen, blocky, clumsy, heavy in the breasts and buttocks, their faces bright with duress, were leaning into a third woman as if she were a stalled car they were pushing down the street. Hands flew like birds, shoulders stiffened, and the third woman—the prisoner—stood erect against her jailers, wedging her own right shoulder between the bars and jerking her wrists against the grip of the handcuffs. All three were shouting and cursing—the familiar lip-pop of "fuck you" running from mouth to mouth, as if it were contagious, like a yawn—and the policewomen were grunting with the effort to force the prisoner into the cell. *Ugh, ugh, ugh*—Dana had no idea what a grunt sounded like, but she saw it as it was written on the page and put it in their gasping mouths. The whole thing, the whole *danse macabre* with its kicks and flailings and ugly exploding violence, went on far longer than she would have imagined, a rocking back and forth, ground gained and lost, until finally the big-shouldered women prevailed and the prisoner was flung spinning into the cell. She took three reeling steps and then collided with the toilet and went down as if she'd been shot.

Both of the policewomen worked their mouths in an angry tearing way while the shorter and stouter one twisted the key in the lock, and then they squared their shoulders and stamped angrily up the hall, where the bolted steel door swung open for them on cue. As for the woman on the floor, she didn't move. She was stunned—or worse. Dana rose tentatively from the cot. Was there blood? No, no blood. What she was seeing was the woman's hair, dark and matted, pooling under the cheek that was pressed to the floor.

She didn't know what to do. The woman needed help, obviously, but what if she was violent or drunk—or both? She was breathing, that much was evident from the rise and fall of her rib cage, and there didn't seem to be any bruise or swelling where her head had struck the scuffed tile of the floor, or not that Dana could see from this angle. She wouldn't have gone down so hard if the police had bothered to remove the handcuffs, but they hadn't—it was a kind of punishment, Dana supposed, tit for tat—and so she'd hit the toilet in mid-stride and pitched headlong to the floor without bringing her hands into play. Dana was bent over her now, trying to control her voice. "Are you all right?" she asked. "Do you need help? Should I call someone?"

It was then that the smell hit her, a savage working odor of the streets, of festering clothes, body secretions, food gone rancid. The woman was wearing a pair of dirty maroon polyester pants that rode up her ankles, a plaid shirt six sizes too big for her and what looked to be men's brogans, cheap and clunky and without laces. She wore no socks, the dirt clinging to her ankles like lichen on a rock. Dana laid a hand on her arm. "Hello?" she said. "Are you awake?"

Suddenly the eyes flashed open, dark eyes, muddy, the color of knots in a pine board, and the lips curled round a snarl. She said something then, something hard and defensive—"Back off!," yes, that was what it was—and attempted to sit up. It took her three tries, her legs sprawled out in front of her, her hands pinned at her back, and Dana said, "Do you need a hand?" and the woman just repeated herself: "I said, 'Back off!'"

Using her elbows for traction, she dug her way across the tile to the near bunk and braced herself against it. In a moment, she was standing, though shakily. She said something else then—"What do you think you're looking at?"—though Dana couldn't be sure because even the Einstein of lip-readers got no more than maybe thirty percent of what was said, despite what the hearing world might think, but what did they know? They knew movies, some waif-like actress pretending to be deaf and holding a conversation like anybody else while her huge imploring eyes consumed the screen in a parody of compassion and need. But it didn't work that way. So many English sounds were monophonous—so many words formed identically on the lips—that it was impossible to tell them apart. Context, context was all. That and guesswork. Dana said nothing. She gave a weak smile and eased down on the opposite bunk, hoping that her body language would speak for her: *I'm no threat; I just want to help.*

For a long while the woman just stared at her. There was

a lump on her forehead, visible now just over her left eye, and the skin there was stretched and abraded. Dana held her eyes because there was nothing else she could do—if the woman were to speak to her again it was her only chance of comprehending and the last thing she wanted under the circumstances was for the woman to think she was ignoring her. Or dissing her, as they said. *Dissing,* from disrespecting.

But now the woman was talking again, asking her for something—her eyebrows lifting with the interrogative. But what was it? Dana said, "I don't understand."

"What, are you deaf or something?" the woman said, and Dana got every word of that because she'd seen the question a thousand times on a thousand pairs of lips. She tried to make her voice soft and non-threatening, though no matter how many sessions she had with the speech therapist it was always a gamble: "Yes," she said.

The look on the woman's face, disbelief wedded to a flare of anger. She might have said, "Are you putting me on?" Or: "No shit—really?" Her lips moved, but she was clearly intoxicated—*Drunk and Disorderly,* wasn't that the way they phrased it in the police reports?—and the faulty mechanics of her lips and tongue would have slurred the words in any case. But here came the interrogative again, tied this time to a gesture, a universal gesture—she worked her hands round to one side, held up two fingers in a *V* and dropped her head to purse her lips as if she were inhaling: *Smoke,* she was saying. *You got a smoke?*

Dana shook her head, shook it with more emphasis than usual. And then, in case her fellow prisoner might misinterpret the gesture, might think she was holding out or maybe even *dissing* her, she said aloud, "Sorry, I don't smoke."

As it turned out, the hours wore on and nobody came for her, not Bridger, not the booking officer or Iverson or a hired attorney inflated with outrage. Nobody came, nothing happened. The drunken woman—her name was Angela—made a number of long, lip-flapping speeches, little of which registered on Dana, and eventually the matron or warder or whoever she was came to the cell with a set of keys, said something to Angela and released her from the handcuffs. A short while later the woman returned with two brown paper bags and handed them through the bars. This was dinner—two slices of white bread encasing a thin sliver of bologna with a dab of ketchup painted like a bull's-eye in the middle of it, spotted yellow apple, sugary fruit drink in a wax carton with malleable straw attached—and when she took the bag, when she held it in her hand and felt the palpable weight of it, Dana came close to breaking down. And she would have broken down if she'd been in private, but there was no privacy here, the warder standing right there with her null-and-void expression, and Angela, at the bars, taking the bag from the warder's hand as if it were filled to the neck with human excrement.

It wasn't so much the contrast between bologna-on-white and pad thai or the ambience of the cell as opposed to the restaurant with its exotic smells and the fish tanks and scurrying waiters and all the rest, or even the absurdity of the situation, the wrongness, the waste, but the fact that if this was dinner it was the first marker of time she'd had since they'd led her in here and locked her up. If this was dinner, then it must be six o'clock, six at least, and nobody had come for her, not Bridger, not a lawyer, not her mother in New York who could have made phone calls, pulled strings, shaken the earth to its molten core in her deaf daughter's behalf. There was nothing. Nothing but the walls and the bars and Angela, who, after an interval, curled up on the bunk opposite and absented herself in a deep drugged sleep.

If she'd been impatient and angry, now she was scared, lonely, distracted. She wanted out, only that, and she found herself pacing again, round and round the confines of the cell, one foot in the trace of the other, like some neurotic animal in a zoo. Something had gone wrong. Bridger couldn't get through to them. He couldn't raise the bail money, couldn't find a lawyer because all the lawyers in town had shut down their offices for the weekend. Worse: more charges kept coming in, this other Dana Halter, whoever she was, off on a regular crime spree. Tulare County. Where in God's name was Tulare County, anyway? Couldn't they see—couldn't *anybody* see—that it didn't have anything to do with her? She hugged her arms to herself and kept pacing. There was nothing else she could do.

At some point—it might have been an hour later or even two: there was no way to know in this place—the door at the end of the corridor swung open and the taller of the two policewomen appeared, her right arm supporting the elbow of a blond woman who looked to be in her late thirties/early forties and who seemed to be having trouble standing upright. Down the corridor they came, the woman leaning heavily into her escort, and then the door to the cell stood briefly open, Angela rousing herself to fire off a few random curses before dropping her head to the cradle of her arms, and their number had grown to three. The door slammed shut with what must have been a boom—doors were always booming in books—and then the policewoman was gone and the blond woman stood there befuddled, as if she couldn't quite make sense of the sequence of events, the arm at the elbow, the opening and shutting of the door, the turning of the key in the lock and the interposition of vertical cylinders of steel between her and the naked gray wall of the corridor.

She looked round her in bewilderment, both hands clinging to the bars, before slowly subsiding to the floor. She was drunk, that much was evident, but as a drunk per se she was the antithesis of Angela. Her hair, which looked as if it had been washed, set and dried at the salon ten minutes earlier, was parted just to the right of center and fell glistening to her shoulders. She was wearing a matching navy blue skirt and jacket, very business-like, with a fresh white carnation pinned to the breast, a white silk blouse and sheer hose, but no shoes—they must have taken her heels away when they booked her. Dana was trying to decide whether she was a lawyer or maybe a real estate lady when the woman fixed her eyes on her and gave her a full, dazzling wide-lipped smile. "Hi," she said. "My name's Marcie, what's yours?"

Angela stirred herself, raised her head and said something in response. Dana watched her lips round and draw back in a grimace. "She's deaf," that was what it was.

Dana ignored her. "I'm Dana," she said.

"Pleased to meet you," Marcie said. And added something she didn't catch.

Angela said something then. "I'm telling you," it looked like. "She's deaf." And then something else. And then, to Marcie, she made the sign for a smoke.

Marcie was still grinning. "I'm drunk," she said, ignoring Angela and staring into Dana's eyes from where she sat on the floor with her knees tucked up under her. She moved her lips mechanically, enunciating as slowly and exactly as she could. "They made me walk the line and sing the alphabet. Isn't that a riot?"

Neither of them had anything to say to that. Even if Dana had interpreted her correctly, and there was no assurance of that, the rhetoric was questionable: they were in jail, all three of them, whether guilty or innocent, drunk or sober. And that was no riot—it wasn't even funny.

At the county jail—a bus had come for them in some dead hour of the night and they were made to line up, submit to leg restraints and handcuffs and shuffle aboard—the three of them were put into a larger cell already occupied by six sleep-deprived, angry-looking women in various stages of degradation and despair. Two of them had the faded blue outline of a scorpion tattooed on the right side of their throats, and one, a massive baby-faced teenager whose head had been shaved to stubble, looked as if she could break through the wall without working up a sweat. The other three—thin Asian girls wearing heavy makeup and all but lost in the orange prison jumpsuits—might have been prostitutes. They all might have been prostitutes for all Dana knew. And what difference did it make? She was one of them now, and if she had to sleep on the floor because a quick calculation showed nine people sharing six bunks, she would. She'd do whatever it took if only she could get through this, if only the nightmare would end.

She was wearing her own orange jumpsuit by now, her clothes—even her shoes and underwear—taken from her and replaced with well-washed easy-care cotton (SAN ROQUE COUNTY JAIL was emblazoned across the shoulders in six-inch letters) and a pair of cheap flip-flops, courtesy of the taxpayers of San Roque County. Angela had come to life the minute they entered the cell—she embraced the big girl as if they were sisters, then immediately trolled for cigarettes, employing the same pantomime gesture she'd used on

Dana and Marcie. That was the last thing Dana remembered clearly, because what followed were two nights and two interminable days of focused aggression. She was repeatedly backed up against the wall trying to explain herself with her lips and her hands while one woman or another breathed some sort of malcontent's tirade in her face. *Didn't she have anything to offer, no cigarettes, lozenges, gum, makeup, nothing? What was she, stupid? Deaf and dumb, right?* And then there'd be an arch look for the rest of the cell and all their faces (except Marcie's: she'd been bailed out the first morning) would twist with the kind of cruel glee Dana had endured all her life. But this was worse. It was special. It was like being on the playground at Burgess Elementary all over again, and they never got tired of the routine because she couldn't answer them, or not quickly enough and not in any recognizably human accent, and so she was their pincushion, their totem, the only animate thing in sight that could make them feel better about themselves through all the long hours of brooding and hate.

On Monday morning, at four a.m. by the clock at the end of a long hall that led to the fresh air and the sick-sweet punishing smell of exhaust that rode heavily atop it, they were herded back onto the buses, women on one side, men on the other. Dana was beyond despair. She felt numb to everything, cauterized against the humiliation of using the toilet in the middle of a brightly lit room while seven other women watched her, dead to the clasp of the chains round her ankles and the cuffs that pinned her left wrist to the big girl's right, rinsed clean of any memory of student papers, her apartment, her job, her boyfriend, even innocence. This was her life, these chains, these abusive, ignorant and foul-smelling women, two slices of white bread, a sliver of bologna, one red squirt of ketchup. This, only this.

43

Four

THAT NIGHT, the night they met, Bridger had stood beside Deet-Deet at the bar and ordered a beer he never tasted. He was trying to look casual, his back to the shining mahogany surface and his weight supported on the props of his elbows, cultivating an air of unconcern, what he liked to call "terminal cool," the beat dragging everyone down as if sound were heavier than air, as if it were some other medium altogether, glue, lead, volcanic ash, but he wasn't succeeding. In fact, as anyone observing him would have seen in an instant, he was locked in on Dana as if he'd been hypnotized. Certainly he looked casual, in his not-hardly-ever-washed jeans, mostly destroyed Nikes and the Digital Dynasty T-shirt with its flaming orange extraterrestrial grinning lickerishly over one shoulder, not to mention his hair, which was growing back in to the point at which random spikes of it projected toothily from his crown, but casual was the last thing he was feeling. What he was feeling, even before Deet-Deet reached out almost blindly for the hand of a doll-sized girl in a yellow tank top and found himself sucked out onto the dance floor, was a peculiar kind of tension—call it anxiety, fear of rejection, the punishment of attraction—he hadn't felt in a very long time.

He waited through three anonymous dance tunes till he was reasonably sure she wasn't with anybody, except maybe a girlfriend with a white-blond ponytail tied up in a high knot on the crown of her head, and then he began to move his shoulders and let the beat infest him as he worked his way through the crowd on the dance floor. He danced opposite her through an entire interminable number, generating a real sweat and working the dregs of the sake back up from his legs to his head, before she noticed him, and when she did notice him it was with a look of surprise tailed by an unguarded smile. Which he took to be a good sign. After the next tune he shouted a few things at her and she shouted back—*Love the way you move; Hot tune, huh?; What'd you say your name was?*—and the wonderful thing, the amazing and insuperable thing, the thing that echoed in his brain even now was that he had no idea she was deaf. Because he was deaf too—everybody was deaf, at least until the lights went up and the DJ took away the thunder.

Deet-Deet was gone and he was standing there in the dissipating crowd and he had Dana by the hand, feeling the gentle pressure of her palm in his while she introduced the girl—woman—with the ponytail and another woman he hadn't registered, Mindy and Sarah, friends of hers from the apartments, and he was lucky, very lucky, because she never would have been out on a Monday except that it was her birthday. Yes, she was thirty-two—she made a face—and wasn't that ancient? Thirty-two? No, he protested, not at all. It was nothing. "Oh, yeah," she said, her whole face opening up to him, the most expressive face he'd ever seen, the most sensual, the prettiest, and he noticed her accent, he did, but thought it was Scandinavian or maybe Eastern European, "then how old are you?" Well, he was twenty-eight. She was still grinning, her eyes crawling all over his face, "You see?" she crowed, and looked to Mindy and Sarah before coming back to him. "You're just a baby."

They didn't get around to exchanging phone numbers, but despite the residual effects of the sake he did manage to commit her name to memory, and when he got home he looked her up in the phone book (*D. Halter, #31 Pacific View Court*). He called the next morning to ask her to dinner but there was no answer and the message on her machine, delivered in her hollow monotone, instructed him not to leave a message but to e-mail her, and gave a Hotmail address. As soon as he got to work he shot off an e-mail, relieved in a way to duck the uncertainty and potential embarrassment of direct contact—he barely knew her and she could turn him down, she could be married, engaged, actively uninterested or so pathologically dedicated to her career she excluded all else—and after typing in a witty line or two about the previous night he made his pitch. To his surprise, she answered within seconds—*Yes, it's just what I want, Italian, but only if you promise not to make me dance off all that pasta afterward,* and gave him directions to her apartment.

The complex was nice, nicer than his, and it sprawled over a hillside with mature plantings—birds-of-paradise, plantains, palms of every size and variety—but the numbers seemed to run in random patterns and he couldn't for the life of him find number 31, which, as far as he could tell, bore no relation to numbers 29 and 30, in front of which he'd already washed up twice. After he'd made three circuits of the place without luck, he stopped a woman about Dana's age who was just going down the steps with a cat on a leash. "Excuse me," he said, "but do you know which apartment is Dana Halter's?"

She gave him a blank look.

"You know," he said, "*Dana?* She's early thirties, about your height, dark hair, really pretty?"

He watched the light come into her face. "Oh, sure, yeah—sorry, sorry. You mean the deaf woman, right?"

It hit him with the force of epiphany. Suddenly it all

made sense: her atonal voice, the non sequiturs, the fluidity of her face when she spoke, as if every muscle under the skin were a separate organ of communication. When he pushed the buzzer at her door it produced a persistent mechanical hum like any other buzzer, but at the same time a light began to flash in the apartment. And suddenly there she was, looking beautiful, her hands fluttering, her voice too loud as she greeted him, and she never took her eyes from his face, a kind of unwavering eye contact that made him feel either irresistible or self-conscious, he couldn't tell which. Then there was the CD he'd agonized over in the car (Would she judge him by it? Did she know the band? Did she like them?) but which she never mentioned, and there were the specials she didn't order, the dinner conversation that drifted from autobiography to mutual interests to politics and the environment and bogged down when he got excited and tried to talk too fast or with food in his mouth, but still he couldn't bring himself to broach the subject of her deafness. No one asked the blind kid at school how he'd lost his sight—he'd tell you in his own time (basement, pipe bomb)—and it would have been unthinkable to quiz the swimmer with the prosthetic leg at the health club. It just wasn't done. It was rude, a way of calling attention to their difference.

For her part, Dana waited till the meal was finished, till the waiter had cleared away their plates and they were both frowning over the dessert menu, before she lifted her head and said, "You know, I don't know if you noticed, but I have to tell you something"—she paused, holding him with her eyes, and then her voice boomed out so that the people two tables over turned to stare—"I'm deaf. Profoundly deaf. They put my hearing loss at close to a hundred decibels. You know what that means?"

He shook his head. The whole restaurant was listening.

"I can't hear a thing."

He fumbled with the response—what could he say: *I'm sorry; It doesn't matter; The tiramisù looks good?*—and she thought it was hilarious. Her shoulders twitched, her eyes caught fire. She was beaming at him across the table, as triumphant as the grand prize winner on a quiz show. "I really put one over on you, didn't I?" she gasped, and laughed till he joined her and they both had to pound the table to keep from floating away.

Things moved slowly from there—she was busy; he was busy—but they graduated from dating (sushi, Thai, the art museum, movies, the beach) to a less formal arrangement, and before either of them realized it they'd come to depend on each other. San Roque was a small coastal city—89,000, if you could believe the population estimate posted at the city limits; perhaps twice that at the height of tourist season—and his apartment was ten minutes from hers on the quiet, uncongested streets. It was nothing to drop by, leave a message, meet for coffee or an impromptu concert (and yes, she loved concerts, classical, jazz, rock, fixated on the body language of the musicians as if she were watching a silent ballet). Rarely did a day go by when they didn't either see each other or at least communicate through e-mail and instant messaging. She was there suddenly, and she filled a hole in his life. He was in love. And so was she, because he could read the signs—her eyes, her hands, the expression on her face when he stepped into the room—and the signs were favorable, they made him feel god-like, as if he were The Kade himself. She'd watch his lips across the table in a coffeehouse and laugh out of all proportion to what he was saying. "Oh, yeah," she'd say in her curious uninflected tones, her voice wavering and tossing till it smoothed out all the bumps, "you're a funny guy. You know that, don't you?" And then she'd quote some statistic she'd found in "Dear Abby" about how the majority of single women above all prized a sense of humor in their prospective mates.

Of course, at the same time, she was quick to point out that in ninety percent of all cases the deaf married their own kind and when they did get attached to the hearing, the divorce rate was stratospheric, and then, needless to say, there was the problem of children. One deaf couple she knew had agonized when the wife became pregnant—"All they could talk about was *'Will it be deaf, will it be deaf?'*" And they had a girl, slick and red and fat and with all her fingers and toes in the expected places, and the parents clapped their hands in her face and shouted till the nurse came running and the whole place was in an uproar, but the child never reacted. "'Thank God,' they said, 'she's one of us.'"

"And what do you mean by that?" Bridger had asked.

She dropped her eyes and her face became immobile. "Nothing."

They were in her apartment at the time, working on their second bottle of wine after she'd whipped up her special crab salad and he'd pitched in with its perfect complement, a bag of Lay's barbecue potato chips. It took him a moment, struggling to decode what she was trying to tell him, and then he reached across the table and took her hands in his till she lifted her eyes again. "But that isn't you," he said, fumbling around the issue. "I mean, you're not like that."

"I don't understand."

"You're not—I mean, you weren't born like that. Right?"

She'd looked as if she were going to cry, but now she forced a smile. "Born like what?"

"Deaf."

She'd gotten up then and left the room. When she came back a moment later she was wearing a T-shirt she'd preserved from her student days at Gallaudet, one he'd seen before, one she wore when the mood took her, when she felt conflicted or defiant. It featured an upraised fist, reminiscent of the old Black Panther logo, and above it the legend DEAF POWER.

At the age of four and a half she'd been stricken with spinal meningitis and barely survived it, her temperature as high as 105 degrees for three days running. The doctors explained to her parents that her aural nerves had been irreparably damaged, that she was now and always would be profoundly deaf. But she was lucky, she insisted, because she was post-lingually deaf, which made it a thousand times easier for her to learn to speak and read and function in the hearing world. What did she remember from that brief period before the fever set in? Words. Stories. Voices. And her father taking her to see *Yellow Submarine* at a revival house.

"Yes," she told him, reaching to bury her hand in the bag of potato chips as if to hide it from him, as if she were afraid of what it might say otherwise, "that's not me." And then, in the flattest tuneless disconnected echo of a voice, she began to sing: "We all live in a yellow summarine, yellow summarine . . ."

He didn't leave the police station till they told him she'd been transferred to the county jail in Thompsonville, and by then it was past nine. Earlier, from his cell phone, he'd called the only lawyer he knew, a friend from college who was practicing entertainment law with a firm in Las Vegas. "Steve," he'd crooned into the phone, "it's me, Bridger," and Steve had instantly begun schmoozing and catching up and pouring the syrup of his top-drawer voice into the receiver until they'd exhausted the trivia and he cleared his throat in a way that indicated that the ticker was running, or should have been running, and Bridger said, "Well, really, the reason I called is I've got a problem." He explained the situation.

"Not good," Steve said. "Not good at all."

"It's not her. She didn't do it. She ran a stop sign, that's all—you understand that, right?"

"You look into identity theft?"

"I don't know: mistaken identity, identity theft—what's the difference?"

Bridger could hear someone else talking in the background. "Yeah, yeah," Steve was saying, "I'll make it short." And then: "Bridger? Yeah, well, the difference is money, big money, because if it's ID theft, you've got to clear the records in whatever jurisdiction this other woman's been committing fraud, and then you've got to go to the CRAs and it can be a real hassle, believe me."

"I hear you," Bridger said, "but what do I do right now? I mean, I can't just leave her in jail."

"You need to call a lawyer."

"I thought that was what I was doing."

"A *criminal* lawyer. Somebody local. You don't know anybody who knows anybody?"

"Nope."

"All right, so you go to the yellow pages, start making calls. But I got to warn you, once they hear the charges they're going to want in the neighborhood of fifty thousand as a retainer and probably ten just to talk to her, and that guarantees nothing, especially with extradition to Nevada and these no-bail holds. But you give them the money and they'll promise you anything."

"But I don't—I mean, I'm doing okay, but . . ."

"What *is* paint and roto, anyway?"

"Hey, it would take too long to explain—it's special effects, that's all. I'll show you next time you're in town, promise. And I like the job, the money's good, but what I'm saying is I don't really have a whole lot in the bank and there's no way I could, well, you know, come up with anywhere near that figure . . ."

There was the voice in the background again, a wash of voices now. Steve shifted from honey to vinegar. "She's in jail for the weekend, nothing anybody can do about that. Monday they'll arraign her and assign a public defender, some troll out of a cave in a cheap suit with a cheap briefcase and a look of terminal harassment, and then you just hope for the best. But hey, listen, great talking to you. Luck, huh?"

On Monday morning, he called in sick (Radko: *Pliss liv a message*) and drove down to the county courthouse, a showcase building erected in the twenties to resemble something out of the Alhambra. It was all stone, stucco and tile with a monumental clock tower and an observation deck on the roof that gave tourists a view of downtown San Roque, from the blue rug of the ocean to the hazy arras of the mountains. At the information kiosk, a beaming old lady with a long flaring nose and the trace of a British accent told him to consult the daily calendar at the far end of the hall, and he saw Dana's name listed there with some eighty or a hundred others. Her arraignment on charges was scheduled for eight-thirty a.m. in Courtroom 2.

The courtroom was the sort of place that inspired confidence in the legal system: vaulted ceilings, dark pews with the rich grain of history worked into them, the elevated jury box to the left, the judge's buffed and burnished high-flown bench in the center under the great seal of the state of California, and a long file of lesser furniture—desks for the court recorders and clerks—tucked in along the right-hand wall, everything very hushed and efficient-looking at five past eight in the morning. Bridger took a seat in the last row. Aside from the bailiff—a tall, muscular, eager-looking cop in a tan cop's shirt with some sort of walkie-talkie pinned to the collar—there were only two other people present, a young couple who might have been college students huddled in the front row over the comics page from the morning newspaper. For his part, Bridger was exhausted. He'd worked all weekend trying to catch up, fueled exclusively by Red Bull, coffee and pizza, The Kade's face so bleakly familiar to him it was like a hallucination, the too-small eyes and the ape-like bone structure of the skull visible to him even when he wasn't staring at the screen. It was a good thing the work didn't require even the smallest modicum of thought, because his mind was as far from Drex III as it possibly could be. All weekend he'd thought of nothing but Dana, Dana locked away in a cell, Dana scared and vulnerable, Dana eating some slop out of a bucket, harassed, put upon, unable to explain herself.

He'd called every attorney in the phone book and got nothing but recordings, *You've reached the law offices of Merker, Stillman; our hours are ten a.m. to five p.m., Monday through Friday; if this is an emergency, please call 565-1608*. It was an emergency and he did call—some fifty-four different attorneys at law—and all but one of the emergency numbers fed him a recording as well. The one that didn't— this was Saturday morning—was answered by an overwrought woman who demanded to know who in hell had referred Bridger to her private number and what was so goddamned earth-shattering that he had to interrupt her on her day off. There were shouts in the background, the thwack of a tennis ball connecting with the sweet spot of a racket. He explained the situation to her and suddenly she was the most reasonable and beneficent woman in the world, outraged over what the legal system had done to his significant other—Dana, that was her name, right? Dana?—

and willing to fight for her till she dropped . . . as soon as she got her retainer in the amount of $75,000, that is.

At eight twenty-five the room began to fill, people of all ages ducking through the door with a nervous glance at the judge's dais before sliding noiselessly into one or another of the pews. Their demeanor indicated how modest, submissive and blameless they were, men and women alike, each of them a dutiful citizen who wouldn't dream of causing the least disturbance or questioning the authority of the court. Their hair was freshly shampooed and they'd made an effort to dress for the occasion, the men in clean pressed shirts, some even with ties knotted meekly round their necks, the women in muted colors and clutching their best purses: these were the people who'd been arrested for brawling in the streets, public intoxication, domestic disturbances and DUIs, the ones who'd been bailed out to sleep in their own beds and see to their grooming and makeup. The others, the ones like Dana, were waiting in the wings somewhere, and Bridger felt his pulse jump each time the door behind the judge's desk swung open.

The cop had been joined by a colleague now—same shirt, muscles, walkie-talkie, but shorter and darker, with a hard incriminatory gaze—and the two of them stood sentry while the clerks filed in from stage left as if this were the opening of a play, which, in some sense, Bridger supposed, it was. When everyone had taken his place, the judge's door flew open and shut and the judge was amongst them and the taller cop cried out, "All please rise and come to order, the Honorable Kathleen McIntyre presiding."

Bridger's hopes rose: a female judge. He studied her face even as he lifted himself from the seat and subsided again, and it was an interesting face, sympathetic, kindly even, poignant eyes, tasteful makeup, tasteful hair. He felt sure this whole fiasco would be resolved as soon as she got a look at Dana—she'd see in an instant that the woman before her was no forger, thief, batterer, no assaulter with a deadly weapon or fugitive from justice. Not Dana. Dana was lithe and beautiful. She was a teacher. She had no record of any kind. She was deaf. And innocent, purely innocent. Surely, Justice McIntyre would see that. Anybody would.

But Dana didn't appear. First a whole squad of lawyers in expensive suits, perfectly groomed, signed in and conferred with the judge on one motion or another or on behalf of so and so, and then the Spanish interpreter gave his spiel to the courtroom and everyone was admonished to watch the fifteen-minute video—first in Spanish, then in English—that explained their rights. Once the video was over, the judge started hurtling through the docket, people stepping forward as their names were called, the judge reading the charges aloud, apprising them of what the DA (cocky, square-shouldered, young, his hair right out of a fashion magazine) advised in their case and asking how they pled. Most, including the male half of the young couple with the comic pages, were charged with public intoxication and/or driving under the influence and most pleaded no contest and got off with time served, a fine and a contribution to the Victims' Assistance Fund. There were more compelling cases—an old woman with madhouse hair and staring eyes who'd been accused of driving on a suspended license, leaving the scene of an accident and failure to appear; a gang-banger sporting the ritual tattoos who'd been charged with distributing drugs in prison and who was there after surrendering on a warrant, only to be handcuffed and led away—but the real meat of the calendar, the serious charges, had to wait until after the noon-hour recess. Bridger couldn't believe it—he'd wasted a whole morning and Radko would have his ass—and for what? He still hadn't laid eyes on Dana since the night before she'd been arrested. He wanted to hit something with a mallet—with the judge's hammer, with a plank torn from one of the pews—hit it and hit it till it splintered.

Then came the afternoon. More lawyers, more criminals, suits, hangdog looks, Justice McIntyre growing sharper and more irritated as the day wore on. Finally, at a quarter past two, the door to the rear of the jury box opened and two long rattling files of prisoners in orange jumpsuits and leg restraints shuffled into the room, men and women taking seats in alternating rows. Bridger half-rose, straining to see as the face of one woman after another appeared framed in the doorway and was replaced by the next. When he did ultimately spot Dana coming through the door sandwiched between a rangy black-eyed woman with a teetering head and angry shoulders and a big butterball of a girl with her scalp shaved to stubble and a silver stud punched through her right eyebrow, he barely recognized her. Her shoulders were slumped, her head down, her hair unwashed and uncombed. There seemed to be a smear of something on her chin.

She sat with the others, her legs shackled, and she never even lifted her eyes to scan the gallery for him. He was riveted with anger, with horror. It was all he could do to stop from shouting out, and he saw too the insidious way the system worked, varnished wood and the grain of history notwithstanding—if you spent the weekend in jail, no matter how innocent you might be, you were doomed to the jailhouse look, to the look of incrimination and guilt. You were dirty, your spirit had been crushed, and if you weren't guilty of the charges against you, you were guilty all the same, of being accused, of being listless, hopeless, dirty and alienated. He made a promise to himself in that moment: never, no matter how much time passed, would he let this rest, never.

When the judge called her name, Dana rose to her feet and cried out that she was present, her voice ricocheting from one side of the courtroom to the other, and there standing beside her and responding in a high redemptive singsong, was her court-appointed attorney, a woman of fifty in a skirt and blazer and with a face that shouted out for justice. "Your honor," the woman sang and it was a song she'd practiced on a hundred other afternoons in court, "I'm Marie Eustace from the Public Defender's office appearing for Dana Halter, who is in custody here beside me, and I'd like to request an immediate identity hearing in this case—it's obviously a TODDI. My client is locally known as an educator here in San Roque, she suffers from a disability and has no record whatever. She's been falsely arrested, Your Honor, and endured a weekend in County, and I'm confident we can fax these jurisdictions for fingerprint and photo ID and have her out of here this afternoon."

And now Bridger saw the second figure there, standing in the row in front of her, a little windup toy of a man almost as short as Deet-Deet, who was interpreting for her in ASL. His hands worked and twisted in small Sign, elbows pressed to his side, and he paused for the judge's response.

Bridger looked to the judge. She was frowning, glancing from the attorney to the interpreter to Dana, her brow creased under a descending wave of professionally dyed and blow-dried hair. "All right, Counselor," she said, letting out a long exasperated breath, "see what you can do and when you've got something to show me we'll proceed."

It was then that he finally caught Dana's eye—she saw him, locked on him; it was unmistakable; she saw him right there in the courtroom doing everything he could do—but the look she gave him wasn't a look of love, gratitude or even relief. She looked into his eyes, burned into him, and then she looked away.

Five

THEY LEFT THE COUNTY JAIL at four a.m., a breakfast of
white bread and processed cheese with a dried-out tanger-
ine and the fruit drink distributed to them in the brown paper sack as they boarded the bus, and she ate every morsel,
though she had to chew gingerly around the bad tooth, and
licked her fingers afterward. She even felt the smallest pulse
of optimism—they were moving, the wheels of justice
grinding forward as the bus lurched and bounced and the
safety glass rattled like a machine gun against the steel
mesh, and she didn't care where they were going as long as
it put distance between her and the hellhole she'd just va-
cated. People let their heads loll against the backs of the
seats, their eyes closed and legs splayed. There was a taint of
exhaust leaching in from under the floorboards and it was
a small mercy because it cut through the human smell. The
only light came from the green glow of the dash and the
pale wash of the headlights beyond and Dana focused on it.
The others might have been asleep, but she sat rigid with
anticipation, staring out over the driver's silhouette to
where the dark slick of the roadway unraveled before them
and the hills and trees opened up on amber streetlights and
the shadowy roofs of condos and tract homes where people
lay dreaming.

The bus deposited them at the courthouse, a policeman
with a shotgun standing guard while they shuffled through

a corridor and into a holding cell located somewhere in proximity to the courtroom itself. Once they were safely inside the cell, a guard released the handcuffs and they were allowed to mingle and gather as they saw fit. Dana kept to herself, or tried to. She made her way to the far corner of the cell, eased herself down on the floor and was careful to avoid eye contact with anyone, but the fat girl was there like a picked scab, dodging into her frame of reference every two minutes, and Angela careened from one group of women to the next, her fingers locked in the nicotine gesture, until finally she collapsed beside Dana and began a long spittle-flecked monologue on a subject—or subjects— that remained mysterious. Nothing happened through the long morning and into the early afternoon, when everyone began to bristle and stir as if an electric current had been switched on, and a man from the Public Defender's office swept into the cell and gave a speech Dana didn't catch at all. Shortly thereafter Iverson appeared, weaving his way through the clutch of prisoners, a woman with a briefcase at his side.

And what did she feel when she spotted him there amidst the crowd swiveling his head from side to side, looking for her? Elation. Pure elation. She might not have liked him, might have assigned him a good measure of the blame for what had happened to her—he should have intervened, should have explained to them that they'd got the wrong person, should have persisted and used his influence and got her out—but she gazed on him now as if he were her savior. Finally, finally something was happening. He introduced the woman, who handed her her card—*Marie Eustace, Public Defender*—and leaned in close to quiz her sufficiently enough to understand that this was all a mistake, Iverson simultaneously translating in his rigid mechanical Sign. It took no more than five minutes. They would establish the identity of the true criminal and have her out of here ASAP, that was the promise, and Marie Eustace put on a look of high dudgeon and told her how outraged she was that the court had fallen asleep on this one. "Don't you worry," she told her, "we'll have you out in no time," and then she moved on to huddle with Angela.

Dana had never been in court before and the flags and the arras and the great seal and all the rest might have impressed her under other circumstances, but all she felt as she sat there in the dock (that was the term, wasn't it?—yes, from the Flemish for *hutch, pen, cage*) was the same shame and anger she'd felt on the morning of her arrest, though it was multiplied now. By the power of ten, ten at least. She couldn't lift her head, couldn't scan the cluster of spectators for Bridger's face, couldn't do anything but go deep and close herself down. All through the weekend she'd distracted herself by mentally conjuring the poems she made a practice of beating out in class for her students so they could feel the music of them, the dactyls, iambs and trochees singing in their heads even as her hands thumped the rhythm on one desktop after another. She did it now, head bowed, vanished from the scene: *Just as my fingers on these keys / Make music, so the self-same sounds / On my spirit make a music too.*

When they finally got to her, after Angela, after the big girl with the shaven head (with the unlikely name of Beatrice Flowers), after half a dozen men who tightened their jaws and flexed their shoulders as they stood before the judge, she came out of her trance long enough to startle the whole courtroom with the unleashed power of her voice: "Yes," she said, standing as Iverson signed that they'd called her name, "I'm present." That was when she looked up and saw Bridger, his face crying out to her, and he was the only one in the courtroom who didn't flinch at the sound of her voice. She gave him nothing, not hope or joy or love. Then she sat down again and dropped her head.

More waiting. Eternal waiting. Cases came and went, charges were read aloud, pleas made and recorded, bail set and fines levied. At four-fifteen Marie Eustace reappeared to confer with the judge and present into evidence faxes from each of the jurisdictions in question, and the judge put on her reading glasses while the court went lax and people studied the ceiling or ducked in and out of the door on urgent business. Then the judge removed her glasses and called Dana's name again, Iverson signing, and Dana found herself edging past people to approach the bench, and at least they'd released her shackles, at least there was that.

The judge's eyes were a milky blue, faded and blanched as if all the vitality had gone out of them, yet she had a smile in reserve, a rueful smile, which she somehow managed to summon for the occasion of this, Dana Halter's exoneration. Dana could see it all before it happened—yes, it was a case of mistaken identity, or worse, identity theft—and the lethargy she'd felt was replaced suddenly by anger, by a rage that built in her till she couldn't contain it. "The court must offer you our deepest apologies," the judge was saying, as Iverson's hands worked and twisted before her, "because this was an ordeal you've been through, I know that, but until the evidence came in"—and here she held up a handful of faxes, the first of which, from Tulare County, showed the shadowy likeness of a stranger, a white male nonetheless, under the tag Dana Halter—"there was nothing we could do. But we do apologize—I apologize—and we will give you every consideration we can in straightening this out. Our victims' assistance people are as good as they come and will be available to you immediately on release."

But she had to speak, had to push it. "Is that it?" she

said, and she had no idea whether she was shouting or whispering. "Is that all you're going to do?"

Marie Eustace blanched. Iverson signed frantically, *That's enough. No more. She's going to dismiss.*

Dana swung round on him, signing back, big Sign, angry Sign, her arms looping and elbows jabbing: *You shut up because I don't need you—and when I did need you you weren't there.* All of it came out then, all the hurt and confusion, and she turned back to the judge and let her voice lash out like a physical extension of herself, of her furiously signing hands: "I've been locked up, I've been abused—I missed two days of work with no way even to call anybody—and you give me this, this *apology* and it's supposed to make everything all right?" Her face twisted. She felt absurd, hateful, a clown in an orange jumpsuit, and she could see the judge's eyes hardening, and what word was on her lips, what curse?—*Shit, shit,* that was what it was, she was about to proclaim it all *shit*—but before she could spew it out Marie Eustace stepped forward and said something to the judge and the judge looked directly at Dana and her lips said, "Case dismissed."

She had no intention of sitting in an airless office disclosing herself to the victims' assistance people, answering their idiotic questions, filling out forms, lip-reading the banality of their clichés while Charles Iverson juggled his hands—she didn't have one more second to waste. Not one. She wanted out of the jumpsuit, wanted her clothes back, her keys, her car—and the papers, the student papers. And she had to call the school and explain herself, had to go in person and throw herself on Dr. Koch's mercy, had to meet her class and do her job—if she still had a job. Because who was going to believe her? People didn't just get thrown in jail for no reason, not in this country, anyway. Even as they began the paperwork to process her out, even as Marie Eustace arranged for the court to provide her with an affidavit proclaiming her innocence, she could picture the look of incredulity and anger on Dr. Koch's face, less than a week left in the term and one of his teachers skipping out early . . .

But what she wanted most of all, sitting mutely in a colorless anteroom somewhere in the depths of the building and waiting for them to file their papers and rescind the charges and give her back her life, was a shower. She worked at her fingernails, one nail under the other, and they were black with the filth of that place, with the filth of those ugly jeering women, the prostitutes and street people and addicts and drunks, common drunks. She'd passed them in the street a hundred times, felt sorry for them, always one to reach into her purse for a handful of change or a dollar bill, but never again. They *were* common, she knew that now, common as in *not refined; vulgar; low; coarse.* And petty. Nasty. With no human feeling and no love but for themselves. The *menu peuple,* the mob, the hoi polloi. That was what they were—it was *Lord of the Flies* in that cell, on the streets, everywhere she turned, and where did that leave her? Where it left Ralph, where it left Piggy. But she was no victim, she refused to be, and once she got home, once she shut the door behind her and locked out the world, she was going to stand under the shower and scrub the dirt off her till the water ran cold and then she was going to call Dr. Koch and go straight to the impound yard, wherever that was, and get those papers out of the backseat of the car. Just the thought of it gave her a pang—she was so far behind. It was insane. Like the nightmares she'd have in the moments before waking, the ones in which she appeared in front of the class with no lesson, no plan, her hair a mess, her clothes fallen in a heap at her feet. Naked. Frozen. Unable to speak with her hands or her tongue either.

She was so wound up she almost forgot Bridger. But there he was, rushing toward her in the hallway as she stepped through the door with Marie Eustace, Iverson and her freshly issued affidavit, his face bleeding sympathy and love. She let him hold her, though she was embarrassed by her odor and furious with him—why hadn't he *done* anything? He was saying something, saying it uselessly—she could feel his breath at her ear as he squeezed her to him—and then she pushed away from him and signed, *How could you leave me in there?*

His signing was clumsy, nearly illiterate—he'd taken a course in ASL just for her, but his hands were like sledgehammers, bludgeoning the language. *I tried.*

Well you didn't try hard enough.

That was when a cop in a brown shirt—the bailiff—intervened. He, Iverson and Marie Eustace conferred for a moment, and then Marie turned to give her a look of consternation. She let her eyes roll and stamped her foot. "What?" Dana said. "What is it now?"

"You're not going to believe this," she said, and she looked to Iverson to interpret, her eyes skittering apologetically between them, "but, well, I'm afraid you're going to have to go back to County to get processed out."

Dana shook her head. Violently. Jerked it back and forth, and they could read that, couldn't they? "No," she said, and she felt her voice go loud, the force of it constricting her larynx till it felt like a hard compressed ball in her throat, and she turned her back on the lawyer and the cop and signed furiously to Iverson: *I am innocent and here's the document to prove it and I will not go back there, never, and don't you or anyone else try to make me.*

Iverson, with the face of a bad actor and his hands that stalled and stuttered, translated for the lawyer and Dana refused to look at her, though Marie Eustace was speaking to her, though she put a hand on her arm till Dana shook it off. She looked to Iverson alone. *There's no way around it,* he signed. *It's the law, guilty or innocent. They brought you here on the bus and they have to take you back on the bus. You need to change out of those clothes and get your own things back, there's paperwork—*

No, she signed, *no. I won't go.* In a fury, she let her hands go silent and began to tear at the jumpsuit, to tear it from her, and she shouted aloud so they could all hear her, the cop and Bridger and the judge in her chambers, "Just take the shitty thing and I'll walk out of here naked, I don't care, I don't care—"

Ultimately, she did care—she was made to care. The bailiff stepped forward and informed her that she was still in custody and that he would have to use the restraints if necessary. Marie Eustace's face was livid. She blew air in the direction of the bailiff and Iverson signed his threats and Bridger just took hold of Dana, as if to shield her with his body. She'd never been so enraged in her life—the absurdity of it, like something out of Kafka, or worse, out of some police state, Cuba, North Korea, Liberia—but what calmed her, what took all the fight out of her in an instant, was the sight of the bailiff's hand on Bridger's wrist. She couldn't make out what they were saying, their lips gyrating, faces red, but she understood in an instant that Bridger himself was a heartbeat away from being arrested for interfering with the duties of an officer of the law or some such nonsense. "It's okay," she said aloud, "it's okay," and the officer took her by the elbow and escorted her down the hallway, through a pair of heavy doors, and then back to the cell itself, back to Angela and Beatrice Flowers and all the rest.

It was nearly midnight by the time they finally released her from the county jail in Thompsonville, seventeen miles from San Roque, and Bridger was there waiting for her in a crowded over-lit anteroom. For a long moment she just held him. She hadn't wanted to cry, but the minute she saw him there, the minute it was over, she couldn't hold back. Then they were moving toward the door and she broke away from him and lunged through it to stand there on the steps feeling the air on her face—salt and faintly fishy, refrigerated by the sea, clean air, the first clean air she'd taken into her lungs since Friday morning. Bridger came up behind her and put an arm round her shoulders, but she pushed him away. She was angry suddenly, angry all over again. "Can you even imagine what it was like in there?" she demanded. "Can you?"

All the way home, all the way to her shower and her bed and the door that locked people out instead of in, he tried to explain himself, but she was getting very little of it because his hands were on the wheel and his mouth was venting like any other hearing person's and that made her more unforgiving still. Finally, her hair in a towel and the beer he'd got her and the sandwich he'd made her set out on the coffee table, he led her to the computer and pecked furiously at the keys, typing out a whole long unfolding apologia that could have been the epilogue of a Russian novel, and she saw what he'd done and how hard he'd tried and that it wasn't him but the system that was to blame—or no, the *thief*, the thief was to blame, and for the first time the image of that face, that dark blur on a slick sheet affixed above her own name, came careening into her mind, a *man*, a *man* no less—and after a while she leaned into him, wrapped her arms round him and began to forgive.

In the morning, Bridger drove her to work. She hadn't got much sleep, her dreams poisoned and antithetical, and every time she woke she had to catch her breath, thinking she was back there again, under the lights, on the hard floor of the cell. As it was, she was twenty minutes late, and if it weren't for Bridger she might have been later still—she'd trained herself to respond to the flash of the alarm clock, but she'd never been so exhausted in her life and would have slept right through it if he hadn't been there to wake her. The first thing she'd done on getting out of the shower the night before, even before she chugged the beer cold from the bottle and devoured the sandwich and half a thirty-two-ounce bag of potato chips, and cookies, a whole bag of cookies, was to e-mail Dr. Koch. The e-mail ran to three pages. She gave him a blow-by-blow account from the moment she was pulled over for running the stop sign to her release in Thompsonville some eighty-three hours later, because she knew she could communicate better on the page than in person, or more fully at any rate, and she had to make her case—Koch was a brooding, tough, sour little man who thought of himself in inflated terms and brooked no nonsense, and he was as demanding with the deaf teachers as with the hearing. Maybe more so. She needed his understanding, that was what she said in conclusion, and she promised to come to him before her first class and bring the affidavit with her too. But there was the problem: she was twenty minutes late and her class started without her—and Dr. Koch was there in the classroom, covering for her, and she'd never seen him look sourer.

He rose from her desk the minute she stepped through the door—he'd had the students reading in their texts while he put his head down and made his way through a pile of paperwork his secretary had handed him as he fled the office—and he gave her a look that needed no translation. The students were seniors, and this was a college-prep course, one of her best classes. There were twelve of them, each with his or her own nascent gift to take out into the hearing world, and she knew their secrets and their strengths and their failings too. *Sorry I'm late,* she signed, flinging her purse and briefcase on the desk. She was out of breath. Her color was high. She pinched her shoulders in apology: *I overslept.*

Koch gave her nothing. He was already at the door, a stripe of sun fallen across the first row of desks as if to slice the room in two. Every one of her twelve students sat riveted, watchful and tense, and Robby Rodriguez, always emotional, looked as if he were about to collapse under the weight of his private agony. For a long moment Koch just stood there, his hand on the latch. Then he signed abruptly that he'd see her in his office during the lunch hour, jerked the door open and stalked out of the room.

Like most deaf schools, San Roque was residential, the student body drawn from all over the country, though the majority came from the West Coast. It was run along the lines of a college campus rather than the standard high school (which to Dana's mind wasn't much better than a reformatory in any case), and when the students weren't in class or attending speech therapy, they were free to do as they pleased—within limits, of course. On Tuesdays and Thursdays Dana met with three classes, one in the morning, two in the afternoon, and in the interval she held office hours, ran errands or stole the odd hour to work on her book. She had a secret hope for this book, an ambition that drove her to obsess over its smallest details, to make it right, to communicate in a way that might have been second nature to the hearing but which for her at least was as new and intoxicating as love itself—not erotic love, but agape, a flowing unstoppable love for all creation. Just to think of it, to think of what she'd accomplished so far and the hazy uncharted territory to come, gave her a secret rush of fulfillment and pride. She wouldn't talk about it, not with anyone except Bridger. It was too close, too personal. Even the title—*Wild Child*—was like an incantation, a way of summoning a spirit and a voice she'd never before been aware of, and at the oddest times she'd find herself chanting it, deep inside, over and over.

As soon as she dismissed the morning class (she gave the group a shorthand version of what had happened to her—*and* to their final papers, which she vowed to have back the next day without fail), she went straight to Koch's office to explain herself. His secretary signed that he was in conference and she signed back that she would wait, taking a chair in the corner of the main office and flipping through the underscored pages of her classroom anthology in an effort to calm herself, but she remained far from calm. Her tooth was bothering her, for one thing—the distant throb had been replaced now with a sharp intermittent pain that seemed to accelerate along with the racing of her pulse—and sitting there in the bright molded plastic chair with her elbows tucked in while the rest of the world went about its business was like being back in the jail cell all over again.

When Dr. Koch did finally see her—at noon, precisely—he was brusque and impersonal, as if she were just another delinquent student. She hadn't expected sympathy, not from him, but courtesy was the one thing she demanded—of anybody, especially the hearing. She'd spent too much of her life trying to communicate with people who turned hostile the minute she opened her mouth to put up with anything less. *Look at me,* she demanded. *Just look at me. And listen.* That was her social contract, and if people didn't like it she was ready to turn her back on them. No exceptions. Not anymore.

He was seated at his desk when she stepped in the door, and he waved a hand to indicate the hard oaken supplicant's chair at the foot of it. She gave him a neutral smile as she slipped into the chair, the affidavit tucked under one arm in a stained manila folder she'd dug out of her filing cabinet in the rush to get to work in the morning. "Good afternoon," she said aloud, but he didn't answer. He was bent over the desk, impressing his precise infinitesimal signature on the diplomas the school would give out at commencement Saturday morning, shifting them from one pile to another, and every time it seemed as if he were about to pause and look up, he reached for another and then another.

The office was pretty much standard issue: a tumult of books and papers everywhere, various certificates and framed photos of graduates leaching out of the walls, the multicolored pennants of colleges the school's students had gone on to—USC, Yale, Stanford, Gallaudet. She was trying to remember when she'd last been in this room—could it have been as long as a year ago, when she was hired?—and her gaze came to rest on a very small portrait, in oil, of Dr. Koch signing to an ill-defined audience in a sketchy auditorium somewhere. The artist seemed to have had a thing for red, and the result gave the subject's face the texture and coloration of a slab of raw meat.

"So this is all very unfortunate," he said, glancing up sharply and signing simultaneously to get her attention. "A real mess. And the timing couldn't have been worse. Really, I mean, *finals* week." A pause, his hands at rest. "Did you even give finals?"

Maybe it was that she was wrought up—her car was still in the impound yard, there was a criminal out there impersonating her, she'd barely slept in three days and if someone had stuck an electric prod in her mouth it couldn't have felt any worse than her own natural dentition did—but his words hit her the wrong way. They entered her eyes and then her brain and there they set off a chemical reaction that caused her to stand up so abruptly the chair fell out from under her and hit the floor with what might have been a thud, if only she could have heard it. *You talk as if I'm the one at fault,* she signed.

He regarded her steadily, his hands folded on the desk before him. He was hearing, but he'd been in deaf education all his life and his signing would have been as proficient as a native speaker's if he hadn't lacked expression. And there was no way to teach that, not that she knew anyway. "I don't know who else is," he said, and his hands never moved.

Didn't you get my e-mail? she demanded.

"I got it. But it still doesn't begin to explain how you could just not show up for classes on Friday and Monday both—and be late today on top of it. You couldn't have called in at least? Couldn't have had the courtesy?"

I was in jail.

"I know. That's why we're having this discussion." He looked down at the desk a moment, picked up a paperweight in the shape of a football (Second Place, Division III Playoffs, 2001) and set it down again. "Don't they give you a phone call?"

One. One only. I used it to call my boyfriend—

"Well, good for you. But couldn't he have called? Couldn't anybody?"

So I could get bailed out.

"You know, your students were upset—the Rogers girl, what's her name, Crystal, especially. We all were. And I think it's pretty unprofessional of you—and inconsiderate as well—to just disappear like that. Finals week too. But you didn't get bailed out, did you?"

*You read the e-mail. There was nothing I could do. It was a case of mistaken identity—worse, identity theft—*here she brandished the manila folder—*and if you think it's a joy* *being locked up you just try it, you'll see. It was the worst nightmare of my life. And now you have the gall to blame me?*

"I don't like your tone."

I don't like yours either.

He brought both palms down on the desk with enough kinetic energy to dislodge a stack of papers and then, as if the impulse had just come into his head, jumped to his feet even as the papers settled silently round his shoes. "Enough!" he shouted, and he was signing now, signing angrily, punching out his hands like a prizefighter. *It's not for you to like or dislike. Let me remind you that you're the employee here, not me—and an untenured employee at that. One that comes in late half the time as it is—*

"Bullshit!" she said, and then repeated it for emphasis— "Bullshit!"—before turning her back on him and slamming the door behind her with such force she could feel the concussion radiating all the way up her arm as she strode past the secretary, down the hall and out of the building.

Six

BRIDGER WAS AT WORK, dwelling deep in Drex III, cruising right along, the mouse a disembodied extension of his brain and his blood circulating in a steady, sure, tranquil squeeze and release, when Dana called. He'd come in early, directly after dropping her off at school, hoping to make up some of the ground he'd lost over the past four days, and he'd already got two hours in before anyone else showed up. Which didn't prevent Radko from lecturing him in front of the whole crew about "the impordance of deamwork" and how he was letting everyone down. This struck him as unfair, grossly unfair, especially when Deet-Deet leaned out of his cubicle and made Radko faces at him throughout his dressing-down, but he didn't say anything in his own defense other than that he'd been there since eight and would stay on through dinner—whatever it took—until he finished up every last frame of this sequence (another head replacement, this time of The Kade's co-star, Lara Sikorsky, whose stand-in did a triple-gainer off one of Drex III's needle-like pillars and into a lake of fire, from which she emerged unscathed, of course, because of a genetic adaptation that allowed her skin, hair and meticulously buffed and polished nails to survive temperatures as high as a thousand degrees Fahrenheit). In fact, he'd been so absorbed in the work he hadn't opened any of the pop-ups from his co-workers or even put anything on his stomach yet, other than coffee, that is.

His cell began to vibrate and he surreptitiously slipped it from his pocket and leaned deep into his cubicle to screen it from anyone—i.e., Radko—who might be passing by on the way to the refrigerator or restroom. Dana had a tendency to text messages that went on for paragraphs, but this time she was terse: *Koch is a real A-hole! I'm quitting. I swear.*

He punched in a response: *Do you want to talk?*

Nothing to talk about. I'm going home.

Don't. You only have four more days.

Nothing. He held the phone a moment as if it were totemic, as if it could project meaning apart from any human agency, and then she retransmitted the original message: *Koch is a real A-hole!*

All else aside, this was a proposition he couldn't deny. He'd met the man four or five times now, at one grindingly dull school function or another (which Dana was required to attend on pain of forfeiture of administrative patience and goodwill), and he was as stiff and formal and unsympathetic as one of the helmeted palace guards on Drex III. And the way he condescended to the deaf teachers—and to the students too—you would have thought his special talent was for humiliation rather than education. Still, he was the man in charge and it wasn't as if she had a whole lot of options: the San Roque School was the only show in town—in fact, it was the only school for the deaf on the Central Coast, as far as he knew. He phoned her back, but there was no answer.

He called every fifteen minutes after that, but she wouldn't pick up, and he took a moment to peer out of his cubicle and determine Radko's whereabouts before e-mailing her as well (*Don't do anything rash,* was the message he left on cell and PC alike). As the morning wore on, though, he couldn't seem to recover his concentration, the mouse moving so slowly it might have been made of kryptonite, the frame before him frozen in an instant that wasn't appreciably different from the instant that had preceded it, the whole movie turning to sludge before his eyes. All he could think about was what would happen to her if she lost her job. At the very least she'd have to move God knew where to find another one—there was a deaf school in Berkeley, he was pretty sure, but the others might have been anyplace, Texas, North Dakota, Alabama. The thought of it—*Alabama*—made his stomach skip, and he dialed her yet again.

When Radko left at three-thirty to drive down to L.A. for "a meeding," Bridger slipped out too. Despite his assurances to the contrary, he had no intention of working straight through, not today—he had to drive Dana to the impound yard to retrieve her car and then sit down with the victims' assistance people and start the process of reclaiming her life, because there was no guarantee she wouldn't be arrested again, not until they caught this jerk who'd stolen her identity. When he pulled into the parking lot at the school, she was sitting on the front steps waiting for him, and that was a relief, though he never really believed she'd just walk out on her classes, no matter what degree of assholery the headmaster attained. That wouldn't be like Dana. She never gave up on anything.

She was having an animated discussion in Sign with one of her students, a weasel-faced kid of seventeen or so who seemed to have given an inordinate degree of thought to his hairstyle (bi-colored, heavy on the gel, naked skin round the ears and too far up the nape), and she looked like her old self as she rose to her feet, gathered up her things and slid into the car. But then her eyes went cold and the first thing she said wasn't "How was your day?" or "I love you" or even "Thanks for picking me up," but "I'm really at the end of my rope."

He lifted his eyebrows in what he hoped was an inquisitive look, though he wasn't much good at pantomime.

"With Koch, I mean."

"Why?" he asked, careful to exaggerate the movement of his lips. "What happened?"

The car—a '96 Chevy pickup he'd bought used when he was in college and had been meaning to service ever since—stuttered, died and caught again. "Never mind," she said. "It would take me a week to explain." The weasel-faced kid gave them a tragic look, a look that ratified what Bridger had already surmised—that he was burning up with the delirium of love and would walk through fire for his teacher, as soon as he could eliminate the competition, that is. She gave the kid a farewell wave and turned back to him: "Just drive. I've got to get my car back—I mean, I'm helpless without it. And the papers"—she did a characteristic thing then, a Dana thing, a sort of hyperactive writhing from the waist as if the seat were on fire and she couldn't escape it—"oh, Jesus, the papers."

At the impound yard—CASH OR CREDIT CARD ONLY ABSOLUTELY NO CHECKS—they waited in line for twenty minutes while the people ahead of them put on a demonstration of the limits and varieties of hominid rage. The office, to which they were guided by a series of insistent arrows painted on the outer wall, was made of concrete block and had the feel of a bunker, dark and diminished and utterly impregnable. Immediately on entering they were confronted with a wall of bulletproof Plexiglas, behind which sat a skinny sallow grim-faced cashier with hair dyed the color of engine oil. She might have been forty, forty-five—an age, at any rate, beyond which there is neither hope nor even the pretense of it—and she wore a blue work shirt with some sort of badge affixed to the shoulder. Her job was to accept payment through a courtesy slit and then, at her leisure, stamp a form to release the vehicle in question. From early morning till closing time at six, people spoke to her—cursed, raved, foamed at her—through a scuffed metal grille. There were no cars in sight. The cars were out back somewhere, secreted behind a ten-foot-high concrete-and-stucco wall surmounted with concertina wire.

The couple who were stalled at the window when they arrived inquired as to whether the woman on the other side of the Plexiglas would take a personal check and the woman didn't bother with a reply, merely raising a lifeless finger to point to the NO CHECKS sign nearest her. There was some further negotiation—Could she accept the major part of the amount on a credit card and the rest in a check?—followed by a second objectification of the finger, after which there was a rumble of uncontained threats (a mention of lawsuits, the mayor, the governor himself) before the couple swung round, murder stamped across their brows, and slammed out the door, vehicleless. Next in line was a man so tall—six-six or more—that he had to bend nearly double and lean into the counter in order to speak through the grille. He was calm at first—or at least he made an effort to suppress the rage and consternation in his voice—but when the cashier handed him the bill for towing and two days' storage, he lost it. "What is this?" he demanded. "What the fuck is this?"

The woman fastened on him with two dead eyes. She never moved, never flinched, even when he began to pound at the Plexiglas with both fists. When he was done, when he'd exhausted himself, she said only, "Cash or charge?"

Dana had observed all this, of course, though she was spared details, the whole business a kind of mute Punch and Judy show to her, Bridger supposed, but when it was her turn she stepped forward, slid the impound notice and her driver's license through the courtesy slit and waited for the woman to return her keys. But the woman didn't return the keys. Instead she pushed an invoice through the slit and said, "That'll be four hundred eighty-seven dollars, towing fee plus four days' storage. Cash or charge?"

"But you don't understand," Dana said, her voice like an electric drill, "I'm innocent. It's all a mistake. It was somebody else they wanted, not me. Look"—and she held up the affidavit, pressed it to the glass. "You see? This exonerates me."

Bridger couldn't be sure, but it seemed as if the smallest flare of interest awakened in the cashier's eyes. There was something unusual here, something out of the ordinary, and for a moment he almost thought she was going to act on it, but no such luck. "Cash or charge?" she repeated.

"Listen," he said, stepping forward, though Dana hated for him to interfere, as if his acting as interpreter somehow exposed or diminished her. She didn't need an interpreter, she always insisted—she'd got on just fine all her life without him or anyone else conducting her business for her. Dana gave him a savage look, but he couldn't help himself. "You don't get it," he said. "I mean, ma'am, if you would only listen a minute—they got the wrong person, is all, she didn't do anything . . . You saw the affidavit."

The cashier leaned forward now. "Four hundred eighty-seven dollars," she repeated, enunciating slowly and carefully so there would be no mistake. "You pay or you walk."

Next it was the victims' assistance office in the back annex of the police station. They were fifteen minutes late for their appointment with the counselor because even after Bridger convinced Dana to go ahead and pay the impound fee and put in a claim with the police later on, there was a delay of over an hour before the car was released, and no one—not a clairvoyant or a president's astrologer or even the public defender—could have said why. As a result, Dana was pretty well worked up by the time they stepped through the door—mad at the world, at the headmaster, the torturer's assistant in the impound office and Bridger too, for daring to speak up for her—and things went badly, at least at first. To give her credit, the woman behind the desk (middle-aged, creases under the eyes, every mother's face) was a living shrine to patience. Her name, displayed on a plaque in the center of the desk, was Mrs. Helen Bart Hoffmeir— "Call me Helen," she murmured, though neither of them could bring themselves to do it. She let Dana vent for a while, offering sympathy at what seemed the appropriate junctures, but of course the soothing soft gurgle of her voice was lost on Dana.

At some point—Dana was clonic with anger; she wouldn't take a seat; she wouldn't be mollified—the woman extracted a three-tiered box of fancy chocolates from the filing cabinet behind her and set it out on the desk. "Would you like a cup of chamomile tea?" she asked, lifting the top from the box and looking from Dana to Bridger with a doting smile. "It helps," she added. "Very soothing, you know?"

So they had chocolates and tea and Dana calmed down enough to take a seat and attune herself to what the counselor had to say. They made small talk for a few minutes while they sipped tea and worked their jaws around nougat and caramel and cherry centers, and then the woman looked to Dana. "You do read lips, then, dear? Or would you be more comfortable with an interpreter? Or your husband—?"

"My boyfriend."

"Of course, yes. Does he—can he translate?"

"Sure," Bridger said. "I can try. I took a course last semester in adult ed, but I'm pretty clumsy with it—" He gave a laugh and the woman took it up. Briefly. Very briefly. Because suddenly she was all business.

"Now, Dana," she said, spreading open the file before her, "as you've already no doubt gathered, you've been the victim of identity theft." She removed four faxes from the file and pushed them across the table. The mug shot of the same man gazed out at them from all four, and Bridger felt a jolt of anger. Here he was, a white male who looked to be thirty or so, with a short slick hipster's haircut and dagger sideburns, his eyes steady and smug even there in that diminished moment in the Tulare County Sheriff's Department, in Marin, L.A., Reno, here he was, the shithead who'd put Dana in jail. "Unfortunately," the counselor was saying, a little wince of regret decorating the corners of her mouth, "the onus is on you to defend yourself."

"Is that him?" Bridger said. His voice was hard, so hard it nearly choked him getting it out. All his life he'd cruised along, high school, college, film school, Digital Dynasty, living a video existence, easy in everything and never happier than when he was sunk into the couch with a DVD or spooned into a plush seat in the theater with the opening credits rolling—Melissa used to call him a video mole, and it was no compliment—but in that moment he felt something come up in him he'd never felt before, because now everything was different, now the film had slipped off the reel and the couch was overturned. It was hate, that was what it was. It was rage. And it was focused and incendiary: *So this was the son of a bitch.*

The woman nodded. A pair of reading glasses dangled from a cord round her throat and she lifted them now to her face and peered down at the photos. "We don't know his real name and he could have been arrested under any number of aliases in the past—"

Dana spoke up suddenly. "What about fingerprints?"

"We haven't run a fingerprint trace. They haven't, I mean. It's because"—here she paused, looking to Bridger to carry her past the sad truth of the moment—"well, I'm sorry to say that a crime like this, a victimless crime, just doesn't merit the resources . . ."

Bridger's hands were traumatized. He had to fingerspell most of it—"victimless" took him forever—but Dana picked right up on it. "Victimless?" she said. "What about me? My job? My students? What about the four hundred and eighty-seven dollars—who's going to pay that?"

Who indeed?

The explanation was circuitous, dodging away from the issue and coming back to it again, and it took a while to unfold. First of all, Dana was a victim, of course she was, but she had to understand just how much violent crime there was in the state of California—in the country as a whole—and how limited law enforcement resources were. There were rapists out there, murderers, serial killers. Sadists. Child molesters. But this in no way diminished what had happened to her and there was a growing awareness of the problem (the counselor—what was her name?—dispensed clichés like confections, like tea, because they were soothing) and there were a number of steps Dana could take to restore her good name and maybe even bring the criminal to justice. At this point, the woman drew a pad and pencil from the top drawer of her desk. "Now," she said, "do you have any idea who this man is or how he might have got hold of your base identifiers?"

Dana hesitated a moment till Bridger had laboriously spelled out "base identifiers," a term neither of them had previously come across. "No," she said, shaking her head emphatically. "I've never seen him before."

"Have you lost your purse or had it stolen anytime in the past few months?"

She read this on the woman's lips and shook her head again.

"What about your mailbox—is it secure? Locked, I mean?"

It was, yes. The mailboxes at her apartment complex were located in a special alcove, and everybody had a key to his or her own box.

"What about at work? Do you receive mail at the"—here the woman brought the glasses back into play and glanced down a moment at the sheet before her—"the San Roque School for the Deaf?"

Dana did. And no, the mailboxes there were in the main office and anyone could have access to them. But Dana hadn't missed anything—her pay stubs were there every two weeks on schedule and there had been no interruption of her mail at home, or not that she knew of, anyway.

The woman looked to Bridger a moment. He'd been so rigidly focused on what she'd been saying and the effort to communicate it to Dana that he'd forgotten where he was. Now he saw that it was getting late, past six anyway, the venetian blinds pregnant with color, thin fingers of sunlight marking the wall like the vestiges of a thief. He thought of Radko. He thought of Drex III. He'd have to go back after dinner, he was thinking, and that thought—of dinner—made his stomach churn in an anticipatory way. When was the last time he'd eaten?

"You see, the reason I ask," the woman went on, holding Bridger's eyes a moment before shifting back to Dana, just to be sure he was with them so that none of this—her spiel, her words, her professional empathy—would be wasted, "is because the vast majority of identity fraud cases come from a lost or stolen wallet or misappropriated mail. In fact, one of the thieves' favorite modus operandi is to get your name and address—out of the phone book, off your business card—and put in a change of address request with the post office. Then they get your mail sent to a drop box in Mailboxes R Us or some such, and there's all your financial information, credit card bills, bank statements, paychecks and what have you."

She paused to see what effect she was having. The fingers of light crept higher up the wall. On her face was a look of transport or maybe of triumph—she knew the ropes and she was in no danger and never would be. "Then all they have to do is make up a driver's license in your name, order new checks, replacement Visa cards, and voilà—you're out an average of something like five thousand dollars nationwide."

Bridger was thinking about his own mailbox, just a slot with his apartment number under it, and how many times had the cretins at the U.S. Postal Service stuffed it with his neighbors' mail by mistake? Or what about the time he wound up with half a dozen mutual fund statements addressed to a woman on the other side of town who had only a street address—196 Berton instead of 196 Manzanita—and a zip code in common with him? What if he'd been a crook? What then?

Dana broke into his reverie. She was getting impatient. She wanted action. That was Dana: cut to the chase, no time to spare. "Yeah," she said, her voice even hollower and more startling than usual, "but what do I do now, that's what we want to know."

The woman looked flustered a moment—this was a departure from the orthodoxy, from the ritual that soothed and absolved—but she recovered herself. "Well, you'll want to file a police report right away and you'll need to include that in any correspondence with creditors, and the credit reporting agencies should be notified if there are any irregularities. Your credit reports. You should order copies and check them over carefully—your Visa and MasterCard and what-have-you as well. But we'll get to all that. What I want you to know, what I want to tell you, is how these things happen—so you'll be prepared next time around." The look of rapture again. She arched her back and gazed into Dana's eyes. "An ounce of prevention, right?"

She held them there for half an hour more, and by the end of it Bridger began to wonder exactly what she was trying to convey. Or even how she felt about it. Her eyes seemed to flare and she became increasingly animated as she trotted out one horror story after another: the woman who had her rental application swiped from the desk in her landlord's office and wound up with some thirty thousand dollars in charges for elaborate meals and services in a hotel in a city she'd never been to, as well as the lease on a new Cadillac, the purchase price and registry of two standard poodles and $4,500 for liposuction; the twelve-year-old whose mother's boyfriend assumed his identity till the kid turned sixteen and was arrested when he applied for a driver's license for crimes the boyfriend had committed; the retiree whose mail mysteriously stopped coming and who eventually discovered that thieves had not only filed a change of address but requested his credit reports from the three credit reporting agencies so that they could drain his retirement account, cash his social security checks and even appropriate the 200,000 frequent flier miles he'd accumulated. And it got worse: deprived of income, the old man in question—a disabled Korean War veteran—wound up being evicted from his apartment for non-payment of rent and was reduced to living on the street and foraging from Dumpsters.

"That's terrible," Bridger said, just to say something. Dana sat rigid beside him.

"Tip of the iceberg," the counselor sang out. "And in your case, honey"—turning to Dana—"it's even worse, or potentially worse, because this isn't simple ID theft, where a drug user or ex-con tries to make a quick score and move on, but what we call identity takeover."

"I don't understand," Dana said, her face lit from beneath as the sun crept up the wall behind her. "Something's over, you're saying?" She turned to Bridger and he was trying to help as best he could when the woman simply scrawled the term on her pad and slid it across the desk.

"Identity takeover," she repeated. "It's when somebody becomes a second you—lives as you, under your name, for months, sometimes years. And if they live quietly and don't get in trouble with the law, they might never be detected—"

"Now *I* don't understand," Bridger heard himself saying. "Why would anyone want to do that—assume somebody's identity—if it wasn't for some credit card scam or something? I mean, what's the point?"

The woman shrugged. Looked down at the telephone on her desk as if she expected it somehow to provide the answer. She began boxing the photocopies between her hands in a brisk valedictory way, then looked up. Her eyes were gray and clear and lit with a strange excitement and they went from Bridger's face to Dana's and settled there. "Think about it," she said in a soft voice. "You're broke, uneducated, you owe child support payments, you've got a criminal record and your credit report stinks—maybe you've defaulted on a loan or gone bankrupt or driven your business into the ground. You find somebody solid—somebody like you, Dana—with good credit references, higher education, no criminal record of any kind at all. You said you had a Ph.D., right?"

Dana looked to Bridger for a translation and he did the best he could: *She says you have a Ph.D., right?*

"From Gallaudet," Dana said after a moment, her voice echoing tonelessly off the walls. She sat up, squared her shoulders. For the first time all afternoon the hint of a smile settled on her lips—she was proud of what she'd accomplished, proud of the recognition it gave her in a world full of slackers and underachievers, and she saw it as a springboard to more, much more. Her ambition was to move up to a four-year college, and not a deaf college like Gallaudet, but a hearing college where she could teach the contemporary American novel and poetry and maybe even creative writing to hearing students. "In English/American studies. I did my thesis on Poe and won the Morris Lassiter Award for Scholarship two years ago, the year before I came here to teach at San Roque." Her voice ruptured—she was tired, he could see that—and she chopped and elided the syllables. "It is un-der consid-eration at a ve-ry pres-ti-gious univ-ersity press my the-sis dir-ec-tor gave me an inroduction to—to which, I mean—but I don't really feel comftable mentioning the name until things are finalized. It wouldn't be right somehow . . ."

"Yes," the woman was saying, and she wasn't really listening, just trying to make a point. She had one of the photocopies in her hand, the one that showed the imposter, the smug thief with his shoplifter's eyes, in sharpest detail. "You see"—she tapped a glittering red fingernail on the stretched skin of the page—"this is Dr. Dana Halter. And you can bet he didn't have to write any thesis to get his degree."

Though he knew he should get back to Digital Dynasty, let himself in quietly and see to The Kade's unfinished business, he couldn't let Dana suffer all this alone. The news had been exclusively bad—No, the counselor had informed them, the city was not liable for the towing and impound fees and the police were within their rights for having arrested her because her base identifiers were the same as the thief's and they could try a lawsuit but it was just about as unlikely to fly as the San Roque phone book on her desk, though they *might* try small claims court for the towing and impound costs, but of course that would depend on the whim of the judge—and he wanted to be with her, even if it was only to order out pizza and sit in front of the TV while she put her head down and plunged through her student papers. Which was just what happened. They drove separately to her place and while he went out for the pizza (extra large, half garlic and chicken, half veggie) and two dinner salads with Italian dressing, she threw down her briefcase and got to work.

It was just after eight when the phone rang—or flashed, actually. He'd been sipping Chianti and watching a re-run of *Alien,* a movie he must have seen at least twenty times (Dana loved the tag line for the trailer: *In space no one can hear you scream*), trying not to feel too guilty about work. His feet were propped up on the coffee table, the fifth slice of pizza had plugged the hole in him, and he was enjoying the fact that he could crank the sound as loud as he liked without having to worry about distracting her. Every once in a while, as the creature retreated in a tail-whipping blur or mugged to the thunder of the score preparatory to ending the existence of one clueless crewmember or another, he would glance up at Dana. She was sitting across the room at her desk, the buttery glow of the lamp catching and releasing her face as she hovered close with her red pencil and then leaned back again, order restored and everything finally at peace—but for the creature, which was doing its thing now with the saliva machine and the multi-hinged jaws. Yes, and then the phone began to flash.

Dana glanced up. "Would you get that?"

He lifted his knitted ankles off the coffee table without shifting his gaze from the screen—they were going to commercial, a direct cut from the drooling teeth to a baby's naked bottom sans irony or even the faintest glimmer of network awareness—stood and crossed the room to the phone. Like most of the deaf, Dana had a TTY, an assistive listening device that was compatible with her cell and allowed her to send and receive both text and audio messages. He depressed the on button and the light stopped flashing, but instead of a text message, a high querulous whine of a voice came stabbing through the speakers: "Dana Halter? This is John J. J. Simmonds, accounts payable, down here at T-M? I'm calling about your delinquent account—"

"*Who?*" Bridger said.

"Because if you're having financial difficulties, I'm sure we can work out some sort of payment schedule, but you have to understand that payment in full must be made each month under the terms of the agreement you signed—"

"Whoa, whoa, whoa," Bridger said. "Hold on now—what account?" He glanced up at Dana; she was frowning over one of her papers, the red pencil poised at her lips.

"Don't give me that crap—"

"I'm not—I mean, we, I mean she—"

"—because deadbeats are one thing we just do not tolerate and I'm sure you can appreciate that."

"I can, yes, but—"

"Good, now we're getting someplace." The voice came right back at him, hard-charging, impenetrable. "Let me give you the straight facts: we're going to need a certified cashier's check in the amount of eight hundred twenty-two dollars and sixteen cents overnighted to our offices by closing time at five p.m. Pacific Coast Time or we *will* discontinue service and we *will* take legal action, and this is no idle threat, believe me."

Bridger could feel the irritation rising in him. "Hold on just one second, will you? What account are we talking about here—can you please just tell me that, *please*?"

"T-M Cellular."

"But she doesn't—we don't even use T-M. Both our phones are with Cingular."

"Don't give me that crap. I've got the past-due deadbeat bills right here in front of me. You understand what I'm saying? Eight hundred twenty-two dollars and sixteen cents. FedEx. Five p.m. tomorrow. This is no game, let me assure you of that."

"Okay, okay." He was watching Dana, her brow furrowed in concentration, the red pencil dancing—she was oblivious to the whole thing. On the screen, the monster was back, the camera gave a sudden jerk, and there was blood everywhere. "Listen, this is probably a mistake—she's just been the victim of identity theft—and if you would just send the bill so we can iron things out—"

"Who am I talking to?"

"This is her boyfriend."

"Boyfriend? You're telling me you're not Dana Halter? Then why in Christ's name did you say you were?"

"But I didn't—"

"You put her on right this minute, you hear me? I mean *now*! You think this is some kind of joke here? You think I'm a clown? Put her on or I'll have your ass too—for, for— *obstruction*!"

"I can't."

"What do you mean 'you can't'?"

"She's deaf."

There was a pause. Then the voice came back, harsher,

louder, a theatrical bray of outrage and puffed-up sanctimony. "I thought I'd heard it all, but you got balls, you really do. What do you think, I'm stupid here? We're talking fraud, felonies, we are going to take legal action—"

"Wait, wait, wait"—an inchoate idea had begun to form in Bridger's head—"can you just tell me what the number is, the number on the account? I mean, the number of the phone itself?"

The voice was exhausted, exasperated, drenched with contempt. "You don't know your own phone number?"

"Just give it to me."

Heavy irony, the world-weary sigh of disgust: "Four-one-five . . ."

As soon as he had the number, the instant the man on the other end of the line gave up the last digit, Bridger shouted "Check's in the mail!" and pulled the phone cable out of the wall. Then, his heart pounding with the audacity—the balls, yes—of what he was about to do, he glanced over his shoulder to make sure Dana was still at her desk, still bent over the papers with a red pencil and a wondering frown, before he pulled his cell from his pocket and dialed the number. There was the distant faintly echoing hum of the connection being made, of the satellite revolving in the sunstruck void, and then the click of the talk button and a man's voice saying, "Hello?"

PART II

One

"Yeah, hi. Is this Dana?"

They were announcing a special over the loudspeakers—*Attention, Smart-Mart shoppers, we're having a blue-light special in the housewares department, our superdeluxe model three-speed blender for only thirty-nine ninety-five while supplies last*—and the clamor distracted him. Plus, Madison was hanging on his left arm like a side of beef, totally sugared-out, her hair in her face, a smudge of chocolate on her chin, chanting *I want, I want, I want,* and where was Natalia? "Hold on," he said into the phone, "I can't hear you."

He gave the place a quick scan, the phone in one hand, Madison occupying the other, the usual chaos prevailing—kids running wild, fat people shoving carts piled high with crap up and down the aisles as if it were some sort of competition or exercise regimen, heads, backs, shoulders, bellies, buttocks, a stink of artificial butter flavoring and hot dogs grilled to jerky—and then he found a small oasis of calm in the lee of the menswear department and put the phone to his ear again. "Yeah? Hello?"

"Dana?"

"Yeah. Who's this?"

There was the briefest tic of hesitation, and then the voice on the other end of the line began to flow like verbal diarrhea: "It's Rick, I just wanted to hook up on that thing we were talking about the other day—"

He didn't recognize the voice. He didn't know any Rick. Madison pinched her tone to a sugar-fed falsetto: "I want Henrietta Horsie. Please. Please, Dana, please?"

"Rick who?"

"James, Rick James. You know, from the bar the other night? The one on, what was the name of that street?"

That was when everything went still, the loudspeakers muted, Madison moving her mouth and nothing coming out, the bare-legged kids charging silently up and down the aisles and even the babies with their purple-rage faces stalled right there in mid-shriek. He felt sick. Felt as if someone had taken a shank and opened him up. And he was trembling, actually trembling, when he clicked the off button and slid the phone down inside the Hanes display case.

His first thought was to find Natalia and get her out of there, to get in the car and make scarce, but he fought it down. It was nothing—or no, it was something, definitely something, something bad—but there was no need to panic. So they had the phone number—that was inevitable. He'd get another phone, no big deal, but then what if they could somehow trace it or get to the house? But no, he told himself, that was crazy. He was safe. He was fine. Everything was fine.

Madison, five years old tomorrow and with the shrunken hungry bewitching face of an elf out of some fairy tale, let go of his hand suddenly and allowed herself to come down hard on the hard shining floor. He looked down at her in that moment as if he'd never seen her before, her eyes contracting with calculated hurt or sullenness, ready for bed—past ready for bed—and then he jerked his head up and scanned the place for Natalia.

William Wilson was thirty-four years old, a pizza genius and a clothes horse, and to his own mind at least, a ladies' man, though his last lady—the lady before Natalia—had given him a daughter of his own whom he loved till it hurt and then turned into a queen bitch and landed him in jail. He'd always hated the name his mother had imposed on him—William Jr. after his father, who was his own kind of trouble—and when he was in elementary school he felt a little grand about it and insisted that everybody call him William and not Bill or Billy, and then in junior high he saw how uncool that was and got a warm-up jacket with Will stitched across the breast in white piping, but that didn't seem to make it either. Will, William, Bill, Billy: it was all so ordinary, so pedestrian—or plebeian, one of his favorite words from history class, because if anybody was the opposite of plebeian, it was him, and Christ, how many William Wilsons were there in a country the size of the U.S.? Not to mention England. There must have been thousands of them there too. Hundreds of thousands. And what of all the Guillaumes and Wilhelms and Guillermos scattered round the world? By high school he'd adopted his mother's maiden name—Peck—and nobody dared call him anything else, because he was quick with his tongue and his hands and feet too, black belt at sixteen, and there was only one kid at school who even thought about fucking with him and that kid, Hanvy Richards, wound up with the bridge of his nose broken in three places. Peck Wilson, that was who he was, and he went to the community college and got his associate's degree and rose up the ladder from delivery boy to counterman to manager at Fiorentino's in his hometown of Peterskill, in northern Westchester, and he traveled too, to Maui and Stowe and Miami. He tried out women the way he tried out drinks and recipes, always eager, always exploring. By the time he was twenty-five he was flush.

Sure, then he met Gina, and it was all shit after that. Or no: to give her credit, because she had an awesome body and a pierced tongue that tasted of the clove cigarettes she smoked and could make him stand up straight just thinking about it, she took him on more of a shit-slide, a whole roller-coastering hold-your-breath-and-look-out plunge into a vast vat of shit and on shit-greased wheels too. But he didn't want to think about that now. He wanted to think about Natalia, the girl from Jaroslavl who never got enough of anything—the shopper extraordinaire, restaurant killer and bedroom champion—with the breathy bitten-off Russian accent that made him itch and itch again and her little daughter by the guy who brought her over and got her her papers, an older guy she never even liked let alone loved.

They were in the car now, the Z4 he'd bought her (black, convertible, with the 3.0-liter engine and six-speed manual transmission), and the trunk was full of Smart-Mart loot and Madison was squirming in her lap. "Why is it we must go so soon?" she said, giving him a look over her daughter's head. When he didn't answer right away because he was fumbling with the packaging of one of the CDs he'd picked up while she was shopping (the new Hives, a greatest hits compilation of Rage Against the Machine, a couple of reggae discs he'd been looking for), she lifted her voice out of the darkness and said, "Dana? Are you listening to me?"

He loved the way she said his name, or the name she knew him by, anyway—down on the first syllable, hang on to the *n* and then rise and hit the *ah* like a bell ringing—and he dropped the plastic CD case into his lap and reached for her hand. "I don't know, baby," he said, "I just thought you might want to go someplace nice, like that seafood place maybe, you know? Aren't you getting hungry?"

Her voice floated back to him, coy, pleased with itself: "Maggio's? On Tiburon?"

"Yeah," he said, and he had to release her hand to shift down. "I mean, if you're still up for it." He gave her a glance.

"And Madison. She could sleep in the car—I mean, she's really knocked out."

She was silent a moment. The engine sang its sweet song as he accelerated into the turn. "I don't know," she said, "too much tourists, no? Already, already the tourists! What about—?" And she named the priciest place in Sausalito.

"I hate that place. Phonier than shit. All the waiters have a stick up their ass." He was remembering the last time, the look on the face of the little fag with the bleached hair when he mispronounced the name of the wine—it was a Meursault and he'd had it before, plenty of times, but he wasn't French, that was all.

"I like it."

"Not me. I swear I'll never go there again. I say Maggio's. I'm driving, right?"

The car thrummed beneath him, everything—every bolt and buckle and whatever else they had under the hood—in perfect alignment. This was the real thing, German engineering, and it made him feel unbeatable. He fumbled a moment with one of the reggae CDs—an old Burning Spear his cellmate used to play all the time—and then passed it to her. "How about a hand here, huh?" he said, and Natalia's sweet smoky arrhythmic voice floated out again—"Sure," she said, "sure, no problem, honey, and Maggio's is fine, really"—and the lights flashed in the windows and the fog came up off the bay and Madison, her hair shining in the draw of the approaching headlights, found her niche in her mother's arms. And there it was: the first light insuck of a child's snore, replete.

He was abstracted all through dinner, but Natalia hardly noticed. She was chattering away about some new appliance she needed for the house—a new microwave oven, that was it, because the old one, the one that came with the place, was outdated and it took her nearly five minutes to boil water for a cup of tea and she just didn't trust the Smart-Mart line since they were a such a *cheapie* place, didn't he think?—and he let her go on, her shopper's rhapsody a kind of music to him. If she was happy buying things, then he was happy paying for them. It was a feeling he liked, providing for her—especially in contrast to Marshall, the dud she'd been with before him and who wasn't the father of Madison and was so stingy and petty she couldn't even begin to talk about it, but of course she always did. She'd been out to the car twice to check up on the kid and sneak a smoke and she managed to tuck herself back into her seat just as the entrées arrived. He didn't say anything, just watched her as she unfolded the white linen napkin with a fillip of her wrist, her shoulders bare, eyes darting round the room—in her element, absolutely in her element. The steam rose from their plates. The waiter materialized over her shoulder—"Grated parmesan? Ground black pepper?"—and faded away. She spread the napkin across her lap, took a sip of wine. "You are the quiet one tonight, Da-na, yes?" she said, giving him a sidelong look as if better to examine him from the angle. "Something is wrong? You usually like this place, is it not so?"

He did like the place. It wasn't in the league of the Sausalito restaurant maybe, but the menu was pretty eclectic and they knew him here—everybody knew him—and if there was a line of tourists or whoever, they always seated him the minute he walked in the door. Which was the way it should be. His money was good, he tipped large, he always dressed in a nice Armani jacket when he came in for dinner and his girlfriend was a knockout—they should have paid *him* just to sit at the bar. He was having the seared ahi, to his mind the best thing on the menu, and it came teepeed atop a swirl of garlic mashed potatoes and translucent onion rings with a garnish of grilled baby vegetables; she was having the seafood medley. The ahi looked good, top-flight, but he didn't pick up his fork. Instead he reached for the wine, their second bottle, a Piesporter he'd always wanted to try, and it was good, light and crisp on the palate, very cold and faintly sweet the way a Riesling should be. "Yeah," he said, "the place is great."

She was neatly slicing a medallion of lobster in two. Her earrings caught the light as she bent her head forward, and he saw her framed there as if on the screen in a movie theater, the selective eye of the camera enriching the scene till the grain of the wood paneling shone behind her and the crystal glittered and her eye lifted to meet his. He'd bought them for her, the earrings, fourteen-karat white gold chandeliers with a constellation of diamonds, to make things up with her after their first fight—she wore them to bed that night and she didn't wear anything else. "You look not so great—like a man who is, I don't know, not so great right now. Are you not hungry? You are feeling discomfited?"

He had to smile. Inside he was still seething at that fuckhead on the other end of the phone—Rick James, yeah, sure, the superfreak himself—but he had to hand it to her: she could make him smile anytime. *Discomfited.* Where in Christ's name had she come up with that one? "It's nothing, baby," he murmured, reaching across the table for her hand, a hand almost as big as his own, the long predatory fingers, the pampered nails in two shades of lacquer, as if a cobalt moon were setting over a maraschino planet in ten fleeting phases. She took his hand in a fierce clasp and brought his knuckles to her lips.

"There," she said, everything about her sparkling, the earrings, the sheer fabric of her dress, her eyes, her lips, "you see? I make it better."

But it wasn't better. He felt sulky, sullen, felt like lashing out at somebody. He freed his hand, picked up his fork and scattered the seared slabs of pink flesh round the plate. "You got your phone?" he said suddenly.

She was sipping wine, the pedestal of the glass hovering like a hummingbird over the bud of her mouth. She liked wine. Liked it even more than he did. She liked vodka too. "Why? Did you lose yours?"

He shook his head, held out his hand. "I left it on the dresser."

"But no—you have it when we are at The Bridge, for cocktails. Before the Smart-Mart. Remember? You are calling for canceling Madison's piano lesson—remember?"

"Maybe I left it in the car."

A theatrical sigh, the bemused frown giving way to a lingering look of chastisement, of maternal tsk-tsking—yes, and wasn't it motherhood that ruined them all, that elevated them to the status of the all-knowing and all-powerful, and reduced everybody else, even grandfathers, dictators and mercenary killers, to the level of feckless children? Even as she dug into her purse for the cell a quick flare of anger burst in his brain, streamers everywhere. Did he snatch it from her? Maybe. Maybe he did. "I've got to make a call," he said, barely able to suppress the rage in his voice. "Be right back."

He was on his way to the men's, shouldering his way past a group of lawyer types at the bar—thirty to sixty, pinned-back ears, faces that glowed like jack-o'-lanterns with their own self-importance, Glenfiddich in their tumblers and bitches on their arms, Berkeley bitches, Stanford bitches, maybe even Vassar bitches—when he shot a glance to the doorway and saw the cutout figure of a little girl with a tragic face poised right there on the carpet in the shadow of the hostess' stand. Madison was barefoot, her sundress askew, Henrietta Horsie dangling by the rope of its tail from the clench of one tiny fist. There was the smell of the sea knifing in through the open door, a smell of cold storage and rot, and it reminded him of where he was, of what it cost to live where you could get that smell anytime you wanted it, day and night. She was crying. Or no, whining. He could hear the faint singsong whimper, and it was like some stringed instrument—cello, violin—playing the same dismal figure over and over. Two couples suddenly entered the picture, looming up behind her looking puzzled and annoyed, as if they'd just stepped in something, and the hostess—Carmela, eighteen years old and as tall and lean and honey-breasted as a fashion model's little sister—was bent at the waist, clearly disconcerted but trying her best to coo something reassuring.

Fuck it, he was thinking, *let Natalia deal with it,* and he swung abruptly to his left, nearly colliding with a fish-faced woman in pearls and a black cocktail dress and half a mile of exposed bosom who was making her way back from the ladies'. "Oh," she gasped as if he'd run her down on a football field and slammed the wind out of her, "oh, beg pardon," and that was all it took—the movement, the distraction—because he heard Madison cry out behind him and then he turned and she was running to him, already sobbing.

The whole place stopped dead, every head raised to see what the commotion was, even the waiters looking over their shoulders as they levitated their trays and paused in mid-step. One of the lawyers might have said something: there was a laugh, a group laugh, at the bar behind him, but he blocked it out, Madison coming straight for him, her sobs brutal and explosive, the bare dirty feet slapping through a minefield of boots and loafers and heels till she was there clinging to his leg like a—what were those fish that fasten on to the sharks? "Dr. Halter, is everything all right?" one of the bartenders said, but he ignored him. And he must have lifted her too forcefully because she exploded all over again and he just tucked her, kicking, under one arm and brought her to Natalia like something he'd caught and trussed up in the jungle and they were laughing at him, he could feel it, everybody in the place, just laughing.

There was one white-haired old shit in the men's, meticulously drying his fat red hands as if he was afraid his skin was going to come off, and Peck gave him a look of such pure hate and burgeoning uncontainable violence that he backed out the door like a crab. The door eased shut on marble, fresh-cut flowers, a smell of new-minted money chopped up and vaporized. And what was that?—opera—playing through the speakers. For a long moment he just stared at himself in the mirror, his eyes vacant, and nothing registered, as if he didn't recognize himself or the place either. Then he realized the phone was still in his hand, Natalia's phone, the one that was stuck to the side of her head sixteen hours a day when she was running up the bill talking to her sister in Russia and her brother in Toronto and her best friend Kaylee whose kid was at the same pre-school as Madison. The phone. He studied it there in the palm of his hand as if he'd never seen it before, as if he hadn't signed on for a thousand free minutes and used it as an extension of himself whenever he had to check up on the ballgame or place a bet or score a little something to make the afternoons go easier with nothing to do but sit in the sun on the back deck and stare at Natalia's sweet brown midriff and tapering legs because how much sex can you have before you go blind and deaf and your tool falls off?

He heard somebody at the door—another white-hair—and he said, "Give me a minute here, will you? Is that too much to ask—a fucking minute's privacy?" And then he opened his hand and began to slam the cell against the marble tile of the wall in front of him, and he slammed it till there wasn't much left to hold, and after that he dropped it to the marble floor and worked it with his heel.

Later, after they'd got home and Natalia put Madison to bed and settled down in front of the tube ("Everything satisfactory? You want that doggie-bagged, Dr. Halter?" "Nah, no point in it—give it to the homeless, will you?"), he took a bottle of beer into the spare bedroom he used as an office and booted up the computer. He went to the T-M site, typed in his password and brought up his account—OVER-DUE AND PAYABLE/SERVICE INTERRUPTION WARNING—to see what he could find there. He'd gotten lazy or incautious or whatever you wanted to call it and now he'd put everything at risk and that was just stupid, stupid, stupid. For a year and more he'd been careful to pay up all his Dana Halter accounts just so something like this wouldn't happen, but he'd had a little cash-flow problem—the condo, the new car, Natalia on the phone and at the mall and the salon and Jack's and Emilio's and all the rest—and things had slipped. Now they were onto him. *Jesus,* the thought of it made him so furious, so rubbed raw and plain pissed off it was all he could do to stop himself from jerking the monitor off the desk and flinging it through the fucking window because the thing wasn't giving him what he wanted. He stared at the screen, at his account, calls out and calls in—incoming, incoming—but nothing more recent than the close of the last billing period. He wanted that number. The number of that fuckhead Dana Halter—or the cop or detective or whoever he was, *Rick Fucking James*—and he wasn't going to wait for the bill and he wasn't going down to the T-M office to pay off the account either. No, he was going to get a new phone in some other creep's name and no one would be the wiser except maybe Natalia ("Will you not give me back my cell, Dana?" she'd said the minute they got in the car; "No," he said, "I need it because I'm expecting a call, okay? Can you just back off? Can you?").

Before he did that, though, he had a little task to perform, the smallest pain in the ass maybe, but not risky, not at all. What he had to do, first thing in the morning, even before he opened a new account and got his five hundred free minutes and no-charge weekends, was go down to Smart-Mart and amble into the menswear department. He'd been hasty, impulsive. He hadn't been thinking. But he could picture it already, some career drudge stocking shelves or pushing a broom and "Hey, bro, can you help me out here—I had my cell balanced right here on top of this display because my arms were loaded down with all this high-quality Hanes underwear and I think it went down there, yeah, there, behind the partition. Hey, thanks, man, thanks beaucoup." Yeah, and then he'd toss it away again, but not before he hit *Calls Received* and got that clown's number. Because who was to blame here, who was the wise guy, who was fucking with whom?

Two

"WHAT DID HE SOUND LIKE?"

Bridger shrugged. She watched his lips. "I don't know—like anybody else, I guess."

It was early evening, she was feeling frayed and beaten and so exhausted her internal meter was barely registering, but her papers were finished and back in the hands of her students and her grades were in. They were at a restaurant, Bridger's treat, the silent careening of the waitresses and the tidal heave of people swelling and receding at the bar a kind of visual massage for her, and as she poured out her second glass of beer she felt herself coming back to life. She'd always liked this place—it featured old sofas and low tables, loud rock music (very loud: she could feel the vibrations in the beer bottle, in the cushions, the table, almost picture the air fracturing around her) and a mostly young clientele from the local college. It was dark, there were dashed-off-looking abstracts on the walls, and it was cheap and good. She'd ordered risotto, about the only thing she could get down without chewing; Bridger was having pizza, the all-sustaining nutriment and foundation of his diet.

"You're hearing," she said, leaning into the table, "and you can't do better than that? What was his voice like?"

He leaned in too, but he wore an odd expression—he hadn't heard her. Because of the music. "What?" he said, predictably.

She gave him a smile. "Just like the night we met."

"What?"

So she signed it for him and he signed back: *What do you mean?*

You're deaf too.

He had an outsized head, castellated with the turrets and battlements of his gelled hair, and sometimes, when she saw him in a certain light, his features seemed compacted in contrast, like a child's. That was how it was now. He had the look of a child, puzzled, unaware, but slowly allowing her gesture to make the words in his mind and bring the meaning back through the circuitry to his eyes. "Oh, yeah," he said aloud. "Yeah."

But what did he sound like?

A shrug. *Cool.*

Cool? The jerk who stole my identity is cool?

Another shrug. He lifted his beer to his lips to give him time with the response, then he set it down carefully and said something she didn't catch.

What?

His clumsy Sign, loose and sloppy, but endearing because it was his: *Suspicious.*

He sounded suspicious? Cool and suspicious?

People were watching them—the girl at the next table over, trying not to stare but nudging the boy with her, college students both, with tiny matching Mickey Mouse tattoos on the underside of their left wrists. People always stared at her, overtly or furtively, when she talked in Sign, and when she was younger—especially in the crucible of adolescence—it used to affect her. Or no: it mortified her. She was different, and she didn't want to be. Not then. Not when the slightest variation in dress or hairstyle reverberated through the whole classroom. Now it was nothing to her. She was deaf and they weren't. They would never know what that meant.

Bridger gave one last shrug, more elaborate this time: *Yes.*

She finger-spelled his name and it was both an intimate and formal gesture, intimate because it was personal, because it named him instead of pointing the right hand and index finger at him to say *you* and formal because it had the effect of a parent or teacher announcing displeasure by reverting to the full and proper name. Charles instead of Charlie. William instead of Billy. *Bridger,* she signed, *you're not communicating.*

She watched his mouth open in a laugh, enjoyed the glint of the crepuscular bar lights off the gold in his molars.

And if you're not communicating, how are we ever going to track down the bad guy?

They both laughed, and her laugh might have been wild and out of control—most deaf people's laughs were described as bizarre, whinnying, crazed—but she had no way of knowing, and she couldn't have cared less. The place was warm. The place was loud. A guy at the bar turned round to stare at her. "But seriously," she said aloud. "The area code was 415?"

"What?"

"Four-one-five?"

He nodded. The music might have been supersonic, the plates rattling on the shelves, people running for cover and whole mountains tumbling into the sea, but a nod always did the trick.

"Bay Area," she said.

"That's right," he said, and he leaned in so close she could feel his breath on her lips, "and it's a 235 prefix."

Another number. She took it from him and repeated it: "Two-three-five?"

"Same as Andy's, my friend Andy? From college?"

"Marin?"

"Yeah," he said. "Marin."

On Friday morning she met with her last class of the semester and felt nothing but relief. They were juniors, so there was none of the tug she'd felt with the seniors on Thursday, the ones who were going out into the world to make a life without her—these kids she'd see next year, and they'd be taller, stronger, wiser, and she'd give them words, words on the page and in the mind and in the residual silent beat of the iamb that was as natural as breathing, *What lips my lips have kissed, and where, and why / I have forgotten.* As she packed up her things, sorting through books, papers, videotapes, she couldn't suppress a sudden rush of elation, the kind a runner must feel at the tape, her first year behind her, the long break ahead and the sting of what had happened over the past weekend gradually beginning to fade.

The other teachers were going out to lunch at a place down by the ocean to celebrate the end of the term with steamer clams, fish and chips and a judicious and strictly medicinal intake of alcohol, but she was going to the dentist. Or rather the endodontist. *Root canal.* Simple dactyl. There wasn't much metaphoric mystery there: the root of the tooth branched down into her jaw like the root of a tree, where the living nerve relayed pain to the thalamus; the canal was to be excavated through the tender offices of Dr. Stroud's instruments, and though she'd be spared the noise that so intimidated the hearing, the stink of incineration would ride up her nostrils all the same even as the bony structure of her cranium vibrated with the seismic grinding of the drill. And the pain—there was no aural component for that. She would feel it as much as anyone, maybe more.

She could see it like an aura, taste it. Pain. Of course, Bridger had a different take on it altogether—and he could afford to, since he wasn't the one undergoing the ordeal. The night before, just to reassure her, he'd told her that the last time he'd been to the dentist he'd named names and given up all his secrets in the first three minutes and still the fiend kept drilling. She'd signed back to him, right hand open, palm in, fingers pointing up, then the fingertips to the mouth and the hand moving out and down, ending with the palm up: *Thank you.* And then aloud: "For sharing that."

She'd avoided Koch since their confrontation on Tuesday, but as she was hurrying down the hall, running late, two cardboard boxes of books and papers clutched to her chest, her briefcase slapping at her right thigh and skewing awkwardly away from her, he emerged from the main office. They made eye contact—he saw her; she saw him; there was no avoiding it—and his mouth began to move. The only thing was, she didn't know whether he was chewing gum or delivering a soliloquy out of *Richard III*, whether he was offering up the apology he owed her or even a threat or insult, because she dropped her eyes and went right on by him as if he were a figure out of a dream.

Because she was late, Dr. Stroud dispensed with the usual ten minutes of banter, gossip and news of the world, and settled her into the chair as expeditiously as possible. Still, he was running at the mouth all the while, filling her in on his wife's fender bender (Dana loved the term, loved the rhyme and the function and the way it snapped on the lips to reveal the grimace of the teeth) at the farmers' market the previous week—she was there for the cut flowers, she was mad for cut flowers, and for beets and broccolini and did he ever tell her about the time she ran out of gas in the middle of the Fourth of July parade?, and some overanxious boutique baby-vegetable purveyor backed into her in his seven-thousand-pound Suburban. Or at least that was the drift of it, broccolini a bit problematic, and that put her back a phrase or two. Before he inserted the rubber dam and the crank device that jammed her jaws open, she was able to respond by averring that broccolini was her single favorite vegetable, sautéed in olive oil with chopped garlic, shallots and a splash of Dijon mustard, and that she hoped the damage to the car wasn't too severe, but by that time he was already onto some other subject, something dental—or endodontal—she gathered, something serious in any case, because his eyebrows suddenly collided and his pupils narrowed. A moment later he and the nurse both snapped on their surgical masks and she felt the sting of the needle as it slid into her gums and after that all communication ceased.

Two hours in the chair. The drilling, the gouging, the fitting of the post and the grinding down of the temporary cap: two hours anyone else would have written off. But not Dana. She was, as Bridger was quick to point out—pejoratively—an A-type personality, as if that were something to be ashamed of, as if civilization hadn't been built on the backs of the A-types, as if armies hadn't been led by them, advances made in the laboratory, in the concert hall, the universities and hospitals and everywhere else. Slow down, people told her—*Bridger* told her—relax and live in the moment, but they were B-types, they were slackers. Like Bridger. And were there only two types then? No, she thought, there must be a third type, type C, for Criminal. That man in the photo staring out at her from the fax in the police station, that was what he was: no need to make and build or lie back and smell the roses when you could just simply steal it all.

So she was an A-type. And she had two hours. She understood that it would be somewhat difficult to focus under the circumstances, what with the dentist's fingers in her mouth and the nurse's face hovering in her field of vision like the moon to his sun—no hearing person could have done it—but she was good at shutting out the world, a champion, in fact, and she'd brought the thin sheaf of *Wild Child* along with her. It had been over a week since she'd had a chance even to think about it in any fruitful way, and that nagged at her. She couldn't hope to write under the circumstances—there was no realistic way and she had no expectations—but what Bridger didn't understand was how vital it was to review and revise, to re-enter that world she'd created and find her way to a destination she couldn't even guess at.

The drill bit, the dam held. Dr. Stroud probed. The nurse loomed. And Dana lifted the manuscript in one hand and banished them both, drifting, drifting now into another place altogether, a place where she wasn't Dana Halter of the San Roque School for the Deaf, but a child of eleven, a boy child, nameless, naked, dwelling in his senses. There was a scar at his throat, a raised ragged island of flesh he fingered because it was there, a scar that preceded all the others and took him back to the moment when he found himself waking for the first time to the swaying of the trees and the rhythmic clangor of the birds and insects, attuned to the fierceness of the wind in the branches and the pitch of every note the branches sang. He lived in France, in the untamed forest of La Bassine, but he didn't know it. Lived eighteen hundred years after the death of Christ, but he didn't know that either. All he knew was to dig in the earth for grubs and tubers, to gorge on berries, grasshoppers, frogs and snails, to crouch over his haunches in a nest of leaves and listen to that symphony of the air and the melody the brooks played and the insects of the day and the insects of the night, the earth spinning for him alone and no human voice, no words, to intrude on it . . .

But Dr. Stroud was there, leaning away from her now, the surgical mask removed, and he was smiling at her—preening himself on a job well done. The nurse was smiling too. "That wasn't so bad, was it?" he said, careful with his lips and teeth and tongue so that she could understand.

"No," she said, her own lips cumbersome and without sensation, "not bad at all."

"Good," he said, "good. Well, you're a model patient, let me tell you." His eyebrows tented. Both his hands were clenched above his shoulders and rocking back and forth in celebration of their mutual triumph. "If you have any pain, Advil should do it. And nothing too strenuous"—yes, that was it: strenuous—"for the rest of the day. Take some time off. Put your feet up. Relax."

She nodded, her mouth frozen in a Xylocaine-induced grimace. And then he went on to tell her an elaborate story about one of his other patients, whom he wouldn't name out of professional discretion, but she was something of a hypochondriac—his mouth gaped over the word—and that was the last thing she caught because he forgot himself and began talking so fast even a hearing person would have had trouble understanding him. A term came to her—motormouth—and she had to smile, whether he misinterpreted it or not. She was on her feet now, at the door, and he was still talking away, but for all she got of it he might as well have been chewing gum.

Three

MADISON WAS AWAY at the piano teacher's, Natalia was sunbathing on the deck and he was poised over the black granite top of the kitchen counter, mixing their second round of Sea Breezes. He stood there in a cocoon of silence (the CD needed to be punched up but he didn't feel like punching it), appreciating one of those moments when the whole world opens itself up to you, when everything you take for granted in the daily hassle to scratch and grab and assert a little dominance is suddenly right there in front of you and the planet poises on its axis, just balanced, just now. And he wasn't drunk, not yet—that wasn't it. He was just attuned to the little things: the taste of the salt air through the flung-open window, the feel of the delicate layer of ice on the neck of the Grey Goose bottle straight from the freezer, the perfume of the split lime, the sweetness of the cranberry juice and the acid pull of the fresh-squeezed grapefruit in the stone pitcher. He looked out over the salt marsh to the bay beyond, the light like something out of a painting—a thousand gradations of light, from the palest driest Arctic stripes at the wrought-iron rail of the deck to the rich tropical gold poured all over Natalia and the chaise longue to the distant white purity of the sails of the boats tacking against the breeze.

For dinner, he was going to make sea scallops braised with scallions and garlic, with a sauce he'd learned years ago while fooling around at the restaurant (a white wine reduction flavored with shallots and a splash of sherry, dollop of butter, fold in the cream at a galloping boil and reduce the whole thing again till it was a fifth of what you started with). He was thinking rice with it, flavored with bouillon, sherry and sesame oil, and maybe a salad and some sautéed broccolini on the side. Keep it simple. He could have done something more elaborate, because everything was fine and he had all the time in the world, and yet sometimes you just wanted to get back to basics and let the flavors speak for themselves. He could have made dinner rolls from scratch if he'd had the inclination, could have done up something for dessert too, but you couldn't beat fresh-picked raspberries in heavy cream with a sprinkle of sugar and a splash of brandy to burnish the taste. This was how life should be, no hassles and strains and worries, time on your hands, time to stroll through the farmers' market and the wine shop and have a cappuccino and croissant with your lady on a sun-struck morning, time to chop and dice and sear and lay out a nice meal for Natalia's friend Kaylee and what was her husband's name? Jonas, yeah, Jonas. Not a bad guy, really, for a loser. They had a chain of exercise studios—Pilates and the rest of that crap—and he supposed they did pretty well, and that was all right. At least the guy appreciated fine cuisine, a good bottle of wine—at least he wouldn't be wasting his time in the kitchen on a couple of zeroes.

The light shifted. The world began to crank round again. His eyes went to Natalia, the sun on her legs, the sheen, the geometry of perfection, and then he came back to the business at hand: cutting two neat pale green wedges of lime to garnish their drinks.

· · · · ·

By the time the doorbell rang, everything was ready to go—Madison back from the piano teacher, fed and in her pajamas, the videos selected, the pans laid out and the scallops prepped—and Natalia got up out of the chaise longue in her two-piece and chiffon robe and drifted through the open French doors like something floating on the breeze. She always moved like that—everything in its own sweet time, *Don't rush me, just look at me*—and he heard the greetings at the door and came out of the kitchen with two fresh cocktails in hand. The kid—the daughter, Lucinda—made a bolt for Madison's room and Kaylee, a bony blonde with pinched little shaded glasses and a frizz of hair twisted up in a bun, pulled him to her for an embrace. "Hey," she was saying, "we just saw the most awesome thing out on the road on the way here, this white bird?—Jonas says it was an egret—just like perched there on the yellow line like it was in the middle of a river or something—"

Peck handed her a Sea Breeze, even as he gave the husband's right hand a squeeze and fitted the cold glass into the socket of his left. "Hey," he said, and the husband—stubble-headed, goateed, going to fat around the ring in his earlobe—returned the greeting.

"Wasn't that an egret, Jonas?" Kaylee was saying.

"It is a white bird," Natalia said, bending to levitate her hand two feet from the tiles as her breasts, on display, shifted in the bikini top, "about this high off the ground, yes? We are seeing them all the time," she avowed, straightening up. "With the binoculars. Common, yes. Very common here."

"Really?" Kaylee lifted her eyebrows, raised the cocktail to her lips. "It's like really beautiful, though," she murmured over the rim of the glass. "Like magical, you know?"

The husband wasn't having it. He just held on to his

grin and said, "Maybe we ought to get one and stuff it for the Corte Madera place."

"Oh, Jonas," the wife said, making a face. She looked to Peck for approval. They both did, the whole party arrested in the entryway, gulping vodka and making small talk about birds.

"Sure," he said, "why not? And we can stuff the tourists while we're at it too."

The conversation at dinner ran to a whole host of mainly numb-brained subjects, from Nautilus machines to stair-steppers, the stock market, the Giants, A's, farm-raised salmon and the new Kade movie to the "like super-expensive" European vacation Jonas was treating his wife to, a whole month and the kid at Grandma's, week in Paris, week in Venice, then the rest of the time on some jerkoff's sixty-thousand-foot-long boat off the Islas Baleares. They'd actually said that, actually given him the Spanish with the rolling *r* and the whole deal, as if they were a tag team of waiters in a Mexican restaurant, first him—*Islas Baleares*—and then her, like an echo. They'd praised the meal—and the wine, and they'd brought two bottles of Talley Char-donnay that wasn't half bad—but as the sun went to bed and the stereo got louder and they began to put a real ap-preciable dent in the bottle of Armagnac that had cost him sixty bucks at the discount place, Peck began to realize he could live without these people. He really could. Kaylee he'd approved of because she kept Natalia occupied and off his back, but the husband was full of shit to his ears—they both were—and he felt himself getting restless, getting edgy, and that wasn't good because it destroyed the mood of the day and made him think of other things, things that had a negative energy, things that brought him down. Like Dana Halter. Like *Bridger,* that asshole.

He'd called the number that morning and got a message—

"Hello, you've reached Bridger's cell; leave a number"—
and he felt as if he'd pulled the handle on a dollar machine
and got two cherries instead of three. Bridger. What kind
of name was that? And why was he playing the game
instead of Dr. Dana Halter? If he was some kind of cop
he wouldn't have been stupid enough to display his
number . . . which meant he wasn't a cop. But then who
was he?

"So, Dana," the husband was saying, fat-faced, red-faced,
leaning into the coffee table as if it were the municipal pool
and he was about to plunge in, "anything new with you?"

He felt the smallest burr of irritation. He gave the guy a
look to warn him off but he was too dense to catch it.

"I mean, with your practice—that office space in Larkspur? How'd that ever work out?"

It wasn't just a burr—it was a thorn, a spike. Who *was*
this clown? And what had he told him? Shit, he couldn't
even remember himself. He reached for the snifter and took
a moment to study the way the brandy swirled and caught
at the glass—it was the color of diet cola when the ice melts
down in it, and how had he never noticed that before?—
and then he realized that nobody was talking. The husband
was staring at him, waiting in his gerbil-faced way for a response, wondering vaguely if he was being dissed, and if he
was, what to do about it—and both girls had stopped jab-
bering away about so-and-so's boob job and were watching
him too. "I don't know," he said finally, trying to control the
bubble that was swelling inside him like one of the bubbles
that punch through the sauce after you fold the cream in,
"with all the malpractice insurance, I don't know how anybody could say it's worth it. Really. Sometimes I think I'd be
better off just staying out of it—"

Kaylee's mouth flapped open as if it were spring-
operated: "But you're so young—"

The husband: "And your training. What about your training?"

They'd moved into the main room from the dining table—"No, no, don't bother," Natalia had said when Kaylee tried to help her clear up, "leave it for the maid"—and he'd taken a certain satisfaction in going round the room and flicking on the lamps to create a feeling of intimacy and warmth, as if lamps were hearths and the twenty-five-watt bulbs miniature fires blazing against the night and the fog creeping in across the hills behind them. He studied the husband just the briefest fraction of a second—was the fat fuck mocking him? Was that it? But no: he could detect nothing but a kind of stubborn booze-inflected obtuseness in the man's dwindling stupid little eyes. He didn't answer.

"But all that work, medical school and all," Kaylee said. She arched her back and did something meant to be furtive that tautened the thin black straps of her bra. "It seems such a shame."

"Oh, no," Natalia cut in, making a moue over the *o* sound and holding it a beat too long. "Dana's job is for looking after me and Madison," and she reached out to caress his biceps. "Is that not so, baby?" She smiled her biggest smile. "A full-time job, no?"

The husband's snifter was empty and he was reaching out his claws to refill it. "Where did you say you went to medical school? Hopkins, wasn't it?"

"Yeah," Peck said. "But I was thinking it might be cool, really cool, to do something with Doctors Without Borders. You know, go to Sudan or someplace. Help people. Refugees and that sort of thing. Cholera. Plague."

"Médecins sans Frontières," the husband said, as if he were licking fudge from between his teeth.

From the back room came the sound of the kids' video, some Disney thing with the seahorses and talking starfish and all the rest, music swelling, the sound of artificial waves. He was agitated, and he didn't know why. The day had been perfect, the sort of day he could have lived through forever, the day—the days—he'd promised himself when he was inside, when everything was gray and the sun never seemed to shine and there was always some self-important officious asshole there to make you toe the line, lights out, everybody up, and the bonehead cons with their pathetic attempts to join the human race, *427, factory, I swear; Nobody changes this channel, motherfucker;* and *How would you like your Jell-O cooked, sir?* But no, he did know why. Everything he had was balanced on the head of a pin, like the collapsible two-story brick house with the three-car garage and the bird in the cage and the yapping dog all folded up in a carpet in one of Madison's videos, swept away in a windstorm that raked the lot where it had stood just a heartbeat before. It was people like this, like *Jonas,* like *Kaylee,* that were the problem. What was he thinking? That he could just waltz in and set himself up and think these people were his friends or something? No. That wasn't the way it was. That wasn't the way it would ever be.

So what did he do? He pushed himself back from the coffee table and raised one foot in his shining new ultra-cool Vans with the checkerboard pattern and set it down right beside Jonas' drink. "Yeah," he said, leaning back into the cushions and giving both arms a good sinew-cracking stretch, "that's right. That's who I'm talking about."

When he first met Gina, things were different. He was twenty-five years old, with two years of community college behind him and stints at restaurants in Maui and Stowe, no record of any kind except for traffic infractions (tickets he tossed in the trash, because really, they were just a scam anyway, a means for local municipalities to raise cash so they could buy more cruisers and more radar guns so they could rob more people in the name of law and order), and he'd just been promoted to manager at Fiorentino's, the youngest manager they'd ever had. Or at least that was what Jocko, the basset-faced old bartender who'd been there since the Civil War, told him. Then Gina showed up. He'd been sitting at the bar, his day off—noon—with Jocko and Frank Calabrese, the owner, and a mini-parade of girls slipped in and out applying for the cocktail waitress job advertised that morning in the local paper. They had the faintly tarnished look of cocktail waitresses, every one of them, and some had experience, some didn't. He wasn't looking for experience. He was focusing on one attribute only—how hot they were, on a descending scale of one to ten. None of the others even came close to Gina—facially, maybe, but her body was right out of *Playboy;* or better yet, *Penthouse.* Jocko and Frank, who could be brutal, didn't give him any argument.

Gina-Louise Marchetti.

She'd gone to Lakeland High School, just outside Peterskill, she was twenty years old, between boyfriends, and living—temporarily, she insisted—back at her parents' place on a twisting black road in the rural tree-hung precincts of Putnam Valley, where absolutely nothing was happening, not then or now or ever. Within a week he was sleeping with her and within the month she'd moved into his apartment. Most nights after work they'd cruise the local bars and then sleep in till noon and on their days off they took the train into Manhattan and hit the clubs. They did drugs together, but not in an excessive way, and only speed and once in a while E, and they began to enjoy some decent wines and experiment with recipes out of a cookbook when they had a night at home. For Christmas she bought him a cherrywood wine rack—"For the cellar you're going to have"—and he gave her a case of red the liquor salesman got him wholesale; they cooked a paella for Christmas dinner, just to be different, and spent most of the night admiring the way the twelve symmetrical bottles of Valpolicella looked in the new wine rack.

That was nice. Very domestic, very tranquil. He was in love, really in love, for the first time in his life and he was making good money—and so was she—and there wasn't a bump in the road. They moved into a bigger apartment, with a view of the Hudson from the nuclear power plant all the way up the river to where it snaked into the crotch of the mountains. He got himself a new car, a silver five-speed Mustang with some real pop to it. Nights—alone, in bed, just the two of them—were special. *You're an awesome lover,* that was what she told him, *awesome,* and he believed her then— believed her now, for that matter. But everything in this life turns to shit, as his father used to say (until he died in his Barcalounger of an aneurysm in the brain, the cocktail glass still clutched in his hand), and Frank, the owner, proved it by getting divorced.

Divorced meant time on your hands, time to pick and cavil and criticize, and Peck didn't take criticism well. He never had—in fact, the surest way, all his life, to make him react, was to call him out on something, whether it was his chores at home when he was a kid, or the dick of a math teacher he'd had in the ninth grade trying to humiliate him at the blackboard or the succession of half-wit bosses he'd had from junior year on and every one of them thinking they were God's gift to the world. He knew differently. No matter what, he was always right, even if he was wrong, and he could prove it with one jab of his right hand. Maybe other people—the losers of the world—could turn the other cheek, bow their heads, suck it up, but he couldn't. He had too much pride for that. Too much—what would you call it?—self-respect, self-love. Or confidence, confidence was a better word. At any rate, Frank started living at the bar, inhaling Glenfiddich all night long and getting nastier and crankier and crazier by the day. And then—it was inevitable—there came a night when Peck couldn't take it anymore (some shit about he wasn't ordering the right grade of parmesan and he didn't know real parmesan—*Parmigiano-Reggiano*—from his ass and he was fucking up and costing his boss money) and the youngest manager in Fiorentino's history went down in flames. There was some name-calling, some breakage, and he wouldn't be counting on a reference from Frank Calabrese anytime soon.

Gina was a rock, though. She threw down her apron, emptied the tip jar and stalked out to the car, and within the week she'd found a storefront on Water Street and hit her father up for a loan and Pizza Napoli was born. The place was an instant hit—you would have thought they were giving the pizzas away—and the secret was Skip Siciliano, the pizza chef with the handlebar mustache and the towering white toque he'd managed to coax away from Fiorentino's because Frank was an asshole and Skip couldn't have agreed more. That and the location. People wanted to look out on the broad rolling back of the Hudson and sit at nice tables with sawdust on the floor and strings of salami and garlic hanging from the racks overhead and eat pizza hot from the oven and they wanted antipasto and calzone and homemade pasta too and they wanted takeout and a nice selection of medium-priced Italian wines. By the end of the first year, he and Gina got ambitious and opened the second place—Lugano, a name they picked after closing their eyes and dropping a coin on the map of Italy. The idea behind Lugano was to make it an upscale place, full menu, osso buco, seafood, cotechino, specials every night, caponata in a cut-glass jar on every table and crostini the minute you sat down.

Then Gina got pregnant and told her father, and her father—a loudmouth and bullhead in a league of his own who'd never warmed to Peck because he wasn't Italian and even if he had been it wouldn't have mattered because nobody was good enough for his girl, not the right fielder for the New York Yankees or Giuliani's favorite nephew—insisted that they get married within the month. From Peck's point of view, the whole thing stank. He didn't want a kid, didn't want to be tied down at so young an age, and he resented Gina for letting it happen in the first place. But he went along, not coincidentally because her father was the controlling partner of both Pizza Napoli and Lugano, and he loved her, he did. At least then he did. They were married at the Assumption church, big reception at the country club in Croton, no expense spared, Peck's mother there in the front pew, drunk as usual, a buddy from high school he hadn't seen in six years—Josh Friedman—standing in as best man, and it was a fait accompli.

The thing is, it all might have worked out, a slow upward climb into maturity and the fullness of a relationship, the kid, a dog, a house in the country, if it wasn't for Gina. As soon as she got pregnant, she stopped sleeping with him. Just like that. She was always sick, always complaining about imaginary pains, and she got sloppy and let herself go. She never washed her hair. Never picked anything up. And sex. Did he mention sex? Sex was about as frequent—and satisfying—as the comet that comes every four hundred years and then you go out on the lawn and gape up at some poor pale pathetic streak of scum in the sky you can barely locate. Big thrill. Big, big thrill.

Could anybody have blamed him, even the pope and his College of Cardinals, if he began staying late at the restaurant? Even now, even after the jail time and the hate and resentment and going underground and all the rest, he had no regrets. Sometimes he'd just close his eyes and see the glow of the bar at two a.m., the front door locked and two or three of those candles guttering in their yellow globes till it seemed as if the whole place had been sprayed with a fine patina of antique gold, and Caroline or Melanie or one of the other cocktail waitresses sitting there beside him having a slow smoke and a Remy, his hand on her thigh or her breast as if he were fitting her for a custom-made outfit. So casual. So slow and sure. The beauty of it: he'd fucked her the night before and he'd fuck her again tonight. Once he got around to it.

"So jazz—you dig jazz at all?" Jonas was saying, and Peck had been away for a moment there, and at first, for the smallest sliver of a second, couldn't quite place him. "The new Diana Krall—did you know she married Elvis Costello?—it's pretty awesome." The man was fumbling in his jacket, the big hand moving like an animal caught in a bag, and then he flashed the CD and handed it across the table. "You might want to put this on. It's pretty awesome. Believe me."

Somehow, Peck's mood had soured. The pans were dirty, the meal stewing down in their guts, the Armagnac evaporated—was the guy using a straw, or what? Plus there was this asshole Bridger, threatening everything, and the first chink in the wall: the credit card he'd laid out on the counter at the Wine Nook was invalid, or so the pencil-neck behind the counter informed him. Natalia—half-playful, half-serious—had accused him of brooding and he'd defended himself, lamely, as in "I'm not brooding—I'm just thinking, that's all." Now he took the CD from Jonas in its compact plastic case and stared at it absently.

"I think you're going to like it," Jonas said, leaning in over the table. He was drunk, sloppy, fat-faced. Peck suppressed an urge to punch him. "Isn't that right, honey?" Jonas said, turning to his wife.

"Oh, yeah," Kaylee crooned, "yeah, I think you'll really like *like* it." She shrugged, a long shiver that ran up one side of her torso to her shoulders and back down again; she was drunk too, and why couldn't anybody sit down and eat a nice dinner without getting shit-faced? She gave him a wide wet-lipped smile. "Knowing you. Your soulful side, I mean—"

Natalia was nestled into the sofa like a cat, her legs drawn up, shoes off, the snifter cradled in the v of her crotch. She let her eyes rest on Jonas. "It is what, standards— is that how you say? Standards? Such a funny term."

No one answered her. After a moment, the CD still balanced in his hand, Peck said that he'd once been to the Five Spot with a girl he was dating ten years ago or more and that the band that night—female vocalist, flute, piano, percussion, bass—was like somebody taking their clothes off in the dark because they're ashamed of the way they look, and then he laid the disc back down on the coffee table and rose to his feet. "Listen," he said, "I just remembered something—if you'll all excuse me a minute. I've got to—got to go out. Just for a minute."

Natalia said, "But, Da-na, it is near to one in the a.m. Where? Where do you go?"

She was laying into him in front of the guests and that rubbed him the wrong way. He wanted to say something hurtful and violent, but he held back. He was all bottled up. He was wrong, he knew it, and so he said something in melioration, something he shouldn't have said: "I need to make a phone call."

And now a whole shitstorm of protest and sympathy

125

rose up, Natalia complaining in a little voice that he'd smashed her cell phone and wondering why he couldn't use the landline and both Jonas and Kaylee whipping out their cells as if the cells were six-shooters and this was the OK Corral. What could he say? Nothing. He just waved them off and backed across the room as if he were afraid they'd chase him down, tug at his sleeves, force their phones into his hand, and he snapped a mental picture of their faces—drunken faces, puzzled faces, a little indignant even—as he slipped out the door.

Outside, the fog had grown thick, obscuring everything. It was cold suddenly, the damp reach of it getting down inside his shirt, and he wished he'd thought to bring a jacket, but no matter. He slid into Natalia's car—*Natalia's car:* the registration was in his name and he was the one making payments on it—turned over the engine and worked the button on the temperature gauge till it read 80 degrees. There weren't many pay phones around anymore—they were a vestige of a bygone era, Frank's era, Jocko's, his own dead father's, and they'd be gone entirely in a decade, he would have put money on it—but there were a couple in the lobby of the Holiday Inn, and that was where he headed.

He stopped at the bar for a cognac and five bucks' worth of change. He had no idea what it cost to call San Roque, and he probably shouldn't have been doing it, anyway—there were easier ways to get what he wanted—but he couldn't resist, not tonight, not the way he was feeling, so sour and disconnected and twisted up inside. The lobby was over-lit, blazing like some meeting hall, but it was deserted at this hour. He listened to the coins fall and the operator's voice and then the ringing on the other end of the line.

"Hello?"

"Bridger?"

"Yeah?"

"I just wanted to confirm that your listing in our guide is correct—can you give me a spelling on your complete name?"

"Listen, if you're selling something, I don't want it— this is my private cell and you better, please, just remove it from your records."

"Oh, I'm not selling anything, not that you want, anyway." He gave it a heartbeat, just to let everything settle. "It's me, Dana. You know, the Rick James fan."

There was a silence, festering, the scab picked, the bandage torn from the wound. It made his heart swell to listen to it, to listen to the shithead dangle on the other end of the line, caught out at his own game. "Yeah, uh, hi."

"Hi yourself, asshole. You think you can dick with me?"

"You're the asshole. You're the criminal. You think you can steal my girlfriend's identity and get away with it? Huh? We're going to track you down, brother, and that is a promise."

*Girl*friend? The quickest calculation. So he was a she and the fish was on the line. Keep it going, he told himself, keep it going. "I guess we'll see about that, won't we."

"So you got my cell, big deal. I know where you live. I know where you're calling from right now."

"Really?"

"Really. You might be calling from anywhere in the 415, but you live in Marin, don't you?"

That froze him a minute—till he realized that was the old cell number, the dead cell number, and what did it matter? A whole lot of people lived in Marin County. Yeah. Sure. But how many Dana Halters? He saw Natalia's face then, her lips, the dark eternally disappointed pits of her eyes, heard her in his head questioning why, why, why do we have to move and what do you mean your name is not Dana? *What do you mean?*

The voice came back at him, a loser's voice, but hard now, hard with the righteous authority of the new kid called out on the playground: "Don't you?"

"Right," he heard himself say, and he looked up to follow a woman in heels and a tight blue dress picking her slow careful way from the bar to the elevators, "and you live in San Roque." And then, though he wanted to tear the thing out of the wall, all of it, the black box with the shiny silver panel, the wires and cords that pinned his voice to this place and this time, he very gently put the receiver back in its cradle and walked out the door and into the fog.

Four

WORK HAD JUST BEGUN on the next project Radko had lined up—a time-travel thing in which a group of twenty-first-century scientists, including one ingenue with inflated breasts, a sexy gap between her front teeth and a coruscating pimple dead center in the middle of her nose that had to be painted out in every frame, discover a portal to Pompeii the day before Vesuvius erupts and have to go around frantically trying to communicate the imminence of the danger in a language no one understands—when Bridger felt someone hovering over his shoulder and looked up to see Radko himself standing there on the scuffed concrete with a pained expression. It was just past ten in the morning. Bridger had spent the night at Dana's and so he'd had a relatively nutritious breakfast (Cheerios with a spoonful of brewer's yeast and half a diced nectarine, plus toast and coffee) and he'd left her hunched over her computer, tapping away at the dimensions of the wild boy's fate. He was feeling relaxed and benevolent, the new project—which no doubt would become as dull and deadening and soul-destroying as the last—engaging him simply because it was new, the computer-generated temples and sunblasted domiciles of Pompeii in diametrical contrast to the burnt sienna gloom of Drex III. He'd been bent over Sibyl Nachmann's face, his mind on autopilot as he painstakingly removed the blemish, a procedure Deet-Deet had already christened a "zitectomy," when he became aware of Radko.

"She is out there," Radko said, his voice deep and bell-like.

Bridger looked to the screen, not certain exactly what he meant—was she off the scale as far as looks were concerned or was she grazing the limits of histrionic expression? "Yeah," he said, nodding, because it was always a good idea to agree with the boss, "yeah, she is."

Radko waved both his hands vigorously, like an umpire declaring a man safe at third. "No, no," he said, "*Dana*, she is out there."

It took him a moment to understand—Dana was in the front office, beyond the uniform line of cubicles and the pouchy droop-shouldered figure of Radko, who was pointing now, his face heavy and oppressed. Bridger pushed back his chair and got to his feet. If Dana was here, then she was in trouble. Something had gone wrong. The first thing he thought of was the man in the picture, the voice on the phone, the thief. "Where?" he demanded, just to say something.

He found her in the outer office, slumped forward in one of the cheap plastic chairs against the far wall. She was wearing the T-shirt and jeans she'd had on when he left the apartment and she hadn't combed her hair or bothered with makeup and there was something clutched in her right hand, papers, letters. Was it her manuscript? Was that it? He crossed the room to her, but she didn't lift her head, just sat slumped there, her shins splayed away from the juncture of her knees, one heel tapping rhythmically against the leg of the chair. "Dana," he said, lifting her chin so that her eyes rose to his, "what is it? What's the matter?"

There was a noise behind him—Radko at the security door motioning to Courtney, the receptionist, a nineteen-year-old blonde who two weeks earlier had dyed her hair shoe-polish black and banished all color from her wardrobe in sympathy with whatever style statement Deet-Deet was trying to make. She gave Bridger a tragic look and excused herself—"I'm just going to the ladies'," she murmured— and then the door pulled shut and they were alone.

Dana didn't get up from the chair. She didn't speak. After a moment she took hold of his wrist and handed him an envelope addressed to herself from the San Roque School for the Deaf. As soon as he saw it, he knew what it meant, but he extracted the letter and unfolded it all the same, her eyes locked on his every motion. The letter was from Dr. Koch and it said that after consulting with the board he had the regretful duty of informing her that her position had been terminated for the fall session and that this was in no part due to any dissatisfaction that either he or the board might have had with her performance but strictly a result of budgetary constraints. He concluded by saying he would be happy to provide her with references and that he wished her success in whatever new endeavor she might embark upon.

"You know it's bullshit," she said, her voice echoing in the empty room. "They're firing me. Koch is firing me. And you know why?"

"Maybe not. He says they're eliminating the position— that's what he says . . ."

Her eyes narrowed, her jaw clenched. "Bullshit. I e-mailed Nancy Potter in Social Studies and she said they're already advertising for a vacancy in high school English. Can you believe it? Can you believe the gall of Koch? And these lies," she shouted, snatching the letter out of his hand. "Just lies."

Beyond the windows, two rectangular slits cut horizontally in the wall to let the employees of the inner sanctum know there was another world out there despite all evidence to the contrary, a woman with six dogs of various sizes on a congeries of leashes was pausing beneath the massive blistered fig that dominated the block. A kid in a too-big helmet went by on a motor scooter, closely tailed by another, the asthmatic wheeze of the engines burning into the silence of the room. He felt miserable suddenly, thinking only of himself, selfish thoughts, the what-about-me? of every contretemps and human tragedy. This would mean that Dana was going to have to relocate, no choice in the matter, and where would that leave him?

She was on her feet now, angry, impatient, thrusting out her arms and jerking her shoulders back in agitation. "It's because I was in jail. He blamed me. He all but accused me of dereliction of duty."

He tried to put his arms around her, to hold her, comfort her, but she pushed him away. "Here," she said, thrusting a second letter at him as if it were a knife, "here, here's the capper."

The letter was from the Department of Motor Vehicles. A month earlier she'd sent in her license renewal, just as he'd done himself two years ago. As long as there were no outstanding convictions or special considerations, the DMV had instituted a policy of renewal by mail without the necessity of being re-photographed. Dana had taken that option—who wouldn't? The price of a thirty-nine-cent stamp saved you a trip to the DMV office and an interminable wait in one line or another. All right. Fine. So what was the problem? "It's your license?" he asked.

Her eyes were hard, burning. "Go ahead, open it."

He heard the door crack open behind him and turned to see Courtney's pale orb of a face hanging there for an instant before the door pulled shut again. He bent to fish the new license out of the envelope, hard plastic, laminated, *California*

Driver License emblazoned across the top of it. They had her name right, had her address too, but the sex was wrong and the height and the weight and the signature at the bottom. But that wasn't the worst of it. The two photos, the larger on the left and the smaller on the right, were of a man they'd both seen before, and he was staring right at them.

There was no question of going back to work. Dana was in a state. Every day, it seemed, the mail brought some fresh piece of bad news, bill collectors dunning her for past-due accounts she'd never opened, a recall notice for a defect in a BMW Z-4 she'd never seen, notification of credit denied when she hadn't sought credit in the first place. And now she'd lost her job, now she'd be driving on an expired license. "What next?" she demanded, her voice strangled and unbalanced, riding up the walls like the cry of some animal caught in a snare, and she took hold of his arms in a grip so fierce she might have been trying to stop the bleeding, only he wasn't bleeding. Not yet. "Back to jail again? Tell me. What do I have to do?"

He wanted to hold her but she wouldn't let him because he was the villain all of a sudden, the stand-in for the bad guy, the nearest warm-blooded thing she could fight against. A man. Hairy legs and a dangle of flesh. A man like the one who'd done this to her. He said, "I don't know, I really don't," and she still held to her grip, her nails biting into the flesh, both of them fighting for balance. All at once he felt the irritation rising in him—she was crazy, that was what she was. Fucking crazy. "Goddamnit, let go of me," he shouted, and he shoved her away from him. "Shit, Dana. Shit, it wasn't me, I'm not the one to blame."

At that moment the door pushed open behind them

and there was Radko, with his heavy face and his cheap shoes and his cheap watch. "I dun't like this," he said carefully, slowly. "Not in my office."

Dana glared at him. Here was another man to lash out at. "I want to kill him," she said.

Radko studied the gray abraded paint of the floor. "Who? Bridger?"

Bridger understood that he was at a crossroads here, that there was a choice he would have to make, and soon, very soon, between Digital Dynasty and this wound-up woman with the tangled hair and raging eyes. A mad notion of stalking out the door flitted in and out of his head, but he caught himself. Conflict was inimical to him, a condition he'd always—or nearly always—managed to avoid. "I'm sorry," he said, ducking his head in deference. "It's just that thing—you know, with Dana and what she's been through? It just won't go away."

Radko lifted both hands to smooth back the long talons of his hair, then he lifted one haunch and settled himself on the edge of the receptionist's desk and began fumbling for the cigarettes he kept in the inside pocket of his jacket. "This thiff, yes?" he said, his voice softening. "This is it? This is the problem?"

Bridger acknowledged that it was.

"So sit," Radko said, gesturing to the plastic chairs along the wall, "and you tell me." And then, to Dana, as he touched the flame of his Bic to the cigarette, "You mind?"

"Yes," she said, "I do," but he ignored her.

Over the course of the next half hour, while Courtney went out for coffee and Plum twice stuck her head through the door to assess the situation and deliver updates to the crew and the cigarette smoke rose and the sun inflamed the undersized windows, Dana, who barely knew Radko, unburdened herself, and when she was at a loss, Bridger was there to offer amplification. Drawing at his cigarette, smoothing back his hair, sighing and muttering under his breath, Radko listened as though this were the plot of a movie he expected to bid on. "You know," he said finally, "in my country this thing goes on all the time. This stealing of the documents, of the people too. Kidnap for ransom. You know about this?"

Bridger nodded vaguely. He wasn't even sure what country Radko came from.

"Let me see that," Radko said, slipping the ersatz license from Dana's hand. He studied the picture a moment, then offered his opinion that the DMV had screwed up and the computer had sent the license to the address of record rather than the new address the thief had given them. "If you get that address," he said, glancing up as Courtney came through the street door with their coffees, "then you get this man."

Dana had become increasingly animated as they worked through the litany of details—how they'd contacted the credit reporting agencies and put a security hold on all her information, how they'd sent out copies of the police report and affidavit to the creditors of the spurious accounts, how they'd gone to the police and the victims' assistance people—and now she wondered aloud just how they might go about doing that. "This guy could have a hundred aliases," she said, removing the plastic cap from the paper cup and pausing to blow at the rising steam. She took a sip. Made a face. "And how do we get the address? They won't even run a fingerprint trace. Not important enough, they said. It's a victimless crime. Sure. And look at me: I'm out of a job."

"Milos," he said.

Courtney had settled back in at her desk, making a pretense of focusing on her computer, and Plum, for the third time, pushed open the security door and let it fall to again. Bridger said, "Who?"

"Milos. My cousin. Milos he is finding anybody."

The next afternoon—a Friday and Radko gone to L.A. for another "meeding"—Bridger left work early to pick up Dana at her apartment. He had to get out of the truck and ring her bell—or rather, flash it—because she wasn't quite ready, and he stood there on the doormat for five minutes at least till she appeared at the door, but the appearance was brief. Her face hung there a moment, wearing a look of concentrated harassment, the door swung open, and she was gone, clicking down the hallway in her heels, looking for some vital thing without which she couldn't leave the apartment even if it were on fire. He wanted to remind her—urgently—that they had an appointment with Radko's cousin at four-thirty and that his office was in Santa Paula, a forty-five-minute drive, but he wasn't able to do that unless he was facing her and he wasn't facing her. No, he was following her, from one room to another, her hair flashing, her arms bare and animated as she dug through a dresser drawer, pawed over the things on the night table, tossed one purse aside and snatched up the next. "I'm running a little late," she flung over her shoulder, and slammed the bathroom door.

Bridger wasn't happy—he resented feeling compelled to speed and risk another ticket—but he was resigned. He put his foot to the floor, the tires chirped and the pickup protested, wheezing and spitting as he gunned it up the ramp and onto the freeway, and he glanced over at Dana to see how she was taking it, but she was oblivious. He remembered how she'd told him that when she'd first got her new car—a VW Jetta—it ran so smoothly she couldn't tell whether the engine was actually going or not and had continually ground the starter without knowing it. Only after she realized that people were staring at her in the parking lot—grimacing, clenching their teeth—did she begin to adjust. It was all about the vibration, and eventually she trained herself to pick up the faintest intimation of those precise valves working in their perfect cylinders and all was well. The pickup was another story. Yet once he got it up to cruising speed and kept it there he was able to make up the time with some creative dodging around the cell-phone zombies and white-haired catatonics whose sole function in life it was to block the fast lane, and they pulled into Santa Paula no more than twenty minutes late for the appointment.

The town was a surprise. Instead of the usual California farrago of styles and build-to-suit outrages to the public sensibility, it seemed all of a piece, like something out of an old black-and-white movie. In fact, it all looked hauntingly familiar, the broad main drag lined with one- and two-story frame buildings that must have dated from the forties or earlier, the hardware store, the mom-and-pop shoes and clothes shops, Mexican restaurants, coffee shop, liquor store and cantina, and he couldn't help wondering how many period pieces had been filmed here. Teen movies, no doubt. Greasers in too-perfect '55 Fords and Chevys, cruising, heading for the hop. Dreary dramas about old people when they were young. World War II weepers where the crippled hero returns to receive a mixed message and the streets run ankle-deep with schmaltz. Of course, all this could be re-created today without ever having to leave Digital Dynasty, but still, it did Bridger good to see the real deal, the actual frame-and-stucco buildings of the actual town. They were rolling down the street, going so slowly they were practically parked, when he pointed to the scrawled sheet of directions in Dana's lap and asked, "What was that number again?"

She didn't respond, didn't glance down at his finger or up at his face. She seemed as entranced as he, her head lolling against the frame of the open window, legs crossed and one foot dangling as if it was barely attached, and that made him smile—here she was, relaxed for the first time in weeks, a little road trip, the prospect of Milos and an end to her troubles working on her like a massage. He had to point again before her eyes went to his lips. "One-three-three-seven," she said, squinting through the windshield to track the numbers on the storefronts.

There was no shortage of parking—the town seemed almost deserted—and they emerged to eighty degrees and sun and a light breeze with a distant taste of the sea riding in on it. The trees bowed and waved. A pure deep chlorophyll-rich square of green crept back from the curb across the street and wrapped itself around some monument to war veterans or a mayor gone down to the exigencies of time. It was all very—what? Very calming. Ordinary. Real.

Milos' office was above a Korean grocery that stocked nothing but Mexican specialties and beer, and Milos himself answered their knock. He was younger than Radko, thinner, with sucked-in cheekbones and tight discolored lips, but he wore his hair the same way as his cousin, gel-slicked and glistening like the nose of something emerging from the sea, with an orchestrated dangle of individual strands in front. It took Bridger a minute, and then he understood: Elvis Presley in *Viva Las Vegas*.

"So, yes," Milos said, in the same dense indefinable accent as Radko, waving them into the office, "you are looking for a thiff, I know, I know."

He offered them seats—two straight-backed wooden chairs—and dropped into a swivel chair behind a desk that might once have been a library table, gouged and pitted and with nothing at all on the barren plane of its surface except for a single old-fashioned rotary phone. The rest of the decor ran to patterned wallpaper, a bookcase filled with what seemed to be birdwatchers' guides and a long unbroken line of phone books, two hundred or more, that climbed up the near wall like some sort of fortification. Dana perched briefly at the edge of her chair, but almost immediately she rose and began pacing, making liberal use of her hands as she spewed out the story, Bridger elucidating and interpreting whenever Milos' gaze seemed to grow distant. It took five minutes, no more, and then she ran out of words and sat heavily beside him. They both looked to Milos, whose face revealed nothing.

"All this I know," he said, and held out his hands, palms up. "My cousin," he added, in a long whistling sigh.

A protracted moment swelled and receded. It was oddly silent, as if the rest of the building were deserted, the grocery notwithstanding, and hot, too hot, the pair of windows behind Milos' desk painted shut and the fan in the corner switched off—or no longer functioning. Bridger exchanged a look with Dana—she was drained, her shoulders slumped, the drama over—and he wondered what they were even doing here. Milos, as Radko had confided, mainly worked divorces, peering through suburban windows, watching motels from across the street, and his office didn't exactly inspire confidence. He was definitely low-tech. And this thief, this man in the photo, this voice on the phone, was as high-tech as you could get.

Milos finally broke the silence. "A man such as this," he intoned, pulling open the drawer of the desk and removing a smudged file folder, "he is not so smart as you think." He took a moment, for dramatic emphasis, and slid the folder across the table to Dana.

Inside was the fax of a police report from the Stateline, Nevada, Police Department and there, leering at them, was the now-familiar face. The man's name was recorded as Frank Calabrese, born Peterskill, NY, 10/2/70, no address given—"Transient," the report said, "Sex M, Race W, Age 33, Ht 6-0, Wt 180, Hair BRO, Eyes BRO, SS# ?, D/L 820 626 5757, State NY"—and he'd been arrested for forgery at a Good Guys store, where he'd attempted to acquire credit in another person's name—Justin Delhomme—and purchase a plasma TV worth $5,000. He was carrying a second driver's license, a California license, that showed him to be a.k.a. Dana Halter, of #31 Pacific View Court, San Roque.

Bridger could feel the excitement mounting in him— here he was, the son of a bitch, *nailed*—and he glanced up at Milos in gratitude and elation, and how could he ever have doubted him? "So his real name's what, Frank Calabrese?"

Milos tented his fingers and looked wistfully at Dana, whose head was bowed as she scanned the report, oblivious. "You are jumping," he said, never taking his eyes from Dana. "Because this is not his name, why would it be?" He shrugged. "Just another alias."

Sensing something in the air, Dana looked up.

"But he is not so smart, you know why?" Milos went on, pointing a finger at Dana. He let out a long breath. "Because he is in love with you."

Dana looked to Bridger as if she hadn't read him right, then turned back to Milos. "Love?" she echoed.

"With *you*," he repeated.

"You mean, he's in too deep—he's got too much invested in this scam or whatever it is to give it up, right?" Bridger offered.

"Who you are," Milos said, everything freighted on his lips, "he is. You can catch him now."

Almost involuntarily, Bridger murmured, "But how?"

The sun glazed the windows, a smear of something suspended there in a tracery of false illumination. Bridger smelled his own sweat, primordial fluid, a funk of it, and he could smell Dana too, prickling and acidic. He wanted a beer. He wanted the beach, the ocean, peace and union and love, and what he had instead was this overcooked room and Radko's cousin who was so cryptic he could have been writing fortune cookies in a factory in Chinatown. "How?" he repeated.

Milos pushed the hair out of his eyes, only to have it spring back again in a spray of glistening black vectors, and then he reached into the drawer a second time and shoved a piece of paper across the table to them. On it was written a postbox number in Mill Valley. "This," he said, drawing it out, "is where bill goes. For cell phone. The address on this account is yours and landline number too, but bill goes here." He was smiling now. "Very friendly man in Collections. I think you know him: Mr. Simmonds?" Another shrug. "It is a small thing."

The clumsy lips, the imbalance of the accent: Dana wasn't reading him, so Bridger translated for her as best he could. She watched him carefully, then shifted in the chair. "But what do we do about it?" she asked, her face drawn down to nothing.

Milos' voice rode a current, higher now, as if a breeze had caught it. "You go," he said. "You are Dana Halter too, no? You have proof?"

She nodded.

"Then that is *your* box."

Sunday morning, early, they left San Roque in Dana's Jetta, headed north. Bridger had meant to tell Radko in person—he'd made his choice, for love, for support, for Dana—but in the end, he opted for the easy way out: e-mail. *Sorry. Gone one week. Emergency. Bridger. P.S. See you next Monday?*

The sun was behind them as they pulled out of town on the Coast Highway, the ocean gathering light and throwing it at the pavement, the car a leaping shadow just ahead of them. Dana sat in the passenger's seat beside him, her face soft and composed, her hair still wet from the shower and pinned up in a way that showed off the line of her jaw, the sharp angle of her cheekbone, her ear, whorled and perfect as a shell. She'd held him a long while that morning and then pulled back and signed *I love you,* the index finger pointing first to her heart, then both hands crossed in an embrace and finally the finger coming back to him, and he couldn't resist her. They'd made love the night before, slow and languorous, the bed a raft at sea in the dark and silence of the room, and they fell to it again, on the rug in the hall after she'd come dripping from the shower and given him the sign: *I . . . love . . . you.*

What was he feeling? Burnished. Shining. Polished like a gem. The radio was cranked and she was bent over her laptop, alternately tapping at the keys and glancing up to stare out over the stacked-up waves with pursed lips and unseeing eyes, isolated from the moment and this place and the world. The music crept into him and he tapped out the rhythm on the dash. An old song, familiar as blood. *Who, who, who, who, / Tell me who are you . . .*

Five

SHE LOOKED UP from the screen and saw the sea spread out before her, the stalled distant waves like interlocking tiles, the spilled milk of the clouds, sun like wax—*metaphor, everything a metaphor*—even as the dim dripping forest of La Bassine dissolved in a blaze of light on water. Bridger was beside her, present and visible, one hand on the wheel, the other beating time on the dash. His chin bobbed, his shoulders dipped and rose. One and two, one and two. And now he was singing, singing in perfect silence, his lips pursed as if he were blowing out a whole birthday cake's worth of candles. She glanced at the LED display on the radio: 99.9, classic rock. He was singing some immemorial song he knew and she didn't, singing to himself, everything about him alive and focused and beautiful, running with the sound. She didn't stop to think what it meant to go there, to that place where the hearing were transported in the way she was when she was writing or reading or locked away in the dark chest of the cinema while the shapes joined and convulsed on the screen and she saw with a clarity so intense she had to turn away from it; no, she just let herself feel it through him, through the weave of his shoulders and the rhythmic slap of his hand, and then she was beating time too.

The landscape sprang away from them. The dash gave and released, their two hands pounding. And then a car appeared in the inside lane and rolled silently past them and he shifted his eyes to her, his smile opening up, and he sang for her, sang to her, more insistent now, more vigorous and emphatic, his lips, his lips: *Who, who, who, who?*

She hadn't thought past the moment, past packing her bags and the two new credit cards she'd got to replace the canceled ones, because it had all seemed so natural, so logical: the thief was in Mill Valley and he had a postbox at Mail Boxes Etc. and they were going to go there and find him, watch him, stalk him. And then what? Call in the police. In her fantasy she saw him striding into the shop to check his mail while they sat outside in the car—they knew his face, but he didn't know theirs—and punched 911 into the cell phone. Or they'd get the mail themselves, find an address, an account number, trace him to his house and nail him there (yes, *nail* him, as you would nail a board to the floor). And in the fantasy she saw a SWAT team swooping down on him, men in flak jackets and protective headgear, candy-apple-red lights flashing on the cars, the helicopter slamming at the air, and she'd confront him then, spit in his face as he was led away in the same inflexible restraints they'd bound her up in, and she'd confront him again in court, the perfect witness in perfect control, the interpreter motionless at her side.

But that was the fantasy. The reality—and it made her stomach clench to think of it—might be less certain, might be dangerous. How stupid was he? How much in love with her base identifiers could he be when he knew he'd been found out? He might be a thousand miles away by now, more than a match for any amateur detective, and with a new name and a new persona. He could be anywhere. He could be anybody. But still, the thought of what he'd done to her without pause or conscience or even a trace of human feeling made her seize with the rage she'd felt all her life, the rage of shame and inadequacy and condescension. Revenge, that was what she wanted. To make him hurt the way she did. Only that.

They'd just passed King City when she looked up next. Bridger was no longer slapping the dash, no longer singing. He had one hand draped over the wheel, fingers dangling, and he was slumped down in the seat, looking tired. Or wiped, as in *wiped-out, eliminated, destroyed*. She touched his arm and he turned his head. "Are you tired?" she asked. "You want to maybe stop for lunch?"

He nodded and that was good enough because she couldn't very well expect him simultaneously to keep his eyes on the road and his lips in her field of vision. But then he turned full-face and said, "What do you feel like—Mexican?"

"Sure," she said.

He was grinning even as he swung off the freeway and onto the main street—the only street—of a town that consisted of a grocery, a gas station, a cantina and two cramped and competing *taquerias* called La Tolteca and El Sitio respectively. "Good choice," he said, turning to her as he killed the engine.

They chose El Sitio and couldn't have said why, no appreciable difference between the two places, both dark inside because electricity cost money, both run by the wives, grandparents and children of the men in the fields. There were four tables shoved up against the wall, a chest-high counter, the kitchen. The smells were dark and lingering, but good, a dense aroma of ancient chiles, refried beans in a pot crusted with residue, peppers and onions and the fry pan that was always hot. One of the tables was occupied by two super-sized white women with unevenly dyed hair—travelers like themselves—who were staring moodily down at the foil-wrapped remains of their burritos and clutching bottles of Dos Equis as if they were fire extinguishers. An old man, lizard-like in a white smock and trousers, sat at the table behind them, tentatively poking a pink plastic fork at a plate of scrambled eggs and beans. There was a handwritten menu on the wall.

Bridger consulted the menu a moment, then turned to the woman at the counter. He said something Dana didn't catch—was he speaking in Spanish, was that it?—and then looked to her. "You know what you want?"

"I don't know," she said, using her hands unconsciously. She looked to the menu and back again. "I can order for myself."

The woman behind the counter, as reduced and small-boned as a child, though her hair was going gray, watched them impassively. She was there to take their orders and their money and to give them a plastic chit with a number on it and to call out the number when the orders came up, and her eyes betrayed little interest beyond that. The menu was in Spanish: *taco de chuleta; taco de rajas; taco de cazuela; tamal de verduras.* It wasn't a problem. Dana had lived in San Roque for more than a year now and she knew the basics of Mexican cuisine as well as she knew Italian or French or Chinese, and to make it easier for her, since she wasn't prepared to wrestle with the pronunciation—English was challenge enough—there was a number attached to each item. She chose the fifth item on the list, *tostada de pollo,* turned to the woman and said, as clearly as she could, "Number Five, please."

For a long moment the woman merely examined her out of eyes so dark there was no delineation between iris and pupil, and then she looked to Bridger and said something in her own language, which Bridger, at first, didn't seem to understand. She had to repeat herself, and then Bridger nodded, the pale bristles of his hair gone translucent in the long shaft of sun leaching in through the door. "She says she'll have the Number Five," he said, and then repeated himself in his high school Spanish.

They took the table behind the two women—What percentage of Americans were obese? Thirty percent? Was that the figure she'd read?—and Bridger got them their drinks. He was having *horchata,* she a Diet Coke, out of the can. The women behind them were hunkered over the table, their faces animated, inches apart, exchanging confidences—gossip—and Dana almost wished she could hear what they were saying about their husbands, boyfriends, their ailments and beauty treatments and the children who invariably disappointed them. Instead, she asked Bridger what the woman at the counter had said. "And why didn't she understand me? Wasn't I clear?"

He dropped his eyes. "No, it wasn't that. Or it was. She's—well, her English isn't too good—"

"Yes? But what did she say?"

He looked embarrassed—or reluctant—and she felt her face go hot.

"It was something insulting, wasn't it?"

"I don't know," he said, and then he said something she couldn't make out.

"It was in Spanish?"

Instead of repeating it again, uselessly, he pulled a pen from his pocket and wrote the word out for her on the back of a paper napkin: *Sordomuda.*

Now she did flush. "Deaf-mute?"

He nodded.

What she wanted to ask was, "How did she know?" but instead she glanced across the room to where the woman sat perched on a stool behind the cash register, her head down, flipping through the pages of a Mexican tabloid; she wore gold earrings, the faintest points of light; a silver cross dangled from her throat on a silver chain. She was perfectly ordinary, like a thousand other women in a thousand other taco stands, Mexican restaurants and *pupuserias,* a woman who knew the feel of the mortar and pestle and the consistency of the *harina* paste shaped to fit the hand and pounded flat between the palms. But who was she? Did she have a deaf son? A deaf sister? Was she deaf herself? Or was she just superior? Contemptuous? Hateful?

Everything was in stasis, but for the right arm of the cook—a man so small and slight he might have been the cashier's brother—which jerked rhythmically as he slid the pan back and forth across the gas burner. After a moment, she turned back to Bridger and signed, *How did she know?* but all he could do was shrug and hold out his hands. When their order came up, he went to the counter and brought back a paper plate and set it before her. The dish it contained didn't look like a tostada. For one thing, there was no shell; for another, no lettuce. Instead, what she got seemed to be some kind of organ meat in gravy and a wash of melted cheese.

"What's wrong?" Bridger asked, his mouth crammed with beans and rice. "Not hungry?"

Very slowly, with the tip of one reluctant finger, she pushed the plate away, and it wasn't worth the explanation. She let her hands talk for her: *No,* she signed, *not anymore.*

"You want to drive?" he asked her. They were standing in the street outside the restaurant, the car glazed with the sun. It was hotter than she'd expected, hotter inland than she was used to on the coast. The heat drugged her and she didn't see the woman watching her from behind the window of the *taqueria* or the pair of lizards chasing one after the other through the dust or the drift of yellowed claw-like oak leaves at her feet. She didn't want to drive. She wanted to stare into the screen and shut out all the rest and she let her hands tell him so. A moment later, the town was behind them and only the vibration of the steel-belted radials, riding on air, told her they were moving.

Six

THERE WERE TWO bona fide bedrooms in the condo, one for Madison and one for Natalia and him, as well as an extra half-bedroom, what the real estate lady wanted to call a sewing room. Or a nursery. "Or"—with a look to him, coy and calculating—"a home office, an office away from the office. For when you get tired of all those patients." It wasn't much, not a whole lot bigger than the cell he'd shared with Sandman at Greenhaven Prison, but it had a view of the bay and the big stippled pyramid of Mount Tam, and Natalia had found him an oak desk, a pair of matching file cabinets and a Tiffany desk lamp on one of her far-flung antiquing forays. So it was an office. He hooked up his computer and his printer and did business here, reserving the computers at the public library for highly sensitive transactions, the things he didn't want to risk having traced. Madison wasn't allowed in this room, for obvious reasons, and he frowned on Natalia coming in to appropriate a pen or a pair of scissors, though once, when he'd forgotten to lock the door, she'd slipped in naked and put her hands over his eyes. She didn't have to whisper, *Guess who?*

He was in the office now, at his computer, Natalia treating herself to a morning at the spa and Madison off at day camp, and he was doing a little research. It was the kind of thing he was good at, better than good—he'd made a nice quiet living at it for the past three years now, and if there was the occasional glitch, like that time in Stateline when he'd been up all night at the blackjack tables and he was wired and burned-out and maybe a little drunker than he thought, he had it covered. Post bail and walk and let them come after somebody else, Dana Halter or Frank Calabrese or whoever. It was nothing to him, not anymore, and if he hadn't fallen for Natalia he could have lived in Marin for the duration, a doctor in a tailored suit and the calfskin duster he'd picked up last winter, *money for nothing and the chicks for free,* wasn't that how it went?

The first time, though, when he was Peck Wilson and in love with his four-year-old daughter—Sukie, Silky Sukie, he used to call her—the law was a clamp, a harness, a choke hold that cut off all the air to his lungs and the blood to his heart. Gina moved out on him and took his daughter with her, right back to the big Bullhead's house, and why? Because he was a son of a bitch, a rat, a scumbag, because he was cheating on her and no fit father and she never wanted to see him again, never. And if he ever dared to lay a hand on her again, if he ever even thought about it—

What she didn't mention, what the lawyer didn't mention, was the way she'd come to treat him, as if he'd been hired for stud purposes only, to broaden the gene pool so the Marchetti dynasty could wind up with a granddaughter and heiress prettier than a queen and smarter by half than anything they could ever have hoped to produce. That, and to go on fattening the bank account by pushing himself day and night till his brain began to bleed out his ears. Without her, and with the unflagging bullheaded enmity of her father, Lugano went down the tubes within six months—the state came and closed the place up for non-payment of sales tax, which he had to hold out just to cover the suppliers—and the pizza place was reeling. But the divorce order, which he hadn't agreed with but was too tired to fight, specified the amount he had to pay for alimony and child support and laid out the hours—minutes, seconds—he could spend with his daughter. Okay, fine. He moved to a smaller apartment, ran the wheels off the car. There was Caroline, there was Melanie, and what was her name, that girl from the bookstore in the mall? On Sundays, he took Sukie to feed the ducks at Depew Park or to the zoo at Bear Mountain or they hopped the train into the city to catch the opening of the newest kids' flick or to see the Christmas display at FAO Schwarz.

Even now, sitting at his desk, watching the information come to him like a gift from the gods, he could remember the way it felt when he found out Gina was seeing somebody. He'd let himself slip—if he was working out more than every second or third day, that was a lot—and he was drinking too much, spending more than he wanted to on women who did nothing for him, letting work eat him up. He was at a club one night after locking up, a local place that featured a live band on weekends, standing at the bar waiting for Caroline to come back from the ladies', thinking nothing, when somebody threw an arm round his shoulder—Dudley, one of the busboys from Lugano, the one who was always in the cooler, smoking out. "Hey," Peck said.

"Hey. 'Sup?"

Dudley must have been around nineteen, twenty, hair corded in blond dreads, pincer eyes, big stoned grin, tattoos to the waist, which was as far down as he'd ever been exposed on the premises of the restaurant, but Peck could speculate about the rest. This was the kind of guy—*dude*—who probably had the head of a dragon staring out of his crotch.

In answer, Peck told him "Not much," and then went on to regale him with a laundry list of woes, not the least of which was his bitch of a wife, and then Caroline came back and they all three had a shot of Jäger and the band pounded away at a Nirvana tune and they just listened, nodding their heads to the beat. When the band took a break, Caroline went outside to have a smoke and Dudley leaned in, his elbows tented on the bar, and opined, "It sucks about the restaurant."

It did. Peck agreed. There was movement at the door, ingress and egress; somebody stuck some money in the jukebox and the noise came roaring back.

"Yeah," Dudley said, raising his voice to be heard above it, "and it sucks about Gina too."

A little fist began to beat inside Peck's right temple. "What do you mean?"

Dudley's face receded, flying away down the length of the bar like a toy balloon with human features painted on it, and then it floated back again. "You mean you don't know?"

The next day, he didn't go in to work. He felt the faintest sting of conscience—they'd be shorthanded, short on produce too, and the dishwasher would just sit around and listen to right-wing talk on the radio and Skip would be so drunk he'd burn the crust off the pies and squeeze the calzone till it looked like road kill on a plate—but the tatters of his work ethic were nothing in the face of the rage he felt. What was he working for, anyway? *Who* was he working for? At first he refused to believe what Dudley was telling him. That she was seeing anybody was enough to light all his fuses, but that she was going out with—sleeping with, *fucking*—Stuart Yan was beyond comprehension. That he was Asian, or half-Asian, had nothing to do with it, nothing at all (and yet he couldn't help wondering just exactly how the Bullhead must have felt about that). The problem, the immediate problem that settled inside him with the weight of a stone, was how he was going to face people, anybody—

Dudley, his friends, former customers, people at the bar—when his wife was fucking some slope and he was paying for it, paying for her to just lie around like a slut and get laid all day.

By ten in the morning he was parked at a turnout just off the road to her parents' house. The season was spring, late spring, and already the vegetation was twisted up like a knot, weeds crowding the front bumper, the branches of the trees in full leaf, but still he was afraid she'd notice the car—metal-flake silver wasn't exactly an earth tone. Cars went by, three and four at a time, as if they were attached on a cable, then nothing, then three and four more. There were birds crowding the canopy of the tree that hung out over the car—tiny black-and-yellow things he'd never noticed before, popping in and out of the leaves like puppets—and he worried briefly that they'd spot the top of the car with the drooling white beads of their excrement, but eventually they faded out of his line of vision and he forgot all about them. He didn't really know what he was doing there parked under a tree on a back road to nowhere, didn't have a plan, and yet every time he heard the hiss of tires on the road his heart started slamming at his ribs. He watched pickups rattle by, cars of all makes and descriptions, a kid on a green Yamaha. There was the smell of the sun on the pavement. After a while he buzzed the window down all the way, let the radio whisper to him, the soft thump of a song he'd heard so many times he might have written it himself. An hour cranked by, two hours, three.

Finally, and he might have dozed for a while, he couldn't be sure, he came up fully alert, just as if someone had slapped him or doused him with a bucket of ice water: there she was. Her car. The metallic blue Honda her father had bought for her, and she was behind the wheel with her ugly black-framed glasses on, two little white fists like claws jerking back and forth though the road ran straight as a plumb line in front of her, and there was the kid's seat in back—Sukie, strapped in and clutching a neon-orange teddy bear, her face a blur—and another face there too, on the passenger's side in front. The car was coming toward him—he'd chosen this straightaway for its sight lines—and the whole thing was over in the space of ten seconds, come and gone, and yet still he recognized that face, round as a beachball, the sleepy eyes, the clamped dwindling afterthought of the mouth, and before he could think he'd turned the key in the ignition and slammed the car into gear.

If she hadn't seen him there at the side of the road, she saw him now. He watched her eyes go to the rearview and then her head bobbed toward Yan's and Yan looked over his shoulder and that was all it took to put him over the line, that unconscious gesture of complicity, of intimacy—*putting their heads together*—and he came up on the bumper of the Honda so fast he had to hit the brakes to keep from tearing right through them. And he might have—might have run them off the road, because he was acting on impulse only, inimical to everything that walked or drew breath on the planet—if it wasn't for Sukie. His daughter. His daughter was there, strapped in with her bear, and he was the one out of line here, he was the one endangering her. He dropped back half a car length—safety, safety first, because Gina was as uncoordinated and ungifted a driver as he'd ever seen—but he stayed there, raw and hurt and put-upon, stayed there, right on their tail, till a gas station rolled up on the right and Gina hit the blinker and pulled in.

As if that could help her.

He was out of the car in a heartbeat, screaming something, he didn't know what—curses, just curses, maybe accusations too—and he had his hand on the driver's side door of the Honda even as Stuart Yan was puffing himself out the other side and some bald suit at pump number 3 shouted, "Hey, what's going on here?" If he recalled anything with clarity from those diced and scrambled moments excised from his life, it was the look on Gina's face behind the rolled-up window and the locked door—pale, distant, afraid, terrified of what was about to unfold—and the look of his daughter. Her face was like a big open wound, hurt and puzzled and caught dead-center in a tornado of emotions. That look—Sukie's look—almost stopped him. Almost. But he was running on fumes at this point, the high-octane stuff, fully combustible, and he lit into Stuart Yan with a kick to the windpipe and then he took hold of the suit—some real estate drone with an inflated opinion of himself—and flung him across the hood of the car. What did it take? The trash can, the first thing that came to hand, metal anyway. He raised it above his head, shit flying everywhere, cups and paper wipes and soda cans, and brought it down against that window, again and again and again.

He lifted his eyes from the computer screen and looked out over the bay to where a string of pelicans blew like leaves across the belly of the water. In the foreground was a gently curving row of palms, just like in Florida or Hawaii, better even; sun glinted off the hoods of the Jags, Mercedeses and BMWs in the reserved parking; sailboats crept by like moving statues. If Gina could only see him now. He was sitting on a condo worth three-quarters of a million dollars, he had a new BMW, money in the bank, a girlfriend any man would kill for, and he was leaning over his antique desk under the light of his antique lamp, doing research, manipulating things, the kind of work that always had a calming influence on him, but then he wasn't calm. And he wasn't happy. Not today. In fact, the more he thought about it, the angrier he got, filled right up to the neck with the bitter concentrate of the very same rage that had come over him the day he'd put Stuart Yan in the hospital. And why? Because he'd been careless, because he'd let himself get sucked in, because Natalia was the one thing he couldn't let go of. And Dana Halter wasn't the problem, he saw that now. Bridger was. Bridger Martin.

Once he had the cell number, the rest had been easy. He went online to a reverse phone directory to get the carrier, then called customer service, claiming to be Sergeant Calabrese of the Fraud Division of the SFPD. The woman on the other end of the line, whether she was in India or Indiana, never asked for verification, though he had a legitimate police code he could have used, and she matched the cell to the account number and brought up the name and address on the account. For twenty-five dollars an online information broker gave him the header information on the credit reports—full name, address, social security number, d.o.b.—and he faxed all three credit reporting agencies on the stationery of one of his ersatz businesses, Marin Realty, asserting that Bridger Thomas Martin, of #37, 196 Manzanita, San Roque, was applying for rental property and ordering up a copy of the credit reports. A little research, that was all. Just watching his back.

He'd been busy since he'd got that phone call at the Smart-Mart, very busy, but it wasn't as if he hadn't known it was coming. The same Realtor who'd sold him the condo would be handling the resale, and though he'd probably get screwed out of a couple thousand here or there, it didn't really matter—he'd already set up an account in New York to handle the transfer of the funds once it sold. And it would sell fast, prime property right on the water, people lining up to get in. The hard part was Natalia. She didn't know a thing about it, not yet. The real estate woman wouldn't be showing the place till they were gone, and he was ready to just walk and leave everything behind, the desk and the lamp and the bedroom suite and all the rest of it, but Natalia was going to put up a fight, he knew it. And that was what made him angry. The thought of it. The thought of losing her. And for what? For Bridger Martin?

A week, that was all he needed. The reports would be in his hands by then and the new credit cards too, though Bridger Thomas Martin, whoever he was, wasn't exactly a tycoon and the credit limits were lower than he would have liked ideally, but that wasn't a worry—he had plenty of cards, cards were nothing. No, he had something else in mind for this clown, something else altogether. A week. A week to wrap things up, and then they'd be gone, and he saw it already, the new car—he was going to look at a Mercedes this afternoon, on the way back from his workout—with plenty of room in back for Madison and her toys and pillows and blankets, he and Natalia sitting up front in style, stopping wherever they liked, first class all the way, a nice little vacation and educational too, good for the kid. See the country. The sights. Pike's Peak. The Great Lakes. Gettysburg. And Vegas, definitely Vegas. Natalia could hardly object to that.

When he'd got what he wanted he shut down the computer, went out to the kitchen and made himself a sandwich. For a long while he stood at the counter, his jaws working mechanically, gazing at the Mexican tile, the pottery and baskets and whatnot Natalia had picked up to give the place a little charm, the new microwave, the Navajo rugs. The light played through the windows and rode up the walls. It was exclusive light, the light of the sun reflected up off Shelter Bay, rippling and fluid, and there were times when he could just sit for hours with a cocktail and watch it move and transform like an image on a screen. He was going to miss it. Miss the fog too, the way it wrapped itself around everything in the visible world, like snow in suspension, making and remaking itself all over again. All the anger he'd felt earlier was gone now—if he felt anything, he felt drained.

But he wasn't going to let it get to him. He had things to do. He rinsed the plate, stuck it in the dishwasher, then dug his gym bag out of the closet. Working out always cleared his head, the endorphins flowing, the reps on the weight machine his own kind of zen, almost unconscious, counting off, counting off again, his breathing deep and steady. When it went well, when he got into the rhythm of it, he almost felt as if he were rooted to the bench—or no, as if he were the bench itself, no more aware than a slab of steel. And after he worked out, he was going to look at that car, and then he had to stop at the market. Tonight it was veal cordon bleu, and he had to pick up the boneless chops, the prosciutto and the Emmentaler he liked to use (pound the veal, bread it, lay on two wafer-thin slices of the ham and two of the cheese, wrap it up, pin it with a toothpick and bake at 350), and he was thinking maybe he'd do gnocchi with a white sauce and a quick sauté of baby zucchini on the side. Or maybe fava beans in tomato and basil. And he'd pick up two bottles of that Orvieto Natalia liked, and if he was in the mood, and if he had the time, he might whip up a couple of almond tortes. That would please her. And some spumoni for the kid.

He went out the door, bag in hand, and didn't look back.

For what he wound up paying for the attorney he could have spent a month in the best hotel in Manhattan, no expense spared, room service, show tickets and bar tab included, but the man got him a shrink to testify before the judge that what Peck had done to Stuart Yan (and the ancillary damage to his wife's car and to the not-so-innocent bystander) was an aberration, the result of temporary insanity, and that it would be ridiculous to say he was a threat to society when in fact he was no threat at all. The attorney talked of mitigating circumstances—the defendant was only trying to protect his family from this interloper, this stranger, Yan, whom he saw, rightly or wrongly, as threatening his wife and child, and he'd over-reacted in the heat of the moment. He accepted his culpability. He was contrite. Willing to make full restitution. Further, he had a clean record and he was a successful small business owner whose incarceration would deprive the community of his services and put at least seven people out of work. But the assistant DA came right back at him, claiming that this was a case of attempted murder or at the very least assault with a deadly weapon likely to produce great bodily harm—the defendant was a black belt in karate, after all, and knew perfectly well what he was doing in attacking Mr. Yan, who, incidentally, had temporarily lost the use of his voice due to damage to his larynx and could very well suffer permanent incapacitation.

Peck had to sit there and take it, but he was seething. Under other circumstances—outside in the street, a bar, anyplace—he would have taken the man apart because he'd never felt such hatred for anybody in his life, not even Yan or Gina. Who *was* this guy? What had he ever done to *him*? As it turned out, though, it was just posturing on the assistant DA's part: neither side wanted to take the case to trial. The outcome—and it could have been foreordained given what it was costing—was a plea bargain.

The judge, a skeletal little dark-skinned man in his forties—his name started with a *V* and went on for six unpronounceable syllables—gave him a five-minute lecture, rife with sarcasm, as Peck stood there trying to hold his gaze. Yan was in the back of the courtroom, wearing a neck brace, and Gina and her parents were there beside him, looking like Puritans ranged round the ducking stool. About the only thing Peck could be thankful for was that Sukie was at a friend's house, because as unforgiving and vituperative as Gina might have been, even she realized there was no point in having her witness her father's public humiliation, not after what had happened to the window of the car and the rain of those splinters of safety glass and the way her father had fired up the Mustang and scorched the pavement till the tires smoked and all the birds blew out of the trees. The judge gave him three years probation and imposed a restraining order enjoining him from coming within five hundred feet of his wife. The order further prohibited him from having any contact whatever with her, not by telephone, e-mail, the postal service or through a third party, except as arranged by the court according to family law and visitation rights for his daughter. At the end of it, the judge leaned forward, and in his high clipped Indian accent, asked him if he understood.

"Yes," Peck said, though it was wrong, all wrong, and he was sick with the aftertaste of it. "I understand."

"Good," the judge said, "because I sincerely hope you do. If you obey the directives of this court and keep out of trouble—any trouble whatsoever—this felony charge will be reduced to a misdemeanor upon completion of probation and payment in full of restitution to the victims." He paused. The courtroom was silent but for the faint distant moan of the air conditioner. "But if I see you here before me again, no matter what the charge, you'd better have your toothbrush with you because I will remand you directly to jail. Do I make myself clear?"

Peck remembered feeling like something scraped off

the bottom of somebody's shoe, even though the attorney seemed pretty pleased with himself and to everyone's mind the incident was closed. His mother was there, with one of her sack-like friends, both of them probably drunk already though it wasn't yet noon, and two of his own drinking buddies, Walter Franz and Chip Selzer, from the ex-bar at the ex-restaurant, had turned up to show support. Lunch, people wanted lunch and a celebratory drink or two, his mother grinning, Walter and Chip crowding in on him, but he wasn't having it. "Hey, congratulations, man," Walter crowed, throwing an arm round his shoulder. "It's over, huh? Finally over."

They were out in the hallway, a crush of people coming and going. Fat people. Stupid people. The dregs. And then he saw Gina and her parents pushing through the swinging door at the end of the corridor, Yan trailing behind them like a retainer, and he couldn't help himself—he shoved Walter away, a shrug of the shoulder that knocked him up against the wall, and when Chip moved in, his palm spread wide for the high-five, he just turned his back and stalked out the door.

For the next few weeks he put his head down and tried to forget about it. Focus on the business, that was what he told himself, shake it off, straighten things out. Though he'd never let it show, the legal convolutions—the endless meetings with the shrink and the lawyer, the postponements, the general level of harassment and pure unadulterated crap—had really got to him, and Pizza Napoli wasn't what it was or what it should have been. Sales were flat, people cooking out and going to the beach, and they just didn't think pizza as much in the summer as when school was on and the kids were sitting there at the kitchen table every night screaming to be fed. For the first time ever, and against his better judgment because in his eyes it reduced the place to the level of

Pizza Hut or Domino's, he gave in to Skip and offered a two-for-one coupon in the local paper.

It didn't do him much good—if there was a blip in the receipts it was too small to notice. But the ad itself (it wasn't even an ad, just a cheesy coupon in the Thursday morning insert), aside from costing him money, seemed to suck the last shred of class out of the place. He hated it. Hated the way it looked on the page, the lame line drawing of a stereotypical grinning potbellied mustachioed greaseball of an Italian chef holding up a vertical pizza in defiance of gravity beneath the legend *Pizza Napoli, Buy One Regular Size Pizza with One Topping, Get the Next One Free.* Christ, he might as well have been selling hula hoops.

And then there was Gina. He wasn't allowed to contact her, but he still had the right to see his daughter every Sunday, all day Sunday, whether Gina liked it or not, and his lawyer contacted her lawyer and worked out an arrangement whereby Gina's mother would bring Sukie to some neutral place and he would pick her up. They agreed on McDonald's—she loved McDonald's, more for the playground than the food, the vanilla shake thick as sludge and the shrunken little patty of whatever it was they slipped between the grease-soaked bun, no ketchup, no mustard, no onions, neither of which seemed to interest her beyond the first sip and the first bite—and Gina's mother was consistently late. He sat there in the Mustang, checking his watch every ten seconds, kids all over the place, but not his kid, and when Gina's mother did show she never apologized or even said word one, handing Sukie over as if she were giving her up to a child molester. Did he hate that woman, with her surgically restructured face and her liposuction and frozen hair and the way she locked up her features and threw away the key as if just to look at him was an ordeal? Yes, sure he did. And he hated Gina for what she'd done to him. And the Bullhead—just hearing his voice on the phone, the hectoring nag of a voice going on and on about the menu at Pizza Napoli, the books, the bottom line: *You're not offering the public what they want. You know why? Because you get stuck on one thing. Listen to me: you're screwing up. Big-time. Wake up, will you?* Not to mention Stuart Yan, who was suing him for damages in civil court. It had to come to a head. A saint would have broken under the pressure, and he never claimed to be a saint.

It was a Sunday and he was sitting in the car outside McDonald's, reading the sports page, watching the leaves change, checking his watch—nine o'clock, nine-thirty, ten— and Gina's mother never showed. His first impulse was to drive out there and do some damage, confront the bitch, tear the house down if that was what it took, but he suppressed it: that was a ticket to jail. He checked his watch again. A guy came out the door, a nobody, a nonentity in flip-flops and shorts, and he had his two kids by the hand and they were one happy family, their Egg McMuffins tucked away and the park or a football game in their immediate future or maybe a cruise up the river to see how the leaves looked against the water. He wanted to call, but that was against the rules too. At eleven, sick with rage, he gave it up and drove to the restaurant to discover a message on the machine: *Just to let you know,* Gina's mother's pinched voice came at him as if she were hollering down a tunnel, *Sukie won't be coming today because of the ballet at Carnegie Hall. The whole family's going.*

He listened to the message twice through, standing there over the phone in his office at the back of the building, struggling for control. There were stains on the wall. The place smelled of marinara sauce, a dark ancient funk of it, and of the grease extruded from the pepperoni and the cheese burned to the walls of the oven. They thought they'd beaten him down, marginalized him, taken him out of the equation—before long, he'd be erased altogether. That was what they thought, but they were wrong. He could have called his lawyer and started up that whole dance again, could have complained, and yet he didn't see what good that would do—they had their own lawyer. Up to this point, he'd played by the rules. Now the rules were off.

In the morning, as soon as the offices were open, he put in calls to the phone company, the gas, electric and water, identifying himself as John Marchetti and ordering a stop service on all utilities at the house. He filed a change of address at the post office, then called American Express and Visa—the two cards he'd seen the Bullhead flash—and claimed he'd lost his wallet and wanted replacement cards overnighted by FedEx. When the new cards arrived at the post-office box he'd set up, he began to order things for delivery to 1236 Laurel: a new washer and dryer; an antique slate pool table that weighed over a thousand pounds; a pair of purebred Dalmatians; a deluxe fourteen-jet hot tub that could accommodate six people comfortably. That was just the beginning. He canceled Gina's cell, canceled her credit cards, went down to the bank and closed out their joint savings account. And Yan. He went after Yan too, but in a more immediate way. A week later, after he'd closed the restaurant for the night and made the rounds of the bars, he found Yan's Nissan parked out front of his apartment and poured six plastic jugs of muriatic acid over the finish, then slashed the tires and took out the windshield for good measure. The night was cold, his breath steaming, the tire iron flashing under the street lamp like a sword of vengeance, and maybe somebody saw him there or maybe it was the post-office box, maybe that was it. He never knew really. In fact, he was still asleep when they came for him, and he never did remember his toothbrush.

By the time he got round to cooking, it was past seven and Madison was distracted and whiny. She sat at the kitchen table, pounding her legs back and forth under the chair as if she were on a swing set at the playground, watching him poach the gnocchi while the cordon bleu began to send up signals from the oven and the white sauce thickened in the pan and the zucchini simmered in olive oil, red wine, garlic and chopped basil, the flame up high just before he cut it down nearly to nothing. There was an untouched glass of milk in front of her and the croque monsieur he'd made her from a heel of French bread and the leftover slices of prosciutto and Emmentaler browned in the pan. He could see the semicircular indentation her upper teeth had made in the sandwich when she'd lifted it to her mouth and then decided she wasn't going to eat it after all because she was cranky and tired and sugared-out in honor of Dunkin' Donuts Day at camp and because he wanted her to eat and her mother wanted her to eat and she didn't want to do what anybody wanted her to do, not in her present mood.

For his part, he was through coaxing her. She could kick away all she wanted and she could pout and mug and whine that the milk was too warm and the sandwich too cold or plead for him to read her a story or at least let her get up from the table and watch TV, but he was in a zone—he was enjoying himself, the meal coming to fruition, two sips left of the vodka martini on the counter and the Orvieto on ice. Natalia had set the table on the deck—it was an uncharacteristically mild evening, the fog held at bay, at least temporarily—and she was out there now, martini in one hand, magazine in the other. After the spa, she'd spent the afternoon shopping with Kaylee, and she'd come home in a delirium of shopping bags, the slick shining colors catching the light, her hair swept back, her smile quick and unambiguous and her mood elevated. Definitely elevated. She insisted on trying things on for him—*Did he like this one? Did he? Was he sure? It wasn't too, too . . . was it?*—and Madison was summoned to try on the three outfits she'd got for her (hence the mood and the lateness of the meal).

He hadn't told her a thing yet, just that he had a surprise for her. While she'd been out shopping, he'd been shopping too, and he'd traded the Z4 in on a Mercedes S500 sedan with charcoal leather seats, burl walnut trim, an in-dash GPS navigator system and Sirius satellite radio, in a sweet color they called Bordeaux Red. There was a price differential, of course—a considerable one, and he knew he was being taken, the salesman pulling some sort of phony accent on him and kissing his ass from the front door to the desk and back again—but that hardly mattered. The Beemer was his down (the pink slip signed over to him by none other than Dana Halter) and there were no payments for the first six months, by which time it really wasn't relevant. Now, as he dodged from one pan to the other, checking the cordon bleu, dipping the gnocchi out of the pot and slipping them onto a greased sheet for a three-minute browning in the oven, he was burning up with the need to show it to her, to show it off and see the look on her face. That was how he'd planned it out, the new car first, the thrill of it, maybe a ride round the block or over the bridge, and then he'd give her the news: Business. An opportunity on the East Coast. But it would be a vacation, a vacation too—see the sights. Didn't she want to live in New York? Hadn't she always said that? New York?

In the heat of the moment—pans sizzling, aromas rising—he didn't hear her come in the door. There was Madison, pouting at the table, there was the deck and the empty chaise, and here she was, Natalia, slipping her arms round his waist. "So what is this surprise?" she cooed, her lips at his ear. "Tell me. I can hardly stand to know."

Flipping off the gas under the burners, he gave the zucchini pan a precautionary shake and then swiveled round in her embrace. Both his hands climbed to her shoulders and he took her to him for a lingering kiss while Madison looked on in mock disgust. "You'll see," he murmured, and in that moment he was sure of her, sure of the feel and the taste and the smell of her, his partner, his lover, the dark venereal presence in his bed. "As soon as we eat."

"Ohhh," she said, drawing it out, "so long?" And then, to her daughter: "It is a surprise, Madison. For Mommy. Do you like a surprise?"

After dinner—Madison managed to get down two forkfuls of gnocchi and half a slice of the veal, though she just stared right through the vegetables—he took them down the front steps to the gravel walkway along the bay. They were holding hands, Natalia on his right, Madison on his left. Madison bunched her fingers in the way Sukie used to, not quite ready to interlock them with his because she was still in a mood and that would have been too conciliatory under the circumstances—the surprise wasn't for her, after all, or not primarily. "What is it, Dana?" she kept saying in a high taunting schoolyard voice. "Huh? Aren't you going to tell?"

"Yes, Da-na," Natalia chimed in. "I am in suspense. It is out here, outside? Something outside?"

He didn't answer right away. He was thinking of Sukie, the last time he'd seen her. It was the week he'd been released. They were at McDonald's, same place, same time, but she wasn't the girl he knew. It wasn't just the physical changes—a year older, a year taller, two teeth missing in front, her hair pinned up with a tortoiseshell barrette so that she seemed like an adult in miniature—but the way she looked at him. Her eyes, fawn-colored, round as quarters, eyes that had given themselves up to him without stint, were wary now, slit against the glare of the sun, against him. He could see the poison Gina had poured into them and see too that there was no antidote—there was nothing he could do to win her back, no amount of fudge on the sundae, not the desperation of his hug or the prattle of the old stories and routines. She was lost to him. He didn't even remember her birthday anymore. "No," he said finally, bending low against the tug of Natalia's hand to bring his face level with her daughter's, "it's inside."

All three of them had halted. Madison's nose twitched. "Then why are we out here?"

"Because this is an alternate way to our garage, isn't it? An acceptable way? A nice way, out here, breathing nice clean air after dinner?" He straightened up even as she let go of his hand and flew across the grass; just as she reached the garage door—unfinished wood gone gray with the sun and sea for the natural look—he clicked the remote and the door swung up as if by magic.

"It is a car?" Natalia said, catching the glint of chrome as they strode across the grass hand in hand.

When they were there, when he'd let Madison in to scramble over the seats and Natalia, her mouth slack, had pulled back the driver's side door to peer inside at the dash, he said, "Top of the line. Or nearly." He paused, watching her run a hand over the upholstery. "I could have gone for the S600, but it's such a gas hog—four hundred ninety-three horses. I mean, think of the environment."

Natalia was giving him a puzzled look. "But where," she said, "is my car?"

"Mommy, Mommy!" Madison shouted, bouncing so high on the rear seat her head brushed the roof.

"I traded it on this," he said, trying to keep his voice even.

"For you. For Madison. You can't have her on your lap all the time, I mean, she's growing up—look at the size of her."

"But I love my Z-car." Natalia's lips were clenched. Her eyes hardened.

"I know, baby," he said, "I know. When we get to New York I'll get you another one, I promise."

Her head came up now, up out of the dark den of the interior, with its rich new smell and the shining screen of the GPS system. "New York? What are you talking about?"

Later, after they'd put Madison to bed, they had a talk. It was the kind of talk he hated, the kind where you were up against the wall, no place to hide, and everything was going to come out sooner or later. He felt vulnerable. Irritated. Felt as if he was standing before the judge all over again, the lawyer, his probation officer.

Natalia had made coffee and they sat across from each other in the living room, holding on to their mugs as if they were weighted against a hurricane wind. She was watching him closely, her eyebrows lifted, both hands clenched round the mug in her lap. "So, you are going now to tell me what this is all about? That I should have to leave my home and tear up—is that how you say it?—tear up my daughter when she is just to start in school?"

"You love me, right?" he countered, leaning forward to set his mug on the coffee table. "You've told me that a thousand times. Did you mean it?"

She didn't respond. Outside, a pair of blue lights drifted across the bay.

"Did you?"

In a reduced voice, she said that she did. One hand went to the throat of her silk blouse; she fingered the necklace there, pearls he'd given her. Or paid for, anyway.

"All right, good. You're just going to have to trust me, that's all"—he held up a hand to forestall her. "Haven't I given you everything you could possibly want? Well," he said, without waiting for an answer to the obvious, "I'm going to continue to do that. No, I'm going to give you more. Much more. Private school for Madison, the best money can buy, and you know the best schools are on the East Coast. You know that, don't you?"

Her face was ironed sober, no trace of theatrics or antipathy. She was trying hard to comprehend. "But why?"

"It's complicated," he said, and he glanced up at a movement beyond the window, a flash of white, the beat of wings, something settling there on the rail—an egret. Was that an egret?

"Yes?" she said, leaning into the table herself now, her eyes probing his.

"Okay," he said. "You just have to—listen, my name isn't really Dana."

"Not Dana? What do you mean? This is a joke?"

"No," he said, slowly shaking his head, "no joke. I—I *adopted* the name. Because I was in trouble. It was—"

She cut him off. "Then you are not a doctor?"

He shook his head. There was the shadow of the bird there, faintly luminous, and he couldn't help wondering if it was a sign, and if it was, whether it was a good sign or bad.

"And all this"—her gesture was sudden, a wild unhinged sweep of her hand—"is a lie? This condo, this coffee table and the dining set? A lie? All a lie?"

"I don't know. Not a lie. Everything's real—the new car, the earrings, the way I feel about you and Madison." He glanced away and saw that the bird was gone, chased by her gesture, by the violence of her voice. "It's just a name."

There was a long moment of silence during which he became aware of the distant murmur of the neighbor's TV, a sound that could have been the wash of the surf or the music of the whales. But it wasn't. It was only the sound of a TV. Then she said, "So, if you are not Da-na, then who are you?"

He never hesitated. He looked right at her. "Bridger," he said. "Bridger Martin."

PART III

One

"IT'S GOOD," Bridger said, using his hands for emphasis. "I like it." He nodded his head vigorously, chin up, chin down. His smile widened. "Really good."

"Really?" she said, and felt the color rise to her face. "You're not just telling me that, are you?"

They were sitting in her car across from Mail Boxes Etc. in the town of Mill Valley, California, just over the Golden Gate Bridge from San Francisco. She'd never been here before, had never in fact done anything more than attach the name to a place she knew vaguely to be somewhere north of the city. It was a pleasant-enough town, she supposed, with its oaks and pines and the mountain that loomed over it, the streets that managed to seem urban and rural at the same time and the carefully cultivated small-town feel— just the sort of place a thief might want to live. Trees to hide behind. Money that spoke quietly. Anonymity.

They'd been here, in the parked car, for two hours now. The day before, they'd checked into a motel in Monterey— Bridger had insisted on taking her to the aquarium there, which she loved despite herself, sharks tapping some hidden energy source with the flick of a fin, fish floating like butterflies in the big two-story tank as if this were the Disneyland of the sea—and they'd got up early that morning and driven straight through to Mill Valley. Bridger's map, downloaded from MapQuest, with a red star indicating the

Mail Boxes franchise they were looking for, took them right to the place without fret or deviation, and if she'd expected it to look sinister, expected the criminal himself to be grinning at her from behind the copy machines, she was disappointed. The store looked no different from any other Mail Boxes Etc. There it was. People going in, people coming out.

But what to do next? Bridger wanted her to go right up to the counter and carry off an imposture, tell them she'd lost her key, show them some proof (if she wasn't Dana Halter of #31 Pacific View Court, then who was?) and see what was in the box, a bill, correspondence, a bank statement, anything that might show the residential address. Then they'd turn the tables. Then *they'd* go to *him*. She knew he was right. That was the logical thing to do, because they could sit here watching the place forever and still the guy might not show up or if he did they could miss him— all they had was a photograph, after all, and photographs offer up one version only, the version of the moment, and what if he'd grown a beard, dyed his hair? Or he might send somebody else for his mail—his wife, his daughter, his gay partner for all she knew. He could be wearing a hat, sunglasses, he could come in with a bag over his head. No, Bridger was right, but she was the one who had to go in there and break the law, not he. All her life she'd had to struggle with social situations, struggle to make herself understood while people gave her that don't-touch-me look, and what if the person behind the counter said, "What number?" *What number?* That would kill the whole thing— they'd probably call the police on her. A woman with a suspicious high bludgeoning voice trying to scam—that was the word, wasn't it? Scam?—some innocent citizen's mailbox key for what had to be a nefarious purpose. What could she say—that she'd forgotten the number of her own box? Another lie to layer it smooth: *I've been out of town and it just slipped my mind, well, because this is my second home up here, my vacation place, actually, and I, well, I don't—I just forgot . . .*

So they were sitting in the car, watching the door of the place—people coming, people going—hoping to get lucky. In the meanwhile, he'd asked her to read him what she'd been writing, because he was curious and wanted her to share it with him, and yes, he assured her, he could listen and keep his eyes on the door at the same time. And so she'd read to him and she watched his face when he told her it was good and maybe she'd flushed red, maybe she had.

"You know," he said, "the writing's really" and she didn't catch the rest.

She leaned in close to him. "What? The writing is what?"

"Cinematic," he said, contorting his face, his mouth, his lips, and he finger-spelled it just to be sure.

"Cinematic?" she repeated, secretly pleased. All at once, and she couldn't help herself, she saw the book as a movie, a whole parade of scenes, not the least of which featured the premiere, the red carpet, she and Bridger in tuxedos—or no, he in a tuxedo and she in a black strapless dress, or no, white, definitely white . . .

His face changed, his eyes sinking away from the smile. "There *was* a movie, you know. Like thirty years ago? By"— he finger-spelled it—"François Truffaut. You know that, right?"

"Yes," she said, holding his eyes, "of course. I've seen it."

"It was called *L'Enfant Sauvage*. We saw it in film school." He brought his hands up out of his lap, as if to use them, and then thought better of it. "And it was good, I re-member. Truffaut himself played the teacher, what was his name?"

"Itard."

"Right, Itard—but you haven't got that far yet, right? What you gave me is as far as it goes—where they find the kid wandering naked in the woods and nobody knows who he is or how he's managed to survive on his own?"

She nodded. It was easy to read him because he was her intimate, her man, and she knew his speech patterns as well as she knew her father's, her mother's—what was hard was reading strangers, especially if they talked fast or with an impediment or an accent. That was why her stomach felt light and her blood raced as if she'd just climbed a dozen flights of stairs: there was a stranger behind the counter in Mail Boxes Etc. and she was going to have to go in there and pretend to be someone she wasn't, pretend to be hearing, pretend to be entitled and maybe even cavalier. *Yes,* she signed, *that's as far as it goes.* And then, aloud: "I want to get to that part, where Itard tries to teach him to talk, to name things, to speak through an acquired language, but first I'm interested in how the child is perceived by the society around him—and how he perceives the world himself. That's the beginning. That's the groundwork."

"He never did learn to talk, did he? I mean, after how many years of exercises like seven days a week and all that?"

And all that. The struggle, that was what it was about, the fight to overcome the deficit, the impairment, the loss. Itard and Victor, the Wild Child, who could barely pronounce his own name. "Five years," she said. And then, finally, her throat constricting, she added, "No, he never did learn to speak."

He ran a hand through his hair and it came away with a faint sheen of gel on his palm. She noticed because he raised both his hands, as if to speak in Sign—he tried for her sake, and it was more intimate, more giving, even than what they did in bed together; in that moment, she felt herself go out to him as if all her tethers had been cut. *Are you going to go to*—he paused, because he couldn't find the Sign and had to spell it out: *France? To see it. For research, I mean?*

She showed him: *Country, foreign country. Europe, European.* "Germany" *is the double eagle,* "for France you flick the wrist like this, like the flicking of a Frenchman's handkerchief out of his cuff. See? It's easy."

His hands were in his lap. His face fell into what she liked to call his "hangdog" look, and she loved the reference, the picture it made in her mind of a dog called out on the carpet—right, on the carpet?—and the way its body collapsed under the weight of all that undisguised doggy emotion. "What?" she said. "What's wrong?"

"You didn't answer the question."

"You mean France?"

A full minute must have gone by and neither of them had even glanced at the door across the street. His eyes were concentrated on her lips, as if he were the deaf one. "No," she said, shaking her head slowly, back and forth, heavy as the pendulum at the bottom of the grandfather clock in her parents' front hall, the one that announced the hour to everyone but her. "I'd love to, but—"

"But you can't afford it. Because you don't have a job. Right?"

She dropped her eyes. Used her hands: *Right.*

Both of them looked up then and studied the façade of Mail Boxes Etc. They might have been architectural students—and she should have thought of that, should have brought two sketch pads and an assortment of pencils, charcoal, gum erasers, the ones that smelled like tutti-frutti. Or maybe they were building inspectors. Or town planners. She wouldn't have put that ugly cookie-cutter thing there if she was on the board, no way in the world. In fact, she'd tear it down in a heartbeat and let the oaks creep back in, put in a fountain, a couple of benches. The frame collapsed and her eyes went to the movement inside, the vague bobbing of shapes screened by the reflection of the sun off the windows, people at work, packages being weighed, mail sent out and received, copies run, an amorphous huddle around the cash register. Her stomach sank. And then she felt his touch: two fingers at her chin, gently shifting her gaze back to him. "Have you thought about what you're going to do?"

"No, not with this hanging over me," she said, gesturing toward the store. "I mean, I get paid through the end of August, but obviously I've got to start sending my résumé out." She watched his face change—he didn't want her to see what he was feeling, but he was a lousy actor. "I don't want to leave, if that's what you mean."

"That's what I mean," he said.

She leaned in to kiss him, the familiar taste and scent of him, lips that spoke in a different way altogether, and then drew back again. "I'd love to go to Aveyron, to Lacaune and Saint-Sernin—are you kidding me?—but the airfare's out of my range, I'm afraid, and with the dollar weak . . . Plus, they'd probably arrest me the minute they ran my passport through the computer." She put on a face. "Dana Halter, batterer and assaulter—it even rhymes."

"But how can you write about a place you've never seen?"

This was easy. She pointed a finger to her head. "I see it here. And I've been there, to the south of France, anyway— to Toulouse, which isn't that far from Aveyron. Didn't I ever tell you that?" She'd been there as a girl, a few years after she became deaf. She must have been ten, eleven—the age of the wild child. Her parents were vacationing in Europe that year and they brought the whole family along—her and her two brothers—for the educational opportunity. Her parents were practical in that way. Her mother especially. And especially with her, full immersion in both Sign and speech right from the beginning—what the people who make their living off the deaf call "total communication"—because there was no way her daughter was going to be a cripple or even the tiniest bit dependent on anybody or anything. Her mother was pretty then, her hair trailing down her back beneath the brim of the suede cowgirl's hat she'd bought on a trip to Mexico, her legs long and naked in a yellow sundress and two boy babies and a little deaf girl compressed in her arms—Dana didn't know whether her memories of that time came from the photographs in the family album or what she'd seen and smelled and felt. When she closed her eyes she could see the fingers of palms etched against pale stucco, a river like an avenue of light, the new bridge (a regional joke: Napoléon had built it) humped over the water as if it were trying to swim.

"You know," she said, trying to hold on to the moment because in the next moment she was going to have to go into that store, "it's easier to learn foreign Sign than a spoken language. Much easier. I picked up FSL right away because my mother thought I should meet deaf French kids."

"Iconicity," Bridger said, surprising her. "Like when you sign 'cup.'" He demonstrated, his left palm the saucer, his right cupped over it. "We learned it in the class I took. German, French, Chinese, whatever—a cup is a cup, right? What about Marcel Marceau—I bet he would have been good at it. Did he know Sign, you think?"

Just then a movement on the far side of the street caught her eye, and she started. A man in a flowered shirt, baseball cap and wraparound sunglasses scrambled up to the door as if he were in a hurry—as if someone were chasing him, as if he were a fugitive—pulled back the door and disappeared inside. "Bridger!" she shouted (or might have shouted; she couldn't tell, but it felt like a shout). "Bridger, it's him!"

She was out of the car before he was, a deaf woman in the middle of the street, cars coming both ways and she staring down a UPS man in a boxy brown UPS truck that was right there in front of her though she couldn't hear his horn or the metallic keening of his brakes, and even as Bridger caught up to her and grabbed her arm she was telling herself to slow down, stay calm, focus. Then they were on the far side of the street, up on the sidewalk, and Bridger might have been saying something, but she wasn't paying attention—her eyes were fixed on the door ahead of them. She saw her own reflection there, a shifting of shapes, the gleaming metal handle of the door, and she took a deep breath and stepped inside, Bridger right behind her.

There were eight people in the place and she tried to take them all in simultaneously, including the heavyset woman behind the desk who looked up and gave her an expectant smile and the old man fumbling for change at one of the copy machines. Her heart slammed at her ribs. The overhead lights seemed to recede, painting a thin pale strip of illumination across the heads and shoulders of the eight figures in their various poses, bending, gesticulating, lips flapping on air—and where was he? Her eyes jumped from one to the other, and then suddenly there he was. There, at the back of the store, where the bank of mailboxes ran in a neat continuous file from waist- to shoulder-level: she saw the bright flash of the shirt first, then his profile under the bill of the cap as he stood over the wastebasket, discarding junk mail. Oblivious. Completely oblivious. As if he were the most innocent soul in the world. The son of a bitch. She couldn't believe it.

She felt Bridger wrap an arm round her waist, an admonitory tightness straining the ligaments of his wrist and fingers. *Calm*, he was telling her, *stay calm*. It took a moment—she was just staring, all the rage and disbelief she'd felt over the way she'd been violated rising in her till she was strung tight with it, ready for anything, the accusation, the physical assault, the spewing up of the deaf woman's shriek that was so caustic and inhuman it could set off all the alarms up and down the block—and then Bridger disengaged his arm and she felt his fingers on her chin, urgently tugging her face around. *That's not him*, he signed.

She looked harder. Small Sign, very quiet: *No, it is. It is.*

Bridger shook his head emphatically and her eyes went from him to the man in the cap and back again. "Not even close," he said.

By this point the man had finished with his mail and abruptly pivoted on the ball of one foot to hurry up the aisle toward them, a sheaf of what looked to be bills and a manila envelope clutched to his chest, and she saw how wrong she'd been—even with the sunglasses and the bill of the cap pulled down low, this man was nothing like the one in the photograph. He was older, hair graying at the fringes of the cap, his nose splayed across his face as if it had been molded of clay, lips bunched round a look of eternal harassment. He wasn't the thief. He wasn't Frank Calabrese or whatever his name was. He was nobody. She watched him plunge impatiently through the door and scurry off down the street and still the blood pounded in her veins.

"All right," Bridger said, swinging her round to face him, "we're going up to the counter now and you're going to be Dana Halter. Okay? You cool with that? Because I tell you, there's no other way."

She wasn't cool with it. Wasn't down with the program or hip to it or copacetic or even just basically willing, but she let him guide her up to the counter and tried on a smile for the heavyset woman, who gave it right back to her. "Can I help you?" the woman said, and that was easy to read—context, context was all.

"Yes, please," Dana said, and dropped her eyes a moment while she extracted her driver's license from her purse and laid it on the counter. "I'm Dana Halter?" she said, looking up again. "I just—I don't know, I guess I misplaced my mailbox key . . ."

The woman was younger than she'd first appeared. She was wearing a pink cable-knit sweater that gave an unfortunate emphasis to her shoulders and upper arms, her skin was pale to the point of anemia and she wore a pair of clunky-looking glasses with clear plastic frames. But her eyes were what mattered, and her eyes were nonjudgmental. She barely glanced at the license and then slid it back across the counter. "No problem," she said, and her smile brightened, and then she said something else.

"I'm sorry, what?"

Dana saw the woman flick her eyes to Bridger and then Bridger said something.

"She said," he repeated, speaking slowly so that she could read his lips, "that there is a twenty-five-dollar fee for replacement keys and I said that was okay. Right, honey?"

"Yes," she said, nodding vigorously and holding the woman's eyes, "sure. That's only fair, and I'm sorry—it was my fault, not my fiancé's." She was elaborating now—lies always required elaboration. "So stupid of me." She turned to Bridger, playing the airhead, the doll-face, the bimbette. "My bad, honey," she said. She was beginning to enjoy this, especially the aftershock of the term "fiancé" on Bridger's face. But then the woman said something else and she had to ask "What?" again.

"Number?" the woman was saying. "What number?"

This was what she'd been afraid of—any honest person,

any normal person, would have had the number on the tip of her tongue, but Dana didn't have it because she was an imposter—she wasn't Dana Halter at all. Or not this Dana Halter. She felt her lips tighten. For a split second she looked away, averting her eyes like a criminal, a liar, a scam artist, and she struggled to control her voice as she repeated the version of the story she'd rehearsed about this being their second home and how they'd been away and how to her embarrassment—Can you believe it?—she'd forgotten the number. But here was her ID—she thrust the driver's license across the counter again, and dug out her social security card and a major credit card too—and she wondered sweetly if the woman could just look it up in her records?

The smile was gone now and the woman's eyes had lost their sympathy. She didn't look suspicious so much as uneasy—an understanding was awakening inside her and Dana recognized it and for the first time in her life played to it. She stood absolutely still, poised at the counter in the silence that was eternal, and let her eyes do the talking for her. *Yes,* her eyes said, *I'm different,* and it hardly hurt at all to see that this time it was the woman who had to look away.

Aside from the usual glut of flyers and one-time-only offers addressed hopefully to "Occupant," there appeared to be three or four legitimate pieces of mail in the box. Dana caught the briefest glimpse of a commercial logo on one of the envelopes—was that a bill?—before bundling the whole business up in two trembling hands and willing herself to walk in a measured way to the exit, even turning to look over her shoulder and wave two appreciative fingers at the woman behind the counter. Bridger was waiting for her outside. Together, they crossed the street, careful to look both ways and present an air of calm to anybody who might be watching, and then they were in the car and the mail—Dana Halter's mail—was theirs.

The surprise was Bridger. He was so wound up he actually snatched the bundle out of her hands and began pawing through it, impatiently tossing newsprint flyers and glossy brochures to the floor at his feet. There was an expression of willed triumph on his face, something hard there she'd never recognized before—from the look of him you would have thought he was the one whose identity had been stolen. He came up with the letters—three of them, addressed to the postbox—but it was she who slipped the bill emblazoned with the PG&E logo out of the pile and lifted it exultantly to the light. He might have said "Bingo!" or "Eureka!" but he didn't have to. They both knew what it meant. They had him now. They had their man.

"Open it," he said.

She could feel the smile aching on her lips. "It's a federal offense."

"Horseshit," he said, or something like it. "What about stealing somebody's identity—what kind of offense is that? Open it." He made a snatch at the envelope then, but she was too quick for him, shifting it to her left hand and secreting it in the space between door and seat cushion. She was afraid suddenly, frightened at the prospect of what was about to be revealed. They were so close. The face of the thief, his mocking eyes, the cocky thrust of his chin, came back to her. So close. Her stomach clenched around nothing, around the remains of the stale croissant and sour coffee they'd got at a gas station hours ago. Bridger said something, terse and urgent—she could feel the force of his expelled breath—but she dropped her eyes and shut him out. He tried to turn her face to him, his fingers at her throat, and she shook him off. Silently, deep in her mind, she counted to ten. Then she tore open the envelope.

The address inside, the service address, stared out from the page, and it gave her a jolt that was almost physical, as if her auditory nerves had been suddenly restored and someone had screamed it in her ear:

109 Shelter Bay Village
Mill Valley, CA 94941

Bridger slammed his hand down on the dash and raised his chin to howl in triumph, and then he pumped his fist twice in the air and pulled his lips back to emit what must have been a hiss of jubilation. Context told her what it was: "Yessss!"

The other envelopes revealed little—the first two proved, respectively, to be ads for real estate and equity loans, addressed in a neat computer-generated script meant to mimic human agency and dupe the addressee into opening it. The third one, though, was more interesting. It was addressed to *The Man, Box 2120, Mill Valley, California*, and inside was a thrice-folded sheet of lined paper torn from a yellow legal pad. A cryptic message was scrawled across it at a forty-five-degree angle in a looping oversized longhand: *Hey, that thing we talked about is on, no problema. See you soon. Ciao, Sandman.*

"'See you soon,'" she read aloud, looking to Bridger.

He had on his wondering look, his features floating across the pale globe of his face like drifting continents. His hair bristled. He ran a hand through it. "Is he going someplace? I mean, Dana, Frank, whatever his name is—is he planning a trip maybe?"

"What's the postmark?"

Bridger turned the letter over. It had been postmarked in Garrison, New York, four days earlier. "Where's Garrison?"

"I think it's near Poughkeepsie," she said. "Or maybe Peterskill. Maybe that's closer."

"So what's that—an hour, hour and a half north of the city?"

She shrugged. "I guess. Yeah."

The sun was on the car and though it was cool enough outside—in the low seventies, she guessed—she began to feel it and turned to crank down the window. When they'd come back to the car, she'd slid into the driver's seat—it was hers, after all, though Bridger had done nearly all the driving to this point—and now she looked out on the quietly bustling street and felt a tickle of emotion in her throat. "What now?" she wondered aloud, and Bridger pulled her to him, awkwardly, across the wheel. They embraced a moment and then he leaned back so she could see his face and the answer there: "We go after him."

"Us?" Now she went cold, but it was a steadily blowing crystalline kind of cold, and her fear was gone. She made the argument for its own sake. "But what about the police? Shouldn't we just give them the information?"

He gave her a look of disgust. "The police? Right, yeah. And go through the same kind of crap we did back in San Roque? Plus, what if he *is* planning to light out for the"—it took her a minute to catch this—"territories? To"—he finger-spelled it—"Poughkeepsie or wherever? Or what if this isn't even his house?" He didn't blink. Just stared into her eyes, earnest, angry, fired up, all his frustration, his attitude, his *love* come boiling to the surface. But was it love? Or was it just some twitch of the male ego, the need to go mano a mano, the testosterone speaking?

No matter. She wasn't going to think past the moment. She had an address and there was a thief hiding behind it. Even as she twisted the key to turn the engine over and grind the starter—and here Bridger provided the ears for her and the facial expression too—she knew she was going to chase this thing down till there was nowhere left to go.

The fog on the hills had an apocalyptic look, as if it were composed of some fatal gas poised to descend over the trees and rob the breath of every living thing, and yet the sun was still high and vital and the breeze untainted. On another day, in another mood, she might have found the fog a palliative, the cornerstone of the Bay Area's charm, but not today, not now. It was five o'clock. They'd gone to Noah's Bagels for lunch, though she wasn't hungry (or she was, but when the food arrived she found she couldn't eat), and that had given them some time to decompress and think out their next move. Or at least consider it, because they both knew that nothing was going to stop them from driving over to Shelter Bay Village, a mere five minutes away. But then what? Would they confront him? Call 911? Knock him down and bind him up themselves?

What they decided, finally, was to reconnoiter the place (scope it out, as Bridger would say, and she had to assume the phrase derived from "telescope" in some way, but then wouldn't it have been more accurate to say "binoc it out"?), just to see what they could see. Now they were here, in front of a recessed bank of semi-detached redwood condominiums constructed to maximize the views, strolling hand in hand along the gravel path that edged the water in a gently sweeping arc beneath a promenade of palms. And yes, those were binoculars dangling from her neck, and if anyone were to ask, well, she was just another innocuous and slightly dotty birdwatcher, and wasn't that a great blue heron out there? And look at the egrets!

Bridger's eyes were fixed on the deck of the near building, the one they'd identified from the front as #109. Was there movement there? He touched her arm and she lifted the binoculars to her eyes, trying to be discreet. At first she saw nothing, sheets of light glancing off the big flat opaque windows till they went from silver to black, and then she recalibrated and a figure materialized before her, the figure of a woman hovering over a glass-topped table. A young woman. Pretty features, dark hair wound up in a coil at the crown of her head, blue top, black capris. She was wiping down the table, that was it, and now—suddenly, heart pounding, Dana swung the binoculars away and pointed a finger out over the water, as if she'd been tracking the descent of a flock of mergansers—the woman was staring right at her.

Dana felt Bridger's hand go to the binoculars and she let go of them—he was playing the mime too, jerking the instrument back and forth as if following the imaginary birds, but what his lips said was, "Who is that? The wife, you think?"

Still focused on the patch of water that lay just beyond the faded redwood deck of #109, she could only nod. "I guess," she said. "If this is the right place."

Bridger's eyes shot to the deck and then went back to the binoculars. "Did you see anyone else? A man? Is *he* there?"

In the end, the tension was too much for her to bear. She gently extracted the binoculars from his grip, let her gaze rove over the surface of the bay a moment, and then swung him round by one arm and led him off in the opposite direction, two bird lovers on the track of something elusive. When they'd gone fifty paces, she leaned into him and they both halted, looking out to the water. "What now?" she asked, and if she could have heard herself—if she were a character in a novel—she might have described her tone as forlorn. Certainly she felt that way. The woman had looked right at her—or had seemed to. There was a face to it now, another face, flesh and blood, dark eyes, dark hair, capris.

Bridger loomed into her field of vision. "I say we ring the doorbell."

He was right. She knew he was. "Couldn't we just . . . wait? To see, I mean. If he shows up, gets out of his car—we could see his car and get the license plate . . ."

"And then what?" His mouth was drawn so thin it was like a paper cut. He was determined, she could see that. A breeze came up then, clean and sweet, and blew the hair across her face so that for a moment she was hidden and what he said next didn't register. But his fingers were there, gently probing, and he brought her back with a sweep of his hand. "Come on," he urged. "We'll go together. Just ring the bell, that's all. We're visiting. Looking for the Goldsteins. Ask her do you know where the Goldsteins live and just see what happens, see if the son of a bitch is there—maybe he'll answer the door himself, and that's all we need. Just that."

She didn't argue. All at once they were strolling again, following the gravel path as it looped back across the gentle grassy undulations and neatly recessed flowerbeds the landscaper had thought to provide so the denizens of Shelter Bay Village could delight in the contrast as they gazed out over the property to the flat shining void of the water and the hills beyond. A woman in jeans and a windbreaker emerged from behind the bank of buildings and jogged toward them, a small black dog scrambling ahead of her on the tether of its leash. Someone was getting out of a car in the lot—another woman, dipping forward to retrieve her purse and a bag of groceries. Dana felt as if she were about to lose consciousness. Something flitted before her eyes, but it wasn't palpable, and then they were on the doorstep—a deep-pile mat, two pots of begonias, brass knocker—and she was glad she couldn't hear the sound the buzzer made in response to the weight of Bridger's index finger.

The door pulled abruptly open and the woman was there, prettier even than she'd looked at a distance, and there was a child there too, four or five years old, a girl, tugging with all her weight at her mother's wrist—her mother, this was her mother, and anybody could have seen that. The woman gave them a blank look. "Yes?" she said. "Can I help you?"

Bridger said something then and for a moment it seemed to immobilize her: "Is Dana here?"

The child kept tugging, chanting "Mommy, Mommy," and something else Dana couldn't read, and the woman's face changed in that instant, the eyes retreating, lips hardening round the bitter savor of the lie. "No," she said, "you must have the wrong house." She glanced away to shoot her daughter an admonitory look and then came back to them. "There is no one of that name here."

Two

"WHAT DO YOU MEAN they asked for me? By *name*?"

He'd just come through the front door, feeling harassed, his shirt soaked under the arms, and he hadn't had a drink yet or anything to eat either and the first thing she said to him was that somebody had been there looking for him. That snapped him to attention, all right. That froze him. Right there in the front hall, the three white plastic bags of takeout Chinese dangling from his fingertips and the unread newspaper pinned to his chest. He'd spent the better part of the afternoon and well into the evening hassling over things, the little details that prick you like multiple beestings till your flesh is scored and bleeding and you barely have the energy or will to do what you have to do— like take three carloads of Natalia's clothes and accessories to the storage unit in Larkspur she'd insisted on renting and FedEx six cardboard cartons of dresses, handbags, shoes and kiddie toys to Sandman's place in Croton—and now she'd sprung this on him. He stood there, stupefied.

She was wearing her martyred look, the look she'd put on two nights ago and hadn't taken off since, the savage dark strokes of her eyeliner crushing the life out of her eyes, her mouth set in a permanent pout, her nostrils flaring with self-pity. "No," she said, "not you," throwing it over her shoulder as she turned away from the door, padded across the room on bare feet and flung herself down on the couch that was strewn with the chaos of her packing. "Not you," she repeated in a withering voice. "Da-na. They want Da-na."

For two days and nights it had been going on like this, the aftermath of his confession a rain of ashes, the village gone and all the people in it, no-man's-land, and he'd had it. Enough. Enough already. Before he knew what he was doing he'd dropped the bags to the floor—and he didn't give a shit if the war wonton soup leaked into the Szechuan scallops and leached right on through to the carpet and if the carpet was ruined and the floorboards underneath and everything else all the way on down to the goddamn basement—and he was there and he had her by the arm, all the rage in him concentrated in the grip of the five fingers of his right hand. "Don't fuck with me," he said, low and hard, tuning his voice to the register of violence the way he'd learned to do when he was inside, when people were holding their breath and listening and the whole place went suddenly quiet. "You just tell me, you understand? No more of this shit."

She looked alarmed—scared—her eyes flaring up and then dwindling down to nothing, and that made him feel bad, but not enough to loosen his grip. He jerked her arm, shook her like one of the big fifty-pound sacks of flour stacked up on the shelves in the back room at Pizza Napoli. She didn't cry out. Didn't protest. She said, "A man and a woman. For you, they ask for you."

Still he held her and he could feel the pressure beating at the sclera of his eyes as if it was too much to contain, as if it would all blow out of him like spew. "How old?" And when she tightened her mouth, a second's hesitation, he jerked at her arm again. "I said, how old?"

"You are leaving a mark." Her voice was cold, distant, as if she were alluding to an arm that was attached to someone else in another apartment altogether. He became aware then of the constricted burst of cartoon voices emanating from Madison's room, a sudden crazed drawn-out cackle of a laugh, crepitating music. He let go. Natalia gave him a look of resentment, as if he were the one at fault. She wouldn't rub at her arm—she wouldn't give him the satisfaction. She was going to suffer. She was a martyr. "The man maybe twenty-five, I don't know," she said finally. "The woman thirty. Tall, pretty. Blue jeans she was wearing and a tan jacket from bebe, one hundred and thirty-nine dollars on special sale. Okay?"

"They weren't selling anything? You're sure, right? They asked for me by name, not 'Mr. Halter' or 'the man of the house' or anything like that?"

In one swift sure movement she snaked away from him, sliding over the arm of the couch and spinning to her feet like an acrobat. Her eyes lashed at him. She clenched her fists at her sides. "What do you tell me—for months, what do you tell me? You want me to be Mrs. Halter. Mrs. Halter! And who am I to be now? Mrs. Nobody? Yes?"

He took a step toward her and she backed up against the double doors that gave onto the deck. "Shut it," he said. "Just shut it. We leave in the morning, first thing. So get this shit"—and here he snatched an armful of clothes from the couch—"in your fucking suitcase and get your fucking suitcase in the fucking car, you hear me?"

"Oh, I hear you," and she was rubbing her arm now, "*Mister* Martin. If that is even your name. Is that your name? Huh, *Bridger*? Is that your name?"

He had no time for this. *A man and a woman,* two nouns that beat in his head with the force of revelation. They knew what he looked like, knew where he lived. They could be out there now, watching him. He looked past her, through the windows and out beyond the deck where the colors were neutering down toward night and the water had blackened along the gray fading shore. Something released in him then—*he had no time*—just as Madison appeared in the doorway calling "Ma-ma" in a piteous attenuated voice and both of them turned to her. "It's all right," he heard himself say. "I got the food. It's right here. Right here in the hallway."

They were sitting at the kitchen table, an interval of peace, lingering, the candles lit, wine poured, the chopsticks at their lips, and Madison, revitalized, telling them the plot of a movie she'd seen about a dog and a cat on a cross-country trek, when the doorbell rang. If he'd allowed his internal motor to idle over dinner—and he didn't care how crazy things got, dinner was sacrosanct, because if you didn't sit down over dinner you weren't even civilized—now it revved suddenly, so suddenly he didn't even know how he'd got through the double doors and out onto the deck, ready to drop down a story into the flower bed below. "I'm not here," he called to Natalia, slipping a leg over the rail, "you never even heard of me." And he eased himself down till he was dangling by his arms, then dropped to the ground.

It took all of sixty seconds, legs and arms pumping, and he was around front, letting the fronds and tendrils of the vegetation conceal him. There were two figures on the doorstep—a man and a woman—and Natalia was just opening the door. The man—he was in his twenties, soft-looking, with spiked hair, a two-tone jacket and the over-sized black jeans the street punks and club aficionados affected—was the one who spoke up, because the woman (and here it hit him: *Dana Halter,* she was *Dana Halter,* in the flesh) just stood there as if she'd been molded out of wax. And she *was* something to look at. She had Natalia's hair, thick and dark, though it twisted out and away from her scalp and hung loose over the collar of her tan jacket and she was taller, slumping her shoulders awkwardly because this was no fun for her. Somebody had assumed her identity, fucked with her life, and she was slumping her shoulders because she was embarrassed by the whole thing. But not so embarrassed she was about to just give it up and let the credit card companies and the insurance people sort it out. That gave him pause. Who was she? Why was she doing this to him? Was it payback, was that what she wanted? And the guy, Bridger—what was it to him?

"You again?" Natalia's tone was peevish, hard. "I told you. I already told you."

"Frank Calabrese," the man said. "Is Frank here?"

"Who?"

He repeated himself. His voice took on a pleading quality. "Look, we've been victims of a crime—or she has." He pointed to the woman. "My fiancée. She—somebody stole her identity. We're looking for Dana Halter. Or Frank Calabrese. You sure he's not here? Frank?"

From where he was hiding, crouched in the bushes, and he would not go down on one knee and stain a good pair of Hugo Boss twill trousers for nothing, he made sure to take a clean mental snapshot of these two, because they were going to pay for this—he was going to make them pay, both of them—and that was a promise.

The light in the entryway shone weakly, casting a jaundiced glow over the little gathering on the doorstep. Natalia's face hardened. She looked ready to do battle, and that was a good sign—she was on his side, at least, and he felt in that moment that she was going to stay there, no matter what he wound up telling her. "Listen," she said, her voice gone higher now, pinched and querulous, "there is nobody of this name, no Da-na, no Frank, nobody. This is not the correct house, understand?" A car pulled into the lot—the cream-colored Lexus that belonged to the Atkinsons, in one-eleven—and for a moment he felt his pulse leap as the headlights swept the bushes and then died. "If you come here to this house again," Natalia was saying, her face a sallow over-laid mask in the rinse of yellow light, "to, to *discommode* me and my daughter, I will call the policeman."

"Yeah, you do that," the guy snarled, trying to tough it out, but this was the same voice that had come at him over the phone and it had nothing behind it, nothing at all, and the door slammed and the night went quiet but for the solitary receding footsteps of Rick Atkinson on the gravel walk.

And then the strangest thing: the two figures stayed there on the doorstep a long moment, conferring, but without saying a word. Their hands—they were working their hands like ghostly shrouded puppets, and it took him a moment to understand. They were deaf. Or she was deaf. She was the one who hadn't spoken and so here she was juggling her hands as if she were molding something out of the air and passing it to him and then he juggled it and passed it back. It was so unexpected, so private and intimate, that Peck lost all consciousness of the moment. He felt like a voyeur—he *was* a voyeur—and his rage at what had just taken place cooked down into a sort of wonder as he watched them walk down the steps and up the path to the parking area. He was going to leave it at that—they were going, that was enough, and by morning he'd be gone too and all this would be behind him—but he recovered his wits in time to slip out of the shadows and follow them. Just to see what they would do next.

Somehow they'd traced him to the condo, but what did that mean? He wasn't Dana Halter anymore, he wasn't Frank Calabrese. *Frank Calabrese*—that gave him a chill. How in Christ's name did they get hold of that? But still, even if they called the cops and the cops came—a remote

possibility—nothing would happen, or at least not immediately. Where was the proof? He'd deny everything, act bewildered. And then, if he had to, incensed. The cops could
see just by looking at him, by the way he was dressed, by the
way he held his ground at the door of his three-quarters-of-
a-million-dollar luxury condo, that they were out of their
league. These two must have known that. But then what
were they doing—playing amateur detective? Looking to run
him down, confront him, settle this outside the law? For all
he knew they could have a gun. Anybody could have a gun,
the rangiest no-chin kid on the street, the old lady pushing
a shopping cart, housewives, mothers—guns were the cur-
rency of society, and he, personally, wanted nothing to do
with them, especially not on the receiving end.

The shadows played to him. He stayed out of sight, following the scrape of their shoes on the gravel path, watching their silhouettes bob against the hard fixed umbrella of
light opening out of the pole at the far end of the lot. He
saw them juggle their hands again when they reached their
car—a black Jetta, California plates—and then they were
speaking aloud, but he couldn't make out what they were
saying, her voice blurred and thumping at the syllables as if
she had a blanket over her head, his voice blending with
hers in a way that made them both indistinct. After a while,
they climbed into the car and the doors slammed with two
soft detonations, one on the tail of the other.

And what was he thinking? He was thinking he could
just step out of the bushes and lay the guy out, break him
up, and her too, some applied discouragement to end it
right here. But no, that wasn't the way. The way was just to
cut his losses and move on. He still had Natalia, he still had
money—and a new Mercedes S500 in Bordeaux Red. Peterskill wasn't Mill Valley, maybe, but he'd missed the leaves
changing in the fall, snow for Christmas, all of that, and it

wouldn't be so bad, not once he got settled. Plus there'd be Florida, Florida in the winter, and they had this whole trip ahead of them with nothing to do but see the country and kick back and enjoy themselves.

For a long while he crouched there in the bushes, watching the back end of the car, letting his mind run— Natalia would be in a state, no doubt about it, and there'd be no rest at all, not till he got her in the Mercedes and pulled the door shut behind him. The story, as it was evolving in his head, the one he would refine at length as they rolled cross-country, had to do with his bankruptcy, the failed restaurants, a fictitious name to smooth things out so he could track his investments, and yes, of course they were going to keep the condo for a summer place, no need to pack the dishes, towels, cutlery, and did she really think he was going to leave his wine cellar behind? He put a fist down in the wet to ease the pressure on his knees. There was a smell of rankness, of knife-shaped leaves and eucalyptus buds going over to rot. Across the lawn, up against the buildings, a bank of sprinklers started up with a hiss of released air. And then, finally, the Jetta's brake lights flashed and the engine turned over and he watched the car back out and glide across the lot to pass on into the black grip of the night.

When he got out of prison he didn't spend a whole lot of time dwelling on his hurts and sorrows, on what could have been and what Gina had done to him and all the wasted effort and sweat and blood he'd put into Pizza Napoli and Lugano or the fact that he was bankrupt and an ex-offender who didn't even have his silver Mustang anymore because he'd sold it and everything else he owned to pay his fish-faced lawyer. No, he was too wise for that. His wisdom had been accumulated through the twelve-ton nights in his bunk and the zombie days doing food preparation and staying out of trouble—and he had to work hard at that. Had to work to rein himself in. Dwell deep. Control the rage that beat in him like a hammer every minute of every day. Because there were some very twisted people inside and the sole meaning and extent of their lives was to fuck with you, and to respond in kind was a lock on extending your sentence. He'd heard the stories. And he put his head down and counted the days off the calendar and when push came to shove he let his hands speak for him, hard and fast, so fast nobody saw it coming and if some dickhead had to go to the infirmary with a pair of sausage eyes and a broken nose, it was nothing to him. He wasn't like the rest of them—of all the put-upon victims of circumstance in the place he was the single one who really truly didn't belong because he hadn't done anything anybody else wouldn't have done in his place and there was no way he was going to complicate things by letting people get to him. That was the beginning of wisdom.

And then there was Sandman. The College of Sandman.

Sandman had been around. His most recent infraction had, regrettably, involved a certain degree of forcible persuasion, which was why he'd been locked up here amongst the violent offenders. As Peck had. The rest of the inmates, to a man, were losers, the kind of scumbuckets and degenerates who deserved what was coming to them—after a year inside Peck felt like a Republican: lock them up and throw away the key—but Sandman was different. He was educated. He believed in things—the environment, clean air, clean water. The man could go on for hours about restoration ecology or the reintroduction of the wolf and how capitalism had sucked up all the resources of the world just to spit them back out as hair dryers—he had a real thing for hair dryers—and greenback dollars. Six-three, tat-tooed over most of his body, with a physique honed in the weight room, Sandman, who wasn't much older than he was, showed him the way. "You know how they say, 'Be all you can be'? In those Army recruiting ads? Well, I say, 'Be anybody you can be.'"

He was talking about the Internet. He was talking about the greed of the credit card companies, online auto loans, instant credit, social security numbers skimmed at the fast-food outlet and the gas station and up for sale on half a dozen sites for twenty-five dollars per. He was talking about Photoshop and color copiers, government seals, icons, base identifiers. The whole smorgasbord. *Be anybody you can be.*

Two hundred dollars. That was the gate money they gave you when you walked out the door after eleven and a half months of chopping cabbage, dicing onions and suck-ing up the reek of the grill, burgers, dogs, sloppy Joe on a bun, strip steak that was like jerky softened in water and then jerked all over again. Most of the morons blew the whole two hundred the first day on women and drugs and then they were out on the street trying on one scam or an-other and the probation officer just begging for a chance to send them back up. But not Peck, not William Peck Wilson.

He went straight back to Peterskill—to the office park on Route 6 where the orthopedists and urologists and pedi-atricians had their offices. Out back were the Dumpsters. It took him maybe an hour, slinking around like an immi-grant bagging cans for redemption, and he had what he wanted: a sheaf of discarded medical forms, replete with names, addresses, birth dates and social security numbers. Then he sat in a bar over a scotch and made a phone call to Dudley, the busboy, because he needed two things: a ride and a connection. Dudley, he reasoned, was the very man to hook him up with a false ID because Dudley had been clubbing since he was sixteen in a state where the drinking age was twenty-one, and he wasn't disappointed. For less than half his gate money, Peck was able to get himself a social security card and driver's license, with color photo, in the name of one of the patients at A&O Medical, and after that it was easy. He opened a checking account with the remaining hundred dollars and started writing checks for merchandise, which he turned around and sold for cash, installed himself in a hotel and applied for Visa and American Express cards. Once the cards arrived he took a cab out to the local Harley dealer. He'd always wanted a Harley, ever since he'd seen *Easy Rider* on TV as a kid, and Sandman had stoked him on the idea during their late-night fantasy excursions, a whole vista opening up in the shadows, blooming like a radiant perfect flower, the vision so intense he could feel the wind in his hair and see the sun spread like liquid gold across the road in front of him.

The dealer was a fat-faced longhair with what they called a hitch in his git-along, wearing a leather Harley jacket over an embroidered white shirt and some sort of racing medallion dangling on a cord from his throat. He was clueless, absolutely clueless. And Peck Wilson sat down with him and neatly signed all the paperwork in his new name, the credit references sterling, the bike—an Electra Glide in black with the Harley logo a sweet blaze of red on the swell of the fuel tank—being prepped even as they ran each other a line of bullshit about unholy speeds and wrecks and wild men they'd known, and then he swung a leg over the thing, fired it up with an annunciatory roar and blew on down the road and out of town. For good.

It wasn't quite dawn yet, the stars gone a shade paler in the eastern sky and Mount Tam to the west still an absence in the deep slough of dark and fog. Nothing had been moving fifteen minutes earlier when he'd backed out of the garage for a run to the coffee shop, and now, as the heavy wooden door slapped shut behind him, he eased himself out of the car with the cardboard tray—the same stuff they made egg cartons out of, and how was it he'd never noticed that before? Balanced there, in the molded slots, were two large double lattes and a hot chocolate with extra whipped cream and a white paper bag of assorted croissants and half a dozen éclairs to glut Madison into a sugary road-enhanced daze. She didn't travel well, and that was going to be a problem, but Natalia had spent a couple hundred bucks on coloring books and a miniature farm set and videos for the TV monitor built into the back of the seat.

The coffee was hot, the croissants still warm, but instead of going right upstairs with them, he set the cardboard tray on the hood of the car and eased open the side door next to the garage. For a long moment he stood there, watching, listening, taking in the cold rich damp scent of the sea for the last time. And then, just to satisfy himself, he took a quick stroll through the lot, checking the cars that sat inert under the thin skin of the dew. He was calm, breathing easily, feeling optimistic about what lay ahead, though he hated having to leave—hated being forced out, hated the miserable interfering sons of bitches who'd come after him and turned everything upside down—and when he'd gone through the lot, he walked the gravel path all the way round the perimeter, the mist (what was it Madison called it?—the breath of the bay) rising up to envelop him and let him go again.

Natalia was perched on the edge of the couch, in a green velvet suit jacket, skirt, stockings, heels, waiting for him. She was applying her makeup—she never went anywhere, not even down to the corner store for a box of crackers, without her makeup—when he came through the door. She didn't smile. Didn't even look up from her compact. "Madison is still sleeping," she said.

He set the tray down before her like the offering it was. "Good. Maybe I can just carry her out to the car and she won't wake up till we get to Tahoe, what do you think?"

She didn't answer. He'd packed everything the night before—early into the morning, actually, and he was exhausted, looking forward to the hotel, the fresh sheets, room service, the blissful anonymity—and he noticed with a tick of satisfaction that the new matching overnight bags, Natalia's and Madison's, had been set by the door. The hassling was over, the pouting, the arguments, the tears, the pleading and the demands, and the new phase was about to begin. They were minutes from being out of here, turn the key and never look back.

"I got her hot chocolate," he said, "the kind she likes, from the bakery? And éclairs. For a special treat."

Natalia was not the sort of mother to buzz over a child's sugar intake. To her mind, whatever you could squeeze out of a glutted overblown capitalistic society was a good in itself, and éclairs were the smallest expression of it. A look for him now, above the mirror. "Yes," she said, faintly amused, conciliatory, "that is very nice. You are a very nice man"— and he could see she wanted to speak his name, wanted to say "Da-na," but checked herself. She bent forward to remove the plastic lid of the takeout cup. "This is the double latte?"

"They both are."

She brought the cup to her lips, the white foam clinging like drift to the waxen sheen of her lipstick before her tongue melted it away. The simple animal satisfactions, sugar, cream, caffeine. He reached for his own cup. The smell of coffee, reminiscent and forward-looking at the same time, filled the room. "Very nice," she concluded, the fingers of one hand probing at the neck of the confectioner's bag even as she sipped at the latte and gave him a glossy uncomplicated smile.

They were complicit. He felt gratitude for that, for what she was giving up for him, for her trust and faith, and he swore to himself in that moment that he'd do everything in his power to live up to it. Easing himself down on the back of the sofa, he ran a hand over the side of her face, caressing an ear, letting her hair sift through his fingers. "I am," he said. "I am a nice guy." And he meant it.

The coffee was still warm in the pit of his stomach when he lifted Madison out of her bed and carried her down to the car. She'd folded herself up in the fetal position, her thumb in her mouth, hair fallen across her face in a silken swirl, and he took the blankets and bedding with her, one big bundle, the warmth rising from the furnace of her, her pupils roaming beneath the lids in dreamtime, and how could he not think of Sukie, of his own daughter, back in Peterskill and as remote from him as an alien on another planet? As he laid Madison across the backseat and folded the blankets over her bare feet, he had a fleeting picture of the two of them together, the two girls, at the park—at Depew Park, in Peterskill—running hand in hand through the dandelions and the long amber grass, white legs flashing in concert.

It was a mistake to go back to Peterskill, he knew it—he'd known it all along. But it sang to him in his blood—it was what he knew—and his daughter was there. And Sandman. There was a house in Garrison, up in the woods and with a view of the Hudson, late nineteenth century, stone, with hand-hewn beams, remodeled in what Sandman called the prevailing bourgeois fashion and dernier cri of consumer convenience, and it was his for the taking, fifty-five hundred a month with an option to buy, Sandman contributing the deposit and talking up the owners, who were retiring to Florida but not yet entirely sure they wanted to give up the house for good, the credit check done and the papers just waiting there for Bridger Martin to blow into town and affix his signature. That was all to the good, and after vagabonding around the country on a nice extended vacation, it would be a relief to get there and start over—the schools *were* good and Natalia could shop till she dropped in Manhattan. He wouldn't want to hit any of the old haunts, though, wouldn't want to run into anybody, even his mother—especially her. Or Gina. It wouldn't do to have people calling him Peck, not anymore. But Garrison was the next town up the line and he figured he'd be spending most of his time in the City, anyway, and with Sukie it was just a matter of hooking back up with the lawyer and getting those Sunday visits quietly arranged again. He was just *Dad* to her, not Peck or Dana or Frank or Bridger, just *Dad,* and no one the wiser. Or maybe that was a dream. Maybe the cops would be waiting for him at McDonald's, because why wouldn't Gina sell him out, why wouldn't her mother?

"You are ready?" Natalia slid into the seat beside him. She was wearing a pink visor with a designer logo that had probably cost fifty bucks, fifty bucks at least. When she saw he was looking at it, she said, "For travel. For the sun. Is there not sun in Las Vegas?"

"Yeah," he said, distracted, "yeah, there is. Good thinking." He flicked the remote for the garage door and the pallid light flooded in. He was thinking of what they were leaving behind, of how everything, from his knives to his saucepans to the Viking convection oven and the new microwave, would occupy their niches until the place was sold and everything the new owners didn't want or couldn't use was dumped in the trash. No regrets, he told himself as he started up the car—one of the finest production cars in the world, in the history of the world—and backed out into the morning.

What he didn't notice—what he failed to notice because he was still there, upstairs, roaming the uninhabited rooms of the condo, lingering in his mind over all the dispensable things they'd accumulated and left in their wake—was the black Jetta, pulling out behind him.

Three

HE'D FALLEN ASLEEP, couldn't help himself, so exhausted he might as well have been drugged, and when he woke the side of his face was pressed up against the window of the car and Dana was clinging to him like a spare set of clothes, the rhythm of her breathing synchronized with his own. There was a faint gray infusion of light. Nothing moved. The yellow lamp at the end of the lot was a blur, perched somewhere in intermediate space, the fog wiping away everything else. His left arm had gone numb where he'd slept on it, and his shirt felt damp and gummy, the price of sleeping in the car. Which smelled stale, as if they'd been living in it for months and not just overnight, and he wondered about that, about the odors of confinement, and for a moment he closed his eyes and the car was a bathyscaphe dangling over an abyss in the dark canyons of the sea, the twisting shapes of the deep fish, the wolf fish and coelacanth, passing in review. Then he opened them again on nothing, on a seep of grayness, and thought to check his watch.

Slowly, with exaggerated care—no reason to wake her yet—he extricated his dead arm and brought his wrist into view. He wasn't surprised particularly to see that it was just before six in the morning—a horrendous hour, an hour he encountered maybe two or three times a year when he lost his head partying with Deet-Deet or Pixel and fell into the old ineluctable videogame trance—but he did feel just the slightest tic of irritation with the fact that he wasn't in a bed in a motel sleeping till noon, noon at least. He'd been the one for giving it up the night before—they had the wrong condo; the guy had moved or died or been jettisoned into outer space—but Dana had been insistent. Even as he was wheeling out of the lot, bent on finding a place to eat and a motel with cable, she was brandishing her worn file folder, inside of which were the affidavit from the San Roque courthouse and the faxes with the thief's police record and photo. "This," she said, spitting it out, "is all we need. Show this to the police and we've got him."

"Right, but we have to find him first," he'd said, exasperated, but still turning his face to her so she could see him form the words. "And when we find him, then what? Where are the cops? You think they'll just happen to be driving by?"

"I dial 911. As soon as I see him. I dial 911 and say there's a crime in progress, a—a burglary, okay? A crime in progress."

"And then what?"

"Then I show them this"—the folder—"because isn't this a crime? In progress? Isn't it?"

They were out on the main road by then, the headlights of the oncoming cars illuminating her face in flashes, as if they were back under the strobe at Doge and he was seeing her for the first time. For a moment, he felt himself slipping into nostalgia, into tenderness—she'd never seemed more beautiful, her eyes struck with light, her lips parted with the onrush of her rhetoric, her face held aloft and glowing in the excelsior of her hair, like a gift in a box—but he resisted it. He was hungry, tired. He was looking for a place to eat, nothing fancy, a burger, anything. She was right, he knew it, but he wasn't ready to admit that yet, not until he had something in his stomach, anyway.

"What are you doing?" she demanded then. "Giving up?"

A fast-food place loomed up on the left and he flicked on the blinker and hit the gas to spin into the lot ahead of the oncoming traffic. All in one motion he nosed into a parking space, jammed the lever into park and swung round to face her. "No," he said, "I'm not giving up. I'm just hungry, that's all. It's been a long day, don't you think? Can't we just sit here for half an hour and have a Big Mac and a Filet o' Fish—no, no, forget the calories, forget the cholesterol and trans fats, let's just gorge for once—and think things out? Because we're close, I know it, you're right, and we can nail this bastard, absolutely, but let's just take a minute to regroup, okay? And eat?"

He didn't know how much of that she got—he never did know with her, but he was always conscious of his lips and his tongue and he liked to think they were communicating. That was the case now. They sat there a moment under the yellow-and-red glare of the big M and he watched her flip the hair away from her face with a quick thrust of her chin. Her eyes narrowed. Her voice went low, so low it was as if she'd just been punched in the stomach. "She was lying, you know."

And so here they were.

They'd stocked up on grease and nitrates and sugar, Dana so anxious she was lifting right out of her shoes while he ordered and paid and then she looked at him as if he were a pedophile when he told her he had to use the men's—*What if we miss him?* she signed. *What if he's coming in right now? Right this minute?* In the car, the brown bag in her lap, her fish sandwich as yet untouched, she kept saying, "You know he's in there, you know it—or wherever he is, he'll be back—and what we need to do is just sit there all night, all day tomorrow, all week if necessary, and keep the binoculars on those windows till we see him for sure. Positive identification, isn't that what they call it? And that's it. We see him, he's"—one of her favorite expressions—"dead meat."

But they hadn't seen him. The curtains were closed when they got back—they hadn't been gone more than half an hour, forty-five minutes—and the curtains stayed closed all night long, though the lights had burned late, very late. So late they were the last thing Bridger remembered, seared into his consciousness like the afterimage of a whole raft of flashbulbs going off simultaneously. He glanced up now. The fog bellied, drifted, pressed and released. The cars were dark humps, the trees erased. Above and beyond him, cutting perfect rectangles out of the shadow of something larger, were the windows—Frank Calabrese's windows—still lit.

When finally the garage door became visible beneath the glow of the windows and finally—suddenly, abruptly—it began to rise in silent levitation to reveal the rear lights of the car glowing there like a visual affront, he thought he was dreaming. It was like a trompe l'oeil, the flat plane of the door there one minute and effaced the next. Was he seeing things? But no, there was the back end of the car, a Mercedes, dealer plates, the exhaust leaching from the tailpipe to vanish in the fog, and now the double punch of the brake lights—and the thing was moving, backing out. He shoved Dana, hard. Pushed her from him and took hold of her face in both his hands, working the swivel of her delicately jointed neck as if it were some instrument he'd found and calibrated, as if it were his: *Look,* he was saying, *look.*

Her hair, her eyes, the sourness of sleep on her breath—none of it mattered. She was there instantaneously, up out of the depths, with him. Her body tensed and she was sitting upright, staring into the mist, her mouth gone slack in concentration. And then, instinctively, she sank down in the seat—and her hands were on him, pulling him down too, her voice blunted and featureless, forced into use before she was ready: "It's him."

The Mercedes had pulled out now, the rear wheels swinging to the left as the driver brought the car around, and there was a figure at the wheel, indistinct behind the windshield and the tatters of the fog, and was it a man? Was it him? Bridger was transfixed. He was sunk so low in the seat his chin was on a level with the armrest, adrenaline surging, hide-and-seek, and then the car righted its course and sliced up the drive in the silence of dreamtime and there he was—unmistakable—the thief, the son of a bitch, his chin cocked, eyes fixed on the road ahead, and the woman, the liar, beside him. For a moment Bridger was frozen there, watching the taillights lift and dip over the speed bumps, and then Dana's hand was on his wrist and her voice was hammering at him in all its weird unmodulated hyperventilating urgency: "Start-the-car-start-the-car!"

Already the brake lights were vanishing in the fog. His hand trembled at the ignition. Once, twice, then the engine turned over and he slammed the thing into reverse, lurched out of the spot and forced it into drive even as he jerked at the wheel and reached for the lights—but her hand was there, her face looming into his field of vision: "No, no—no lights, no lights!"

There wasn't any traffic, and that was a good thing, because he was so intent on the taillights ahead of him he didn't even give a glance as he swung out of the drive and onto the blacktop road. He hit the gas. The wheels spun and grabbed with a chirp, and there was that familiar feeling of the headlong rush, the g-forces, the sudden heaviness in the flesh. Two red spots. He was chasing two red spots. The fog parted, jumped and swayed and gave up its substance, and then it closed in again, and he was having trouble gauging where the road gave way to the shoulder, to the ditch running alongside it, and that would be something, wouldn't it, to veer off the road and blow a tire, break an axle, ram a tree—a whole forest? She was saying something, the words garbled with her excitement, and her hands were moving in frantic semaphore, but it was all he could do to keep going, no lights, no lights, the two red spots his only means of orientation.

The road swept round to the right, then a hairpin to the left, and the lights vanished and came back again. "Stay back!" Dana was saying. That was what it was: "Stay back!"

His own voice was strangled with the tension, and his tone—the abruptness of it, the quick snap and release—startled him. "I am, for shit's sake. What do you think I'm doing?" And then, the wheel riding through the clench of his fingers: "I can't see. Shit. Fuck. You want to wind up in a ditch?"

But then the taillights dilated suddenly, right there, right there ahead of him, and his foot slammed at the brake—it was a stop sign, a stop sign emerging fuzzily from the mist, and the man in the Mercedes was observing the law, full stop, though there wasn't another car on the road—and here was Dana, unbelted and lurching forward like a loose sack of groceries. The sound of her head striking the windshield was like a thunderclap, an explosion. He heard himself curse even as the wheels locked on the fog-slick pavement and the car spun across the road, the taillights of the Mercedes moving away now, dwindling, and he wanted to say "Are you all right?" but she wouldn't have heard him, anyway.

The car was running. They were on the road—in the wrong lane, maybe, but on the road. His eyes swiped at her and he saw the blood there, just beneath her hairline, a fresh wet shock of it, but his foot was on the accelerator—he couldn't help himself—and she, clapping both palms to her head so he couldn't see anything of her eyes or the wound either, let her voice jerk free: "Just go!"

There were other cars now, dragged forward on chains of light, moving like submarines in a reconfigured sea. The wheel felt heavy in his hands. There was the muffled hiss of the tires, his heart in high gear still, a pair of yellow fog lights glowing in the rearview, the Mercedes just ahead. He must have asked Dana twenty times if she was all right—did she need a doctor, should he take her to the hospital—but she wasn't looking at him. Her eyes were fixed straight ahead, on the back end of the Mercedes. She was belted in now and she'd dug a T-shirt out of her bag and pressed it to the wound at her hairline; when he glanced at her, all he could see was that shirt, and it wasn't white any longer. On the inside of the windshield, where her head had hit, a crystal star had formed, a thin tracery of lines radiating from its center in rays of prismatic light. He took one hand from the wheel and tugged at her knee till she turned her face to him. "You're bleeding," he said. "The shirt is full of blood."

Her voice wafted to him as if from a great distance, the tires hissing, the wipers beating time: "It's nothing. A bump, that's all."

"A bump? Didn't you hear me? You're bleeding."

"We can't stop now," she said, turning away from him, and that was that. Discussion over. For a moment they went on in silence, cars emerging out of the gloom, a Safeway truck humping along in the opposite lane, its hazard lights flashing. And then suddenly she was doing something with her hands, something manic, and the shirt dropped away from the wound, a raw spot there, a slit like a mouth, red and raw. "But look, look," she was saying, and his eyes jerked back to the road, "his blinker. He's heading for the freeway."

The wheel was concrete, it was lead, it weighed more than the car itself, but Bridger managed to crank it round and follow the Mercedes up the ramp and onto 101, headed north, the roadway opening up across its lanes to a jerking unsteady convoy of trucks and the sleek shot arrows of pickups and cars homing in on some unseen target in the distance. "Eureka," she said, her voice charged with excitement. "He's going to Eureka. Or Oregon."

He said, "Yeah, maybe," and fell back to allow a battered blue pickup to insert itself between him and the Mercedes.

"He's leaving town. He's running."

Was he? Had they got to him? Had they put a scare in him? Suddenly he felt exhilarated, felt as if he could do anything—he was The Kade and this guy, this bad guy, was an extra in a lizard mask, a walk-on, nothing. He gritted his teeth, bore down on the wheel. *This time, brother,* he said to himself, *you're the one going to jail, and we'll just see how you like it.* But then what was the plan? Should they call 911? His mind was racing. What would they say? That there was a criminal loose, that he'd stolen someone's identity—Dana's identity, a young woman's, a deaf woman's—and he was right ahead of them on 101 in a red Mercedes with dealer plates? That he was running. That he was getting away. But where was the proof? They would have to be there when he was pulled over, because if they weren't the cops would just let him go—he wasn't even speeding. This guy—and Bridger could just make him out in silhouette through the back window of the pickup and the intervening lenses of the pickup's windshield and the slanted rear window of the Mercedes—was driving as if he was on his way to church. And maybe he was. Maybe he'd pull off the freeway and amble up to some big glass and stucco cathedral and they'd roll in behind him and have the cops nail him right there when he was down on his knees cleansing his soul. Wouldn't that be ironic? Because that was him, definitely him, and as long as they stayed with him there was no way he was going to get out of this.

"Yeah," he said, but he was saying it to himself because she wasn't looking, "maybe."

Before he could think, before he could put together two consecutive thoughts, the Mercedes swung onto Sir Francis Drake and merged onto the 580, heading for the Richmond Bridge. The blue pickup veered off and Bridger fell back as the fog began to dissipate and the Mercedes picked up speed. "Call the cops," Dana said, "call the cops," but he flicked his turn signal and moved out a lane, accelerating to keep pace and yet careful not to attract notice—if it came to it the Mercedes would leave them in the dust. "Not yet," he said. "We have to see where he's going, we have to be there."

It was only after they'd followed him onto I-80, going east toward Sacramento, that Bridger thought to glance down at the fuel gauge—there it was, right there in front of him, a simple continuum from empty to full, from go to no-go, and at first it didn't register on him. He was dull, he was unfocused, he wasn't thinking of gas—gas was a given. And so it took him a moment, his adrenaline surging, to understand that the needle was pinned all the way to the left; even as he watched, the warning light blinked to life. Empty. He was incredulous. Outraged. And his first thought was to blame someone, to blame her—*Who'd been driving last? Out of gas? He never let his car dip below half a tank, never*—but he put his foot down instead, his heart rattling, and heard himself say, "Quick, give me your phone!"

They shot up on the Mercedes before he let off on the gas, and he saw the back of the thief's head quite clearly, an average head, oblivious beneath its Mr. Hipster haircut, and the thief's shoulders and the long swaying fringe of the thief's wife's hair as she leaned forward to adjust the radio, and he had to make a snatch for Dana's arm because she wasn't hearing him. "The phone! Quick, the phone!" He was one lane out, falling back now, drifting, allowing a silver Toyota to interpose itself between him and the Mercedes, the warning light on the fuel gauge burning a hole in the dash. Then the phone was in his hand and he punched in 911.

It picked up on the first ring and a woman's voice said, "Nine-one-one, can you hold, please?"

"No!" he shouted, but the connection gave back static and the needle held fast and the thief cruised along in the inside lane as if it had been funded, surveyed, poured and striped for his exclusive use. There was an exit coming up fast on the right, gas, food and lodging, a Chevron station showing its badge, and he didn't know what to do. Dana was watching him, her eyes wide with excitement, a thin red furrow of blood leaching out of the black slit at her hairline. "What do they say?"

"Hold," he shouted. "I'm on hold. And we need gas. Didn't you—?"

"Nine-one-one," the voice came back at him. "What is your emergency?"

"A thief," he said, and he was shouting still, he couldn't help himself. "A theft. Identity theft. He's—he stole my girlfriend's, my fiancée's, identity, and he's here, we have him in sight, we—"

Dana's voice, fluting in its highest register, clambered atop his: "A red Mercedes. Tell them a red Mercedes!"

"What is your location?"

At first the question didn't register. Location? "We're in

a car," he said. "On the freeway, the I-80, and he's—we're running out of gas . . ."

"You're running out of gas?"

"Yes, and he's—"

"Sir, this is an emergency line only. I'm sorry. You're going to have to hang up immediately."

The connection went dead, the exit blew past. A crazy thought of battering the Mercedes off the road flew in and out of his head, something he'd seen in a movie, a dozen movies, but there was no one to paint out the wires here, and the blood on Dana's forehead was real. "How accurate is this gauge?" he demanded, flinging the phone back at her. "How many miles do we have? Does it go right out or is it just a warning and you get twenty miles or something? Do you know?"

She said, "What?"

He repeated himself slowly, and she said, "You mean the gas gauge?"

He nodded.

She was leaning over him to check the gauge for herself, to get the angle on it, when the Mercedes suddenly swung out into their lane and he was so startled he nearly let go of the wheel. Had he seen them? Was that it? Bridger tapped the brake, drew back until the car behind him sped up to pass. But no, the guy wasn't looking in his mirrors, wasn't doing anything but staring straight ahead except to dip his head toward his wife's, as if they were conversing. He didn't have a clue. They were okay. Everything was okay. Until they ran out of gas.

When it happened, he was almost surprised, expecting miracles, the loaves and fishes, the Hanukkah oil, good triumphing over evil despite the odds. The car suddenly seemed to waver, as if a gale had swept up off the roadway to fling it back, then the engine choked and died and he was coasting to a stop on the shoulder, as powerless as one of the lizard lords of Drex III.

For a moment he just sat there, his hands trembling on the wheel. Beside him, her knees drawn up to her chin as if she were bracing herself against some unseen force, Dana gave him a long slow look that cut right into him. Disbelief was there—that was part of it; he felt it himself. Disappointment. Sorrow. And something else too: disgust. She looked disgusted. With him. He couldn't suppress a quick flare of anger. "What? What is it? You want me to get out and run him down on foot?"

The gash on her forehead had begun to crust over, a yellowish contusion swelling beneath a ragged badge of dried blood. Her hands snapped at him: *No, I want you to get out and get gas.* And then she was pointing to a building in the near distance, on a side street that ran parallel to the freeway, a gas station, Shell, and how far was it? A quarter mile?

He'd already cracked the door—he was already on his way—but he couldn't resist coming back at her because he was as wrought up and furious as she was and how dare she blame him, as if this whole mess was his idea, as if he were the one who should have seen to the maintenance of the car when it wasn't even his in the first place. "What's the point?" he said aloud. "You think he pulled off to wait for us? You think we'll ever see him again? Huh? Do you?"

A truck blasted by, sucking all the air with it, and the car shook on its springs. Her face twisted. Her hands flew at him and she was signing angrily and forcing out the words at the same time: "Shit," she said, "shit, shit, shit! Just go, you idiot, you jerk, you—" But he was already gone, the door slamming behind him, and he hadn't walked ten feet before he broke into a sprint, as angry as he'd ever been—murderous, crazed—but for all that glad to be out of the car and away from her.

The whole thing—the whole fiasco—cost them maybe twenty minutes, half an hour, he couldn't say. He jogged back to the car with a gallon can that was as heavy and awkward as a cannonball, and then he left a strip of rubber burning on up the freeway to the next exit so he could double back and fill up the car, and he had to ask her for cash because they wouldn't take his credit card and he was in no mood for an argument. And then, without discussion, without debating whether they should call the cops with a description of the car, fill out a police report, drive to the hospital to see if she needed stitches or sit down to some breakfast, some nourishment, bacon, eggs, Tabasco, coffee for Christ's sake, they were hurtling up the freeway, uselessly, hopelessly, and the Jetta hardly rattled at all when he hit a hundred and left it there.

Neither of them spoke. He felt strangely calm, beyond the law, beyond the grasp of the pedestrian drivers in the slow boats of their sedans and convertibles and pickups as he blew by them, shedding their quick startled looks of bewilderment and outrage, hammering the car from one lane to another, using one pedal only. The day was clear now, sun glancing off the hoods of the line of cars and trucks stretching off into infinity, the roadside a blur of golden-brown vegetation and the searing intermittent flashes of aluminum cans hidden in the weeds. He was sweating. His fingers ran loosely over the wheel, attuned to the slightest variation, manipulating it with all the finesse and superior hand-eye coordination he brought to his PlayStation, and what game was he playing now?

Twenty minutes into it, twenty minutes after he'd pinned the accelerator to the floor, she spoke for the first time since they'd left the gas station. And what she said was, "Take this exit—U.S. 50, to Lake Tahoe. He's going to Lake Tahoe, I know it. I feel it. Pull off, pull off!"

Why would he go to Tahoe? He was running, and he was on I-80, heading east—he was going back to New York, obviously. To hide out. To get away from them. They'd been to his house, they'd knocked on his door, and now he was running. "That's crazy," he said.

Her face floated there, inches from his, and it was clear that she wasn't concerned about reason or logic or even likelihood. "Just do it."

"Shit, why not just use a Ouija board?"

"Do it."

He took his foot off the accelerator and it was as if they'd been flying ten feet above the roadway and come crashing to the ground. Everything was moving in slow motion. Cars began to overtake them. Signal lights flashed. People's faces cohered behind planes of glass. He was on a highway, he could see that now, the sun in his eyes, tires rippling beneath him, the air conditioner wheezing in his face. An SUV slid by on the left and two kids, brother and sister, waved to him from the rear window as their dog—some sort of terrier that looked as if it were wearing a false mustache—popped up between them. And then, and he didn't know why, he merged with the traffic heading for Tahoe.

And what was it—luck? Fate? A fine-tuning of the music of the spheres? He couldn't say, and all his life he'd remember the moment, because when they came up on the first exit, right there, as if it had been parked purposely in front of the family restaurant with a FOR SALE sign scrawled on the side window, was a Bordeaux-red Mercedes, dealer plates attached.

Four

MADISON SLEPT the whole way to Sacramento, past San Quentin and over the bridge, through Richmond, Vallejo, Cordelia and Vacaville, the hot chocolate gone cold, the éclairs untouched. He'd kept the music low so as not to wake her—a reggae mix he'd downloaded himself, mostly Marley, built around live and studio versions of "Rebel Music," a tune he couldn't get enough of—and that was a real onus because he felt so loose and liberated, so purely on fire, and he wanted to make his new top-of-the-line Bose speakers just burn with it. But Madison asleep was infinitely preferable to Madison awake, and he restrained himself. And though he wanted to open the car up, see what it could do, he kept to the inside lane and held it at seventy—there'd be plenty of open road on the way down to Vegas and across the high desert, heading east. He saw himself for a moment then, a snapshot of the future, purple-edged clouds closing over the claws of the hoodoos and the dead dry mountains, Natalia asleep with her head in his lap and Madison silent in back, the beat driving the speakers and the unbridled horses under the hood all pounding in unison. Who was that masked man? Was that a jet or just thunder?

He was feeling good. Better than good. He laid a hand on Natalia's thigh, where the skirt rode up over the dark silk of her stockings. "You know what I want to do, first thing, when we get there?"

She was reading a magazine, her hair thick and shining as she bent over it, her features alive. "What you always want to do?" she said, giving him a coy sidelong glance.

"That's for tonight." He slid his hand down, gave her knee a squeeze. "No, I want to go straight to the pool and then the hot tub and the sauna, sweat a little, and then get a rubdown—a massage, twin massages, you and me. How's that sound?"

Her smile was for him and him alone, the sharp perfect cut of her lips, down-dwelling and in-dwelling, pure invitation, pure lust. "Will we not eat first?"

"And then cocktails," he said, running on ahead of her, "early cocktails, maybe even a piña colada or something in the massage room, dress for dinner, of course, best place in town, and then over to Stateline to hit the blackjack tables."

"And Madison? What of Madison?"

A glance to the rearview mirror: a pickup there, half a dozen cars behind that, spread out across the roadway, a big off-white eighteen-wheeler gearing up to pass on the left. "Oh, hell—I don't care, we'll load her up with videos and get one of those in-hotel babysitters. We're celebrating, right? No expense spared? This is a vacation, baby, and we'll make it last as long as you want—"

"Yes," and the smile began to fade though she tried to keep it intact, "and that will be when we arrive in a new home, yes, a house in the forest, a house all to ourselves—and Madison is enrolled for her school. That is when the vacation will finish." She paused, glanced beyond him to the road and addressed her words to the windshield: "It is a nice house?"

"You've seen the pictures, are you kidding me? It's class, pure class. Two acres, it sits on. With a pool. And a built-in bar."

"Nicer than the condo?"

"You kidding? It's like an estate."

"And this option to buy?" He watched her lips as she formed the words; she always homed in on the central proposition, infallibly. "You will exercise it if I like the place—*we* will exercise it, yes? In my name too?"

She was making her bid, and he couldn't blame her. He didn't mind. Sure, why not? He'd need to turn over the profit on the condo, anyway, and he had a few things going, this scheme Sandman had outlined for him, for one thing, and he might get lucky at the tables—in fact, he knew he would. He could feel it, the whole trajectory of it, up, up and up. He couldn't lose. And there was the car—he'd get clear of that, pick up another one. Two cars, a new Z-4 for her, and something for him too, not a Mustang, though—and not a Harley either. "Right," he said. "Yeah, of course. And you're going to love the shopping—there's no place in the world like Manhattan."

"Not even Jaroslavl?"

"Well, I don't know. Is that the place with twenty million people and Bergdorf's and Macy's and Tiffany's and the Diamond District?"

She was grinning. She shook her head. "I don't think so."

"Grand Central. The Empire State Building? Le Cirque and Babbo and the Oyster Bar?"

"No," she said, shaking her head till her hair swung free, side to side, "no, I don't think so."

He loved this kind of banter, loved to see her like this, all the shrewd compacted energy of her wired to the moment, smiling, loose-limbed, beautiful. And content. Content, for once. He felt his cock stir. He wanted her in bed.

"Tell me about Bergdorf's," she said.

The Mercedes hummed, the sun painted the highway before him on into the distance. He was aware of Bob Marley, faintly delineating his rage under the sweet fractured musicality of her voice as she shifted from one subject to the next, from Manhattan to drainage problems with the basements of old houses to the cat she wanted to get—a Bengal cat; had he ever heard of the breed? Just four generations out of the wild. A beautiful animal. Exquisite. And maybe she'd get two of them, a male and female, to breed them, and she'd send a kitten to Kaylee and maybe one to her brother in Toronto. FedEx. Did they FedEx live animals?

He felt the pulse of the music, nodded, touched her, kept his eyes on the road. And before he knew it they hit the turnoff for Tahoe.

He didn't realize Madison was awake until he glanced in the rearview mirror and saw the etiolated little kernel of her face centered there. She was sitting up, perched on the edge of the seat, straining the limits of the seat belt—which he'd insisted on fastening while she was asleep. There was a red crease on one side of her face and her hair looked like something washed up out of the sea. For the moment she was recalibrating, wearing that dazed and disoriented look of children everywhere when they climb up out of the caverns of sleep, but he knew that it was just a matter of time before the whining started in. He was no child psychologist and he couldn't begin to imagine what it must have been like with the last jerk Natalia was attached to, but the kid seemed excessively needy, a complainer, a whiner. Not at all like Sukie. Sukie was a stalwart. Even as a baby she settled into herself, slept through the night, ate when she was fed and gurgled at the mobile over the crib for hours at a time. She walked early, talked early, knew how to entertain herself, and right from the start seemed to understand that adults sometimes needed a few minutes of peace in their lives. But not Madison. She wanted and wanted and wanted. Just like her mother.

Maybe ten seconds passed before she started in. "Mommy, I have to pee," she announced, her voice reduced to its doleful essence. Of course she had to pee. He understood that, he was no monster, but he'd been hoping to make it as far as Rancho Cordova, to the hotel there, for lunch, and once he got going he didn't like to stop. And once they stopped she'd be hungry—and, perversely, and just this once, not for éclairs, because they were warm now and mushy—and they'd wind up eating some third-rate roadside crap and he could forget about the filet he'd had on his mind for the past half hour. He cranked the music a notch and watched the road as Natalia swung round in the seat.

"Can you hold it, honey?"

"No."

"Dana—I mean *Bridger*—got you some nice éclairs. You want an éclair?"

"I have to pee."

He was staring straight ahead, absorbing Marley, but he could feel her turning her face to him. "We must stop. Next exit."

Softly, because he didn't want to spoil the mood, he let out a curse.

"I know," she said, "but what can we do—wet her pants?"

"Mom-*my*!"

He said nothing, but already he was flipping the turn signal, looking for the next exit, even as Natalia added, "And she will need to eat something." To Madison: "You want eggs, honey? Scrambled eggs and sausage, your favorite? With ketchup? All the ketchup you want?"

There was no answer, no answer was immediately forthcoming, but the whining struck a new note of urgency and he gave it up, merging smoothly with the line of cars pulling off the highway and into the lot of Johnny Lee's Family Restaurant, Open 24 Hours. *Hey, Mister Cop / Ain't got no birth cerfiticate on me now.*

"So," Natalia said, leaning into him with the sway of the car, her voice rich with satisfaction, as it always was when he did what she wanted him to, "we must forbear your filet mignon in Rancho Cordova—"

"Forgo."

"Right, forgo. And instead we dine at the family restaurant. How is it you say? No big thing, yes?"

He took the exit ramp maybe a hair too fast and something—a toy—skittered across the dash, struck the window and caromed to the floor at his feet. He gave her a look—he was irritated, despite himself, but he wasn't going to show it. "No big thing," he said, and he even managed a smile.

It was worse than he'd expected, one of those hokey theme places (wagon wheels on the wall, sepia photographs of prospectors and the hind ends of their mules, waitresses in cowgirl hats and outfits that could have been lifted out of the Dale Evans Museum). Natalia took the kid straight to the restroom while he put in their name with the hostess and then they had to wait fifteen minutes in line with an assortment of copper-haired old ladies and clowns with bolo ties and checked shirts while Madison squirmed and jerked at her mother's hand and fell to the floor and refused to get up because she was hungry, the non-stop chant of *When, Mommy, when are we going to get a table?* rising up out of the forest of old people's legs like the squall of some misplaced sylvan thing that was dying or about to be killed. The buoyancy he'd felt earlier, the high that was compounded in equal parts of relief at getting out of Shelter Bay Village before things went disastrously and irreparably wrong and the anticipation of kicking loose on the road, was gone now. Breakfast on the road was always the weakest link in the culinary chain, a kind of deprivation of the senses that reduced every possibility to a variant on eggs/ sausage links/silver-dollar pancakes and maple-colored Karo syrup. It bored him. Made him angry. Even in a decent hotel, where you could get quiche, eggs Benedict, a crab-and-feta omelet, fresh-squeezed orange juice, the meal was still a bore. But this—he looked round him with a sudden cymbal-clang of hate—this was the worst.

"Martin?" the hostess called out, and the line stirred, heads swiveling round, feet shuffling impatiently, and for a moment he didn't realize she was summoning him till Natalia nudged him and he raised his hand like a third grader in the back of the classroom. By the time they were sliding into the booth with its butt-warmed benches and the red Formica tabletop strewn with the refuse of the previous party, he was feeling murderous.

"I want a sundae," Madison announced, her face composed, eyes wide and unblinking and perfectly serious. "Like that girl." She pointed to the next booth over, where a whole rat-pack of kids—six or seven of them—dug into various ice cream concoctions while their parents, two interchangeable couples with porcine faces and a lack of style that was nothing short of brutal, roared over their coffee and grease-spattered plates as if they'd been drunk for days.

"No sundae," Natalia said automatically. "Eggs."

Madison repeated her demand, her voice pinched higher.

"Shut it," he hissed, leaning into the table, because you could only take so much shit in this life, one dried and cubed block of it stacked atop another till the whole thing came tumbling down, and he'd been under some pressure lately, he realized that. And because he realized it, he was able to restrain himself from reaching out for her boneless little wrist and giving it the kind of squeeze that would have opened up a whole new world for her. But he didn't have to get physical—one look, the look he'd laid on Stuart Yan on the courthouse steps—was enough to silence her. It was a look he'd practiced, the don't-fuck-with-me look he'd worn for eleven and a half months at Greenhaven. "You'll eat what you get."

The compromise was something called Pancakes Jubilee, three rubbery thin wafers of griddle-compacted dough buried under a mound of strawberries and about three feet of whipped cream. Natalia, whose appetite always astounded him, had the Cattleman's Breakfast, four eggs sunny-side up with a sixteen-ounce steak, ranch beans, pico de gallo and a basket of flour tortillas. He had coffee, black.

"Do you not want to try a bite of my steak?" Natalia kept asking him. "Did you not say you wanted a steak? Here, try. It's good."

He was furious—acting like a child himself, he knew it. "No," he said, "I don't want your steak. Tahoe. I'll eat in Tahoe. Okay?"

Across the table, Madison wore a beard of whipped cream, whipped cream to her nostrils and beyond. Her eyes were glazed with the sugar fix and the fork was stuck to her hand. Breakfast was over.

Outside, where people stood around on the faux ranchhouse porch picking their teeth and grinding mints between their molars, the heat seized him. It must have been a hundred already, though his watch showed just past ninethirty in the morning. The sun was a hammer. It wanted to take everything down, flatten it right to the ground. There was a smell of incineration, of grease blown out through the kitchen fans, of the kind of death that mummified you before you hit the ground. He watched a crow, its feathers the color of coal dust, dance around something crushed on the pavement as he shrugged out of his sport coat and folded it over one arm. Jesus. How could people stand this shit? How could anybody actually live here? he wondered, tensing up all over again, and no, the coffee hadn't helped, not a bit. He took Natalia by the arm. Down the three bleached wooden steps they went, to the burning lake of the parking lot. Predictably, Madison said, "Mommy, I'm *hot*."

It was then, at that precise moment, that the black Jetta pulled into the lot and he saw the two faces suspended there behind the sunstruck windshield. *A man and a woman.* Everything went silent, the speakers hidden up under the support beams piping out a thin tinny jangle of country guitars, the whoosh of the traffic on the highway, the jet poised overhead. He'd trained himself to stay cool, be cool, to hide the least tic of emotion behind an immobile face and the stark stabbing outraged sheen of his eyes, pure aggression, and he stared right at them, stared hard, though he was scared, afraid they might swing out in front of the restaurant and try to run him down, and spooked on a deeper level too: how in Christ's name did they know he was here? Here, of all places? Even he hadn't known he was going to be here.

Seconds, that was all he had, because the woman—Dana Halter, Dr. Dana Halter—was bent over her cell phone and if the cops stepped in and checked his ID against hers *or his, Bridger's,* there was no hope of talking his way clear of this. Even as he increased the pressure on Natalia's arm, even as she said, "What is the hurry?" and he silenced her with a look, snatched up Madison as if she were an overnight bag and set a brisk pace for the car, it came to him that they must have been hidden somewhere in the lot and followed him when he pulled out of the condo. He cursed himself. He was lax, he was stupid. All of this shit—and he was so wired suddenly it was as if he'd grabbed hold of a high-voltage cable with his bare hands—all of it, all of it, he'd called down on his own head.

But there was the car, a hundred feet away, Madison squirming in his grip, Natalia gone white with the fear that sprang up full-blown out of his frantic headlong urgency, seventy-five feet, fifty, and the two of them were out of the car now, shouting something, brandishing cell phones—both of them, they both had phones, as if Cingular wireless was the supreme force in the universe. "No," he spat, "no," as he flung Madison sprawling into the back, jerked Natalia in beside him and slammed the door, "no time"—he meant the belts, the seat belts—and so what if the buzzer cried out to warn him, and these people, these creeps, were looming up in the rearview, the doors were locked, the engine cranked, and with a flick of the wrist he was out of the parking space, straight ahead, up over the concrete bumper and on into the dirt lot beyond it, heading for the highway in a plume of crushed weed, flying cans and airborne dust.

Strangely, perversely, he found himself worrying about the paint job as he caromed across the vacant lot, thumped through a gully and bore up onto the ramp, cutting off two dickheads in an old hearse with a band logo filigreed across the back panel even as the tires took hold of the pavement and began to sing. The car didn't matter. It was nothing. He'd have to lose it anyway, and soon. There was the blast of the dickheads' horn and then he was right up on the rear end of a Winnebago doing about two miles an hour where the ramp narrowed before merging onto the highway. A glance at Natalia's grim bloodless face, and then his eyes went to the rearview, where the hearse was gunning up on him, horn squalling and the two dickheads stabbing their middle fingers at the windshield. They didn't interest him. What interested him was the black Jetta tearing out of the parking lot and up onto the ramp behind them.

Natalia didn't say a word. Even Madison, rough handling and all, seemed to be holding her breath. Directly ahead of them was the creeping beige, white and lemon-yellow wall of the Winnebago, bicycles, lawn chairs and cooking grills strapped to it as if in some frenzy of reenactment, and right there on their bumper was the hearse. Foot by foot, yard by yard, the ramp fell under the wheels, no room to maneuver on either side because the narrow sweeping arc of it had been cut through rock the color of dried blood, and there were two horns competing now, the Jetta on the bumper of the hearse, arms waving, mouths flung open in rigid oral display. He heard his own voice then, just as the ramp began to broaden out to the highway: "Put your seat belts on."

What amazed him about it later was the way the Jetta had stayed with him. The hearse fell back as if it were hooked to a chain and the Winnebago was just part of the scenery, but the Jetta came on even as he put his foot to the floor and cut everything else away from him. When he hit a hundred and ten, he was aware of a movement beside him—Natalia, her mouth clamped and her eyes in retreat, sliding in back to cling to her daughter—but the gesture meant nothing, not now. At a hundred twenty the car discovered what it was made for, all those German horses, the Autobahn, *cruising speed*. There was a part of him that knew he was in trouble, knew that they could be punching in 911 and telling the dispatcher anything, that there was a drunk driver up ahead, a reckless driver, a deranged life-endangering criminal in a wine-colored Mercedes with dealer placards that might as well have been flags whipping in the wind, but there was another part, a larger part, that just didn't give a shit, the part that ran on adrenaline and pushed his foot to the floor.

Later, after the Jetta had become a memory and Natalia had run out of breath bitching at him and he'd filled whole cauldrons with qualifications and sophistries and outright lies (Oh, hey, they were bad people, people he'd done a real estate deal with who didn't want to honor their contractual obligations, and didn't she know real estate people were the worst?), after she fell asleep wrapped up in back with her daughter and he eased off the main road at Placerville to take the Gold Country Highway back on up to I-80, he began to think about the immediate future. Tahoe was out, definitely out, and he'd have to ditch the car as soon as he could, but 80 would take him to Reno and from Reno he could find a road south to Vegas—it would be a long drive, a lot longer than he'd counted on, and it would involve some elaborate explanation and days of worship at the altar of her, but it was necessary at this point. He'd had a close call. A learning experience.

That was behind him now. The scenery was improving. He cranked the music, let the wheels roll under him. After a while he found himself singing along, keeping time with the flat of his hand against the dash, the adrenaline slowly draining from his veins even as the road climbed and the trees thickened and the naked faces of the mountains began to catch and shape the light. He hit the accelerator to blow past an RV sleepily towing a car behind it and made himself a promise: there was no way anybody was ever going to find him again.

Five

ANGER DIDN'T BEGIN to describe what she was feeling. It was rage, cold and clear-eyed, unwavering, ecstatic, the rage of the psychopath, the soldier under fire, the wielder of the blade. Never in her life had she felt anything like it, not when she was a child sitting across from her mother at the kitchen table in her witch's black rags and the ghoul-green facepaint she'd spent half an hour on, burning to fly out the door on her broom and go trick-or-treating with her school friends, and her mother making her sit there through ten repetitions of her vowel drill, ten full repetitions, though it was Halloween and she pleaded and spat and stormed up to her room and felt the house shudder with the violence of the door splintering the frame; not when she'd been locked up in the county jail with the drunks and degenerates and no one to listen to her; not when she'd stood in the hallway at the courthouse and watched her lawyer's face go slack as they took her back into custody though she'd been cleared of all charges and everyone knew it was a farce and she could have screamed till the walls came crashing down around them. This was different. This was incendiary.

Just the sight of him, that was all it took. The look on his face, the way he walked, the clothes he was wearing. After all the tension and anticipation, after working herself up so she could barely breathe, after taking it out on Bridger and feeling her stomach clench with loss and hate and frustration, there he was, standing right there in front of them—Frank Calabrese, or whatever his name was—in his pin-striped designer shirt and buffed red leather Docs, his jacket thrown carelessly over one arm, his wife the liar and their kid at his side, and *he* tried to stare *them* down as if they were the ones who'd stolen from him. And then he'd turned his back and ignored them, ignored their shouts and accusations as if he were deaf too—"Thief!" she'd screamed, over and over, bursting from the car and charging across the lot, her arms waving as if she were calling down an airstrike, and she thought they had him, finally had him, because people were beginning to turn their heads and somebody would call the police, she would, Bridger would, and he was trapped there in the parking lot in the unforgiving blaze of nine-thirty in the morning and nothing he could do about it. She felt a thrill go through her. He was doomed. Dead in the water. *Dead meat.*

Yet everything about him, from the sway of his shoulders to the thrust-back arrogance of his face, said it was no trouble at all, no problem, somebody else's affair. He was steady, brisk, steering his numb-faced wife and the kid toward the car with quick efficient strides, for all the world no more concerned than if he were out taking a little exercise after church in the languid hundred-degree heat. She and Bridger were nothing to him, less than nothing, and the thought of it made her seize with hatred. If she'd had a gun, she would have used it. Or she could have. She really believed she could have.

She had something on him, though—evidence, a totem, an artifact. Even as he mounted the cement curb in the Mercedes and took off across the vacant lot, she saw it lying there on the pavement, right where he'd slid into the car and slammed the door behind him. His jacket. Marooned in the rush to escape. Dropped. Forgotten. She was sweating, her heart pounding, already shortening her stride, and she bent without thinking to snatch it up before reversing direction and breaking for her own car with everything she had.

All the while, caught behind the Winnebago as Bridger pounded the horn and she leaned out the window shrieking and gesticulating as if she'd come unhinged and the road opened up and the Mercedes pulled steadily away from them until it was a faint gleam in the distance and then, heartbreakingly, gone altogether, the jacket lay on the floor at her feet. It was there as Bridger swerved in and out of traffic, dialing 911 to shout lies to the dispatcher—"Drunk driver!" he yelled into the phone, "Drunk driver!"—there all the way through the long ascent to South Lake Tahoe while she fixed her eyes on the road, rounding each curve with the expectation of seeing the blinking lights of the highway patrol and Frank Calabrese up against the car with the handcuffs on him. Then they were in the town itself, cruising the streets, scanning the parking lots and back alleys, rolling in and out of motel lots, scrutinizing every red car they came across, and she was so intent on the chase, so wound up in what she was doing, she never gave the jacket a thought. Or the slash on her head either. It was just there, part of the world in its new configuration.

The altitude at Tahoe was 6,225 feet, according to the sign posted at the town limits, and the weather was radically different here. There were streaks of snow on the mountains above the lake, the sky was socked-in and the air coming through the vent felt chilly against her face. Bridger was hunched over the wheel, steering with his wrists, looking beaten. For a long while they said nothing, the car creeping past shops, supermarkets, gas stations, condos, one street after another. "Let's face it, we lost him," he said finally, his eyes rimmed red with exhaustion. "He could be visiting a friend in one of these condos, he could be in a casino in Stateline, he could—" He shrugged, said something she didn't quite get. "The license—you know, the dealer plates—do you remember what they said, I mean, the dealer name? I think it was Bob-Something Mercedes?"

"Bob Almond Mercedes/BMW," she said. "Larkspur."

He'd put on his thoughtful look. They were going so slowly they might as well have been walking. "Because I was thinking—I mean, this isn't getting us anywhere—we could call Milos and he could maybe check out the dealer and see who bought the car, what name, I mean—"

"I don't want to go back there," she said, surprising herself. "And besides, he wouldn't use his real name, would he?"

"Get a serial number or something—a vehicle identification number."

"What good's that going to do?"

He didn't answer. Instead, he said, "What about the jacket?"

The jacket, yes. It was flung at her feet like one of those mats they put down to protect the carpet. She reached for it, smoothed it in her lap: raw silk, in black, with red detailing. A smell of cologne rose to her nostrils, and something else too, something deeper, denser: the smell of him, the smell of his body, his underarms, his skin. "Hugo Boss," she announced, turning over the label. "Nice to know the bastard has taste, huh? Did you see him," she said, running a hand through the inside pocket, "the way he looked at us? The balls?" There was something there, something hard—sunglasses, Rēvo, two hundred fifty dollars a pair. She held them up so Bridger could see.

He gave them a cursory glance and then his eyes

jumped suddenly to the mirror—someone must have beeped at him—and he hit the blinker and pulled into a No Parking/No Standing Zone as a little black car, a Mini, shot past them. After a moment, he took the glasses from her and held them at length as if examining some dead thing he'd found under the sink, then clapped them on his face. They were wraparounds, metallic silver. "Yeah," he said, checking himself out in the rearview, "I hear you."

She plunged her hand into the outer pocket on the left side and came up with a comb to which a straggle of dense dark hairs adhered, a Sharpie pen that looked unused and a thin wad of tissue. An odd feeling came over her, even as Bridger turned to her and said, "How do I look?" She slid her fingers over the teeth of the comb, lifted it to her nostrils—there was the smell of him again, of his scalp and the shampoo he used, and it was as if she knew him in some elemental way, as if she'd been with him, the violation mutual.

A light rain began to spot the windshield. Bridger's head floated there beside her, but he wasn't Bridger exactly, not with the slit reptilian orbits of his eyes, the reflective lenses slashing at his features, reducing him. "Take them off," she said.

He swiveled his head and removed the sunglasses, and even as he said, "Is that it?" she dug into the other pocket and came up with a slip of paper, a receipt from Johnny Lee's Family Restaurant, and held it up to the light.

"What is it, a credit card receipt? That could be something. What does it say?"

It took her a moment, the print blurred and pointillated, but then it came together, the total, the tax, the account number and the slashing confident signature under the cardholder's name: *Bridger Martin.*

. . . . .

"We have to get rational about this," he was saying, or at least that was what she thought he was saying. *Rational,* wasn't that it? Of course he might have been talking about *Rashomon,* the Kurosawa film, and for the tiniest sliver of a second she wondered just how the three of them—she, Bridger and the thief—fit into that scenario, with its shifting perspective and deconstructed narrative. She saw Toshiro Mifune, his mouth a rictus of fear and aggression, flailing his sword, and then she was back to Bridger, who was saying something else now, something she was too tired to process.

They were in a nondescript restaurant, fake wood paneling, lights so dim you could barely make out the menu, tuna on rye with a sliver of dill pickle for $9.95 and three dollars for iced tea. It was late in the afternoon now, high summer but wintry for all that, a damp high-altitude gloom hanging over the town as if this weren't California at all, but someplace perennially dreary. Like Tibet. Was Tibet dreary? Her mind was wandering. She was exhausted—and hungry—and here was the tuna sandwich she'd ordered herself in a voice that must have lost all control of the long vowels and those nearly impossible fricatives (a side of french fries) because the waitress had given her the interplanetary stare and she felt like some animal on a leash, but she didn't care: this was her life and there was nothing she could do about it. Not in her present condition. Plus she had Bridger to deal with—she'd dragged him into this, and now he was a victim too (*I don't even have a Citibank card,* he protested, and she imagined him whining, his voice reduced, plaintive, weak). Bridger was upset—she couldn't blame him—but her eyes dropped to the sandwich and shut him out.

He hadn't stopped talking even to draw breath since she'd pulled that charge slip out of the jacket pocket, and what was the term for that? *Logorrhea.* Yes, another SAT word to drill her students with, but she didn't have any students, not anymore. She was wandering, again she was wandering, and she was thinking, unaccountably, of the talk fests they used to have in the dorm at Gallaudet, in Sign mainly, but with people speaking aloud too in a way that was all but unintelligible to a hearie, a kind of sing-along moan that underscored the signs. *Talk talk.* That was what happened when the deaf got together, a direct translation into English—they talked a lot, talked all the time, talked the way Bridger was talking now, only with their hands. Index finger of the four hand at the mouth, tapping, tapping to show the words coming out. *When deaf get together talk talk all the time.* Communication, the universal need. Information. Access. Escape from the prison of silence. Talk, talk, talk.

Bridger's hand was on her wrist, the wrist of the hand that held the tuna sandwich as it moved to her lips. "You're making those noises," he said.

She looked around her. People were watching. She tried to suppress the impulse, but it was almost unconscious, autonomic, a reaction to stress that most deaf people shared: she was emitting, had been emitting, a soft high-pitched keening sound, as if she were a dolphin washed ashore, and it embarrassed her. Her own throat produced these noises, her own larynx, and she had no control over them. "Sorry," she said, and signed it too, right hand, palm facing in, the slow circle over her heart.

"You're not listening," he said.

"I am," she lied.

He looked away in exasperation, his features pinched, eyes rolling upward, and that made her angry, but she didn't want to make a scene, or any more of a scene than she'd already made with her dolphin noises, so she wiped her face of expression and focused on him. What he was talking about, the gist of it anyway, was that they were both tired and incapable of making a decision at this point ("I'm not going back," she interrupted him, "and that son of a bitch is not going to get away with this, I swear, even if I have to crawl on my belly—or my abdomen, my abdomen—from here to New York, I'm going to nail him, you hear me?"), and that they needed to check into a motel, get some rest and decide what to do in the morning, because they were just frustrating themselves driving around looking for nothing, for a car that was a hundred miles away by now.

"I found him before," she countered. "Didn't I?"

"Yeah, I know—the deaf have some kind of ESP, right? And it *was* amazing, I admit it, but you don't really believe in all that, do you?"

"No," she said.

"Because if you do, maybe you can tell me what this jerk is going to do next, maybe you can visualize it, picture him cruising down the open road with our money in his pockets, free money, everything free—he doesn't have to worry about looking for the cheapest motel in town, does he? No, he's going to stay at the Ritz Carlton, he's going to—"

She set the sandwich down so she could use her hands. "He's Frank Calabrese," she said, finger-spelling it beneath the words, "and he's going back to New York. And you know what?"

He lifted his eyebrows, leaned in close on the twin props of his elbows so that his face was inches from hers. The waitress, probably nineteen or twenty but so petite and baby-faced she looked more like twelve, darted her eyes nervously at them, and Dana felt distracted. There was a TV mounted on the near wall, ghost figures going through their silent motions. She felt a wave of depression crash over her even as Bridger threw it back at her: "What?"

"There's nothing to discuss. I don't care if I have a hundred nights' sleep in a row, I'm not going to change my mind." Then she closed her mouth, shot a withering glance round the restaurant, and used her hands exclusively: *Whether you come along or not, I'm going after him.*

They checked into the Gold Country Motel with her credit card—neither of Bridger's was good, both maxed out thanks to Frank Calabrese—and she showered and then stretched herself across the white slab of the queen-size bed and stared at the ceiling like a zombie while Bridger paced back and forth, one hand pinning the phone to his ear while the other swooped, plunged and snatched at the air to underline the specifics of his distress. First he dialed the credit card companies, and then the CRAs, and it seemed to take him forever. She couldn't sleep. Couldn't even close her eyes. Her head throbbed where she'd hit the windshield and she seemed to have irritated something in her left knee when she slammed her way into the car in the parking lot of the restaurant outside Sacramento. At Bridger's insistence they'd stopped at a drugstore and picked up a tube of Neosporin and a package of Band-Aid sport strips, and she'd spent ten minutes dabbing at the wound—it was a purple blotch, like a birthmark, with a crusted gash in the center of it—but it was superficial and it was already healing and she didn't really want to call even more attention to herself by walking around with a shining square flesh-colored patch stuck to her head, so she'd parted her hair and combed it over to at least partially hide the contusion.

At some point, exhausted, she did manage to fall asleep, and when she woke some indeterminate time later, she found Bridger lying unconscious beside her. He was on his back, his mouth open wide, and he was breathing with the ponderous tranquillity of the heavy snorer, though it was nothing to her. She remembered his warning her that he snored when they'd first started sleeping together—other people had complained about it (i.e., girlfriends), but she wouldn't complain, would she? He'd offered up the proposition with a smile and she'd given him the smile back and said that she was afraid she'd just have to tough it out.

She'd pulled the blinds for privacy when they'd checked in, but the spaces between the slats still showed the same insubstantial light she'd fallen asleep to, so unless she'd slept through the night and this was dawn she was looking at, it must have been eight or nine or so. Well past dinnertime. She felt her stomach rumble—*peristalsis,* and there was another word—and realized with a sudden keen apprehension that she was hungry. Starved, actually. She'd been too keyed up to eat much of the ten-dollar tuna sandwich and the last time she'd eaten before that was the previous night when they went out for fast food and left Frank Calabrese his window of opportunity to slip back into his garage—or maybe he'd been there all along, lying low. Plotting. Stealing. Working himself up for his big car-chase scene. The thought of him stuck in her mind like a dart—he was right there in her moment of waking, the last thing she thought about when she fell off to sleep and the first when she opened her eyes; before long she'd be dreaming about him.

She pushed herself up to a sitting position. The motel was so cheap there was no clock radio, with its LED display, to orient her—they'd scouted three other places before settling on this one, which was twelve dollars less with her Triple-A discount—and she wondered what she'd done with her watch. She'd taken it off, hadn't she, when she'd showered? That was the first thing she'd done, the minute the man behind the counter (bearded, with a turban and a nose ring clamped round a red stone, a garnet, or maybe it was just glass) had given them the key and she'd flung open the door and dumped her suitcase on the bed, because the whole business of the past two days had made her feel unclean, dirty right down to her bones, and at least the water had been hot. Now she let her feet find the floor and went into the bathroom to look for her watch, because the first rule of motels was that everything had to be put away at all times or you'd wind up leaving half of it behind. She was in her bra and panties, her clothes balled up on the wet linoleum of the bathroom floor, and there was her watch, on the cracked, vaguely white porcelain of the bathroom sink: eight forty-five. Her stomach stirred again, and as she strapped the watch round her wrist, she was already moving back into the room to wake Bridger.

He hadn't moved. He was stretched out atop the covers, his limbs splayed, looking helpless and bereft, a faint quivering about his lips and nostrils as the expelled air shook through him. She felt bad for him. Felt bad for herself. But he was there for her, at least there was that—if ever anyone had passed the test, it was him. She spent a moment standing over the bed, gazing down at him, not thinking about love, not consciously, but stirred nonetheless by a rush of hormonal assertions, imperatives, desires. After a while, she bent forward and pressed her mouth to his and held it there, just held it, as if she were resuscitating him.

The restaurant they chose for dinner was a bit more upscale than the lunch place—softly lit, big Kentia palms in earthenware pots, linen-covered tables, clean plaster walls painted a shade of apricot—and when they'd paused outside before the recessed shrine that displayed the menu, she liked not only the prices but the vegetarian bill of fare. "Enough fast food," she said, swinging round on Bridger as couples strolled by and the light began to fade over the mountains, "enough burgers and fries. Let's have something healthy for a change."

He shrugged, in full passive mode. He'd canceled his cards, put a security alert on his credit reports, slept, showered and used the toilet, but he was still in shock. As they pushed through the door, her arm looped through his, he said something she didn't catch, and in the momentary distraction of addressing the hostess and following her to their table, he didn't repeat it.

Now, as they sat there over the menus—she'd ordered a glass of white wine; he was having a beer—she said, "I didn't catch what you said back there at the door."

Another shrug. "Oh, it was nothing. I just—I don't think I have more than fifty bucks on me. Toto."

"No problem. My treat." Her hands unfolded to harmonize with her words. "It's all on me, everything—at least until you get your new cards. They can overnight them, right? And you can still use the cash machine—"

"Overnight them where?"

That was when the waitress returned with their drinks, and on her face the look Dana knew so intimately. It was a look borne out of the drink order and maybe some long-distance reconnaissance from the waitress' station, the probing look, the ready judgment. "Who had the white wine?" the waitress asked, just to hear Dana say, "That's me," though with a party of two—one man, one woman—even a mental defective on her first day on the job would have divined that the wine was for the lady and the beer for the gentleman. Not to mention the fact that she was the one who'd taken the order in the first place.

"Are you ready to order?" she asked, and that was easy to read, because what else would she be asking, poised as she was over her little notation pad, one hip cocked forward, a look of spurious interest on her face. And the next thing she would say, once they'd made their selections, would be "Oh, excellent choice" or "That's the best thing on the menu." *Hearing people.* Sometimes she couldn't help thinking the world would be a better place if everybody were deaf.

But yes, they were hungry. And yes, they were ready to order—the veggie shish kebab on basmati rice for Bridger, the hummus/couscous/baba ghanoush pita platter for her—and the conversation died while Dana fought with the pronunciation and finally resorted to using her finger to point out the item on the menu. Every six months or so she went back to the speech therapist for a couple of weeks just to keep herself sharp—and she tried to practice regularly before the mirror, but with the insane pace of her life, teaching, writing and now this, the practice was the first thing to go. Really, though, *baba ghanoush*? Even the speech therapist had to have problems with that one.

She looked back to Bridger as the waitress drifted away. He was saying something, and he stopped, seeing she hadn't understood him, and began again. "I was saying, yeah, I do have, maybe, I don't know, a couple thousand bucks in my account—unless this creep has got to it—and I will try the cash machine, just to see. Because I don't—"

"Don't?" she echoed. "Don't what?"

"I don't want you to have to pay for me, because if we, if we're—"

"We're going to."

"Yeah, well, I'm going to have to phone Radko—and you can bet I'll be out of a job when we get back." He grimaced, then lifted the bottle of beer to his lips, ignoring the frosted mug that had come with it.

"How long does it take to drive cross-country—a week?" She took a sip of the wine—it was bitter, tannic. She was watching him intently.

"I don't know. Four and a half, five days if you drive straight through."

"Could you stand that?"

"No. Could you?"

She thought about that a moment, one person asleep while the other drives, the shell of the car so fragile against the night, the eternal silence and nothing to distract her, and what if she nodded off? What was the name of that band, years back—Asleep at the Wheel? Bridger had his music, the radio, books on tape, and she had her laptop, but not at night, not when she was driving. And what if the car breaks down? What if it overheats in the desert or—what was the term—throws a rod? She was about to ask him that, about the car, about the rods, whatever they were, but she didn't get the chance because there were two other people hovering over them suddenly, a man and a woman in their twenties, dressed nearly identically in big jeans and big jackets over T-shirts trumpeting some band, and Bridger was up out of his seat as if he'd been launched, clasping the man to him in a bear hug.

She watched with a puzzled smile—or bemused, a bemused smile. *Bear hug,* she was thinking distractedly, and where had that come from? Who had actually seen bears hugging? *Did* bears hug? Or did they do it doggie style—or bearie style?

The man's name—Bridger was lit up, beaming, trembling with the information—was Matt Kralik, and he finger-spelled it for her while Matt Kralik and his girlfriend, Patricia, stood there gaping at her. Matt, he said, looking from Matt to her and back again, had been his roommate and best bud at SC, and what was he doing here? His parents had a place on the lake. But what a coincidence! Awesome! No, no, no, they had to join them for dinner. Bridger insisted.

There was the usual clumsy shuffle of place settings and chairs, the waitress looking on while a darting dark quick-blooded busboy studiously set them up and then they were all seated and Matt Kralik and Patricia had matching martinis in front of them, except that Matt's was officially a Gibson because he had a cocktail onion in his and Patricia preferred the traditional olive. For a moment no one spoke—this was what hearing people referred to as an "awkward silence," but then no silence was awkward for Dana and her gaze quietly passed from Matt Kralik, seated on her left, to Bridger, across the table from her, and finally to Patricia, on her right. Patricia had an eager, almost ribald expression, her features too heavy for the taut athletic body that supported them—she looked cartoonish, all the weight above her shoulders, nothing below. "So," she said, pursing her lips, "Dana—it's Dana, isn't it? I mean, I'm terrible with names—"

"Yes, that's right."

"What do you, ah—*do*? For a living, I mean."

All three of them were watching her as if she were one of the seals from Sea World propped up in a chair and about to balance a cane on her nose in expectation of the slippery reward of a fresh sardine from the trainer's hand, even Bridger, who was wearing his blunted look where a moment before he'd been transported, giddier than she'd seen him in a week, a month. She said, enunciating as clearly as she could, "I'm deaf. I teach in a deaf school. Or at least I used to."

"Oh, deaf," Patricia said. "That's interesting. That's really interesting."

Matt Kralik was saying something. He'd once known a

deaf kid, in high school, and the kid had been a super base-ball player, center fielder, ran like the wind—and some-thing, and something—and he made triple-A ball, but not the majors. "Like that guy that was on the Angels last year, what was his name?"

Bridger supplied the name. And he thought to finger-spell it for her: *Pride,* that was his last name, but he couldn't remember the guy's first name.

"Not Charlie Pride," Matt Kralik said, and she would have missed it—everyone burst out laughing—if Bridger hadn't finger-spelled it too.

"No," Patricia said, gulping back her laugh and steady-ing herself with a delicate sip of the martini. "He was that black country-and-western singer. My father used to have his records, I remember."

"But this guy on the Angels, they could heckle him all they wanted and it was nothing to him. Can you imagine that? They could be cursing his mother and he wouldn't know it."

Bridger shrugged. "Yeah, but what about when they cheered?"

And then Matt Kralik said something and Bridger said something back and Patricia joined in, the conversation wheeling off in unforeseen directions even as the food came and Bridger's hands got busy with his shish kebab and Dana lost track of what they were saying. Eventually, she just lowered her eyes and concentrated on the plate before her.

After dinner, there was chai sweetened with honey and con-densed milk and more talk and then they all insisted on go-ing out to a bar—Matt Kralik knew this place with the best music in town—and she went along though her head had begun to throb until the term *concussion* rose up in her mind as if written in big looping letters on the blackboard in her classroom, a medical term: *jarring of the brain, spinal cord, etc., from a blow, fall, etc., derived from the Latin* con-cussio, *meaning shock.* But no. She was just tired. And defeated. And angry. And the bar—it was like any other bar anywhere else in the world—was a place she didn't want to be. It was loud and raucous, she supposed, and Matt Kralik, Patricia and Bridger responded to it by jigging their heads to the beat of the music that was most likely pounding through the big speakers hung in the corners and opening their mouths wide to (presumably) shout at one another. She took her shoes off and danced twice with Bridger and once with Matt Kralik, but some clod stepped on her right foot with one of his engineer's boots and the liberation of movement, which usually made her experience a kind of boundless high, did nothing for her. She just couldn't shake loose of the image of Frank Calabrese. Bridger could, though—he was having a time, she could see that, and she didn't begrudge him. Or maybe she did. At any rate, after half an hour of watching everybody's mouths chew air, she told him she wanted to go back to the motel and he gave her a look she didn't like and she walked the six blocks alone and let herself into the sterile little box of a room, got under the covers and turned on the TV.

She was awake still when he came in two hours later, drunk, with his sweatshirt misaligned and wearing a stifled little grin caught somewhere between repentance and defiance. She watched with cold indifference as he fumbled into the bathroom and peed, not bothering to shut the door, and she didn't say anything when he stepped back into the room, watching his feet as if he were walking a tightrope, and stood just to the side of the TV, mesmerized by the movement there. A slasher flick was playing, the only thing she could find at this hour aside from the late-night talk shows that seemed to define their own vacuum of irrelevance, and she was no fan of the genre and wouldn't have given it a second glance if she weren't stuck here, bored and agitated and unable to sleep. "We need to get up early," she said, trying to control her voice. "We need to leave this place. We need to get on the road. Get out of here."

She watched him scratch the back of his head, reach down to hike up his oversized jeans. He said something to the TV, mumbling no doubt, then swung round so she could read him. "I don't know," he said, making a half-hearted attempt to sign under his words. "I don't know, I hate this."

"You hate it? How do you think I feel?"

"I've got to get back. Got to call Radko."

She gave it a minute. "You don't have to do anything," she said finally, and she was angry suddenly. Her voice might have risen, she couldn't say. "You claim you love me, you'll stand by me, but it's just words, because if you do—if you did—you wouldn't hesitate."

And now his face flared with his own anger, a deep gouge slicing into the furrow between his eyes, his lips pulling back from his teeth, the scene brightening to an orangey yellow on the TV and imparting the color to his skin so that he looked jaundiced. "Yeah?" he said. "If it wasn't for you," he said, but she dropped her eyes to the screen and shut him out.

The yellow there darkened to gold, to honey, to a deep hungering sepia as the killer in his mask flailed the too-white blade at his victim, the heroine in her midnight-blue teddy, who could only run and crouch and hide, bare-legged, her painted toenails gathering in every particle of light as if to shut the camera down. *Dog barking,* the caption read.

Glass breaking.

A quick close-up of the victim, her makeup smeared, eyes dilated with terror.

Sobbing continues.

PART IV

One

As soon as he laid eyes on the house, he knew he had to have it. Even when he'd been living with Gina and making out pretty well, king of his own domain, envious of no one, he'd be going one place or another—running errands, dodging between the two restaurants—and glance out the car window and see a house like this and feel something move in him. Awe. A kind of awe. To think about the people who lived there, doctors, lawyers, old money, the real class acts with blue-chip investments handed down through the generations and the Jag and the SLK280 sitting side by side in the garage. They came into Lugano sometimes, people in their forties, fifties, even sixties, and they knew their wines and never needed help with the menu or the pronunciation of anything, whether it was Italian, French or German. Then they went home to a house like this, the slate roof, the mullioned windows, shrubs a hundred years old clipped and tamed as if they were an extension of the walls, flower beds, ivy, wisteria—and always a hill studded with trees. To look down from.

And here it was, right before him. The real deal. This was no development house thrown together with two-by-fours and plasterboard, no condo, no rambling Peterskill Victorian that had been divided up two generations ago into dark stinking run-down rat warrens inhabited by welfare mothers and crackheads, this was where the rich people lived, where they'd always lived. And rich people built their houses out of stone. That was the first thing he saw, the stone—a sun-striped bank of silvered gray stone glimpsed through the trees as they followed Sandman and the real estate lady up the gravel drive—and then the poured water of the windows, the slate roof that shone as if it were eternally wet, the ancient copper downspouts with their tarnish of green.

Natalia said, "It is a nice set, yes?"

The sunlight pooled in the drive where Sandman and the real estate lady—Janice Levy, short, bush-haired, expansive—were just getting out of the car. "Setting, you mean," he said. "And look at that—look at that view." He was pointing now, as the lawn unscrolled to a line of trees that dipped away to give up the river and the mountains beyond.

"I hate it." Madison was leaning forward, her face intent, eyes roaming over everything. "Mommy, I hate it. It looks like a witch's house. And there's nobody to play with."

For once, Natalia ignored her, and then they were climbing out of the car, Sandman grinning and Janice Levy watching them with the keen eyes of a behaviorist, watching for nuance, the slipup, anything that would give him away. "Wait'll you see inside," Sandman was saying. "This place is you, man, I told you."

Sandman was right. It *was* him, sure it was, no doubt about it. Even if the inside was as vacant as a barn or redecorated in motel revival with cottage cheese ceilings and lime-green paint he would have taken it on sight, the deal already done and awaiting only his approval. And Janice Levy's approval of them, on behalf of the Walter Meisters, who were already in West Palm Beach because Mrs. Meister, at seventy-two, could no longer take the winters and didn't care how muggy and buggy Florida got, it couldn't be any worse than a New York summer, even with the breeze off the river. Muggy was muggy. At least that was what Janice Levy told them, pinching her voice just this side of caricature to impersonate the old lady as she showed them through the place, pointing out the amenities and spewing away non-stop.

Sandman—he looked good, looked respectable, his tattoos covered up under a long-sleeved button-down shirt in a pale banker's blue that brought out the color of his eyes and his facial hair reduced to a single strip of dirty blond soul beard depending from his lower lip—grinned and tugged at his sleeves and dropped his baritone down to its most soothing pitch as they shuffled through the rooms and Janice Levy waved and jabbered and professionally ingratiated herself. "And the bar," he said. "Look at the bar."

They were in the main room, with its fireplace and views out to the river, oak floors, golden with age, the bar—sink and mini-fridge beneath it—tucked in against one white-plastered wall. "Yeah," he heard himself say, "nice." He was wearing his expressionless expression beneath the new mirror shades he'd picked up in a mall someplace in Utah, give nothing away, though the price had already been set and there was no reason or room for bargaining, sign the papers or walk. But this was how he did business: never let them know what you're thinking.

Natalia ran a hand over the burnished surface of the bartop and turned to Janice Levy to ask about storage space. "Are there not closets?"

Balancing one elbow in a cupped palm and tilting her head in what was meant to be an ingenuous way, Janice Levy assured her that the closets were more than adequate, though, of course, in an old house—a classic house—you did have to be creative. And didn't she know just the antique dealer to find her some real period pieces, wardrobes, chiffoniers, breakfronts, but really, a house like this—

That sold Natalia right there—that and the kitchen, which, as Sandman had promised, had been upgraded to the highest haute bourgeois standard (the Meisters were real foodies, Janice Levy confided, with over five hundred cookbooks alone). The kitchen pleased him too—granite countertops, a prep island, hooks for the saucepans, the big Viking range every bit the equal of the one they'd left behind—and he made the mistake of saying so.

"Oh, are you a foodie, then, Mr. Martin?"

He gave her a stare, then removed the shades to fix his eyes on her, to show her he was sympathetic, handsome, dashing, a ladies' man, nobody to fear. "I wouldn't go that far," he said. "I like to cook. And I like a good restaurant too."

Natalia was fully warmed up at this point—he could see the let's-go-shopping look settling into her pretty dark whiskey-colored eyes, a whole new house to fill, a real house, a country estate surrounded by antique dealers and Manhattan just over an hour away. "He is the best. A cook to dream for. And wine. His own sommelier."

Janice Levy was watching him. So was Sandman. The time had come to sign the papers, two-year lease with an option to buy, break open the Perrier-Jouët and get the real estate lady out the door so she could drive overfed couples around in her white Land Cruiser and sell, sell, sell. She knew all about him. Knew the amount he kept in his bank accounts, knew how much equity he had in the condo in Mill Valley, knew he was clean, debt-free, and that he was twenty-nine years old and had a degree from the USC film school and money to burn. "So," she said, laying her briefcase on the bar and snapping the latches with a practiced flip of both thumbs, "what is it you said you did? For a living, I mean?"

"Investments."

"Oh," she said, "of course. Yes, I knew that." She was marshaling the papers for his signature, the handing over of the check, the first six months paid in advance, Sandman to get his deposit back, when she mused: "You're in the film business?" In the background he could hear Madison's piping skirl of a voice, *Mommy, Mommy, there's a swing set!*

"No," he said, moving up to stand beside her and run his gaze over the first page of the agreement, "that's an amateur's game. It's like gambling, know what I mean?"

Her eyes—they were green, sharp, attractive, definitely interested—shifted to him. He could smell her perfume. Like all real estate women she had terrific legs, which she showed off in a skirt that fell just below the knee. "No, not really. But I do have a client looking for a house now who works in TV, in Manhattan, and he—"

"Investments," he repeated. "Keep it real."

"Yes," she said, nodding vigorously. "Oh, yes. Definitely."

The trip cross-country wasn't exactly what he'd envisioned—they'd stretched it out to two weeks and a day, and they did manage to see the Great Salt Lake, an Amish village and the world's biggest longhorn steer, all for Madison's benefit, but there was no Tahoe and no Vegas. Once he'd got back on I-80 he just kept going, his mind working round the sharp edges of what had happened back there outside of Sacramento, and after he crossed the state line he began to rethink things. For one, there was no real reason to dawdle—a little R & R, sure, please the kid and Natalia too—but the sooner he got settled in New York and started making some real money again, the better. And the car. He'd been in panic mode there for a while, the adrenaline scouring his veins and seriously impairing his judgment. He had ID. He had papers for the car. It was his, no question about it, and once he was out of California he didn't have to worry about the cops either—if that was even a worry to begin with—and plus he had money in the thing. He'd paid ten thousand down, cash, on Natalia's Z4 and had better than a year's payments in it too, and so no, he wasn't going to unload the Mercedes. Dealer plates were nothing—he'd just toss them, make up a phony pink slip and register the thing in New York. And when Bob Almond of Bob Almond Mercedes/BMW wanted to know where his payments were, well, he could go on down to San Roque and try to shake them out of Bridger Martin, the asshole.

And so he'd kept going, Natalia dozing, Madison awake now in back and playing her videos over and over, the maddening rupture of the kiddie soundtrack better than the claws-bared assault of Natalia's nagging, and that wasn't over yet—she was just giving her vocal cords a rest. Scenery—or lack of it—fled by the windows. He kept his foot on the gas and his eyes on the rearview. It must have been four or so before Madison started whining and Natalia lifted her head to give him a stare that burned right through him, Winnemucca bleak, Elko bleaker, and in a withering voice wondered if he intended to drive all day and all night without stopping even to perform their natural functions or consume—that was the word she used— anything of nourishment. "Are you planning to stop," she said, and he wouldn't look at her, his eyes on the road, "or are you still running?"

"I'm not running."

"Then what are you doing?"

"Driving."

"Driving, yes. I see that." She looked out the window on high desert scrub, the world bleached of color, the sun as persistent as a nightmare. "But this is not Tahoe."

"No," he said, "no, it's not. Change of plan."

"This is not Vegas." He stole a glance at her and her face was set, angry, all the soft opalescent beauty drained out of it. "What is this? This is nothing."

An exit blew by, trucks drawn up in a steel ridge, a hundred cars and milling stupid people like stick figures in an artist's rendering of the ultimate truck stop, gas, food, lodging, condoms, pigs in a blanket, tequila. A sign for Indian jewelry, ONLY 20 MILES. And then scrub, more scrub, and the long dwindling slash of the road.

"You stop," she said, and she turned her wrathful face to him. "At the next place you stop and I don't care what it is, you stop."

"A pool," Madison chimed in. "I want a place with a pool. Can I go swimming, Mommy, can I?"

He heard himself say, "Sure, no problem. Next place. Next place with a pool."

For a moment, all three of them fixed their gaze on the road ahead, the gleaming chain-link of cars and trucks vanishing into the horizon, cartoon characters whinnying and chortling in the background, the tires faintly humming. "Something is wrong," Natalia said then.

"Nothing's wrong."

"Then why not Tahoe. You promised Tahoe."

"I told you, I changed my mind."

"Those people—"

"Fuck those people."

She drilled him with her eyes. She didn't want him cursing around Madison, and he knew that—that was one

of the rules. No cursing around Madison. "Those people—"
she repeated.

"Fuck those people."

And so it went, ad nauseam, for two weeks and one day.

Their first night in the house, after four in the local motel
and five full days of shopping, hassling with the utilities, ar-
ranging furniture and unpacking the big cardboard boxes
sent on ahead from California, he decided to inaugurate the
kitchen. A little Thai/Chinese fusion was what he was thinking: three-flavor stir-fry (scallops, monkfish, tiger shrimp),
pork spring rolls to start and a nice medium-spicy squid
salad that would have enough push to it to satisfy Natalia
and yet not overwhelm Madison's tender young palate.
Though Madison was learning—he had to give her credit
for that. Ever since her mother had moved in with him he'd
been weaning her off the bland stuff, slipping her a slice of
daikon or Vidalia onion when he was cooking, an extra
portion of wasabi and pickled ginger with her sashimi—
and then a bowl of green-tea ice cream to cool and com-
pare. Or having her do the taste test with a tiny sliver of the
tan chipotle mecos he liked to use in his chicken enchiladas
or the dark red coil of a smoked serrano, and always an ice
afterward. She was getting to be a little champ, actually, insist-
ing on a dollop of jalapeño jelly instead of cinnamon on her
butter-drenched toast in the morning.

The supermarket wasn't what it was in California, of
course, but he'd found an Asian market in Fishkill (a little
bit of a haul from Garrison, but he tried to restrict his shopping to the north so as to stay away from Peterskill, for obvious reasons) and got pretty much everything he needed,
from the cellophane noodles to the sweet chili sauce, spring
roll wrappers, fresh cilantro and gingerroot. It had rained

earlier, the clouds gathering atop Storm King and fanning out to sink low over West Point, and that was something he'd missed, the suddenness and violence of the thunderstorms; now, standing at the kitchen counter, he caught the indefinable scent of his boyhood drifting across the lawn and through the screens, the smell of the woods, sumac, mold, rot, the superabundant water sitting in its pools in the hidden places, everything in ferment. He was happy suddenly, feeling as if a load had been lifted from him, a load that had worn him down this past month and more, happy to be cleaning squid with one of his sharp new J.A. Henckels ice-hardened knives and having a glass of Champagne at the window, the sky close and gray and the grass spread out beneath him such a dense green it was almost black. Happy about the Champagne too, the price on the Perrier-Jouët so good he'd gone ahead and bought a case, the French wines cheaper here by far than on the west coast, thinking he'd be drinking a lot more French from now on, not to mention Italian and even Spanish. He was feeling all this, alternately plying the knife and setting it down to lift the Champagne flute to his lips, when Natalia slipped up noiselessly behind him and wrapped her arms round his waist.

"Hey," she murmured. "How is it going? Looks good. Squid, yes?"

There was a saucepan on the stove, the heat up high—he was making a fish stock from the scraps of the monkfish, a little white wine, butter, garlic and green onions to flavor the squid—and his hands were full. Normally, he didn't like to be bothered when he was cooking—cooking required your full concentration or things were apt to go wrong—but he was feeling so good he just leaned back into her to enjoy the feel of her long-fingered hands on his abdomen, up under his rib cage and where he was especially sensitive, on his chest and nipples. "Feels nice," he said, turning his head for a kiss. "You want a glass of Champagne?"

"Fine," she said, moving away from him now, "yes, I would like that, but I am looking for the hammer I have just bought—have you seen this hammer?"

She'd found a set of musty-looking turn-of-the-century prints in one of the local antique shops, featuring two children, a boy and a girl, in various poses—swallowed up in a maelstrom of brooding vegetation, strolling hand in hand like lost waifs, kicking their bare feet in a snarling stream, gazing up into the heavens as if for guidance—and she'd spent the last hour trying to decide where to hang them. "No," he said, "I haven't seen it, but would you mind—the Champagne's in the ice bucket there and my hands . . ." He held up both palms, wet and slimed with the exudate of the squid, in evidence. "And that saucepan on the stove there—would you turn the heat down? To low. All the way to low."

She was wearing a pair of capris to show off the perfect swell of her calves and her beautiful ankles and feet, open-toed sandals and a white blouse hiked up and knotted under her breasts—and she'd put her hair up too, no nonsense here, a whole house to whip into order. He crosshatched the flattened slabs of squid to tenderize them and watched her glide across the floor to the stove and then pour herself a glass of the wine. And what was he feeling—love? Lust? The quiet seep of fulfillment and domestic bliss?

"Toast?" he proposed, putting down the knife to wipe his hands on a towel and then taking up his own glass.

The sun had fingered its way through the clouds, suddenly illuminating a patch of woods beyond the window—up came the light as if wired to a rheostat—and then just as quickly it faded. A snapshot. With a very long exposure. She was watching him intently. Poised on one foot, the glass at her lips. "Toast to what?" she asked, her face changing. "To, to"—and here it came, the flush along the cheekbones, the sheets of moisture to armor her eyes—"to a man who will not even make the introduction to his mother? In his own hometown? Of his fiancée? Is that the toast you want? Is that it?"

He said her name, softly, in melioration.

"Because I cannot stand this shit, and that is what it is, *shit.* You hear me?"

"Please," he said, "not now."

"Yes, now," she said, spreading her legs for balance and then throwing back her head to drain the flute in a single gulp as if she were back in Jaroslavl with a glass of no-name vodka. "I don't believe you. I don't believe anything you say. This money. Where do you get this money? Is it drugs, is that it?"

He just stared. He didn't want to get into this.

"Will I—am I to go to prison, then? Like Sandman? And you—you have been in prison too, I know it."

"It's a long story," he said.

"Yes. But you tell it to me. You tell me everything." She poured a second glass for herself, and he could see her hand tremble at the neck of the bottle. "Because I swear, if you don't . . . You are ashamed of me? Why? Because of my accent? Ashamed of me so that I can meet only Sandman and not your own mother?"

"It's not that," he said, and still he hadn't moved, the squid lying there on the counter neatly prepped, his flute empty, the pan simmering on the stove. "Okay, you're right," he said, and he moved to cut the heat under the pan and pour himself another glass, "I guess it is time, because you're just acting crazy now—drugs? Me? Have you ever seen me do any kind of drug, even pot—even a single toke?"

"Cocaine."

"That's nothing. A little toot now and again, just for fun. What, once a week—once every *two* weeks?" He spread his arms wide in expostulation. "You like it too."

She gave him a tight smile. "Yes. Sometimes."

"I'm no bad guy—you think I'm a bad guy? What happened to me is no different than what happened to you. I just hooked up with the wrong person, is all. My wife. My ex-wife. That was the beginning of it, just like you—just like you with what's his name, Madison's father?"

She took a seat at the table they'd just bought the day before—oak, 1890s, six matching chairs, two with hairline cracks that had been glued and varnished over—and they finished the bottle and opened another one and he told her as much as he could, because he wanted to be honest with her; he loved her, and really did believe that people in a relationship needed to be straight with each other. What he didn't tell her was that his real name was Peck—Bridger was good, Bridger was fine for now, though he'd run the creep's credit into the ground because he couldn't resist putting it to him and before long he'd have to be somebody else—or that it wasn't the investment business he was planning on running out of the big paneled aboveground basement or that he couldn't bring her to see his mother not only because his mother was irrelevant to him but because she might call him Peck or even William and he just needed to take things step by step right now.

At some point, he'd got up and started chopping cilantro, green beans, garlic and chiles, and he deveined the shrimp and put on a pot for the rice. She didn't have much to say. She sat there running the tip of her index finger round the rim of the glass, wearing her brooding look. He was feeling a little light-headed from the wine. The pleasure of the hour, of being alone with his thoughts while things sizzled in the pan, was lost to him and the taste of the

Champagne had gone sour in the back of his throat, but at least, he thought, he'd laid the issue to rest. He'd opened up. Been as forthcoming and honest as he could be, under the circumstances. And she seemed satisfied, or at least placated.

For a long while neither of them said anything. There were the faint sounds of life in the country—birdsong, crickets, the wet rush of a lone car's tires on the road out front. And what else? The rhythmic squeak and release of Madison's swings, a sound as regular as breathing. Everything seemed to cohere round that rhythm, slow and sure and peaceful, even as he moved back to the stove, busy there suddenly. When the wok was good and hot he dumped in the garlic, ginger, green onions and chiles and the instant release of the flavor scented the air in a sudden burst that made his salivary glands clench. Behind him, at the table, Natalia cleared her throat, poured herself another glass of wine. Then, in her smallest voice, she said, "I still do not see why I cannot meet your mother."

Two days later, he was in a place across the river, in Newburgh, buying a high-end color copier with a credit card in somebody else's name, after which he intended to check out an authentic old-country German butcher shop Sandman had turned him on to—he thought he might make Wiener schnitzel, with pickled red cabbage, spätzle and butter beans, just for a change, though on second thought it was probably too heavy in this heat and he might just go with potato salad and bratwurst on the grill—when he decided on a whim to stop in at a bar down by the waterfront. He had a couple of hours to kill and that was nice. It was calming. As was the feel of the sun on his back as he loaded the copier into the trunk of the car, the underarms of his shirt already damp with sweat, the heat and humidity sustaining him in a way the refrigerated air of the Bay Area never could have. He felt like a tourist on his own home turf. A dilettante. A man of leisure taking the air before ensconcing himself on a barstool and having a cold beer or two in a conical glass beaded with moisture while the TV overhead nattered on about nothing and he spread a copy of the newspaper across the bar and mused over the little comings and goings of the Yankees and Mets.

Natalia was shopping. He'd dropped her off at a mall the size of Connecticut and she said she'd call him around two for lunch. They'd found a day camp for Madison, though she hadn't wanted to go, of course, and she'd clung to her mother's legs and shrieked till the snot ran down her nose and generally caused a monumental pain in the ass for everyone concerned, but at least they didn't have to worry about her till five—or was it five-thirty? He thought about Sukie then, couldn't help himself—it hurt to be so close and not see her, but he didn't dare risk it, not yet, anyway. Her face was there, rising luminous in his mind, and then just as quickly it was gone. He checked his watch—quarter past twelve—and stepped into the bar.

Or it wasn't a bar, actually, in the strictest sense of the word—it was a bar/restaurant, looking to go upscale, part of the interconnected complex the city fathers had built along the riverfront to attract tourists and the locals who had a little money in their pockets and thought they were getting something special because the waiters wore starched white aprons over dress shirts and ties and the Hudson was right outside the window. And he wasn't complaining—he loved to drift into places like this, the Varathane still fresh on the pine wainscoting, the owners young and uninitiated and looking to score big. It was like a busman's holiday for him, studying the menu, the wine list, seeing what they were getting for what they were putting out, but it was strictly for comparison. He'd never own a restaurant again. Too much shit. Too much heartache.

It took a minute for his eyes to adjust, and then he nodded at the hostess (eighteen, natural blonde, with a butterfly tattooed on the wing of her left shoulder, and he hated that, hated tattoos on women, especially when they wore them in intimate places—it just suggested traffic to him, that was all), removed his shades, swept a hand over the crown of his head to settle his hair and pulled up a stool at the bar. The place was fairly well crowded and that surprised him. The bar was full of business types in light-weight summer suits, plus a couple of secretaries and three or four of the local lowlifes—you could pick them out at a glance, despite their bright-colored shirts and the watch-me-behave-myself looks on their faces—and maybe two-thirds of the tables were filled, mostly with women, mostly drinking iced tea and picking at the crab salad served on half an avocado. What was the word he was looking for? Déclassé. It wasn't Sausalito, that was for sure.

He'd just ordered his beer and half a dozen cherrystones, just spread out the paper on the bar and glanced up at the TV screen to see somebody somewhere hitting a home run on yesterday's highlight reel, when he felt a hand on his shoulder and swung round on the stool as if he'd been burned, jumpy—crazed, freaked—despite himself. For a moment he didn't know whose eyes he was staring into, some stranger's, some jerk who wanted to just have a glance at the sports page or politely ask if he might not mind shifting down a stool so he could—

"Peck, man—don't you recognize me?"

It was Dudley, Dudley with his hair cut short and his earring banished, dressed in a white apron over a long-sleeved shirt and tie. He didn't know what to say. Tried to stare right through him, hello, goodbye, *You talkin' to me?* But it wasn't working, wasn't going to work. He was William Peck Wilson, and though he hadn't been anywhere near Peterskill in three years, he'd already been sniffed out. *Newburgh.* Jesus Christ. It was twenty-five miles away and on the other side of the river. Who would have thought anybody would know him here?

Dudley was standing there grinning as if they'd just gone in together on a winning Lotto ticket. His eyes were like grappling hooks. His lips were drying out. "Yeah," Peck said, ducking his head, "yeah. Good to see you."

"Oh, man, I can't believe it. So you're back, huh?" And then, before Peck could answer, he was calling down to the bartender, "Hey, Rick—Rick, give this man anything he wants. What do you want? A little nip of that single-malt scotch—what did you used to drink?"

The name stuck in his throat like a wad of phlegm. "Laphroaig."

"Yeah, right: Laphroaig." He stole a glance over his shoulder. "I'm not supposed to drink while I'm working, but hey, this is special, a special occasion." He shifted on his feet, took a step back to widen his view, then reached out a balled-up fist to rap Peck on the shoulder. "Shit!" he barked. "Shit, Peck, it's great to see you. Balls up, man. Balls up!"

He couldn't help himself—something just snapped at that point—but suddenly he seemed to have Dudley by the arm and he was gripping that arm in his right hand as if he wanted to crush it and he was pulling Dudley to him so that he could drop his voice to that Greenhaven register: "Don't call me that," he said. "Don't call me by name. Not ever."

The light banked in Dudley's eyes, then came back in a soft glimmer of recognition. "Yeah," he said. "Yeah, I can dig it."

Then they had the Laphroaig. Then they made some

very quiet, very general conversation until Dudley had to excuse himself to go back to work. There was that moment of farewell and goodbye and see you next time, but Dudley just wasn't ready to let it go yet. "So," he said, already leaning toward the kitchen, "am I going to see you around, or what? Are you back?"

Peck watched two women get up from their table by the window and fuss around over their purses and shopping bags and whatever else they'd dragged into lunch with them, their backsides tight in their skirts as they bent down and came up again. Beyond them, out on the river, a lone high gull coasted on the streaming currents of the air. He stood, tucked the paper under his arm. "No," he said, "just passing through."

Two

THEY WERE SOMEWHERE in Utah, staring out at the salt flats that were so blanched and bleak and unrelieved he might have created them himself for the backdrop to some post-apocalyptic thriller, but he was too tired, sweat-slicked, dehydrated and vaguely feverish even to guess at the storyline or get beyond the long-distance shimmer of the (hackneyed) opening shot. Dana was driving. She'd been gazing into her laptop all day as if it were the crystal ball in *The Wizard of Oz,* and then they'd stopped to gas up and use the restroom and she'd taken over the wheel. For the last couple hundred miles he'd been steeling himself to call Radko, just to see how things stood, though he knew in his heart that by now somebody else would be occupying his cubicle and plying his mouse. It was hot, the car's air conditioner barely functioning, the sun glancing off the hood, the dashboard, the buttons of the radio. His under-arms were clammy and abraded and his T-shirt was stuck to his back and he kept playing with the vents to maximize the minimal airflow, without much success. He took a mo-ment to glance at Dana, her jaw set and hands rigid on the wheel, then pulled out his phone, punched in the number and raised his eyes to the white vacancy of the horizon.

The phone picked up on the second ring. "Rad," Radko announced, delivering his standard telephonic greeting, as if pronouncing the two syllables of "hello" were a waste of time.

"Rad?" Bridger repeated stupidly. He'd been listening to talk radio out of boredom, some reactionary demagogue of the airwaves spewing about communists and liberals and Mexicans in a high inflammatory voice, and though he'd turned down the volume, the noise was still there. The term "eco-Nazis" rose up out of the chatter and fell away.

"Who is this? Bridger? Bridger, is that you?"

"Yeah, uh—hi."

"Where are you?"

"That was what I wanted to talk about, what I wanted to tell you—"

"You tell me nothing. You are at airport, you are in your house, you are standing in lobby of this building where I am running a business and paying the rent, and it does not matter, does not"—he paused to snatch at the word—"register. And you know why?"

"I'm in Utah."

"Utah." There was an infinite sadness in the way he pronounced it, as if Utah were a prison or a leper colony.

"That's what I wanted to tell you, I'm sorry, but Dana, I mean, Milos—"

"No, do not bring my cousin's name into this."

"We have to go to New York, because this thief—"

"Thiff, thiff, always this *thiff*—give it up why don't you? Already, enough."

"He's got *me* now—somehow he managed to get hold of my identity, taking out credit cards in my name and I don't know what else, and if anybody comes there looking for me, creditors or collection agencies or whatever, I want you to know it's not my fault. I'm not guilty. Don't blame me."

"Blame? Who is blaming? I want to tell you something, that there is a woman, very young woman, sitting in your workstation right now, a quick worker, bedder, I think, than you—if you are even here, is what I mean." Bridger tried to cut in, but Radko had raised his voice now, hooking the words on the caps of his teeth and spitting them into the receiver. "But you are not here, are you?"

"I understand. I know where you're coming from. I just want to say that this is all way beyond my control, and, well, I guess when I get back I'll give you a call. Just in case—"

"In case what?"

"You need me. Again."

"When *do* you come back?"

The voice on the radio flared and died. Dana hadn't moved, even to blink her eyes, everything stationary except the shapes of the distant cars and trucks ever so gradually enlarging on the far side of the divider. "I don't know. As soon as I can."

"You don't know?" Radko paused for effect. "Then I don't know too," he said, and cut the connection.

That was Utah. Then there was Wyoming, and after Wyoming, Nebraska and Iowa and the worn green underbelly of Illinois and on and on, the road a whip and the car clinging to it like a drop of sweat or blood or both. They alternated behind the wheel, one of them unconscious in back as the other fought the tedium, and he tried to take most of the burden on himself because it was especially hard on her with conversation a virtual impossibility and no radio to distract or absorb or infuriate her. She wasn't a bad driver—the deaf, as she'd pointed out to him a hundred times, were more visually alert and spatially oriented than the hearing, hence better drivers, hands down—but he couldn't help worrying she'd drift into a trance and do something regrettable, if not fatal. Exhaustion crept up on him, though. And the heat. It seemed as if they were follow-ing a heat wave all across the fat wide hips of the country, hardly a cloud in the sky and not a drop of rain.

They stopped one night at a motel in a college town in western Pennsylvania, both of them so keen to escape the torture chamber of the car they no longer cared whether Frank Calabrese got to New York ahead of them or if he'd defrauded another half-dozen people in the interval or set himself up as President and CFO of Halter/Martin Invest-ments. For his part, Bridger was ready to let it go, give it up, repair the damage and move on, but Dana was intractable. "You're like Captain Ahab," he said, clumsily finger-spelling it for her as they stood in line at a Subway crammed with students slouching under the weight of their backpacks.

I am not, she signed.

"You have to know when to cut your losses"—he tried to make a joke of it—"otherwise you wind up with a peg leg, or worse: you go down with the whale. You don't want to go down with the whale, do you?"

She didn't laugh. Didn't even crack a smile. For a mo-ment he wondered if she'd understood him, and he was about to repeat himself, though nothing falls flatter than a joke reiterated, when her eyes went hard. Her shoulders were cocked toward him, her hair fanned out as if a sudden breeze had caught it, and when she spoke her words were stamped with the impress of her teeth: "It's not funny. You're not funny."

They'd come to the glassed-in counter now, Dana next in line, and the shrunken harried-looking woman in plastic cap and gloves, whose job it was to layer meat, cheese and vegetable matter on the customer's roll of choice, was say-ing "Next" in vain. *You're not funny.* Jesus, did she have to be so negative all the time? Couldn't she lighten up? Even for five minutes?

Of course, he wasn't in the sunniest of moods himself (they were both wiped, both in need of food, a shower, a couple hours comatose on a king-size bed in front of a pulsating TV screen) and something in him, the first flicker of a cruel impulse he never knew he possessed, made him wait till the woman had raised her voice—"Next!" she cried in exasperation, "Next!"—and finally reached across the counter to poke Dana with her plastic-clad index finger. No one likes to be ignored, that was what he was thinking—that was what he was communicating here, a little lesson, tit for tat—even as Dana gave him a savage look, then turned to the woman and ordered, pointing out the items she wanted because pointing was the norm in this establishment, the whole process of shuffling down the line and creating the sandwich a cooperative pantomime between customer and worker punctuated by the odd verbal cue: *Six-inch or twelve? Balsamic-cheddar whole-grain or regular Italian? To drink?*

He waited till they were back in the motel, shoes off, sunk into the bed under the tutelary eye of the TV and working on the sandwiches, before bringing up the subject again. "I don't know," he said, looking her in the face. "I just wonder what the plan is, that's all."

She was at a disadvantage, because it took both hands to compress a twelve-inch submarine sandwich and keep it from disintegrating into its constituent parts, but she was game. She paused to swallow, then leaned over to take a sip of the extra-large diet soft drink clenched between her legs. He saw that her face was relaxed now, the tension and fatigue beginning to loosen their grip. She came up smiling. "The plan," she said carefully, "is to stay at my mother's and let her spoil us for a few days." She opened wide, took a foursquare bite of the sandwich, chewed, swallowed, both hands engaged. "Then," she said, gazing from him to the TV screen and back, "we get in the car, go up the FDR Drive to the Deegan Expressway to I-87 to the Sprain Brook and take that to the Taconic. If memory serves, it's 9A after that and then Route 9 right on into Peterskill." She bent forward for another bite, a baffle of bread, Swiss cheese and smoked turkey blunting her diction. "It's a scenic route," she said, chewing, "beautiful trees, dogwood, wildflowers. You're really going to love it."

It was past noon when they woke, the room frigid and dark, as remote from the world as a space capsule silently drifting across the universe, and they might have slept even later if Bridger hadn't become aware of a muted sound, a rhythmic thumping insinuating itself in the space between the low groan and high wheeze of the air conditioner. At first, he didn't know where he was, everything dim and robbed of color, a sensation of wheels sustaining him, of motion, but then he was fully awake and the noise—someone was knocking at the door, that was it—rousing him to action. He slipped into the pair of shorts he'd flung on the carpet the night before, the feel of them cold against his skin— cold, and faintly damp with yesterday's sweat. The knocking seemed to intensify. He glanced at Dana. Her face was wrapped in sweet oblivion—nothing could wake her, and the thought made him feel tender and protective. What would have happened if he wasn't there? The place could have been on fire and she'd never know. He fumbled his way to the door and pulled it open.

A woman was poised there before him, her fist arrested in the act of knocking—a woman with indignant eyes and her black hair pulled back in a knot, and why did she look so familiar? For a moment, he was mystified, but then he took in her sandals and the tangerine-colored sari, and began to understand. "What?" he said, squinting against the assault of sunlight. "What is it?"

"Checkout time is eleven a.m.," the woman said.

"Oh, yeah," he muttered, "yeah, sorry." The heat, gathered up off the pavement and filtered through every creek, pond and mosquito-infested puddle in the neighborhood, rose up to stab at him till he winced: *humidity*. He'd never really known what it meant except in the abstract. He was sweating already.

"For your information, it is now twelve twenty-five in the afternoon."

"Sorry."

The look she gave him was drained of sympathy. "Don't make me charge you an extra day, do you understand what I'm saying?" Her eyes flicked to the bed and the bundled form of Dana, then flew at his face. "Don't make me do that."

Then they were in the car again, back on I-80, back in Purgatory, back on the road that never ends, and it wasn't until they hit a truck stop outside Bloomsburg that they had a chance to comb their hair, brush their teeth, put something in their stomachs. It was a joyless meal, a mechanical refueling of the body little different from filling up the gas tank. He drove the final leg, trying to extract some entertainment value from the radio, one alternative channel after the other fading out till he gave up and tuned in the ubiquitous oldies. The sun was right there with them all the way, relentless, pounding down on the roof of the car through the long afternoon, the cranked-up DJs in their air-conditioned studios making jokes about the heat— "Triple digit!" one guy kept shouting between songs—and they must have heard "Summer in the City" three or four times rolling through New Jersey. Or he must have heard it.

Dana didn't seem to mind the heat—or the silence either. She sat beside him, enfolded in her own world, tapping away at her laptop—this was her chance to work on her book, she told him, didn't he see that? "Enforced solitude. Or not solitude," she'd added with an apologetic smile, "that's not what I mean." He knew what she meant—and he wasn't offended. Not particularly. She was trying to make the best of things, as if anything good could come of all this. He wished her well. Hoped she finished her book, sold it to the biggest publisher in New York and made a million dollars, if that would make her happy. Because there was no doubt that Frank Calabrese and the whole insane enterprise of running him down wasn't making anybody happy, not her, not him, not Radko. Or the thief either.

The thief. He'd almost forgotten about him, almost forgotten what they were doing here and why. The trees were dense along the road, traffic building, his eyes enforcing the distance between cars, and all he could think about was the power this single individual had over them, how he was the one who'd put them here, in this car, in the glare of New Jersey on a hot July afternoon. He saw him then, saw the guy's face superimposed over the shifting reflection of the windshield, saw the way he walked, rolling his hips and shoulders like some pimp in a movie, like Harvey Keitel in *Taxi Driver,* and felt something clench inside him, a hard irreducible bolus of hatred that made him reverse himself all over again. He'd been tired the night before, that was all. Tired of the road, tired of the hassle, tired of Radko—tired even of Dana and the way she shut him out. But yes, they were going to find this guy. And yes, they were going to see him put behind bars. And no, it didn't have all that much to do with Dana, not anymore.

The sun was behind them when they rolled across the

George Washington Bridge and into Manhattan, a place he'd seen only in movies, and here it was, the whole city bristling like a medieval fortress with a thousand battlements, each of them saturated with the pink ooze of the declining day. Dana directed him through the narrow canyons cluttered with nosing cabs and double-parked trucks, the evening lifted up and sustained on a tidal wave of cooking, a million fans blowing mu shu and tandoori and kielbasa and double cheeseburger and John Dory and polpettone up off the stove and out into the street. There was a smell of dogshit underneath it, of vomit, rotting garbage, flowers in bloom, diesel. He cranked down the window to absorb it. "Turn here," Dana said, using her hands for emphasis. "At the next light, turn left." The parking garage (they were somewhere on the Upper East Side, and he knew that because she told him) cost as much overnight as an entire month's parking had cost him in college, but Dana was paying and it didn't seem to faze her all that much, and then it was twilight and the lights of the city came to life as if in welcome.

There was a negotiation with the doorman, a logbook in the lobby that had to be signed, and then they were stepping out of the elevator on the nineteenth floor, and Dana's mother was there to greet them. She was shorter than her daughter by two or three inches, her hair the color of those copper scrubbers you buy at the supermarket, insistently slim, twice divorced, with a face that had to reshape itself every time she smiled or grimaced, as if it hadn't yet discovered its final form (a reaction to her new dentures, as he was to learn within two minutes of stepping through the door of the apartment). As for the apartment, it was bigger than he'd expected, one door leading to another and then another like something out of Kafka. Or Fincher. It had that claustrophobic cluttered three-shades-too-dim hazy atmosphere Fincher liked for his interiors and Bridger wasn't especially happy with it. If it had been something he was playing with on his computer, that would be another thing, but as it was he was almost afraid to sit on the couch in the living room for fear of sticking to it. So what did he think? Like mother, like daughter—Dana wasn't exactly the most organized person he'd ever met.

"Nice to meet you, Mrs. Halter," he said, standing awkwardly in the middle of the front room. The shades were drawn. There was a smell of cat litter—or, more properly, cat urine.

"Call me Vera," Mrs. Halter said, pushing him down in an easy chair strewn with knitting projects in various stages of completion and fussing over a bottle of wine—she couldn't seem to get the cork out—and a can of mixed nuts that featured Mr. Peanut against a midnight-blue background, but she wasn't Mrs. Halter anymore, anyway. "Dana's father left me for an *older* woman, if you can believe it," she told him, "but that was ten years ago."

"Mom," Dana said. "Don't start. We just got here." She'd draped herself across the couch in the corner, her bare legs pale against the dark pool of cracked green leather.

"Somebody at work. He's a lawyer, I don't know if Dana told you that . . . Anyway, I took my second husband's name—Veit—not because I have anything against Rob—that's Dana's father—but because I got used to it. It's punchier too: Vera Veit. V.V." She set the wine bottle down on the coffee table to mold a figure in the air with the white slips of her hands. "Kind of sexy, don't you think?"

"Mom," Dana said, and it carried no inflection, a complaint that had hung in the air since she was a long-legged preternaturally beautiful teenager who could never hit the right key, never influence a discussion or argument or participate in the roundabout of family ritual without involving her hands and her face and her body. He noted that, noted the way she became a teenager all over again the minute they walked in the door and her mother embraced her and held her and swayed back and forth in perfect harmony with her internal rhythms. It was all right. Everything was all right. For the first time since they left Tahoe, he could relax.

For the next half hour the conversation bounced round the room like a beach ball they were all intent on keeping in motion—a few questions about Bridger, his profession, his income, his prospects, leading to Vera's expressing her outrage over "this identity theft thing" and implying that Dana must somehow have called it down on herself through her own carelessness, to which Dana responded in the angriest, most emphatic Sign he'd ever seen—and then the ball dropped and the three of them sat there staring at one another like strangers until Dana's mother stood up abruptly and said, "So you must be hungry. You didn't eat on the road, did you? Dinner, I mean?"

Until she mentioned it, he hadn't realized how hungry he was. They hadn't stopped, even for a Coke, since breakfast (technically lunch, and he had a queasy recollection of grilled cheese, fries and a side salad with a dollop of very old ranch dressing), pushing on through just to get it over with, as if the drive were a prizefight and they were punch-drunk and reeling and praying for the bell at the end of the fifteenth round to release them. He heard himself say, "Sure. Yeah. But don't go to any trouble—"

"Oh, it's no trouble," she assured him, reaching for the telephone on the table beside her. "I'll just call Aldo's and have them send something up. You do eat meat, right?" she asked, looking to Bridger, and then, without waiting for an answer, she turned to Dana. "Is the osso buco okay with you? You always liked osso buco."

Dana didn't respond—she wasn't even looking.

"And soup. Anybody want soup? They do a nice pavese—you want soup, Bridger? Salad? Anything to start—crostini? Calamari, maybe?"

After dinner, which they ate off of heavy china plates balanced on their knees while sipping what Dana's mother kept calling "a really nice Bardolino," Dana made a show of taking the things out to the kitchen to wash up. Bridger had risen from his chair in a half-hearted attempt to intercede, signing *Let me do it,* but Dana ignored him even as her mother sang out, "No, no, you sit down, I want to talk to you." She had a coquettish look on her face as she added, "So we can get acquainted. All right? You don't mind that, do you? Getting acquainted?" And then she rose and refilled his glass, murmuring, "And have some wine. It's good for you. Good for the heart."

The first thing she did was inform him of the grim statistics—he knew, didn't he, that ninety percent of the deaf married their own kind and that of the ten percent who married into the hearing world, ninety percent of *them* wound up divorced?

"Yes," he said, leaning back in the easy chair and taking a moment to wet his lips with the wine, "that was one of the first things Dana told me after we met. After we started dating, I mean."

"Not a happy number."

"No." The Bardolino had gone to his legs—he'd already drunk too much—and he felt paralyzed from the waist down. Not that he was uncomfortable, not anymore. Or not especially. The place was growing on him—so was Dana's mother. The food had been good, great even, still hot when she artistically slipped one item after another from the sealed Styrofoam boxes onto the plates, and the wine was whispering its secrets to him in a way that made the tensions of the road fade away to nothing.

Dana's mother was leaning forward, both elbows braced on her knees. "So you're not the type that's easily daunted—and you love her. You love my daughter. Or am I wrong?"

He could feel the wine rising now all the way up through his torso to his face, which was hot, and his forehead, which was on fire. "Yes," he said, "or no, I mean—you're not wrong," and he tipped back the glass and drained it.

"Because," she went on as if she hadn't heard him, "as beautiful and independent and smart as she is—and she *is* brilliant, I hope you realize that—there are problems, little frustrations that add up, you know what I mean?" Her eyes were shaped like Dana's, closer to round than oval, and they were the same deep rich color suspended somewhere between brown and gold; when he held her gaze, when he looked into them, he saw Dana just as surely as if he were re-creating her on his computer screen. From somewhere below them, distantly, there was the sound of a siren. "She can be stubborn," she said.

From the kitchen, down the hall and two rooms away, there was the thump and clatter of things being shifted around, a sudden crash, a curse. "What?" he said, distracted. And drunk. Drunk for sure.

"She can be stubborn. But you already know that."

He shrugged. This was neither the time nor place for a critique.

Vera—could he call her Vera?—seemed deflated suddenly. Her own wineglass was empty and she rose to refill it and gestured toward him, but he laid his palm over the rim of the glass and shook his head. Her face composed itself. She sat heavily. For a long moment she said nothing and he was beginning to think the interview was over when she waved her glass and said, "Cochlear implants. For example. Take cochlear implants."

He'd never heard the term before he took his Sign language course. It was the first night, and one of the students wanted to know why the deaf didn't just go out and get implants and dispense with Sign altogether. The teacher—she was married to a physicist who was pre-lingually deaf and used a combination of speech, lip-reading and Sign to communicate—pointed out that not everyone was a candidate for implants, for one thing, depending on the extent and pathology behind their hearing loss, and that among those who were, the results were often mixed. She went on to explain the procedure—the patient would have a receiver and electrodes surgically embedded in the mastoid bone and cochlea in order to pick up sounds from a tiny microphone located behind the ear. In the best-case scenario, these sounds would be transmitted to the auditory nerve and the patient would have some measure of hearing restored, perhaps enough to allow him to function almost normally in the hearing world, especially if he'd lost his hearing later in life. For the rest, it might be enough to improve lip-reading and enable them to talk on the telephone, hear alarms and car horns, that sort of thing. It wasn't a magic bullet.

"You know about cochlear implants?"

He nodded.

"Well, Dana . . . and this really frustrated me and her father too, and maybe frustrated is too mild a word because I was ready to scream"—she paused to give him a brittle smile—"but of course Dana wouldn't have heard me no matter if I screamed all day and all night for the rest of my life. But the point is she refused to be evaluated. Wouldn't even go to the otologist, not even to find out if she was physically capable of improvement—wouldn't hear of it." Another smile. "Listen to me. Just the way we talk, the expressions we use—"

"I hear you," he said, and for a moment she looked startled. Then her features rearranged themselves again and she slapped the arm of the chair and they were both laughing, the siren playing distantly beneath them, keening as if to split the night in two.

Three

ALL THE RIVER TOWNS looked the same, block after block of rambling top-heavy old houses in various states of disrepair, derelict factories sunk into their weed lots, the unemployed and unemployable slouching along the cracked sidewalks while the sumac took hold and the ceremonial parking meters glinted under the sun. Peterskill was no different. Unless maybe it was worse. She'd been here before, when she was a girl—her parents had rented a bungalow on Kitchawank Lake one summer and every Saturday they'd take the family out to a restaurant in the heart of downtown Peterskill, her father irrepressible, shouting "Cucina Italiana, the real deal," mugging and rubbing his abdomen in broad strokes till she and her brothers would break up laughing—but that was twenty years ago and nothing looked even vaguely familiar to her now. The lake she remembered. She'd had a canoe to fool around in that summer—it had come with the house—and she remembered taking it into the little coves on the far shore whenever she could pry it away from her brothers, and she would just drift sometimes, reading, nibbling at a sandwich, feeling the breeze on her face and taking in the intoxicating scent of the lake, the scent of decay and renewal and the strangely sweet odor that lingered when the speedboats had gone.

"I want to go out to the lake when this is over," she said. "Or, I mean, when we're done here."

They were sitting in the car beneath one of the big shade trees planted in some long-gone era of boosterism and hope, and Bridger had a map of the town spread across his lap. He looked up at her out of his too-broad face and ran a hand through his hair. "What lake? What are you talking about? You mean the river?"

She watched for the words, but already the impulse was dying away. After a moment, after he'd turned back to the map, she said, "Never mind. It's not important."

On the way up from the city she'd quizzed him about her mother and how they'd seemed to get along so famously. "What did you talk about?" she asked him.

He was squinting against the glare of the road, his eyes jumping to the mirrors and back—traffic was heavy and it made him tentative. "You," he said. "What else?"

"Yes?" She laid a hand in his lap and he glanced at her before coming back to the road. It was muggy, overcast, threatening rain. "Tell me. What did she say?"

She couldn't read him in profile, but she saw his lips move.

"I didn't hear you," she said. "What?"

He swung his face to her, gave a little smile. "She said you were stubborn."

"Me? Don't believe everything you hear, my friend, especially considering the source. Especially from your girlfriend's mother—"

"Girlfriend? I thought you were my fiancée?"

"Your fiancée's mother." She glanced out the window on vegetation so dense they could have been in the Amazon—less than ten miles from the city and there was nothing visible but a fathomless vault of green. "So I'm stubborn, huh?" she said, turning back to him. "What brought that up?"

A shrug. "I don't know. That first night, when you did the dishes and went to bed right after we ate—?"

His head was tilted forward, eyebrows cocked. Was he asking a question or making a statement? "I'm not following you," she said.

He glanced tensely at the rearview, then brought his face round so she could see the words: "When-you-were-in-bed."

"Yes?"

"Cochlear implants. She said you wouldn't even go in to get examined."

It took her a moment, the sweet smell of chlorophyll flowing at her through the vents, the sky closing in, darkening like a spread umbrella. She said, "She would think that. She was always pushing, pushing. But you don't understand—she didn't understand. It was my decision and nobody else's."

"What about now? Would you do it now?"

She let out a laugh, the kind of laugh that was meant to be bitter, mocking, but it might have sounded like a scream for all she knew. "No way," she said, and she relished the brevity and finality of the phrase, so much intransigence packed into two little syllables.

"Why not? Other people—"

She signed it: *You sound like my mother.*

He gave her a look and took both hands from the wheel. *Other people do it,* he signed. *Why don't you? Then*—the car began to drift and he made a quick grab for the wheel—"then we could talk," he said aloud, his eyes darting to the rearview mirror.

"We are talking."

"You know what I mean."

"No," she said. "No, I don't. You mean I have to talk on your terms, in your language, is that what it is?"

"It's just that it could be better, that's all I'm saying."

"Listen," she said, "even if I wanted to let somebody

open up my head, and I don't—would you want somebody to open up yours? Even if I did, even if I could hear something, anything, the best things in the world—music, my own lover's voice, your voice—I wouldn't do it. This is me. If I could hear, even for an hour, a minute, I'd be somebody different. You understand what I'm saying?"

He nodded, but his eyes had that vague look, as if she were speaking in some foreign language, and then he snatched them away and focused on the car ahead of him. Maybe he hadn't heard her properly, maybe that was it. Whenever she got passionate, whenever she got wound up, she tended to garble her words. She repeated herself, the whole speech, because her mother was wrong—she wasn't stubborn, just determined. And decisive. Even as a child she'd known which world she wanted to live in—the world she'd created for herself, the one she'd built block by block around her till it was impenetrable—and there was no one, not her mother or father or the nimblest and most persuasive audiologist in the world, who could tell her different.

Now, sitting in the car beneath the tree in the midday swelter while Bridger frowned over the map, she came back to the present and thought of what they were doing, what they were about to do, and felt her heartbeat quicken. There were two Calabreses listed in the Peterskill directory, an F.A. at 222 Maple Avenue and an F.R. at 599 Ringgold Street. "Which one do we do first?" Bridger asked, turning to her, his finger stabbing at the map. "This one"—she saw the diagonal slash of the road heading southeast, out of town— "is F.A., and this"—his finger slid across the map, indicating a street due south of where they were—"is F.R. Looks like F.A. is closest, but it doesn't really matter because the town isn't all that big . . . What do you think—you choose."

"I don't know, it's a toss-up," she said, and the image of the flipped coin rose and settled in her mind. "F.A., I guess."

Bridger looked over his shoulder, put the car in drive and swung out onto the nearly deserted main street of Peterskill, and she asked herself why she was so keyed up, so nervous, why her hands had begun to tremble and she was having trouble catching her breath. They didn't even know if the guy's name *was* Frank Calabrese—it could have been just another one of his aliases—and whether or not he was headed for Peterskill, no one could say. That was just their best guess. There was the evidence of the police report Milos had given them (*Frank Calabrese, born Peterskill, NY, 10/2/70*), and the cryptic letter from somebody called Sandman postmarked just up the line in Garrison, and what had *he* said? See you soon. That could have meant anything—he could have been flying to California or they were going to meet someplace in between or go to some crooks' convention together in Arkansas or Tierra del Fuego.

She flipped open the file folder, just to see the words there on the page, as if staring at them long enough would reveal their hidden meaning: "Hey, that thing we talked about is on, no problema. See you soon." Was that enough? No problema? See you soon? Did they really expect to find this guy waiting patiently behind the screen door on Maple Avenue or Ringgold Street? It was crazy. Everything that had happened in the last month was crazy. And where were the cops—wasn't this their job?

Bridger's lips were moving. He was leaning into the windshield, counting off numbers: "Two-sixteen, two-twenty—there it is! Look, that place with the faded siding. Right there, see?"

He'd pulled in at the curb across the street and her heart seized all over again. She was staring at the most ordinary-looking house in the world, a pale gray Cape Cod that had no doubt replaced one of the tumbledown Victorians in the fifties or sixties in some kind of misguided attempt at urban renewal. There were weathered streaks under the drainpipes, a lawn that seemed to recede beneath an even plane of dandelion puffs, a tumble of kids' bicycles flung down on the blacktop drive beside a very ordinary car scaled with rust. Bridger took hold of her hand, and he was saying something, repeating it: "Do you want me to handle this? Because you can stay here if you want—it's probably nothing anyway, right?"

"I'm going." She reached for the door handle, but he hadn't let go of her hand.

"But we need a plan here," he said. His features were pinched, his eyes staring wide. He was trying to be cool, she could see that, but he was as agitated as she was. "If it *is* him in there, and chances are it's not, I know—we have to just back away, I mean, *run*, and I'll call the police on my cell. Okay? Don't say a word, don't talk to him, nothing. Just identify him and call the police."

"Yes," she said, "yes, I know. He's dangerous. I know that."

Bridger was saying something else, using his hands now to underscore the words. "'Assault with a deadly weapon,' remember? That's in the police report. We do not mess with him like back there in that parking lot in where was it, Sacramento? That was insane. We're not going to do anything like that, you understand? Just identify him and call for help. Period."

The sky had closed up, and as she slid out of the car and crossed the street with Bridger, feeling light-headed, the first few spatters of rain began to darken the pavement. At the last moment, when they'd already started up the walk, she wanted to hang back, reconnoiter the place—or the joint, case the joint: isn't that what they said in the old movies?—but then they were on the porch and Bridger was knocking at the screen door and there was a dog there, a shih tzu, all done up in ribbons, and it was showing the dark cavern of its mouth, barking. A moment later a woman appeared behind the screen, not a pretty woman, not young and dark-eyed and stylish, but the sort of woman who'd live in a house like this and find the time to tie ribbons in her little dog's hair.

Bridger did the talking. Was this Frank Calabrese's house, by any chance? No? Did she know—oh, the "F" stood for Frances, Frances Annie? Uh-huh, uh-huh. He was nodding. Frank, the woman thought—and she didn't know him, they weren't related—lived over on Union or Ringgold, one of those streets on the other side of the park.

It was raining heavily by the time they got to Ringgold Street, dark panels of water scrolling across the windshield, the pavement glistening, the gutters already running full. The house Bridger pulled up in front of wasn't appreciably different from the one they'd just left, except there were no bicycles out front and the car parked in the drive was a newer, more expensive model (but not a Mercedes and not wine red). And what had she expected, to see the thing sitting there sparkling in the rain with its California dealer's logo framed neatly in the license-plate holder? She felt deflated. Felt depressed. This time she stayed in the car while Bridger hustled up the walk, his shirt soaked through and a newspaper fanned out over his head. She saw him at the door, saw a figure there behind the screen—a shadow, nothing more—and she was frightened all over again. It was him, she was sure it was . . . but no, they were talking, some sort of negotiation going on, and now she could see the faint pale oval of the man's face suspended against the matte darkness of the interior, a naked forearm floating beneath it, gesturing, and in the next moment the door was shutting and Bridger was dodging his way back down the walk. She reached over to fling the car door open for him.

The rain came with him, the scent of it, his hair flattened across the top and hanging in loose wet strands around his ears. "Well?" she said. "Not him, right?"

"He's at the restaurant. That"—he turned the engine over, put the car in gear—"was his cousin, I think he said."

"Restaurant? What restaurant?"

"Fiorentino's. On South Street—we passed it earlier, don't you remember? I guess he must work there or something . . . the guy that answered the door was maybe, I don't know, forty, forty-five, totally overweight—he had this huge belly. In a wife-beater, no less. Could you see him from here? No? Anyway, he just looked at his watch and said, 'You'll catch him over at the restaurant at this hour.' I asked him what restaurant and he said Fiorentino's before he thought to ask me what I wanted with Frank—and that was when he started to give me the suspicious look."

"What? What did you tell him?"

"That I was a friend. From the coast. From California."

She could feel her heart going again. "But what if he calls and warns him?"

"Shit," Bridger said, and they were out on the street now, water planing away from the tires, "if he does, he does. We don't even know if it's him—and it's probably not, because you're telling me he already has a house and a job? I mean, how likely is that?"

Fiorentino's was on the far side of a broad street a few blocks down, and as Bridger hung a U-turn and pulled up at the curb in front, she had the feeling she'd been here before, déjà vu. Could this be the place, the one her parents had taken her to? The thought made her feel queasy. If this *was* it, then the whole thing got stranger and stranger. She imagined the thief, the guy with the sideburns and the cocky walk, shrunk down to the dimensions of a child, watching her from the kitchen, watching her eat and sign and roughhouse with her brothers, pizza on a shining silver platter, and memory like the taste of it.

She climbed out of the car, fumbling with her umbrella, and looked up at the façade. The restaurant occupied a pair of storefronts somebody had tried to unify with lateral strips of varnished wood that set off the windows like a big picture frame and the sign over the main entrance had been hand-painted in a flowing script. Each of the tables, dimly visible through the screen of rain, featured artificial flowers and a Chianti bottle with a red candle worked into the neck, but it was all so generic. Once she stepped inside, though—a long L-shaped bar to the left, an alcove and then the dining room to the right—she knew. And as if her visual memory weren't enough, there was an olfactory signature here too—some peculiarity of the pizza oven, the imported pomodoro and homemade sausage, the spices, the spilled beer, the mold in the back of the refrigerator in the farthest corner of the kitchen—who could say? But this was it. This was definitely it. She took hold of Bridger's hand and squeezed it. She wanted to say *No more, stop right here,* but her throat thickened and her fingers felt as if they'd been carved of wood.

What she saw was a typical neighborhood bar, half a dozen men in short-sleeved shirts, the white-haired bartender with his flaming ears and red-rimmed eyes, the cocktail waitress in a little skirt and net stockings, bored, her elbows propped on her tray. The TV was going—baseball—and nobody was eating. Too early yet. Too hot. Too rainy.

She stood beside Bridger, her hand locked in his, as he leaned in at the end of the bar and waited for the bartender to acknowledge him. There was a suspended moment, people giving them furtive glances, the quick assessment, her blood racing with fear and hate even as she felt crushed by a kind of trivial nostalgia for the place, for the way she was then, as a girl, when her parents were still married and her brothers were contained by these very walls, and then the bartender made his slow way down the skid-resistant mat and she saw his lips shape the obvious question: "What'll it be?"

She couldn't bear to look at him—she was watching Bridger, as if that could protect her, expecting the thief to step out of the shadow of the alcove and put an end to it all. "Is Frank here?" he asked. And then the movement caught her eye and she was watching the bartender's head swing back as he called down the bar and the cocktail waitress, buried under the glitter of her nails and the sediment of her makeup, awakened briefly to drift to the swinging door of the kitchen, lean into it and convey the message, the name passed from mouth to mouth: "Frank," she imagined her saying, or maybe shouting over the noise of the dishwasher, the radio, the tintinnabulation of pots and pans, "Frank, somebody wants you."

Frank Calabrese turned out to be a disappointment. He wasn't who he was supposed to be, not even close. The door to the kitchen swung open and she caught her breath, expecting the Frank Calabrese she knew to emerge wiping his hands on an apron, hiding out here in his father's or uncle's or cousin's third-string Mafia restaurant till the heat was off him and he could ruin somebody else's life, a mama's boy, a failure, wasted and weak, and this time she would be the one to stare him down, but the face she saw in the doorway was the face of a stranger. This man was short, broad-shouldered and big around the middle, and he was too old—forty, forty at least. He looked to the waitress, then to the bartender, and followed the line of sight from the bartender's pointed finger to herself and Bridger.

He was deceptively light on his feet for such a big man, this Frank Calabrese, and he glided down the length of the room as if he were wearing ballet slippers, his features composed, his eyes searching hers. "Hi," she said, and held out her hand. "I'm Dana, and this"—indicating Bridger—"is my fiancé, Bridger. You're Frank Calabrese, right?"

"That's right," he said, and he'd caught something in her speech that made him narrow his eyes and cock his head ever so slightly as if to get a clearer picture. "What can I do for you?"

Bridger started in then—Bridger, her spokesperson. He dropped her hand and unconsciously ran his fingers through his hair, trying to smooth it back in place. "We're looking for this guy—"

She cut him off: "Criminal. He's a criminal."

"—this guy who I guess must have used your name as an alias, because—"

She couldn't make out the rest, but she knew the story anyway, not just the gist of it, but the whole of it in all its sorry detail, and she watched Frank Calabrese's face till the rudiments of awareness began to awaken there—Yes, somebody had used his credit cards without his knowledge, and yes, it had been a bitch to straighten it all out; he was still getting bills in the mail and this was three years ago already—and then she unzipped her black shoulder bag and extracted the file folder. Frank Calabrese stopped saying whatever he was saying. Bridger gestured to the bar, meaning for her to lay the folder there and display the evidence. Everyone was watching now, the customers, the bartender, the waitress. She took her time, almost giddy with the intensity of the moment, and then she leaned forward to spread open the folder on the counter, making sure that the police report, with its leering photograph and parade of aliases, was right there on top.

The moment was electric. Frank Calabrese laid a hand on the rail of the bar to steady himself and she could see the current flowing right through him, his face hardening, eyes leaping at the page, and before she formulated the question she knew the answer: "Do you know this man?"

"Son of a bitch," he said. "Son of a fucking bitch." He looked up at her, and it was as if he didn't see her at all. "You bet your ass I know him," and his fist came down on the bartop with a force she could feel through the soles of her shoes. She didn't catch what he said next, the key they'd been looking for all along, the base identifier, the name Bridger repeated twice and then reproduced for her with his rapidly stitching fingers so that it hung like a banner on the air: *Peck Wilson. William Peck Wilson.*

Four

HE KNEW he should never have come back, knew it was a disaster in the making, knew that the forces ranged against him—Gina, her fuckhead father, Stuart Yan, the cops, the lawyers—were still in place, merciless and unyielding, and that they'd strip him down to nothing if they had the chance, but it was his choice, wrong or not, and he would have to live with it. Could Dudley be trusted? No, he couldn't, though he'd try his best to be cool about it and that would last all of maybe forty-eight hours or until he ran into somebody from the old days and had his first drink and smoked his first number and started laying out his disconnected version of life under the sun. *Hey, man, this is for your ears only, and don't tell anybody because it's supposed to be like a secret or whatever, but guess who I ran into the other day?*

But he had come back. And he liked the feeling and he liked the house and all that went with it, the shopping and settling in, the smell of the grass as he traced one row after the other on the riding mower that came with the place, the contented squeak and release of Madison's swings pulling hard against their chains, the propulsive thrust of Natalia's figure as she lined the couch up under the picture window or slid the astrakhan rug into place in front of it. And there was Sandman too. Geoff. Geoffrey R. He'd missed him, missed having a buddy, a confidant, somebody he could hang loose with without having to worry about slipping up, because there were times when he looked in the mirror or slapped a credit card down on a waitress' tray and didn't know who he was. William, Will, Billy, Peck, Frank, Dana, Bridger—and the new one, a winner worth something like fifty million Sandman had sniffed out, M. M. Mako, as in Michael Melvin. The name was so ridiculous it had to be real.

All right. Fine. He'd made his choice and he wasn't concerned, not particularly. Even if he got pulled over, the cops had no way of knowing who he was. All they knew was what the license told them: he was Bridger Martin, with a pristine driving record and no outstanding warrants, solid, fiscally responsible, and he was just passing through on his way to Nantucket, a little vacation, and thank you, Officer, yes, I'll be sure to watch my speed. Still, as he carried his mug of coffee and the newspaper down to the office he'd set up in the basement, he couldn't help feeling the smallest tug of uneasiness when he thought of Dudley and Dudley's big mouth and whose ears might be cocked in anticipation. What he wanted—and it came home to him more than ever as he settled in behind his desk, folded back the financial section and looked out on the woods and the river and the pair of squirrels chasing each other across the lawn in quick darting loops—was to live quietly, anonymously, to live in this house with this car and this woman and not have to put up with any shit from anybody ever again. Go north. Go south. Stay invisible. Establish a base in the city, maybe get a little apartment in the Village or TriBeCa, an efficiency, anything, just to have a place to spend the night, because if they were going to go out, if they were going to party, have a nice meal, that was the place to do it. Not that Westchester didn't have plenty of fine dining—and Putnam and Dutchess too—but the real life was down the line, in New York, and nobody would recognize him there. Running into Dudley was a fluke, that was all, and it could happen again or maybe never, not for years. He lifted the paper to the light, took a sip of coffee. Yeah, and what if it was Gina? What if it was Gina he ran into?

It was then—just then, just as he was holding that thought—that there was a rap at the door behind him, the door that gave out onto the lawn. This was a French door, eight panes and a grid of painted mullions. A flimsy thing, old and unsteady on its hinges, a door anybody could see through, anybody could enter. He started—he couldn't help himself—and when he swung round in the chair, a little lariat of coffee sloshed out of the mug to spatter the front of his shirt.

"Hey, man, I didn't mean to startle you"—it was Sandman, the door cracked open, his hand on the knob, his face hanging there in the void, and he was grinning, his eyes winnowed down to two sardonic points of light—"and I wouldn't want to be the one to criticize, but maybe you've had enough caffeine for one morning. I mean, you practically launched out of that chair."

He felt a tick of irritation. He'd been caught unawares, his guard down, caught fretting and worrying and wringing his hands like some paranoiac, some loser. He managed a tight smile as he reached for a wad of Kleenex to dab at the stains on his shirt. "Yeah," he said, "you're right—too much caffeine, who needs it?"

Sandman crossed the room, his big shoulders bunched under a theatrically ducking head, as if he were afraid he'd scrape the ceiling—and it *was* low, only six and a half feet from the floor to the exposed pipes overhead, but this was all exaggerated, all for show—and then settled one haunch down on the corner of the desk. "Right, but I wouldn't mind a cup of mud myself, if you could spare one. Or Natalia. If the pot's full, I mean. If you've got coffee, some of that Viaggio mocha maybe, maybe with real cream and brown sugar? Two lumps. Or honey. I could do honey." He lifted one eyebrow, stroked the strip of fur beneath his lip. "Because you know me, I wouldn't want to be the one to impose—"

He was doing his Sandman thing, always just this side of sincere. Everything a joke and every line delivered with a smile, as if he couldn't just walk upstairs and pour himself fifty cups of coffee if that was what he wanted, or move in permanently or borrow the car and take it to Maine or ask for a pint of blood and get it without stint or question. He was testing. Just testing to see if you were still with the program. And sometimes, like in Greenhaven, the program could be brutal. That smile, that Sandman smile, could freeze you at a hundred paces.

"Shit," Peck said, ignoring him. "I ruined my shirt."

"So buy another one."

"If you didn't come creeping around like some fucking meter reader or something—"

"Me? I'm not creeping. Shit, I just rolled over here with the top down because it is one fucking day out there, and then I slammed the door and *stamped* down that driveway like Paul Bunyan . . . look"—he raised one leg—"I'm wearing my boots, see that? I've been stomping and stamping all morning, man."

Peck was still in the chair, still dabbing at his shirt. He reached for a new wad of Kleenex. "I ran into Dudley," he said.

Sandman gave him a puzzled look.

"This guy I used to know, this kid—he used to work at the restaurant. I saw him over in Newburgh—he's waiting tables at a place over there."

Sandman let out a sigh. "Is that what it is? Is that what's bothering you?"

There was the whine of a motorbike going by on the road out front, the blat-blat-wheeze of a two-stroke engine shifting gears, some geek on his way to carve figure eights in the dirt down by the railroad tracks. They both looked up to follow the sound. "I don't know," Peck said. "I just don't want any hassles, that's all. Don't want any talk, you know?"

"You didn't give him your business card, did you? Your home phone? E-mail? Your bank account number?" Sandman pinched his shoulders and flashed both palms for emphasis. "No worries, come on, man—he doesn't even know your name." A long beat. He patted distractedly at his pockets, as if he were looking for a smoke, but since he didn't smoke anymore he let his hands drop to his lap. "So what did you tell him?"

"What do you think I told him?"

"All right, all right. Fuck it." Sandman got up from the corner of the desk and made a show of shaking out his legs, as if he'd been cramped in the middle seat of a jetliner for the last six hours. "What I wanted to know is, number one, where's my coffee? And number two, do you want to take a ride on the most beautiful day in the history of mankind with the top down and the breeze in your hair?"

"Where to—the library?" He was pushing himself up now, stretching. He took a final dab at the shirt and dropped the Kleenex and newspaper into the trash.

And here was the grin, opening wide. "Yeah, that was what I was thinking. Maybe cruise across the bridge over to Highland Falls or someplace like that, Monroe, Middletown, whatever—they got a library there, right?" Now there was another bike out on the road—or two more bikes, a whole mini-motocross thing going on, the summer morning sawed lengthwise and then sawed through again. Sandman shifted his weight, tented his fingers in front of his nose. "No big deal, nothing strenuous—use the hookups there for a couple hours, make some money, that sort of thing, you know. And then maybe lunch and a couple brews or a nice bottle of wine, I mean, if Natalia doesn't need you to haul furniture around or anything—how about that place up along 9W there where you sit outside way high up and look down on the whole valley?"

"Like gods?" He was smiling himself now too. The tension, whatever it was, had slid away from him like a wet coat in the foyer of a very good restaurant.

"That's right," Sandman said. "Like gods."

Sandman's latest scheme was built on a solid foundation of research ("Research I was doing while you were dicking around in California," he said, but with a grin, always with a grin), and it made sense both logically and financially. Instead of picking up IDs in an almost random way—off the Internet, out of the innards of the Dumpster, paying some kid three dollars a pop to skim credit card numbers at the gas station or the Chinese restaurant—Sandman was looking to target the rich and the super-rich and make the kind of connection that could pay the bills for a whole lifetime to come. "Why not?" he insisted. "If it works small, it works big, right?" Peck had to agree. He was ready to graduate. More than ready.

Because women found him interesting (and he found them interesting in turn; he'd been married something like four or five times), Sandman was able to extract certain small favors from the ones he felt especially close to. At the moment, he was simultaneously seeing two women Peck had never met, and never would meet, both of whom worked in the financial sector. One of them was some low-level functionary at Goldman Sachs—a secretary maybe—and the other, who was divorced and had two kids who were monumental pains in the ass, was an analyst at Merrill Lynch. What did they do for him? They provided stationery. And a legitimate address.

At the library, Sandman eased himself into a chair, booted up one of the computers and showed him how to access the files of individuals the Securities and Exchange Commission kept on its website as a public record. Then they migrated to separate ends of the row of computers and went to work. Once they were in possession of this information, they would use the stationery to request credit histories on selected individuals, and this would give them access to the brokerage account numbers. Then it was easy. Or it should be. Go to the Internet, transfer funds from existing accounts to the ones they'd set up elsewhere, let things rest a couple days and transfer them again, taking it deeper. Then close it all down, in and out, and nobody the wiser. And nobody hurt, except a couple of fat cats so fat they couldn't keep track of their own sweat trail. And they were crooks, anyway. Everybody knew that.

It was past two when Sandman came up behind him and laid a hand on his shoulder. He didn't know where the time had gone. Rather than print things out—and he was still a little paranoiac here—he was copying the files by hand into a notebook he'd brought along for that purpose, and he must have had a good hundred names already, but it was like fishing in a deep hole where they just won't stop biting. Or better yet, picking up nuggets off the floor of a gold mine. When have you got enough? When do you stop? He could have sat there all day and all night too.

"Hey, buddy, time for lunch, what do you say?"

Peck just stared at him, his eyes throbbing and the first faint intimation of a headache blowing like a sere wind through the recesses of his skull.

"Some fun, huh?"

"Yeah," he said, but he couldn't elaborate, not yet, still in thrall to the munificent and all-encompassing kingdom of information. He glanced to his right, where another library patron, a titanic black woman with a pretty face and a sweeping curtain of dreads, was maneuvering her mouse so delicately she might have been peeling a grape with one hand. She looked up then and smiled at him, a smile surfeited with sweetness and simple pleasure, and he smiled back.

"But it's okay, we got enough," Sandman was saying, his voice dropping to a whisper. "Tomorrow we type some letters and then we move, get in and out quick before anybody knows what hit them, because you know they're going to pull the plug on this, they got to. I mean, I can't believe we're the only ones—"

"Yeah," Peck said, his voice sounding unnatural in his ears as he turned back to him and logged off the computer. He was so charged up he could barely breathe. "I know what you mean."

Then it was back down what had to be one of the most scenic highways in the world, the road sliced right out of the side of the mountain like a long abdominal suture holding the two pieces together, and the view had never seemed so exotic to him, sailboats on the river like clean white napkins on a big blue tablecloth, the light portioning out the sky in pillars of fire. Sandman had the radio cranked, the car—a new yellow T-Bird he'd nicknamed "the Canary"—was taking the turns as if it were riding on air and the two of them were as high as lords and they hadn't touched a drop of anything yet. It was glorious. It was golden. It was good to be back.

They pulled up the long gravel drive just after six, the sun shuddering through the trees, the air heavy, saturated, offering up a feast of odors he'd forgotten all about, from the faint perfume of the flowers along the path (and what were they, daffodils?) to the one-part-in-a-billion offering of a skunk's glands and the fresh wet unchlorinated scent of rainwater in the barrel under the drainpipe to the wafting glory of top-quality angus beef hitting the grill on somebody's hibachi two or three houses over. He felt new-made. Felt unconquerable. It didn't hurt that he and Sandman had shared two bottles of the best wine on a pretty poor list in a pretty poor restaurant with the best view in the universe, because the second bottle, a Sauvignon Blanc chilled to perfection so that it went down cold enough to refresh you but not so cold that you couldn't pick up on its body and the subtle buttery oakiness of the cask it had resided in, lifted his quietly buoyant mood and made it soar. Was he drunk? No, not at all. His senses were awakened, that was all. The world was putting out its vibes, and he was receptive to them.

He hadn't given a thought to Natalia all afternoon, except to consider, somewhere in the back of his mind, that they'd have to go out to dinner because he really hadn't had time to plan anything. She had the car, so she would have been out shopping and she would have picked up the kid and probably taken her for a sandwich someplace. He was thinking alfresco, if the mosquitoes weren't too bad—there was a place in Cold Spring, right on the water. Maybe they would try that.

The first thing he noticed was that the sprinkler was going on the side lawn—Madison had been dancing through the revolving sheets of water in her shorts and T-shirt and he must have told her ten times already to be sure to shut the water down when she was done because it pooled there and made a mess of the lawn—and then he saw that Natalia, in her haste to haul her loot into the house, had left all four doors of the car wide open. Or no, it was only three. She was improving. Definitely improving. When Sandman pulled up beside the Mercedes and cut the engine, the first thing Peck did was get out and slam all three doors before ducking round the corner of the house to shut off the water and retrieve the sprinkler. In the process of which, he got his Vans wet.

Sandman was standing there in the driveway grinning at him, his aviator shades throwing light up into the trees. "Good to be home, huh?" he said. "The comforts of the hearth and all that."

"You mocking me?" Peck said, feinting as if to toss him the bright yellow disc of the sprinkler. "Because you set the record there, my friend. How many wives was it? I mean, I only knew Becky . . ."

"Yeah," and he was already turning to the house, "but I'm a bachelor now. But hey, you got any of that French Champagne left? Because I think we ought to be celebrating here, don't you?"

They were in the kitchen, and Peck was removing the foil from the neck of the bottle when out of the corner of his eye he spotted something anomalous on the kitchen counter, something that might have been a dollop of raw meat or— "What the fuck is that?"

Sandman was slouching against the refrigerator. He clipped his shades with two fingers and dropped them in his shirt pocket. "That? I don't know, it looks like shit to me, some kind of animal shit. Raccoons? You're not keeping raccoons here, are you?"

At that moment, the mystery revealed itself. A cat he'd never seen before—spotted like a leopard, with outsized paws and unhurried eyes—slid into the room, followed by a second one just like it. The two of them came right up to him, lifted their heads and began to yowl disharmoniously for food.

That set him off—he couldn't help himself, cat shit on the counter where he prepared the meals, where he kept his knives and his cutting board and his infuser and his grape-seed oil and extra-virgin cold-pressed Ravenna olive oil in the cut-glass decanter—and before he knew what he was doing, right there in front of Sandman, he lost it. His first kick—a reflex really—caught the near cat and sent it spinning into the cabinet across the room; the second kick caught only air. "Natalia!" he shouted, and the cats were gone now, vanished like smoke. "Goddamnit, *Natalia*!"

Sandman seemed to find the whole thing pretty amusing, holding the Champagne flute to his lips as Natalia, utterly unconcerned, drifted into the room in her own good time and stood there watching him, hands on hips. "You are shouting," she observed. "I do not like this shouting."

He was trying to keep it in, trying to keep his cool, trying to remember what he'd learned inside, what he'd learned from Sandman, but he couldn't. "What is this?" he hissed, outraged, gone already, and he pointed to the lump of soft wet excrement on the counter. "What the fuck do you call this? Huh?"

Small, slim, dark-eyed, her feet bare and her breasts heavy in a stretch top—she'd always claimed they were natural, but now it suddenly occurred to him how gullible he'd been to believe her—she shrugged and crossed the room to tear a wad of paper towels from the dispenser. "It is called shit," she said, bending to engulf the redolent little patty and drop it into the wastebasket beneath the sink. Then she extracted the disinfectant, sprayed the countertop and wiped it dry with another towel.

"The cats," he said. "I didn't, you didn't—"

"They are my Bengals," she said, sweeping his glass from the counter and emptying it in a gulp, Russian-style. "I have found them in an ad today, this morning, the male and the female. Don't worry," she added, grinning at Sandman, "you will love them. I know you will love them. But that is not the issue—"

"Issue? What issue? What are you talking about?"

"I am hungry. Madison is hungry." Another look for Sandman. "And you have been partying without me."

There were gulfs here, whole gulfs of unreason and bitterness opening up between them, and he was sour now, no question about it, but he threw in a peace offering: "I thought we'd go out."

She was at the refrigerator, her back to him, pouring herself a second glass. "I do not wish to go out. I wish to stay home. With my daughter." She turned to him now, her eyes burning, and he could see this went deeper than he'd thought—his mother, if she mentioned his mother again, he didn't know what he would do.

"We just got back," he said. "I didn't pick anything up. I thought we'd go out."

She ignored him, but she was playing to Sandman, trying to make him look bad.

"If you're so hot to eat at home, why don't you get off your lazy ass and do something for a change, huh?" He wasn't shouting, not yet—that wasn't his style—but he could feel himself slipping. The look of her infuriated him, the hard little nugget of her face, the way she gazed off into the distance and lifted the glass to her lips as if he didn't exist. His voice rose. He couldn't help himself. "Instead of shopping all the time. Instead of bringing home these fucking cats to shit on the counters, and where else are they shitting, I wonder? Tell me that."

Another shrug, more elaborate than the last. "I will

make the omelet, soup, anything. Tunafish. I will make tunafish." She moved to the cabinet, her jaw set, and began to shift pots and pans around.

That was when Sandman set his glass down on the counter. "You know, I just remembered I got to go. Really. I just remembered this was the night I was going to pick threads out of my carpet." The grin. The mockery. And then he clamped on his shades and was gone.

Everything was still for a moment, then Peck heard the car starting up in the driveway and somewhere beneath it, from Madison's room, the sound of the TV. He went to the refrigerator, took the bottle by the neck and poured himself a glass of Champagne. He was going to celebrate and he didn't give a good goddamn whether she liked it or not. She was at the stove now, turning up the heat under an empty pan. "Who you fooling?" he said.

When she turned round, her face was composed and when she spoke, finally, her voice was so soft he could barely hear it: "Nobody," she said. "I am fooling nobody. Because I am not your wife and I have never seen your mother."

Two days later, at eleven-thirty in the morning, he drove into Peterskill, though it was against his better judgment. Natalia was sitting beside him, leaning forward to study herself in the mirror on the back of the sun visor, sucking in her cheeks and rounding her lips in concentration as she reapplied mascara and eyeliner. She was wearing a shiny cobalt blue dress that clung to her figure, matching heels, stockings (though it must have been ninety degrees out already) and she'd deliberated for half an hour over taking along her silver nylon jacket, just, as she put it, to make a good impression, but finally decided against it. They'd dropped Madison at camp on the way and then driven the few miles into town along the old scenic road with its views of the mountains, the river and the humped gray domes of the nuclear power plant. Natalia had wanted to bring her daughter along—"She must meet her new grandmama because she will love her"—but he told her he didn't want to make his mother too nervous this first time with the kid around and she gave in because he was giving in to her and she was making an effort to be reasonable. And sexy. Very sexy. She'd climbed all over him the night before and he'd woken to her taking hold of his cock beneath the sheets and trailing her lips down his chest and abdomen in a flurry of hot sucking kisses. What he hadn't told her was that when he'd called his mother to tell her he was in town (but just briefly, briefly, just passing through) he'd asked her to see if she could set something up with Sukie. On the quiet.

His mother, for all her obvious flaws, had been good about that, staying a part of her granddaughter's life, and so Gina and her parents wouldn't be all that suspicious and as it turned out Gina's screaming hag of a mother was down with bursitis and Gina was working and the Bullhead was too busy making money to bother with babysitting and if Alice wanted to come and pick up Sukie for the day that was fine with them. So it was settled. Sukie would be there. And how did he feel about that? Strange, yes, but hopeful. It had been something like three years now and she would have had a chance to grow up and see things with a bit more perspective instead of just adhering to the party line Gina would have fed her. He was her father, after all, and he wasn't some jerk like Stuart Yan or whoever Gina was seeing now because how could she stay with Yan, how could she have even seen anything in him in the first place? But there'd be some other tool, some moron her father found on a jobsite someplace, somebody she'd met at work . . .

But they weren't Sukie's father, whoever they were. He was. And no matter what it cost him he was going to try to hook that up again.

"No," Natalia was saying, "you are not listening to me. I am not going to go there, to the house of your mother, unless I have Russian vodka to give to her—export, good Stolichnaya, no pepper flavor, no vanilla, no nothing—and flowers. Roses I will give her. White roses, three dozens, with the long stem. And you stop. You stop—there. There is a store."

"You don't understand," he said, his eyes locked behind his sunglasses, "but this town is a slum, nothing like that here. No florists, no liquor store that sells anything more than the cheap shit in the pint bottle. This is forty-ouncer territory, malt liquor, Miller High Life in the tall can."

They were in downtown Peterskill, sitting at a light. He'd already taken a little detour past Pizza Napoli—boarded up, scrawled over with graffiti, the big red-and-white sign he'd spent twenty-five hundred dollars on still in place, still proclaiming the optimism he'd felt back then—but he didn't say a word and Natalia, busy with her face, didn't even notice.

"Then you go right back out of this town to anyplace, I don't know, the mall, the supermarket, and a good quality of liquor store. I am telling you. I will not get out of this car."

It was all right. It was fine. In a way, it was a relief to flick on the blinker, hang a left and cruise up Route 6 a couple miles to the upscale mall because he was tentative about the whole thing, about exposing himself not only to whoever might be looking for him to glide up in front of his boyhood home and see his mother but about Sukie too. About that first instant, that beat of recognition. Would she come to him? Would she even know who he was?

At the mall, he parked at the far end of the lot and stayed in the car while Natalia trooped off in search of fatted calves and burnt offerings, but not before a colloquy that was like a KGB inquisition. ("And why will you not come?" she wanted to know. "I don't want to run into anybody, that's all." "Your ex-wife, is that who? Or some policeman? Is that it?" "Just anybody," he said. "I don't want to see anybody, okay? What's your problem? You see the store? There's the fucking store.") It took her a good hour or more, the pavement radiating heat till the whole vast oceanic lot shimmered and blurred in mirage and he ran the car for the air-conditioning till it began to overheat. He had no choice but to crank the windows down—and there was that smell again, the smell of his boyhood, of all his years here when he didn't know the rest of the world existed. People stalked by, wrapped up in the private resentments and narrowing back rooms of their own personalities, mothers and children, Jewish, Italian, dark hair, dark eyes, retirees, punks in their street racers and the girls they performed for, everything a performance.

It came to him then that he was being crazy, purely crazy. Nobody knew him here. Nobody would recognize him. He could stroll right in there and buy all the flowers they had, cases of vodka—drink it in the lot out of the open bottle. Sure. Beg for it. Beg for them to come and lock him back up for violating his parole and running out on his child support and the Harley and whatever else they could dig up. At least he'd got rid of the cardboard plates with the dealer logo and the chrome license-plate holder with Bob Almond's name on it and the Larkspur address because that was flying naked. If anybody wanted to know he had the temporary registration taped right there in the lower right-hand corner of the windshield as per California regulation and the plates were on the way—though he did have to get on the stick and see about registering the thing in New York. Driving without plates was just asking to get pulled over. Right, tomorrow. He'd do it tomorrow. And then it occurred to him—it hit him, hammered him with a kind of flaring panic that got his stomach fluttering all over again—that he had to get out of the car and go into that store, or one of those stores, because in his fog he hadn't thought to pick up anything, no toy, no doll, no candy, nothing, for his own natural sweet little daughter, for Sukie.

The house hadn't changed at all, at least as far as he could see—maybe some of the trees were taller, the weeds thicker along the edges of the lawn. He was standing there at the door of the car, caught in a shaft of sun that was like a spotlight, a box of Godiva chocolates in one hand, the flowers in the other, and the stuffed toy he'd bought for Sukie wedged under one arm, giving the place a quick scan as Natalia, running the brush through her hair one final time, made him wait. His father had always spent an inordinate amount of time and money on the place, putting on the addition with its brick fireplace, pouring a new concrete walk, repainting the exterior every three or four years and the trim every two, as if that could forestall the declining property values, and though he'd been twelve years dead now, the effort still showed. Decay had settled in, that was inevitable. And his mother certainly wasn't about to worry over it—as long as the roof didn't fall in on her she'd be happy to sit there in front of the TV with her bloated friends and a vodka and Collins mix and watch the water stains creep down around the fireplace where his father had screwed up the flashing despite the best of intentions.

"All right," Natalia was saying, and there she was, her shoulders squared and breasts outthrust, looking commanding and beautiful and throwing back her head so that her hair rose up in a fan of light and settled in perfect array on the perfect white skin of her bare shoulders. And the bones there. The exquisite bones. The scapulae, the muscles, the ligaments that flashed and moved under her skin. He had a moment of revelation that took him out of himself and he saw her as a sculptor might, some genius of line and form with a block of marble and a hammer ready to hand. "Well?" She was giving him a crucial look, a look that asked, *Am I beautiful? Am I ready? Do you want me?*

"Yeah," he said, "yeah, yeah, you look great," and she held out her arm for him and they turned to glide up the walk, the most natural thing in the world, everything in its place, and then he saw the arc described by the screen door as his mother leaned into it—his mother, with the nose he looked at in the mirror every morning and her hair gone silver and cut in a liquid fall at her jawbone so she looked like some stranger out of a silent movie—and the other figure there at her side, so small and delicate, with the unappeasable eyes and the blanched unforgiving face of the hanging judge.

Five

To EXPECT TRUTH, justice, the closure official victims were forever demanding on the little screen as the captioning played out dispassionately beneath their grim tight faces, to expect anything other than chaos and frustration, was delusory and she was foremost among the deluded. Life frustrates. Eternally frustrates. How could it be any different? That was what Dana was thinking as she stood in the rain on a stranger's lawn and watched Bridger poised at the top of the front steps, knocking at yet another door. When Frank Calabrese's fist had come down on the bartop with the pure uncontainable force of vengeance in all its shining potentiality, she was sure they'd come to the final turning at the final corner. He knew the thief. He named the thief. He knew where he lived. And ten minutes later they were at Peck Wilson's house—the house he'd grown up in, where his mother lived still—and she and Bridger had got out of the car in the rain, every individual blade of grass standing up stark and violently green, the twigs of the trees curled into claws and her heart about to explode, and then the knock at the door and the sky darkening and darkening till it was like night in the afternoon . . . and now, after all that? Nothing. Nobody home. No silent footsteps, no noiseless drop of the latch or presumptive squeal of the hinges, no face appearing behind the dark screen that was like the scrim of a confessional or the veil of maya. None of that. Nobody home.

She watched Bridger shift his weight from foot to foot. His face was drained of color, his upper lip and the flesh at the base of his nostrils drawn tight. He knocked again, waited, his head cocked and eyes lowered as if to concentrate his hearing. They exchanged looks, another moment elapsed, and then he signed, *I'm going to go around back,* and she felt strange all of a sudden, vulnerable, felt like a criminal herself, and darted a quick glance up and down the street. In the rain, and with nothing moving anywhere except the water in the gutters, she almost missed the figure on the porch next door. A faint rhythmic movement caught her eye and she looked up to see a woman there, a big-armed old woman in wire-frame glasses, tilting back and forth in a cane rocker and staring right at her. For an instant she was frozen—to shout out would be too obvious—and then, urgently, she was clapping her hands together to warn him. He swung round, his face blank. *There's somebody watching,* she signed.

Bridger looked in the wrong direction. He'd come down the steps now and was arrested there in the rain, his hair limp, the shirt she'd given him for his birthday—the retro look, broad vertical bands of gray and black with an outsized collar—hanging off him like a shower curtain. *Where?*

Her face was wet, water dripping from her nose. She felt ridiculous. The rain intensified, sweeping down the street in successive waves. *Over there,* on the porch, she signed, and then retreated for the car.

The interior of the car smelled as if it had been dredged up out of the ocean. There was mud on her shoes—a pair of Mary Janes in teal blue she'd picked up on sale two days ago—and her clothes clung wet to her skin. She felt a chill go through her and she slid into the driver's side and started the car to run the heater as Bridger, reduced by the rain and the layer of condensation frosting the windows, waved cheerily to the old woman and cut straight across the lawn, stepped over the line of low shrubs that divided the properties and stood just under the projecting roof of the porch to snap his jaws and wave his hands while the old woman snapped her jaws in return.

It took forever. Bridger was out there chattering away as if the skies were clear to the roof of the troposphere and the sun beaming down in all its glory, and the old lady, rocking in the shadow of her porch, chattered back. And what could they possibly find to talk about, the hearing? All this chattering. Peck Wilson: was he there or not? That was all that needed to be conveyed. She was frustrated, angry, shivering in her wet clothes as the heater, out of use since January, added its own furtive metallic reek to the mix. For a long while she stared out the window, first at Bridger, then at the house—an old place, two stories, with a mismatched addition and a stepped roof—where the man who'd invaded her life had played and worked and grown into the fullness of his thieving manhood.

She began chanting to herself, a little Poe, which always seemed to calm her—*And neither the angels in Heaven above, / Nor the demons down under the sea, / Can ever dissever my soul from the soul / Of the beautiful Annabel Lee*—and then she felt the car rock and Bridger was sliding into the seat beside her. "Well?" she said.

"Her name's"—he finger-spelled it—"Alice."

She was confused. "Whose? The old lady's?"

He swept both palms up over his face and into his hairline, then threw his head back and shook out the water like a diver emerging from a pool. "No," he said, turning to face her. "Wilson's mother. Peck Wilson's mother. Her name's Alice."

"Yes, but where is she?"

"The old lady—she was really nice, by the way—said she was away for the weekend, up at Saratoga or something. At the racetrack with her friend—not her son, her friend."

"You didn't—"

"No," he said. "I didn't tell her anything. I just wondered aloud, as a friendly neighbor, if she could tell me where Mrs. Wilson was because she was a friend of my mother's and my mother told me to look her up if I ever got to New York." He shrugged, toweling his hair with a sweatshirt he snatched out of the tumble of dirty clothes on the backseat. "The usual bullshit. She was old, that's all."

"And she believed you?"

Another shrug. "Does it really matter at this point?"

She gave him a long look, then dropped her eyes to put the car in gear. She was angry, frustrated, the whole thing boiling up in her—yes, it mattered, of course it mattered—and she accelerated too quickly, the back end shearing away from her on the slick roadway, everything out of kilter suddenly, and though she did manage to avoid the two parked cars on her right, the truck, the bright orange and white moving-truck with the U-Haul logo plastered along its gleaming steel midsection, was another story altogether.

Afterward, her most vivid recollection of the accident wasn't the way her car looked with its trunk radically compressed and jammed up under the belly of the truck as if some negligent giant had been at play with it, but standing there in the rain half a block from Peck Wilson's house—from the thief's house—while a joyless policewoman from the City of Peterskill Police Department tried to put her through the drunk test and Bridger waved his hands and flailed his lips at the bare-chested bodybuilder in shorts and flip-flops who'd rented the truck and left its front end projecting halfway across the street. "I'm not drunk," she kept saying, "I'm deaf. Deaf. Don't you understand?" And the policewoman kept saying, "Spread your legs, hold out your arms, close your eyes, touch your nose."

People had emerged from their houses up and down the block and gathered under umbrellas to savor the spectacle, barefooted little girls in shorts and summer dresses knotted behind the neck, their bulging mothers and smirking brothers, an old man in a straw hat. Dana wasn't hurt, nor was Bridger. Thankfully. But she'd been driving and she was the focus of attention, all those shallow shifting eyes judging her, the drunk—or no, worse than a drunk, a freak, a babbler, someone to instinctively shy away from. She knew what they were thinking, knew what they'd say over their hot dogs and coleslaw at dinner that night, a passing reference, the recollection of a little anomaly in an otherwise uniform day: "But she looked just like anybody else, pretty even—until she opened her mouth."

The policewoman—she was of mid-height, Dana's age, with a rangy, asymmetric build, thick glasses in severe frames, eyes that could have been pretty with a little makeup—finally seemed to come round. Bridger had shifted his attention away from the man with the U-Haul and had stepped in to enlarge her understanding of what Dana was trying to communicate, while her partner, an older guy with fading eyes and hair the color of a lab rat's, hunched over his pad and began writing up the accident report. Dana watched them go back and forth, Bridger nearly as expressive as one of the deaf himself. "The truck isn't where it's supposed to be," Bridger was saying. "They should never have parked it there in the first place." The policewoman—Dana saw now that she had a nametag clipped above her breast pocket: *P. Runyon*—didn't seem particularly interested. To her it must have seemed an open-and-shut case, so routine it would have been a snooze but for the spice of the California plates and Dana herself— slick roads, excessive speed, the truck parked and locked and on the other side of the road nonetheless.

She turned abruptly to Dana and said something. What was it? Insurance? Yes, she had insurance—she fumbled through the glove box, her hands trembling, and finally produced the papers—and no, she didn't need to go to the hospital, she was perfectly all right, thank you. P. Runyon didn't seem satisfied. She stalked around in the rain, the water beading on the polished uppers of her standard-issue shoes, alternately glaring at Dana and turning her back on her to sweep the onlookers as if to assure them that things were in hand here, despite appearances, and that they'd all better look out and take a step back or they'd wind up with their cars stuffed under a truck too.

Then it was the tow truck, the crowd dissipating and the patrol car slithering off down the street, a spate of small talk in the solid high cab of the truck and finally the garage with its ancient chemical smells and the once-white shepherd-mix curled up on the floor. The repair estimate? No way to tell yet, but it looked as if the rear axle stub was broken— "Do you see that," the service manager asked, pointing to where her car crouched against a low wall covered with ivy, "the way the wheels are canted like that?"—and of course there was going to be some fairly extensive body work, both back fenders, trunk, bumper, replace the rear window. By the time it was over, by the time they took a cab to the train station and caught the next southbound train and she was pressed safely up against the window and looking out on the pocked gray hide of the river, it felt as if a week had passed in the course of a single day—and it would be a whole lot longer than that, two and a half weeks, to be exact, before she would get her car back. "And that's night and day," the service manager told Bridger over the phone at her mother's while Bridger cupped the receiver and translated, "night and day. A real rush job. Because I know how anxious the little lady must be to get back to California."

In the interval, she tried to relax. Here was an opportunity to spend some time with her mother, work on her book, think things out—and if she was going to teach again she'd better clean up her CV and start making some inquiries, too late at this juncture for a hearing position, and certainly not at the college level, but there were deaf schools in Riverside and Berkeley she might try. If she did want to stay on the coast. She wasn't so sure anymore, wasn't sure about anything. Two months ago she was in love, blissfully involved in her research and her book, secure in her job at the San Roque School and beginning to feel the pull of the environment—mojitos on an outdoor patio in January, a bugless summer, the incalculable gift of the vernal light as it glanced off the stucco walls and red tile roofs of the buildings on campus and rode out to sharpen over the waves. Now she didn't know. Now she was living with her mother, without a car or a job. It scared her how quickly everything had turned against her.

She was being paid through the end of the summer and she'd been issued new credit cards, so she was all right there, at least for a while. Her credit was still a mess, though—she couldn't begin to imagine the depth and breadth of the heap of threatening letters and demand-payment notices piling up in one of those heavy plastic mail carriers in the back room of the San Roque post office, each one of which would have to be addressed at some point. The onus was on her, whether that was her signature on the credit card slip or not—and what did they care? They wanted their money.

Period. The victims' assistance woman had gone into dark mode when she talked about the greed of the banks and credit card companies—*Easy Credit, Instant Credit, No Refusamos Crédito*—and how pretty soon everybody would have to have some sort of implant, like the ones they inserted up under the napes of cats and dogs, to prove their identity. Bridger had said, "Just like *1984*," and the woman gave them a blank look.

But the mail. The mail was a problem. They'd left San Roque in such a hurry she hadn't really planned beyond the moment and so she'd put a four-week vacation hold on her mail delivery. She supposed she should have it forwarded, but that would be a kind of defeat, a giving-in to her mother and the easy way out—and she really didn't want to deal with the mess of her finances. The mail was nothing but bad news, and right now—on a muggy Tuesday afternoon a week after the accident, as she sat at the desk in the spare room of her mother's overstuffed claustrophobe's nightmare of an apartment and fiddled with the knobs on the air conditioner, hoping for just a degree or two of refrigeration—she wanted to focus on other things. Like her book. The laptop was propped open before her, giving back the words she'd dredged up out of herself, the imposture they represented, the incremental silent means of recasting her own uncertain self in Victor's image, in Itard's, but they were old words that slipped and elided and clashed like mortal enemies till she couldn't look at them. "*Wild Child,*" she said aloud, just to feel the buzz of the words on her lips. "*Wild Child,* by Dana Halter," she said, as if it were an incantation. She repeated herself over and over again, but it was no use. Because in her mind, a husky deep contrarian voice kept saying, *Peck Wilson, Peck Wilson, Peck Wilson.*

She felt the door open behind her, her old trick, and turned to see her mother and Bridger standing there in the doorway, looking apologetic. *Can we come in?* her mother signed clumsily.

"Yeah, sure," she said, grandly waving them in. She felt a quick sharp stab of embarrassment. Had they stood there listening? Had they knocked? Had they heard her rehearsing the name of her book? And her own name? Had she said "Peck Wilson" aloud?

Almost done? Bridger signed. His face was soft, open, and she could have read his expression as loving and supportive, but he wasn't fooling her. This was a guilty look, edged with alarm, a look complicit with her mother's—they *had* heard. An irrational anger started up in her: her own lover, her own mother.

"Yes," she said. "Or no, not really. I'm just getting nowhere, that's all. Spinning my wheels, right?" And what was that, a racing term? Or was it when you were stuck in the snow or the mud? "Why, what's the plan?"

Her mother had taken to Bridger in a way Dana would have found gratifying under other circumstances, making it her sworn duty to show him every tourist site in the city, from the Statue of Liberty to MoMA to the American Indian Museum, Ground Zero and Grant's Tomb. She'd even taken him on the Circle Line tour around the Battery and up the East River, through the lively corrugations of Spuyten Duyvil and back down the Hudson on the West Side while Dana was—ostensibly—working. Her mother's smile strained till it blew up in her face. "I don't know," she said, "we were just thinking we might go to a matinee, something light—a musical, maybe. Bridger's never been to a show and it would be a shame if he—"

"We don't have to go," he said, slumping his shoulders and fixing his smile, and of course what he meant was that they did have to go or he would never get over it. "Can you handle it?"

"What do you mean 'can I handle it'? It's not a revival of *Children of a Lesser God*, is it?"

They both laughed. But these were strained laughs—she could tell by the way their eyes flashed at each other like those kissing fish in an aquarium. "We were thinking maybe *The Lion King*," he said. "Or *Rent*, if we can get into it."

"*Equus*," she said. "What about *Equus*?" She was being cruel, but she couldn't help herself. She was remembering the first time she'd ever seen the National Theater of the Deaf, when she was a freshman at Gallaudet, the year Deaf Power came into its own and swept the university. For the first time in Gallaudet's history, all the way back to its founding in 1864, a deaf president was installed after the entire student body took to the streets to protest the naming of yet another hearing chief executive. They marched in the streets for a week, chanting "Down with Paternalism!" and "We Are Not Children!" "No More Daddies," they shouted, "No More Mommies!" The wind stung her eyes. The cops came on their silent shuddering horses. She'd never felt more caught up and passionate in her life. And when the curtain opened on the play on that final night, the night of their triumph, the house was full to the rafters and she had to find a seat on the floor, everyone holding their breath in anticipation. It took her a moment to understand: this was no parade of mimes, no revival of *Death of a Salesman* or *The Glass Menagerie* in dumb show, but a new play, commissioned and written in their own language, the language of their new president. She exchanged a look with the girl sitting next to her, her roommate, Sarah, whose eyes flew back to the stage while her hands lay motionless in her lap, and she began to breathe again.

And now they wanted her to sit through *The Lion King*?

"No," she said, "I think I'll just stay here and kill myself instead."

"Come on," Bridger said, and when he put a hand on her shoulder and ran it up the back of her neck, she pulled away from him. "It'll be fun."

"You go," she said.

Her mother's face hovered over her. "Lunch?" she offered. "Why don't we all just go to lunch then? What do you say?"

"No, really," she said. "You go."

On the day they picked up the car, the day she planned to sign over the insurance check to the man in the garage, retrieve her keys and then, no matter what Bridger or her mother or anyone else might have to say about it, go directly to Peck Wilson's house in the hope of spotting the Mercedes there in the driveway, the sun seemed to rise right up out of the front room of her mother's apartment, already riding high and scorching the earth by the time she and Bridger arrived, on foot and sweating, at Grand Central. Bridger had talked her into walking—for the exercise, of course, but there was no reason to be wasting money on cabfare when neither of them had a job and their credit was mutually shot. She bought three plastic bottles of water in the one-liter size while Bridger saw to the bagels in the brown paper bag and picked up the *Times* and the *Daily News* and then they settled into the Metro North car like reverse commuters. The other passengers looked bored and enervated, nobody talking, and that pleased her in an odd way, their silence layered over hers. She was imagining the other sounds—the rattling of the undercarriage, the hiss of the automatic doors—when Bridger tapped her on the arm and asked for one of the bottles of water.

She watched him unscrew the plastic cap and hold the bottle to his lips until he had to come up for air. The sweat stood out on his upper lip and his hair had thickened with it. "It's hot," he mouthed. "Wow, it's hot." He handed her half a bagel, neatly sliced in two. Outside, beyond the moving windows, the river looked as if it had just been refilled with pure clean tap water instead of the usual gray-green bilge. "You know those pictures of—?" he said, but she didn't catch the end of it. A place name, long word.

"What?"

"Afghanistan," he said, spelling it out. "From the war, like, when was it—couple of years ago? Did you notice that every mujahedin carried three things into battle with him—a Kalashnikov rifle, a rocket launcher and a liter bottle of Evian, just like this?"

"Yeah," she said, "yeah, it was funny. Just goes to show you what you value when you have nothing."

"Right, you have nothing, no water, no trees, nothing but rocks. That's why you bomb the World Trade Center. That's why you carry weapons—so you can take what you want."

"Like Peck Wilson."

He gave her a look. The train lurched over a bad section of track, jolting the bagel he'd been gesturing with. She watched it float up against the backdrop of the Hudson, tightly clamped in the grip of his floating fingers. "I guess," he said. "Yeah."

"Do you think he has a gun?"

He shrugged. "He's an ex-con, isn't that what Frank Calabrese said?"

"So yes?"

"Which is all the more reason to stay away from him. I mean, look what it's got you, what it's got us—ruined credit, running all over the country, no money, no job, and now your car."

"But we are going to drive by, right? Or maybe park around the block and just walk by in case he recognizes my car"—he was saying something but she wasn't watching—"just walk, that's all. And if we see him, or the car—the car would be the key—we call the police."

"Oh, yeah," he said, "yeah. They've been real friendly and understanding, haven't they?"

She felt that burr of irritation again, couldn't help herself. She made an effort to control her voice, breathe in, breathe out. "I'm not giving up," she said, and she had no idea what she sounded like. "Not now. Not when we're this close."

It took him a minute. He turned his head to gaze out on the river and the distant fractured cliffs of the Palisades, then swung back to her, his eyes compact and hard. "That's all we're going to do," he said. "Just walk."

It was quarter past eleven when they arrived at the Peterskill station and it must have been a hundred already, or close to it. Bridger wanted to walk to the garage—"It's only like a mile," he said, and she said, "No, it's more like two, two and a half." The station was right on the water, but there was no breeze and the sun ricocheted up into their faces. Cars pulled in and out of the lot, moving with slow deliberation, their windshields glazed with light. A knot of people crept past them with their shoulders slumped, borne down under the weight of the heat and trailing suitcases and elastic children. To make it worse, something was rotten, something dead along the shore, and the reek of it was calibrated to a persistent smell of frying from the café adjoining the depot. For a long moment they both just stood there glaring at each other until finally she said, "We're taking a cab and I'm not going to argue about it." And she couldn't help adding a little sting to it. "It's my money, anyway."

At the garage, everybody was moving in slow motion, from the mechanics to the service manager who went over the bill with them to the secretary who typed it up and had Dana sign here and here and here. She and Bridger made a show of looking over the car, which had just come back from the body shop that very morning, and she wondered about a ripple effect in the paint you could only see in a certain light and from a certain angle, but the service manager assured her that there was nothing wrong and even produced a pristine high-quality cotton-fiber rag and buffed it for her. "You see?" he said. "What'd I tell you?" And while she watched his lips and face and understood what he was saying, she couldn't see any appreciable difference—the ripples were still there. But it was hot. Mortally hot. And she didn't say anything.

Bridger kept telling her to make sure everything felt right with the rear end and she put it in reverse and jerked back a few feet, nearly running over the once-white dog that lay comatose in the shade of the retaining wall, and then she was out on the street, feeling liberated. She had her car back. She was mobile. She could go anywhere she wanted, up the coast to Maine or back across the country to San Roque, or even down to Gallaudet, to show Bridger the campus where she'd spent something like nine years of her life. Or to that street where the moving van was, or had been—Peck Wilson's street.

Bridger poked her. "How does it feel?"

"Fine." It was a car—how should she know how it felt? It negotiated the bumps and potholes, responded to the pressure of her hands on the wheel, took her where she wanted to go.

"It's not pulling, is it?"

She didn't answer. There was hardly any traffic, a dead town on a dead day—a Saturday—and she was looking for a stretch of road where she could open it up a bit, feel the breeze tear through the windows and take hold of her hair, but there were just city streets and hills and stoplights. "You feel like lunch?" she asked, turning to him. "Before we— before we take our little walk? Our little stroll? Hmm? Lunch? Does that sound good?"

They found a diner in the middle of town, a real authentic one—*echt*, wasn't that the word?—fashioned from an old railway car, and sat there in the stultifying heat with their clothes sticking to the leather-backed seats while they ordered sandwiches they barely touched and downed glass after glass of pre-sweetened iced tea. Both doors were open and an old upright fan was going in the corner. There were flies everywhere, legions of them gang-piling on the window ledges and drifting haplessly in and out the doors. She'd ordered tuna on rye, not the best choice for a tropical day in a place where the refrigeration might be suspect, which was why Bridger had said, "I'm sticking with the bacon on a hard roll," but it wasn't bad—it was good, even. And when the waitress, big in the hips, cheery and efficient, brought her face into view and asked, "What's the matter, honey, is everything all right or is it just the heat?," she smiled and said, "Just the heat."

In fact, she was feeling good. Feeling lucky. This was the day, she knew it, and in the cramped cubicle of the ladies' that was no bigger than a shower stall, she reapplied her lipstick in the scratched-over mirror and gave herself a big relaxed smile, a beautiful smile, the smile her mother always said would be the making of her—"With that smile," she'd say, "with that face, you'll go anywhere," as if a smile could make up for her fried cochlea or disarm the stranger who looked at her as if she'd been just let out of the zoo. But here it was, her beautiful smile, consummate and full-lipped, staring back at her from the mirror, the very smile she was going to lay on Peck Wilson when they were leading him away in chains.

They didn't want to risk driving by the house, so she took a parallel street and found a spot to park under a big over-spreading maple in a long row of them. Bridger climbed out of the car and stretched as if they'd been driving for hours instead of minutes. He was wearing a T-shirt from one of the Kade films, red on black, featuring the hero's outsized head in some sort of leather helmet, and though The Kade was meant to look menacing she found the representation faintly ridiculous. He looked constipated. Looked weak and old and at the mercy of his agents. "Nice T-shirt," she said. "Did I tell you how much I love it?"

He grinned from over the roof of the car. "Yeah," he said. "You did. But The Kade is my man, you know that. If it weren't for him Radko'd probably be out of business by now."

"I hear you," she said, and they both laughed. She was wearing a T-shirt herself, also black, emblazoned with the name of a band she liked. Or would like to like. And a pair of shorts, loose-fit but not nearly as baggy as Bridger's. Despite the heat she had on her running shoes—or better yet, walking shoes. Her first impulse that morning was to go with something open-toed, sandals, flip-flops, but she'd caught herself: you never knew what the day would bring or just how involved this little stroll was going to turn out to be. The thought of it, coming back to her now as she tucked her purse under the seat and locked the car door, made her stomach clench. "You have your cell?" she asked.

Bridger whipped it from his pocket and held it aloft.

"Okay," she said, "then I guess we're ready."

The houses here weren't as dominating as the peeling

Victorians closer to the center of town, but they seemed to be from the same general period—they were just scaled down, as if the people with more modest incomes had wound up here while the brewers and factory owners and bankers expressed themselves more grandly. And conveniently. Or maybe she was all wrong. She didn't know much about architecture, and she would have been the first to admit it. But certainly generations upon generations had lived here, unlike in California, and she could see that reflected in the grim stature of most of the houses, gray and nondescript but still standing after all these years.

They turned right at the corner and there, at the far end of the block, was Peck Wilson's street—what was it called again? Division? Division Street? That was fitting, wasn't it? Or how about Jailhouse Road? Thieves' Alley? Hadn't she seen a street on the map called Gallows Hill Road? That's where he should have lived, the son of a bitch, Gallows Hill Road. She was going to mention that to Bridger, lighten his mood, but she saw that his eyes were fixed on the corner ahead and he'd unconsciously quickened his stride. She skipped a couple of steps to catch up to him, then took hold of his hand and squeezed it hard and moved in to match him stride for stride.

A car went up the street and turned at the corner, leaving a taint of exhaust heavy on the air. Two kids on bicycles chased each other up the opposite sidewalk. The leaves of the trees curled in on themselves. And then they were on the street itself, Peck Wilson's street—an abrupt right at the corner and there was the house where the U-Haul had been parked, and there, across the street and half a dozen houses down, partially obscured by the shrubs and trees and the line of cars parked along the curb, was the house they'd come to visit. She felt Bridger tense at her side, both of them straining to see as they strolled hand in hand up the walk, each step bringing them closer. Bridger stripped off his sunglasses—Peck Wilson's sunglasses—as if to see better. They were directly across from the house now, trying to act casual, but there was nothing to see as far as she could tell.

"What do you think?" Bridger said.

They were still walking, moving past the house and heading for the end of the block, the sun lying in stripes across the sidewalk ahead of them, somebody's sprinkler going, a dog showing its teeth from behind a rusted iron fence. "I don't know," she said, feeling all the air go out of her, "it looks closed up to me."

He had his shoulders thrown back, his head cocked in a way she recognized: he was agitated, keyed up, almost twitching with all that testosterone charging through him. She remembered a lecture she'd attended in college—an animal behaviorist, a woman who'd worked with the chimps of Gombe and the bonobos in the Congo, showed a film of the males working themselves up in threat display, and all the students, all of her deaf compatriots, had burst into laughter. They didn't need to go to Africa to study body language—they saw it every minute of every day.

"Yeah, but all these houses look closed up," he said, bringing his face so near she could smell the residue of the bacon on his breath, "because everybody's just hunkered down in front of the TV with the air conditioner going full blast. We need to"—but she missed the rest of it because they were crossing the street at the corner now, nice and square, nice and rectilinear, up on the far sidewalk and swing left, the cars idling at the light with their windows rolled up and their own air conditioners delivering the goods. The heat rose up off the pavement and hit her in the face as if she were walking through a wall and letting it crumble round her.

And then everything suddenly speeded up, fast forward to the end, the sun, the trees, the sidewalks and cars all dissolving in a blur that crystallized in the rear bumper of a wine-red Mercedes shooting past them, the right turn blinker on and a little girl's limp doll pressed to the window in back.

PART V

One

HE WAS SO BOUND UP in the moment, so intent on the faces at the open door and hyper-aware of Natalia preening and swelling at his side, so busy struggling with the stuffed toy and the candy and the flowers and fumbling toward the semi-coherent murmur of the half-formed phrases on his lips, that he didn't see it coming. Didn't look over his shoulder. Didn't clear his sight lines. Didn't watch his back. "Hi, honey," he was going to say, "remember me?" And would she come to him? Would her face open up the way it used to when he was the heart and soul and dead glowing center of her universe or was she going to freeze him out? And his mother. His mother with her new haircut and big swaying gauzy blouse that bunched at her hips and gave way to the trailing skirt and the pipestems of her legs. "Hi, Mom," he was going to say, "this is Natalia. My fiancée. My fiancée, Natalia." And Natalia would be giving Sukie the fish eye, putting two and two together, working herself up over her own daughter's exile at that overpriced camp at the end of the dirt road that left a tattered blanket of dust clinging to the car every day and yet drawing all her strings tight to make a good impression in front of his mother and still riding high on the current of those three soaring syllables, *fiancée*. There was all that. All that and the heat too.

He'd just shifted the toy from his right arm to his left— it was ridiculous, the biggest thing in the store, a life-size stuffed replica of a sled dog, replete with the blue glass buttons of its eyes—to take hold of Natalia's hand and lead her up the walk, when there was another face there, two faces, hovering suddenly at the margin of his peripheral vision. His and hers. He cut his eyes right and there was a single lost beat in there somewhere before he felt the shock knife through him. It was as if he were ten years old all over again, thrilling to his first slasher flick, no children under sixteen allowed without parent or guardian, the theater gone silent, the maniac loose—and then the scream, stark, universal, collaborative. Rising.

The stuffed dog fell to the ground. He let go of Natalia's hand even as she said, "What, what is it?" and turned to follow his eyes and see them there sprung up out of the concrete walk not twenty feet away like figures out of a dream, a bad dream, terminally bad, the worst, and though he was cool, always cool—Peck Wilson, never ruffled, never at a loss, never weak—he couldn't help himself now.

He didn't stop to think how they'd come to track him here, how they were like parasites, how they wouldn't let go and could never learn no matter how many times he taught them, because this moment was beyond thought or resentment or fear, a moment that broke loose inside of him in a sudden ejaculation of violence. Ten steps, too quick to blink, the heart of the panther his tae kwon do instructor always talked about beating now in place of his own, his hands doing their thing independent of his will, perfect balance, and the fool was actually coming to him, flailing his arms like a fairy. And cursing—"you motherfucker" and the like—as if he had breath to waste. The first blow—the *sonnal mok anchigi*, knifehand strike to the neck—rocked him, and then two quick chops to drop his arms, ride back on the left foot and punch through the windpipe with the right.

Somebody screamed. The heat ran at him, all-encompassing, a sea of heat at flood tide. Another scream. It wasn't Natalia screaming, it wasn't his mother or Sukie either. This was like nothing he'd ever heard, ugly, just ugly. And there was the bitch emitting it, right there watching Bridger Martin jerk on the grass and clutch at his own throat as if he wanted to throttle himself, two quick kicks to the ribs to make it easier on him, and it was just the two of them now. Just him and Dana Halter, in her shorts and T-shirt, her face twisted with the insoluble conundrum of that unholy voice wedded to that hard moment. And then, as if it had all been decided beforehand, he went for her and she dodged away and they were both running.

There was nothing in his mind but to lash out, hurt her, bring her low, crush her, and he almost had her in the first furious rush, a snatch at her trailing arm and the fine articulated bones of her flashing wrist, but she was too quick for him, and the fury of his failure—*the bitch, the bitch, the relentless bitch*—burst behind his eyes in a pulse of irradiated heat so that he was blind to everything but the tan soles of her pumping shoes and the fan of her retreating hair. He burned, burned. Every cord in his body snapped to attention. He was in shape, good shape, but so was she, running for her life, running to beat him, humiliate him, wear him down, and they'd gone the length of the block and she was still ten feet beyond him.

Up ahead, the light was turning red. He saw it and calculated his chance because she would have to pivot to go left or swing right and cross the street with the green and that would slow her a fraction of a second, just long enough—but she surprised him, hurtling straight through the intersection without even turning her head, and the blue pickup, coming hard, had to swerve to avoid her and he was the one who lost a step, dodging round the rear bumper while the driver cursed and the horn blared. What he should have done, if he'd been thinking, was double back and pack Natalia in the car and make scarce before somebody called the cops, but he wasn't thinking. She was fleeing, he was chasing. He was going to run her down by the end of the next block, that was what he was going to do, run her down and have his sixty seconds with her, payback, and then he'd be gone.

He could hear the torn sheet of her breathing, the slap of her feet pounding at the concrete walk. Her shoulders rocked, her hair jogged as if it had come loose from her scalp. And more: he could smell her, the torched ashes of her fear, the sweat caught under her arms and running like juice between her legs. He gained a step, but the heat rose up to put two hands against his chest and push at him even as he tried to close the gap and slam her to the pavement from behind. Faces drifted by behind the windshields of the cars easing down the street, there was somebody on a porch, the thump of the bass line from a hidden boombox, voices, music, the buzz of a cicada. The blood shrieked in his ears. He wasn't even winded.

At the next corner, the car—a white Chevy van—was moving too fast, gunning on the yellow to make the light, and the woman at the wheel hit her horn, laid into it, but this was a game of chicken now and he never hesitated. He had her, actually had his hand locked in her hair, the van sliding by like a bull brushing the cape, when the other car, the one he hadn't seen, plunged in on the bumper of the van. That put an end to it. Where there had been nothing but air the strangest sudden act of prestidigitation interposed a plane of steel, chrome and safety glass, and they both hit it and went down to the smell of scorched rubber.

. . . . .

Two black dudes. Young, angry-looking, scared. People had run crazy right into the side of their car, and they were smelling the scorched rubber too, slamming out of both doors while the traffic froze and Dana Halter jumped up like a rabbit and he jumped up too, absolutely capable of anything, *anything*. But then the siren whooped and the lights flashed and the patrol car was right there, sliding in to block off the intersection, and there was nowhere to go. For one instant he stared into her eyes, brown eyes, the black irises dilated with her fear and now her hate and now her triumph, and the cops were getting out of the cruiser, a tight-assed woman in schoolteacher glasses and an old guy, looking grim. Peck just stood there, sweating, trying to catch his breath. His left arm stung where he'd slammed it against the car and his pants were torn at the knee. He could have run, and wound up in jail—or shot. But he didn't. He went deep and he focused and the cool descended like a long sheet of windblown rain because he saw the look on the lady cop's face when she saw Dana, the flash of recognition there, and already one of the black dudes was starting in, overexcited, hysterical, his voice rising up and rising up until you could hear nothing else.

"What's the trouble here?" the lady cop said, ignoring the black guy, looking from Dana to Peck and then settling there, on him. She had both her hands on her belt, as if it weighed more than she did. He knew the type. All bluff. And bullshit.

"I don't know, Officer," he heard himself say over the jabber of the black dude, "it was this lady"—he indicated Dana—"I think she's crazy or maybe retarded or something? She ran out into the street like she was out of her mind and maybe she was trying to commit suicide, I don't know, and I just tried, well, I grabbed for her, I mean, just out of instinct—"

The bitch cut in now. Her hair was stuck to her face, both her knees scraped and bleeding. She looked the part, looked demented, looked like they'd just let her out of the pyscho ward. She talked too fast, too loud, spinning out something unintelligible. "He, he—" was all he got. She was pointing at him. "Chase me," she said. "I mean, chas*ed* me."

"Crazy lady ran right into the side of my car—they's a dent there in the back door, you can look for yourself, Officer, and, I mean, it's not me. She ran right through the light and she didn't even look one way, I mean, she never even turned her neck—"

"He's a thief," the bitch said, jerking her arms and stamping her foot in emphasis. "He, he—" and the rest was gone, just gibberish.

The old cop was there now, fumbling with his little pad and tamping his ballpoint pen against his open palm as if it held the key to the situation. Peck waited for him to look up, then glanced from him to the lady cop and shrugged, as if to say, *Hey, she's a mental case, can't you see that? Could it be any clearer? Just listen to her.*

He had maybe sixty seconds, two minutes max, and then there'd be somebody coming up the street from two blocks down, from his mother's house, and he prayed it wouldn't be Natalia, prayed she'd have the sense to get in the car and disappear. He listened as the bitch went on, her voice settling now, getting clearer, and he gave the lady cop an indulgent smile. "Maybe she's on drugs or something," he said. "I don't know. I'm just a guy on my way down to get the paper—I mean, if she wants to die . . . And you know something else," he said, and he pointed at the black dude now, the driver, "this guy was running the red light. Yeah, what about that?"

That stirred the brew. This man—he was in his twenties, wearing a basketball jersey and a doo-rag—was clearly not going to take this kind of shit, and his voice went up an octave and his buddy joined in even as the lady cop focused on the bitch and a whole crowd of people materialized. He saw his chance. Everyone was shouting, even the police-woman, trying to assert herself, apply some order, and he took two steps back and found himself on the fringe of the crowd. Two more steps and he was a bystander. Then he turned his back and ducked down the driveway of the near-est house and went up and over the fence in back, dropped down into the alley and took off running.

He must have gone three or four blocks, the change ringing in his pockets and his lungs on fire, before he slowed to a walk. A walk was better. A walk was just right. Because no-body would have mistaken him for a jogger in his taupe silk suit and checkerboard Vans and if he wasn't a jogger then why was he running? Especially with that siren coming in over the trees like a jet plane on fire and caroming off the windows and spoiling the ball game on the radio? He forced himself to keep it under control, though his heart was banging and he'd sweated right through his clothes and he must have looked like shit with his eyes staring and his pants torn at the knee and his arms swaying as if he was some moron going door to door with magazine subscrip-tions or vacuum cleaners. But he didn't have a vacuum cleaner or a briefcase or a sheaf of order forms or anything else. Just sweat. And torn pants.

People were sitting on their front stoops or in little patches of yard with their cooking grills and plastic lawn chairs, and what day was it, anyway? Saturday. Cookout, clambake, cold beer in the cooler. Two kids squatted in the shade of a street tree, cupping a cigarette. They both glanced up and gave him a look—they knew who belonged on their block and who didn't—but he just put his head down and kept walking, angling toward the river, one block south, one block west, repeating the pattern till the sirens began to fade. He guessed somebody must have called the ambulance for Bridger Martin—and the cops too, because there'd been another siren going there for a while, and once they sorted things out they'd be looking for him. Without breaking stride, he fished out his shades, then shrugged out of the jacket and threw it over one shoulder. When he turned the next corner, he was on a street that dipped steeply down toward the train station—there was a bar there he knew, an old man's bar in an old hotel that had been around forever—and he figured he'd slip in there where it was quiet and dark and nobody would even look up from their drinks. Order a beer. Sit at the bar. He'd be safe there and he'd have time to think things out.

He needed to call Natalia's cell, that was his first priority, but when he patted down his pockets his own cell was missing and it came to him that he'd left it on the dash of the car—he could see it there, just as if he were re-running a video. And why was it there on the dash and not in his pocket? Because he'd called her from the car in the parking lot at the mall to tell her he was going to run into the toy store a minute because he had to get something and she'd said, "For Madison?" and he'd said, "Maybe," and she'd said, "That's sweet. You're sweet. And I am sorry to be so late for you and I will be only one minute more."

Right. But where was she now? Did the police have her? Were they asking her for ID? Asking about her immigration status? Asking who had assaulted Bridger Martin even while she told them it was Bridger Martin as if she were reliving some sort of Abbot and Costello routine? And who was the car registered to? And where did she live? And then there was Sukie. And his mother. Madison at camp. It was a nightmare, and he couldn't see any way out of it, because even before this bitch had showed up on the scene and sent everything into orbit he'd been wondering how he was going to cover himself when his mother called him Peck, or worse yet, Billy, and Natalia locked those caustic eyes on him.

He glanced up and there was the river, indented along the near shore by the roofs and projecting angles of the buildings spread out below him, the train station coming into view now, a line of cars creeping up the hill as if hauled on an invisible cable. The sidewalk here had been lifted by the roots of the trees, slabs of concrete shuffled like cards all the way down the long hill, and he felt the strain in the back of his calves and the long muscles of his thighs as he worked his way over the rough spots. Then he was down in the flat, at river level, crossing against the light and moving along the walk in the lee of a restaurant he'd never seen before— upscale Italian, it looked like, and even in the fever of the moment he felt the sting of the irony—and then finally, with a glance in both directions, he pulled back the door of the old man's bar in the old hotel that had been converted to efficiency apartments and Rooms by the Week Only, and let the cool sweet mid-afternoon funk of the place suck him in like a vacuum.

The last thing he wanted was to get hammered or even the slightest bit discomposed, but the first two beers went down like air, and then he had a glass of water and ordered another beer—all in the first five minutes. "It's a bitch out there, huh?" the bartender observed, working his hands in a bar rag, and a couple of the patrons looked up long enough to hear Peck confirm it. The Mets were on the TV. The jukebox was going. It could have been the most ordinary day of his life. He took a sip of the third beer, his thirst waning now—he'd never been so thirsty—and then he drifted back to the men's to clean himself up and get some purchase on things.

The light and fan went on when he opened the door, the smell of the place barely masked by the urinal cake and the gumball deodorizer. His knee was scraped where he'd gone down in the street, but he didn't bother with it, just dabbed at the dried blood on his pantleg and then threw some water on his face. When he looked up, he didn't like what he saw in the mirror. What he saw was not Peck Wilson but some soft scared pukeface whose mind couldn't stop running up against the bared teeth of the moment. What if they searched the car? What if they got his phone? They'd have Sandman's number then and Sandman wouldn't like that. And the house, what if Natalia gave up the address and they searched the house? The key documents were in a safe-deposit box, his bankbooks, passports and the like, but there was plenty there for them to find—the list of names and account numbers in his notebook, for one thing, though there was nothing incriminating in that because nothing had happened yet. They'd find papers though, utility bills, credit card receipts—M. M. Mako, Bridger Martin, Dana Halter. The lease. The car. And they'd trace that back to Bob Almond and the condo and the real estate lady. The fan clacked and stalled and clacked again. The deodorizer hissed. For a long moment he stared at a yellow streak on the wall where somebody had smashed a roach.

But maybe he was getting down over nothing. Maybe Natalia had done the smart thing and got out of there. They had his mother, of course, and his real name and his record now, but she didn't know where he lived, and the thought of that—of where he lived—just opened up a hole in him till he couldn't look at himself in the mirror. There was no chance of keeping the place now—or was there? If he stayed strictly away from Peterskill, just as he'd intended to do in the first place, and made some real money so he could keep it for a weekend retreat or something . . . But then there was Bridger Martin. There was Dana Halter. And how in Christ's name had *they* found him?

He was so wound up he jumped when the door pushed open and some old man with shoulders the width of a straight rule brushed past him to use the urinal, but then the sound of the jukebox—just a snatch of a tune, Marley, "No Woman, No Cry"—came to him and he caught his own gaze again in the mirror and he was Peck Wilson and he was all right. Very slowly, very carefully, all the while holding his own eyes, he washed his hands in a tight clench of powdered soap and lukewarm water, then took his time with the paper towels as the old man spat in the urinal and waited for his bladder to give it up. When he was finished, he went to the pay phone bolted to the wall in the narrow hallway just outside the men's room, and dialed Natalia's number.

While he listened to it ring, he gazed down the tunnel of the hallway to the deeper tunnel of the bar and his half-empty beer glass sitting there on the counter above the vacant barstool as if he were already gone, already wearing a different face in a different life in a different town. Three rings, four. And then there was a click and he got her voice mail: *This is Natalia, I am not here now, please. Leave a message. Once the beep.* He cursed, hung up, dialed again. "Pick up," he kept saying under his breath, "pick up," but she didn't pick up. He must have tried five or six times in succession, pinning the heavy molded plastic receiver to his ear and getting progressively more frustrated and angry and scared each time he dialed, and then the old man blundered out of the bathroom and clipped him on the elbow with the edge of the door and he lost a quarter to the machine and felt as winnowed down and barren and empty as he'd ever felt in his life.

He went back to the bar, drained his beer and ordered another, and that was brilliant—get shit-faced. Sure, why not order a shot to go with it? Fuck up. Get loud. Stumble out into the street and take a cab straight to Greenhaven. "On second thought, cancel that," he said, raising his voice so the bartender, who was already at the tap, could hear him. The man—forties, bald, chinless—looked over his shoulder and gave him a pained look. "I'm too bloated," he said in apology, and the guy next to him, some fish-faced clown who might have looked familiar, glanced up, "you know what I mean?" He heard himself then, heard his voice taking on the local color, his accent coming back the way it did when he talked to Sandman on the phone from the coast. "Just gimme a Diet Coke, huh? Diet Coke, yeah. Lots of ice."

Every five minutes for the next hour he went to the phone, trying her number over and over without success, and he was stalled, checkmated, because there was nothing he could do until he got hold of her and gauged the extent of the damage. He tried to think positively, tried to picture her backing out of the driveway and making her way through the grid of streets till she found Route 9 and went home and buried the car in the garage and waited for him to call. But if she was waiting for him to call, then why wasn't she answering? And would she have taken the initiative to get out of there in the first place—or would she have just stood there, horrified, worrying about his mother and rehearsing his sins and watching Bridger Martin twist and kick on the grass while the sirens started in and people began to stick their heads out the door? Would she have waited for him, thinking that was the thing to do? Maybe. And in that case they were fucked, both of them. But he could also see her exploding in a fury of depilatory Russian curses, jerking round to stamp the flowers into the walk with her heel and then tearing off down the street in the car and everybody—him, especially—be damned. How he hoped that was the case, how he hoped . . .

The clown next to him—he could have been the bartender's twin—kept saying, "You know, you look familiar," and Peck kept denying it. Now the man leaned in till they were shoulder to shoulder and said, "I could swear—didn't you go to Peterskill High?"

Peck shook his head.

"You have a brother, maybe?"

"No, no brother. I'm from California. Just trying to get hold of my wife—we're going into New York, catch the sights. Times Square, that sort of thing, you know?"

He looked dubious. "But you grew up here, right?"

Peck made a show of shooting his cuff to glance at his watch. "No," he said. "San Francisco. But my wife, you know?" he said, pushing himself away from the bar and making his way back to the phone. He dialed again, staring at the dirty buff-colored wall and the graffiti he'd already committed to memory, and it rang once, twice, and then she picked up.

"It is Natalia."

"It's me."

Silence. Nothing. He heard the low buzz of the transmission, staticky and distant, and behind him the jukebox starting up and a sudden shout of laughter from somebody at the bar. "Natalia?"

"I hate you. You son of a bitch. I *hate* you!"

He shot his eyes down the length of the bar, cupped the speaker in his hand. "Where are you?"

"You are a liar. And a—a crook. Just like the crooks on TV—bad TV, daytime TV. You are—" and she began to cry in short drowning gasps.

"Where are you?"

"You lie to me. And to your mother. Your own mother."

"Listen, it's all right, everything's going to be fine. Did they—did you drive home?"

Her voice came back at him, strong suddenly, fueled with outrage. "Drive? Drive what? They have taken the car. No, they have impounded, they say. And I am a sweated woman. I am hungry. And who is to pick up Madison from camp, tell me who?"

"What did you tell them? Where are you now?"

She said something in Russian then, something grating and harsh, and broke the connection. He felt himself sinking. It was all over. Everything was over. That was when he felt a pressure on his arm, somebody poking him, and looked up into the face of some bloated loser in a black motorcycle T-shirt and a whole regalia store's worth of rings, pendants and armbands. "You done, man? I mean, can I—?"

Jesus! He had to restrain himself here, because things could get very dark, very quickly. "One minute," he said, redialing. "I got disconnected."

But this clown wouldn't take a hint. He just stood there, arms folded. "Don't I know you?" he said.

"You don't know me," Peck said, and maybe he did. Was there a motorcycle involved here someplace? "Fuck off."

"It is Natalia."

He turned his back on the guy, cradled the receiver—and if he made a move, touched him, anything, he was dead—and tried to control his voice. "Take a cab," he said. "Wherever you are, take a cab and meet me—"

"Wherever I am? I am in some, some ugly place in your ugly town where you grew up to be a liar and I do not even know your own name. Bridger Martin? The policeman says you are not Bridger Martin. You are not Da-na. William, does that ring a bell? Huh, William?"

"Hey, man, listen—" The loser was there at his back, but he was nothing because he understood what was going down here, what Peck was radiating, and the discussion was over. "I mean, this isn't your fucking living room, man—give somebody else a chance, you know? *Public*. It's a *public* phone."

One look for him, one look over his shoulder, the Sandman look, and the guy backed off, taking his fat-laden shoulders and fat wounded ass back to the bar, putting on as much of a show as he could muster. Settling himself on a barstool now, picking up a glass of whatever shit he was drinking and scowling into the mirror in back of the bar as if to remind himself what a badass he was underneath his fat exterior. "Never mind about that, not now. I'll make it up to you, I will—"

"No, you won't."

"I will."

"No, you won't." She paused to draw in a breath. "Do you know why? Why is because I will not be here. I am leaving. I am picking up Madison in the taxi and I am going to my brother because he is not a liar and a crook. You hear me?"

"What did you tell them?" he said. "Did you tell them where we live?"

There was a silence. He thought he could hear her breaking down again. The smallest voice: "Yes."

"Oh, fuck. Fuck. What's wrong with you? Huh? Tell me. Why would you tell them where we live?"

"I was scared. They are threatening. They say they will—" Her voice fell off. "My green card. They will take my green card."

He felt cold suddenly, the air-conditioning getting to him, the beer weakening him till he could barely hold the phone to his ear. "What did you tell them about me?"

"What I know. That you are a liar. And a thief."

He wanted to get a grip on this, wanted to command her, but he couldn't find the right tone of voice and he felt the control slipping away from him. "Please," he heard himself say. "Please. I'll tell you where to meet me—you can be here in ten minutes. We'll pick up Madison together and—"

"I am going now," she said, very softly, as if it were a prayer. And then she broke the connection.

He dropped the phone. Let it dangle on its greasy cord. Then he turned and walked the length of the room as if he were walking the gauntlet and when the loser at the bar tried to block his way, tried to say something about a Harley Electra Glide, he just set him down hard and went out the door and into the heat, and if he slammed a shoulder into some drunk in an aloha shirt who was trying to light a cigarette and negotiate the door at the same time, well, so what? He wasn't responsible, not at that moment. Not anymore. And how he managed to wind up with the guy's cell phone tucked away in the inside pocket of his jacket, he couldn't have begun to imagine.

Two

In those fleeting furious seconds Peck Wilson spoke to her without words, spoke as clearly and unambiguously as if he were tapped into her consciousness, his internal voice wrapped round her own till it shouted her down and made her quail. He'd lost control. She could see it in his eyes, in his movements, in the look that passed between them like the snap of a whip, and Bridger had lost control too. No matter that he'd lectured her over and over on keeping their distance, keeping their cool, identifying the man and his car and staying clear till the danger had passed and the police could move in and handle the situation—when it came down to it, the sudden proximity was too much for him. They were walking hand in hand through the pall of heat radiating up from the saturated earth, trying to look casual and pedestrian, and then the car appeared right in front of them, pulling into the drive and sliding to a stop just clear of the walk. The engine died. Both doors swung open. And there he was, Peck Wilson, emerging from the car, the rigid barbered slash of hair at the back of his neck and the tapering dagger of a sideburn, his summer suit and open-necked shirt. He had the stuffed toy under one arm and he was looking straight ahead, his eyes on his mother and the little girl standing there on the porch. And then his wife the liar got out too, dressed as if she were going to a cocktail party. Dana froze in mid-step.

That was when Peck Wilson swung his head reflexively to the right and the look passed between them, the first look, the look that went from shock to fear to rage in an instant, and before she could think or act Bridger was rushing him. The toy fell to the ground. The sun stabbed through the trees. There was the sudden clash of their bodies, a dance Peck Wilson knew and Bridger didn't, balletic and swift. And then Bridger was down and thrashing from side to side and Peck Wilson stood over him, aiming his deliberate kicks, and she was screaming, all the air inside her compressed and constricted and forcing its way through the squeeze box of her larynx. He glanced up at her, and there was the whipcrack of that second look so that she knew what he would do before he did, and when he came for her, when he snatched at her wrist, she wasn't there. She ran. She had no choice. Bridger was on the ground. Her blood recoiled and she was gone.

In that moment, she was cleansed of thought: there was nothing in her head but to run. She had no plan, no focus or rationale. Escape, that was all. Get away. Run. Suddenly she was running, and she'd never run harder or faster in her life, unable to hear the ragged tear of his breathing and the propulsion of his footsteps or to gauge where he was, afraid to look over her shoulder, afraid of everything, and why wouldn't somebody stop him? She wanted to cry out but she had no breath to spare. Her arms pumped, her legs found their rhythm and she went straight through the intersection, snatching a glance over her shoulder finally to see him right there, right behind her, sprinting for all he was worth and no quit in him, his eyes cold and dead, his lips drawn tight. She didn't dare look again. Her gaze ran ahead of her, scanning the uneven slabs of concrete for the fatal snag, looking to the old woman shuffling toward her with her shopping bags strung over both arms, calculating her chances at the next light and then the next one beyond that, because there was no stopping no matter what, no hope but to out-run him, out-maneuver him, out-last him. If he caught her he was going to hurt her, swiftly, deeply, without quarter or restraint. He'd told her that much already. And there was no mistaking his meaning.

The van—the white van, the moving wall of it that appeared and stretched and snapped till it was gone—cost her a step, a beat, and his fingers tore at her hair and she felt her head jerked back and she couldn't have stopped if she'd wanted to. Then there was the other car, the force that slapped her, stung her, knocked her to the pavement, his body flung there beside hers and the heat of him rising to her nostrils like some toxin. She was up again, bewildered, dazed, both knees scraped and bleeding and her palms and forearms on fire—*Run!* a voice screamed inside her, *Run!*—but she didn't have to run, didn't have to do anything, because the police cruiser was sliding into the intersection and Peck Wilson was done.

For one long thundering moment she held his gaze, saw the vacancy there, the fear, the retreat, and she trembled all over, the most ridiculous thing, as if she'd caught a chill on the hottest day of the year. She didn't know where she was. Didn't know what was happening to her. "You go to hell," she said, feeling the triumph surge up in her.

They stood there side by side, not two feet apart, as the men from the car, the black men, came at them, flailing their arms and working their mouths, people gathering, the door of the police cruiser catching the light as it flung open and everyone looked to the blue-black uniform, the nightstick and revolver and the visored cap. He was going to run, she knew it. He was going to run and she had to stop him. She jerked round, too wrought up to notice who was inhabiting that uniform and fingering that nightstick or to see where this was going, where it had been going all along, inevitably, one long downward spiral from the day the microbes invaded her body and she stopped living in the world of the hearing. She watched his face change. Watched his eyes settle. And then the cop stepped between them and she was looking into a face she recognized, fury there, fury and disbelief, and she knew she was on trial all over again.

What she remembered most, what she would always remember, was the way they failed her. She tried to marshal her words but she was overwhelmed, heaving for air—"Him," she kept saying, jerking a finger at Peck Wilson, "he's the one, arrest him"—but P. Runyon wasn't listening, and at some point in the silent shuffle of bodies and faces and the shock of the way P. Runyon seized her arm and held it in a tight unyielding grip, she looked up and saw that Peck Wilson wasn't where he'd been a moment before. He wasn't in the cruiser or in the custody of the other cop, the older one with the drooping face, who was busy with the two black men and their windmilling arms and snapping teeth. She felt the panic rising in her and she jerked her arm back. She looked wildly round her, spinning once, twice, the crowd giving back her stare out of indifferent eyes, the trees whirling overhead, shirts, blouses, jeans, shorts. Officer Runyon laid a hand on her again and again she jerked back. Couldn't they see what was happening here? "Peck Wilson," she shouted as if it was the only name she knew, and she shouted it again and again, till all the air had gone out of her.

By the time the interpreter arrived, it was too late. She'd tried to tear away, burning with her urgency, tried to thread through the crowd and fling herself back down the street to that house and the silver-haired woman on the porch—*Ask her, she'll have the answers, ask her*—but P. Runyon wouldn't hear of it. Only then did she think of Bridger. Was he hurt? Or was it just bruises, aches, something he could shake off the way people did in the movies? She felt a flutter of fear rise in her throat: why wasn't he here, why wasn't he adding his voice to the mix? He could explain. He could tell her, this lady cop with the starved lips and grabby hands and the eyes that started at zero and went down from there. Where was he? Where? She had her answer a moment later when the ambulance nosed up to the curb, lights flashing, and P. Runyon waved the driver angrily on, releasing her grip on Dana's arm to point down the street in two quick chops as if she were flinging something away from her. "Who—?" Dana asked, but couldn't finish the thought.

Officer Runyon actually had her handcuffs out—she was shaking them in Dana's face, warning her to calm herself down or she'd have no choice but to take her into custody—when the interpreter pulled up in a nondescript black car with the city logo on the door. She was small, neat, young, her features already in motion as she crossed the street and stepped between the two of them. "What's the matter?" she asked and signed it simultaneously.

"He was chasing me. He wanted to hurt me. Peck," Dana said, "Peck Wilson."

The interpreter looked to P. Runyon and she just shrugged. "That's all she can talk about. She's hysterical."

Who is Peck Wilson? the woman signed, turning to Dana and shutting out the officer.

The thief. He stole my identity. And he chased me, he— Where is he?

Where is he? The question cut right through her. She couldn't help herself, couldn't pull away from it, the rage and frustration and the sick irony that was like some sort of cosmic joke, and suddenly she was sobbing. The interpreter dropped her hands to her sides and then lifted them again and embraced her. There was a long suspended moment, the stranger clinging to her in a crowd of strangers, and then she gently disengaged herself. She didn't brush the hair away from her face or dab at her eyes, but instead brought her right hand to her forehead and swept it out, open-palmed: *I don't know,* she signed. *But I know where his mother is.*

At the hospital, she sat in a hard plastic chair in the emergency room with the interpreter on one side and a detective from the Peterskill Police Department on the other. It was evening now, Saturday evening, and there was a momentary lull in the drift of patients pressing bloodied rags to their shins and arms and foreheads as the late afternoon gave way to night and the alcohol-fueled trauma to come. She was feeling jittery—she'd drained three cans of diet cola and was thirsty still—and her right knee was stinging where they'd dug bits of gravel and dirt out of the pad there and cleaned and dressed the wound. She had a matching square of gauze beneath the left knee, but the right seemed to have taken the brunt of it—that was where the pain was, anyway. The interpreter—her name was Terri Alfano, she was twenty-six years old and possessed of a pair of dark wide-set eyes that absorbed hurt and confusion and delivered up absolution in their place, and Dana didn't know how she would have gotten through this without her—had asked for some clarification on the timing of the incident, and the detective who'd posed the question, his pen poised over a pad of paper, seemed to have drifted off as they signed back and forth.

The problem now—the concern, the worry, the fear that was booming inside her with a dull echoing horror—wasn't

Peck Wilson or his mother or wife or the wine-red Mercedes the police were impounding until legal ownership could be established, but Bridger. Bridger was somewhere behind the swinging doors in back of the nurse's desk, beyond the expressionless patients slumped in the rows of molded plastic chairs and the TV on the wall that was tuned, in another sick intrusion of irony, to an over-wrought drama about emergency room doctors. They hadn't told her much, and what they had told her she wasn't getting at all until Terri Alfano wrote it down for her: Bridger, it seemed, was having trouble breathing and they'd done an emergency tracheotomy. He'd suffered laryngeal trauma and they were going to have to operate in order to clear the air passage and repair damage to the thyroid carti-lage. That was the problem. That was why she was sitting here watching the clock and the swinging doors and the face of the nurse every time she jerked her eyes to the phone and picked it up.

An hour crept by, then another. The detective was gone now, long gone, and the waiting room had begun to fill again. Dana paged through a magazine and watched people's faces as they shuffled in and out the door on the arms of relatives and friends, their features tugged and twisted round the flash point of their suffering eyes. There had been no news of Bridger, and as the light failed beyond the windows and the night settled in, she turned to Terri Alfano and told her she might as well go home. "You don't have to sit here and keep me company, you know," she said aloud, though she didn't mean it. She was glad for the company, desperate for it. She was confused and hurting, crushed with guilt over Bridger—it was her fault, the whole thing, involving him in this in the first place and then drag-ging him all the way out here, and for what? She shouldn't have been so hardheaded. She should have let it go. Should have left it to the police and the credit card companies instead of playing amateur detective, instead of taking it personally, as if the thief could have cared who she was, as if it mattered, as if *she* mattered. What was she thinking? But the worst thing, the thing that haunted her as she stared at the floor and shifted in her seat and raised her eyes to look at the nurse and the clock and the swinging doors that never swung open and gave up nothing, was leaving him when he needed her most, when he couldn't breathe, when he was clutching at his throat and thrashing on the pavement with the pain that should have been hers. There was a moral calculus here, and she'd failed it.

"It's all right. I'm fine." Terri was idly turning the pages of one of the magazines Dana had been twice through already. She sat very still, her back arched, exuding calm. She was wearing a gray skirt with a matching jacket and a rose-colored blouse, very professional, prim almost, but she wasn't cold or rigid in the least, unlike so many interpreters—Iverson and his ilk. Little people who wanted to make themselves big at the expense of somebody else, somebody they could dominate in an ongoing psychodrama of mastery and dependency.

"Really," she said, setting down the magazine. "I know you've got better things to do—"

Terri shrugged, held her palms out, smiled. They'd already talked about her boyfriend, how she could barely think of anything else though it had been six months since he'd moved to the Midwest for a job opportunity he just couldn't pass up and how she was waiting for him to come back for her. They'd talked about her parents, both of them deaf—*mother father deaf,* she signed—and how she'd been interpreting for them all her life, talked about shitty pay and long hours and the obligation she felt to the deaf community. And the guilt. Not to mention the guilt. They'd talked about Bridger, about the San Roque School. About Peck Wilson. "Believe me," she said, signing under it, "it's okay. I want to stay. What if the doctor needs to tell you something—I don't know, something important? Crucial even?"

"I can read him."

"Medical terms?"

"He can write them down."

There was a pause. They both looked up to watch an elderly woman in slippers and housedress navigate the room to the admittance desk like a sad old prow on a breezeless sea. Terri's face bloomed. *Do you really want me to go?* she signed.

Dana shook her head. And then, for emphasis, two quick snaps of the index and middle fingers to the thumb: *No.*

It was past nine when the nurse who'd first spoken with them came through the swinging doors. She was wearing scrubs, replete with the soft crushed hat, and there was a suggestive stain, something dark and blotted, knifing across one hip. They both stood to receive her and as she made her way across the room, Dana could read her expression and her body language—she was satisfied with herself; everything was okay—so that when the nurse was standing there before them with a propped-up smile and telling them that Bridger was going to be fine, she already knew the gist of it. The details were something else. They'd implanted a polymeric silicone stent—"Could you write that down, please?"— to prevent granulation tissue from forming on the exposed cartilage, but he'd be released the following day and the prognosis was good. Full recovery. Though he wouldn't be able to speak for a period of two to three weeks and there might be some residual voice change.

"Residual voice change?" Dana looked from Terri to the nurse.

"He may sound different. That is, he may not have the full vocal range he had before the accident—or the injury, I mean. But maybe not. Maybe he'll recover fully. Many do." She paused to let Terri catch up with her, though Dana was reading her and leaping ahead. The nurse was middle-aged, with sorrowful eyes and a pair of semicircular lines bracketing her mouth—which vanished when she smiled, as she did now. "He's not a singer, is he?"

"No," Dana said, shaking her head even as the image of him in the car rose up before her, his lips puckered round the unknowable ecstasy of the tune generated by the radio, sweet melisma, the owl song: who who, who who.

Earlier, with Terri's help, she'd put in a phone call to his parents, people she'd never met. They lived in San Diego. His father had something to do with the military there, that was all she knew. She'd watched Terri's face as she'd translated, watched as she listened and the emotional content of what she was hearing transferred itself to her lips and eyes and the musculature beneath her skin. The parents hadn't heard from Bridger in a month. They were unhappy. The mother was flying out on the next plane. Was there blame attached? Was there ill will, rancor, animosity? *A deaf girl? He'd never mentioned he was seeing a deaf girl.*

And maddeningly, no matter how many times she punched in the number, her own mother wasn't picking up the phone—or she had it off. Terri kept getting her voice mail and each time she left a message to call back. Nothing yet. Dana had tucked her phone deep in the side pocket of her shorts where she'd be sure to feel the vibrator, and now she felt for it, just to reassure herself, and it was still there, still inert, still made of plastic, metal, silicon. A cold thing. All but useless. Maybe she should have brought a couple of carrier pigeons with her.

Terri saw her hand go to her pocket. She smiled, thanked the nurse, who was already shifting her weight to start back toward the swinging doors, and lifted her eyes to Dana's. "Still no luck?"

She shook her head. "I think she was going to go see a show some night this week, but I don't know—"

The moment hung there between them, and then Terri, signing beneath her words, said, "My place is small—and it's nothing really, nothing much—but there's a fold-out couch in the living room. You're welcome to stay. Really."

She woke at first light, sweating, to an apprehension of movement just beyond the thin grid of the window screen. The atmosphere was heavy, tropical. There was a smell of dampness and mold, the fertile rejuvenate scent of things working in the earth, flowers unfolding, the insect armies stirring in their nests and dens and beneath the leaves of the trees crowded against the house. It smelled like rain, like ozone. For a moment she lay motionless, her eyes on the ceiling—she was getting her bearings, tracing backward through the rosary of events to the hospital and Terri, Bridger, Peck Wilson climbing out of his car and the fear that had exploded in her brain and chased her down the street—and then her eyes went to the screen. There was something there, a shadow, movement. Her heart was pounding. She sat up. And when she felt the door swing open behind her she nearly let out a scream—or maybe she did, maybe she did shout out—until she saw that it was only Terri, her shoulders slumped beneath the quilted fabric of a pale blue robe and her face dull and empty, half-asleep still, on her way to the bathroom. *Are you okay?* Terri signed reflexively.

"Sorry, I must have been dreaming," Dana lied, each word an abstraction nobody could possibly understand, words lifted from the page and an ancient repository of memory in a hopeful way, in the way Bridger must have dredged up his high school Spanish at the taco stand or the car wash. He always felt relieved, he told her—or no, not just relieved, but amazed—when people understood him, as if they were communicating in a code that was indecipherable except in that one serendipitous moment.

The bathroom door opened and then closed on Terri and it was as if she'd never been there, an apparition faded away into insubstantiality, and there was the movement at the screen again, the movement that had woken her, but it wasn't Peck Wilson, at large still and come to sniff her out and finish what he'd begun, and it wasn't the afterimage of a dream either—it was just a squirrel, bloated with the easy pickings of high summer, dipping its head and manipulating its paws against the dark sheen of the wet and silken grass.

It was still overcast when she woke again. Terri was standing over her with a cup of coffee, a soft muted smile pressed to her lips. She was dressed and made-up, her hair brushed, jade earrings catching what there was of the dull light from beyond the window. "I didn't want to wake you," she said, handing her the coffee. "There's cream and sugar if you want—I didn't know how you took it."

"What time is it?" Dana asked, sitting up to cradle the cup in both hands.

"Ten-thirty."

"Ten-thirty? I can't believe we slept so late—"

"All that running—you were tired." Her teeth flashed. It was a joke. "But not to worry, it's Sunday, the one day of the week when people can sleep in."

"What about the hospital? What about Bridger?"

Terri's face—her pretty, mobile, animated face—showed nothing. "I called fifteen minutes ago. No word. He's resting, that's what they said. We can visit anytime."

The coffee was too hot, bitter—she preferred tea and when she did have coffee she drowned it in cream—but Dana lifted the cup to her lips, blew the steam away and drank, thanking Terri with her eyes. She felt overwhelmed suddenly. This girl, this young sweet-faced confiding girl, a stranger to her twenty-four hours ago, was her best friend in the world, a good person, genuine, caring, compassionate—*mother father deaf*—and for that she was grateful, infinitely grateful, grateful to the point of tears. But Terri was a crutch too, and her own mother would have been the first to point it out to her. "You don't have to babysit me," she said.

Terri was drinking from a souvenir mug with the words *Fort Ticonderoga* superimposed in red over a wraparound stockade. "It's not a problem. And I'm not babysitting you, don't think that. I want to help, that's all."

Dana couldn't resist a smile. "Above and beyond the call of duty?"

Terri shrugged. "Sure," she said. "Why not?"

"Nothing better to do?"

"I don't know—you want breakfast? Eggs? Cereal?"

Dana swung her legs away from the mattress, fished her shorts off the floor and slid them on. She needed a shower, her skin prickling with the residue of her sweat—she felt as if she'd been rolled in sugar like a doughnut—but the shower could wait. "No," she said, looking up from lacing her shoes, "don't go to any trouble"—and she held up a hand to forestall the reply—"but I do need to call my mother. Just to let her know—"

Terri lifted her eyebrows and all the deaf expression flooded back into her features. "You want me to interpret—or are you going to text?"

"If you just tell me when she picks up, that would be great—I can talk and she can text. It's better that way, anyway—I wouldn't want to subject you to all that, because I'm sure you know the way mothers are. And my mother's a hundred times worse."

Her mother picked up on the first ring. "Hi, Mom," Dana said into the void.

Where are you? I was worried.

"Peterskill. Still. And don't worry, the car's fine, but we had to stay overnight because"—and she stalled a moment, feeling the emotion rise in her—"because Bridger, I mean, Peck Wilson. Peck Wilson came and beat him up and he's in the hospital."

Hospital?

"He's all right. It's his throat. He got hit in the throat."

There was nothing for a moment, then the LCD flashed across the miniature screen: *Didn't I tell you? You're always—*

"He's okay. Everything's okay. We're going to the hospital in a minute and they said they would release him this afternoon so I guess you'll see us tonight."

Who's we?

"Me and Terri. She's the interpreter from the police."

Did they catch him?

Again the hesitation. It was as if she were the one who'd been kicked in the throat. "No. He—he got away."

I'm coming up there.

"No, no—you don't have to. I can handle it, don't worry."

What hospital?

She gave a little speech then, about independence—how her mother had always preached independence and here she was treating her like a child. How she was thirty-three years old and could handle herself. How anybody could

370

have been the victim of a thief like this and it had nothing to do with her difference or her capability or the way she handled her finances and planned for the future or anything else. "Mom, listen," she said finally, "I'm going to repeat this so you understand: I don't want you to come. Okay?"

What hospital?

The first thing she saw when she walked into the room, Terri at her side, was the flowers. A jungle of flowers, dahlias, tulips, lilies, gladiolus, roses—so many flowers it was as if they'd taken the wrong door off the corridor and wound up back outside again. The next thing was the snaking wiry form of a woman she'd never seen before rising up out of the floral riot to throw her a challenging look, and then she saw the bed, the monitors, the IV apparatus, and finally Bridger, reduced there against the null white field of the sheets. There was a bandage at his throat, whiter yet, folds of pristine gauze wrapped to his chin so that his head seemed separated from his body. His right eye was swollen shut. In fact—and she had to catch her breath as she came closer—she saw that the whole right side of his face was damaged, a dark striated cloud of scab scudding across the jaundiced bruise that sustained it. She felt stricken: he was hurt, badly hurt, and he wasn't going anywhere.

The woman—his mother, she knew this was his mother even before she looked in her face and saw his features replicated there, the nose, the eyes, the retreating bone structure and the pale orbicular expanse of the flesh—tried to stand in her way, tried to question her right, assert authority, but she shoved past her and went to him, her hand finding his and her lips pressed to the side of his beautiful

371

ravaged face. "Oh, God," she said, "oh, God, I'm so sorry," and the tears were there, burning like acid, while things went on behind her, peripheral movement, gestures, his mother and Terri Alfano, her deliverer, working through the niceties. She lifted her head to look him in the eye, the good eye, the one that was dilated and clear. "Are you okay?" she asked from deep inside her, and the words didn't feel right, too pinched, in the wrong register, but she didn't care.

It was only then—only when he lifted his right hand to reply—that she noticed the cast on his forearm, and the sight of it was like an accusation, a pointed finger, a curse. The closed hand, up and down: *Yes.* And then: *Are you okay?*

She nodded.

Did they get him?

She watched his face darken, the color seeping out of the bruise to mottle his jaw, his cheek, the orbit of his open eye. He already knew the answer. Already knew that the pain, the frustration, the anger and hate and obsession—and the fractured ulna and the crushed larynx too—were in vain. He could see it in her eyes.

"He got away," she said, signing under it. "But they got his car—"

His car? Is that all? Shit! He pounded his fist against the cast in a quick violent jerk of the arm and then he tried to say something, his eye glaring and his jaws grabbing at the air, but he wasn't saying anything, she could see that, she could feel it. Bridger. The gauze at his throat, the cast on his arm. He was furious, angry, angrier than she'd ever seen him, and before she had a chance to question it—was he blaming her, was that it?—his mother was there, sweeping her roughly aside to hammer at the nurse's buzzer and then the nurse was propelling herself into the room and doing something to Bridger, to his mouth, his throat, his oral cavity, that Dana didn't want to see. Even as she turned her head, Bridger's mother took hold of the bed curtains and pulled them shut.

For a long while she just sat there beside Terri and stared at the pleated white folds of the curtains on their aluminum track. She felt as if she'd been slapped in the face. She'd felt bad enough as it was—her fault, everything her fault—and now she just wanted to sink through the floor. *Don't worry,* Terri signed. *He'll be all right.*

She didn't respond. She was feeling too low. And tired. As tired as if she hadn't slept in a week. The light drew down suddenly—a cloud passing over the sun beyond the window at the end of the room—and she glanced up and for the first time noticed the second bed there. It was nearly walled off by the masses of flowers Bridger's mother had marshaled round the room, and those flowers represented another level of accusation—she hadn't thought to bring so much as a daisy herself, but then how could she? She was going through this too—she could have been murdered, didn't they know that?

The curtains on this second bed were drawn too, but she could see through a gap at the near end that there was someone there, visible only as a pair of crossed ankles and two bare feet with their canted yellowish soles and ten yellowed toes hanging from their joints like decayed fruit. Those toes fascinated her, those anonymous feet, and her eyes passed over the easy attraction of the flowers to fixate on them—who was back there, she wondered? Some auditory voyeur, silently attuned to the drama playing out round Bridger's bed, the cries of the mother, the gagging of the patient, the wet fleshy wheeze of the nurse's ministrations. Nothing wrong with him at all—you could tell that by the way he'd crossed his ankles. He'd just come here and hidden behind the curtains in witness. That was what she was thinking, watching those feet and letting her thoughts pull her down, when she felt the familiar tactile squirming of the cell in her pocket.

It was her mother. *Peterskill Station,* she messaged, *3:45,* and cut the connection.

Terri was watching her. "Your mother?"

"Yeah. She's coming in at three forty-five." She shrugged, dropped her eyes. "I guess I'm going to have to pick her up."

There was a suspended moment, and then Terri tapped her wrist with a single finger to get her attention. "I can drive you to your car if you want. You remember where you parked it?"

She saw the street suddenly, the shade trees, the cracked sidewalk and the kids on their bicycles and it was like the mise-en-scène of a play she'd seen somewhere a long time ago. "Yes," she said, and she nodded her head for emphasis.

The nurse emerged from behind the curtains then and reached up to draw them open with a brisk snap of her wrists. The mother was there too, rising to her feet from the chair beside the bed, her face strained and eyes leaping out at them as if to say, *What do you want here?* And Bridger—the crisis had apparently passed, and he was watching her, his face flushed beneath the mask Peck Wilson had crafted for him, his scalp so red she could see the individual hairs in relief against the skin. He'd been coughing. Coughing or gagging. The man with the feet would have known as much, Terri and the mother and anybody passing by the door would have known, but not Dana. Because the curtains had been closed.

"Is he all right?" she said now, coming up out of the chair and taking a step toward the bed. The nurse gave her an odd look, ducked her head and left the room on her quick padded feet. Bridger's mother wore her face as if it weighed a thousand pounds, as if it had been hammered out of concrete. She angled away from the bed, moving ever so subtly—perhaps even unconsciously—to interpose herself between Dana and her son. Her mouth was in motion: "What? What did she say?"

She was asking a question, but she wasn't asking it of Dana. She wasn't even looking at her. She was looking at Terri.

Terri said something then, and Bridger's mother said something back. Bridger was flushed. His hands were still, his good eye open and staring.

She felt Terri's hand on her arm and turned to her. "Mrs. Martin says he's having trouble breathing," she said. "They think maybe it's just an adjustment to the surgery, but it's possible maybe a suture"—she finger-spelled it— "came loose, inside, and they might have to reinsert the breathing tube, but it's probably not that and it's nothing abnormal, really—"

"Tell her," Bridger's mother said, waving her arms as if she were flagging a cab, "that they're going to have to run some tests and he'll be here overnight, one more night at least—"

Dana reached for the woman's arm, a simple gesture, to take hold of her if only for an instant and tell her that she understood, that she could talk directly to her, that they were both involved in the same struggle, the same hope, the same love, but Bridger's mother shrugged her off and gave her a look she knew only too well. Dana watched the pale blue eyes, Bridger's eyes, focus on Terri. "Tell her he needs to rest now," she said, and Dana read her perfectly.

And Bridger? He never raised his hand—no, he didn't so much as lift a finger.

· · · · ·

Then they were out on the pulsing streets with the heat in their faces and the too-green trees closing in overhead, the hateful oppressive trees and denunciatory shrubs and the screaming lawns, and she was back in the conduit of the nightmare, hurting all over again. There was the intersection, the first one—"No," she said to Terri, directing her, "turn right here. Yes, that's right, and at the end of the block hang a left"—and the sidewalk scrolled by and the cars parked along the street announced themselves one by one until she saw the Jetta, right where she'd left it, front wheels turned into the curb, the windshield black with the shade of the trees.

Three

HE WAS IN HIGH GEAR NOW, pedal to the metal, any last
vestige of cool blown right out the tailpipe when he took
that moron down in the bar, and he might as well have sent
up one of those balloons they float over the used-car lots
with a big inverted arrow pointing to the bull's-eye on the
back of his head. Another mistake in a day full of them. But
he had no choice except to back down and he never backed
down, no matter what the cost. And he was angry, he'd admit that. Angry at himself, at Natalia, at Bridger Martin and
Dana Halter and the whole sad scary circus he'd somehow
got himself involved in. He'd gone low on the guy, for the
knee, because the big blowhards with the flabby tits and
bowling-ball heads were always top-heavy and they went
down fast. The only problem was the guy was swinging as
his knee buckled and he'd grazed the side of Peck's face with
the plane of his fist and his assortment of biker rings, the
silver swastika and the death's head and the like, and now
there was blood there.

Head down, walking crisply, with purpose, he crossed
in the middle of the block and came down the street toward
the station, past the outdoor café with a bunch of people
chewing as if their lives depended on it and the area reserved for taxis—and when he saw the cabs idling there and
the northbound train sitting at the platform the idea came
into his head to slide into one of the cabs and hustle out of

there, but he dismissed it. The police would arrive in a matter of minutes, once the clown got himself up off the floor and the wreckage settled and the bartender dialed emergency, and the cab would have to go right by them. He saw all that, moving forward, never breaking stride, though people were looking at him—blood on his face, his pants torn and dirty—and he mounted the platform and stepped onto the train, taking a seat on the far side. A minute later he was in the restroom, dabbing at his face with a wet paper towel, hearing sirens—or was he imagining it? A minute after that the train jerked forward, the wheels taking hold, and then the car was swaying as if under the influence of two competing and antithetical forces and the rattling started and they were under way, heading north.

The cut—it was a scrape, really, with a thin slice down the middle of it—traced his right cheekbone all the way to one very red ear and it was bleeding more than it should have, and that was inconvenient. There was little chance that whatever cop responded to the scene at the tavern would connect him with the incident and even less that they'd bother with the train because it was just a bar fight, after all, one of a million, but still he didn't want to draw attention to himself unnecessarily. If they had the Mercedes they'd be at the house with a warrant and there'd be somebody there for a few days at least waiting for him to turn up, but he wasn't going to turn up, he had no intention of turning up—at the house or anywhere else. He wasn't that stupid, though he was getting there. When he'd stanched the bleeding, he took a fresh wad of paper towels, soaked them through, and waded out into the lurching car, taking an empty seat on the near side now, so as to present his left profile to the conductor when he came round taking tickets.

They were making the big sweep round the base of Anthony's Nose when the conductor came up the aisle behind him. "Beacon," Peck said, turning to him, the wadded-up towels pressed to his cheek. The conductor—a black man, older, with distant eyes and a fringe of processed hair hanging limp under his cap—didn't ask, but Peck said, "Hell of a toothache," and he handed him a bill and the man punched his ticket and gave him his change and that was that. For the moment, at least. But what next? And why had he said Beacon and not Buffalo? Or Chicago?

When they stopped at the Garrison station—a little nothing of a stone building, a row of houses, the flat hand of the river and a big empty parking lot—and there was nobody waiting for him, no cops and no Natalia, he began to understand. There was unfinished business here, and the thought of it twisted at him and soured the contents of his stomach, the flat beer out of the twelve-ounce glass, stale bar mix, the Coke that ate right through him like battery acid. Natalia had left him. She was gone. It was over. For all he knew she could be on this very train, connecting to Toronto. But no, that wasn't her style, and he tried to picture her, the little moue of a kissing mouth she would make when she was concentrating on something, doing her eyes or working a crossword puzzle, Natalia, stepping out of the bath or tipping back a glass of Beaujolais Nouveau or worked up and fuming at him, as capable of action as anybody he'd ever met. She would take a cab to Hertz or Enterprise, rent a car, pick up Madison and go back to the house. Where she would brood and fling things on the floor and swig vodka, squat and murderous and stomping around in her bare feet till she passed out and the cops came in the morning with their warrant and turned the house upside down. And then she'd suck down more vodka and take Madison out to lunch and go shopping and eventually she'd find herself back in the house, sorting out the damage. She'd look out the window and see the rental car there, something nice, something sporty—a Mustang, maybe, or a T-Bird, because why would she deny herself as long as the credit cards still worked?—and before long she'd start packing the car with everything she could carry. And then she'd be gone.

As the train rattled through the remnants of the day, the declining sun striping the looping arc of tracks ahead and picking out individual leaves in the treetops while the rest faded to gray, his mind began to close a fist over that picture of Natalia and he found himself getting angry all over again. The house. He hated to lose the house as much as he hated losing her—and the things he'd collected. The car. The names in the notebook, pure gold, every one of them. His business. And Sukie. That was over too. And that was another thing: how quickly it had all turned on him. This morning he was on top of it, waking up in a mansion, six months paid in advance and a lease to buy, climbing into an S500 and taking his fiancée to meet his mother and his daughter he hadn't seen in three years. That was when the image of Dana Halter rose up before him and he saw her there on the sidewalk, the look in her eyes, knowing what he was going to do before he knew it himself, and then the way she'd run, making a chump out of him, a fag, somebody's girlfriend. He wanted to hurt her. Hurt her the way he'd hurt Bridger Martin. Even the score. One parting shot. And out.

It was still light when he got off the train at Beacon, a real shithole of a place, crap blown up along the tracks, crap floating in the river, graffiti all over everything as if nobody cared about anything, not even their own human worth, and where were the cops when you needed them? Why weren't they nailing the little punks with their spray cans instead of busting his ass? For that matter, why weren't they out here cleaning up the trash and painting over the gang signs and obscenities instead of burning up the taxpayers' gasoline to drag their bloated carcasses from one doughnut shop to another? Oh, he was in a mood. He recognized that. What he needed was a car, a change of clothes, something in his stomach. He hadn't eaten all day, not since break-fast—too wired, too scared, too outraged even to think about it—but now, suddenly, he was starving.

The streetlights began to make themselves visible, an amber glow bellying out into the shadows, and already the insects were there, drifting like snow. There were a couple of people milling around, white T-shirts faintly glowing against the fade of the light. He heard a girl laugh aloud and turned to see a knot of teenagers perched on the concrete abutment, passing a bottle in a brown paper bag. He didn't see any cabs and so he started walking up the hill toward the lights of the town—always look as if you have a pur-pose, that was a rule—and before he'd gone three blocks he saw a yellow cab pulled up in front of a tavern and crossed the street to it and leaned in the driver's side window. A Puerto Rican kid with a heavy scruff of acne was behind the wheel, the radio spitting up a low-volume spew of hip-hop. "You waiting on somebody?" Peck asked.

The kid's eyes, naked and too big for his face, skirted away from him. He mumbled something in reply.

"What?"

"Supposed to be."

Peck jerked a finger toward the tavern. "Somebody in there?"

The kid nodded, his eyes flashing white in the dark va-cancy of the interior.

"Forget about them," Peck said, fishing a twenty out of his wallet and handing it to him. "Here, this is for you. I need you to take me someplace where I can rent a car at this hour on a Saturday night. What about the airport? You know the airport on the other side of the river? They got to be open twenty-four/seven, right?"

More mumbling. Something about Hertz in Wappingers.

"But they're closed at this hour, right? On a Saturday?"

"I don't know." An elaborate shrug, the eyes ducking away. "I guess."

The door of the tavern swung open then, a rectangle of light with two people in the center of it, a couple holding on to each other as if they were wading into the surf at Coney Island, and Peck ended the discussion by easing round the hood of the car and sliding into the seat next to the driver. The people at the door—they were twenty feet away, sallow-faced, drunk—made a move toward the cab, but Peck just gave the kid a look to focus him, to let him know what was going down here, and then he said, "Hit it," and the cab pulled away from the curb with an apologetic little chirp of the rear wheels.

The girl at the desk ran his platinum Visa card without even looking up and he showed her his California driver's license decorated with his own smiling photograph and M. M. Mako's name and address, and filled out the rental agreement. He chose a black GMC Yukon because the seats folded down and he was thinking he might wind up sleeping in it—there were dirt roads up in the hills in back of Beacon that might as well have been in Alaska for all the traffic they took and nobody would bother him there—and when the girl asked him if he wanted the supplemental collision insurance, a by-the-book standard rip-off, he just smiled and said, "Sure." Then he went to a diner and had a Greek salad and two burgers, alternately thumbing through one of those freebie real estate magazines and watching himself chew in the reflection of the darkened window. His face floated there in the void, disembodied, a handsome face, a face that could have belonged to anybody, and he chewed and watched himself and let the tension drain out of his eyes. All things considered, he didn't look too bad, the cut drawn pink and thin at the edge of his cheekbone and fading into the sideburn there—for all anyone knew it might have been a scratch he'd got while picking raspberries in the woods or playing with his cat.

Or his girlfriend's cat.

The thought of her started up the whole process all over again, one thought butting up against the next till the momentary calm the food had given him burned off like vapor and he had to stand up, throw a bill on the table and stalk out the door without bothering with his change. Cash he had—he always carried a thousand in hundreds, against the unforeseen and unfortunate, against moments like this, like this godforsaken interlude in a parking lot in New Windsor, New York, under a sky that was black to the molars of the universe and no forgiveness anywhere—but it would begin to be a problem in a few days, because he couldn't risk going into a bank for a cash advance, but that wasn't his immediate worry. His immediate worry, he realized, as he started up the car and put it in gear, was Sandman. He had to call Sandman and warn him about what was coming down, and the thought of that made his stomach churn. It wasn't so much that Sandman was going to be upset in a major-league way about the risk he'd put them both in and the hundreds of thousands of dollars he'd just extracted from their mutual pockets because he'd given in to the impulse to run down that bitch and everything was unraveling like a big ball of concertina wire, but that he'd have to admit to it in the first place. He'd have to squirm and he didn't like squirming. He'd have to breathe into the phone and tell Sandman how weak and stupid and shortsighted and amateurish he'd been and then he'd have to say goodbye, permanently, to maybe the only friend he had left in the world.

Yes. And he actually had the cell out, looking to punch in the number as he cruised down the dark street toward the highway and the bridge back across the river, when he stopped himself. He heard his own voice playing in his head—*Hey, Geoff, it's me. Hey, I fucked up. Don't. Don't say anything because I just got to warn you*—but then he folded up the phone and slipped it back in his pocket. He would call him later. Once he got where he was going—but where was that?

Without even realizing what he was doing, he'd turned south on Route 9 once he crossed the river, idly punching through the stations on the radio while the trees rose up on either side of the road in a vast black continuum broken only by the occasional gap where there was a restaurant or gas station or a business with its lights muted and parking lot empty. He'd passed North Highland some time back, a line of cars behind him, headlights coming at him in intervals, and he was in no hurry, floating there in the dash-lit cabin as if that was all that was expected of him. When he came to the places where the road opened up to an extra lane he hugged the dark shoulder and let the whole line of them pass. The musical selection wasn't much—oldies, mainly—but he found a station playing reggae, a Black Uhuru tune followed by Burning Spear and then, who else but Marley? His spirits lifted. He felt almost human. And when he spotted a deli open alongside the road he swung into the lot and went in and bought a bag of barbecue chips and a six-pack.

He had no intention whatever of going anywhere near the house, but when he came to the turnoff that would take him down to 9D and the run along the river from Cold Spring to Garrison, he found himself flicking the right-hand turn signal and then he was in the deeper precincts of the continuous forest, the blacker road, the less-traveled path, listening to reggae till the station faded out and tipping back his second beer. And then he was sweeping past the old church and the cemetery with its ancient stone markers, everything quiet, under wraps, the moon showing now over the trees, quarter of eleven on Saturday night and only the occasional car running toward him and shuddering on by. It was quiet out here, which was why he'd chosen the area in the first place, and he slowed to just under the speed limit and rolled down the window to feel the glutinous air on his face and come alive to the roar of the insects. When the headlights picked out the black sheen of his mailbox and the flitting sparkle of the gravel drive, he felt a sensation of loss so immediate and immitigable it was like a physical blow that reverberated from his brain on down through his torso to his legs and the foot that hit the brake and brought the car to a near standstill before he came to his senses and speeded up again even as a car swung out behind him with a tap of the horn and shot on past.

What was he doing? He didn't know. But he pulled in at the next road, a driveway servicing half a dozen houses that showed now only as vague scatterings of light through the black-hung trees, and he swung up on the shoulder and cut the engine. He fought the impulse to crack another beer—beer, he didn't even like the taste of it, and it bloated you, slowed you down—and pulled out his cell. For a moment he thought he was going to call Sandman, but then he thought he wouldn't. Maybe he wouldn't call at all. Maybe he'd just let it go. Vanish. Fuck everybody. It wasn't his fault that this woman—this deaf woman, this freak—was like a bloodhound. That was one in a thousand, one in a million. All right. Fine. He was sitting in the dark a quarter mile from his own house, feeling the effects of two beers and refusing himself the third, his fingers grainy with the residue of the potato chips, every flag waving and every buzzer going off in his head—*Get out, get out now!*—and so what he did was hit Natalia's number for the hundredth time that night.

The insects roared. The moon cut through the trees like a laser and sliced the hood of the car in two. And suddenly her voice was there with him, the sweet bitten breathy words: *This is Natalia, I am not here now, please. Leave a message. Once the beep.* The rage came up then, a violent impulsive hot cautery of rage burning through him till it was all he could do to keep from pounding the phone against the dash till there was nothing left. He was breathing hard. His eyes felt like they were about to crystallize. And then, as if it were foreordained, as if it were what he'd come to do all along, he cracked the door of the car, eased out into the night, and started through the trees for the house.

He told himself he was only reconnoitering, only trying to gauge the extent of the damage, to see if they were there yet. Moving deliberately, one slow step at a time, he felt his way through the patch of woods that separated his property from the near neighbor's and emerged from the trees in a hurricane of mosquitoes, angling silently along the edge of the lower lawn, the lawn he'd mowed himself, his Vans wet with the dew, his eyes fixed on the looming vacancy of the house. There were no lights, everything quiet, brooding, ordinary, and in the dark, with the moon draped over the roof, he could see the cool green glow of the LED display on the alarm panel in the kitchen. For a long while he just crouched there in the shadows, thinking how he could slip in through the window in the basement without activating the alarm and get the notebook with the names and anything else he could find that might be incriminating, credit card bills, Dana Halter, Bridger Martin, but if they were watching he wouldn't have a chance, what with the moon and the pale outline of his suit—if he'd thought ahead he could have gone to Kmart and bought himself a black sweatsuit, with a hood, but he hadn't thought ahead. That was the problem. That was what had got him here in the first place.

He was just about to step out onto the lawn when the faintest noise cracked open the night, a mechanical wheeze feeling its way along the dense compacted air from the direction of the driveway out front to fan across the individual blades of the grass and find surcease in the baffle of the woods at the edge of the lawn. To his ears, fanatically attuned, it sounded like the stealthiest all-but-silent easing open of a car door, the hand at the latch, dome light switched off, nothing but the unlubricated protest of the hinges to betray it. *Jesus! What was he doing?* He sank back into the shadows. On hands and knees, aware of every stick and fallen branch that might betray him, he crept along the inside verge of the lawn, heart thundering in his ears, determined now to see for himself—because it could have been Natalia, in his fantasy anyway, Natalia unwilling to leave without him, and waiting there for him so they could pack up the essentials in the dark and make for the next town before the pigs showed up in the morning with their search warrant.

Another sound. So distant and muted he couldn't be sure he was hearing it. He froze. Strained his eyes to see across the moon-dappled lawn and into the dark clot of shadow that was the driveway, the shape there, a deeper shadow, denser, the blackest hole of the universe. What was it—a car? A car pulled up under the trees where nobody could see it? And then that sound again, faint but distinct, the further protest of pea stone compacted underfoot, one stealthy sole down and then the next, and the flaring itch of a zipper worked and finally the sound of water hitting the gravel in a fine directed stream. That told him all he wanted to know. That hardened him. The alcohol burned through his system and evaporated as if it had never been there, replaced in that instant by the adrenal discharge that fueled him to fight, kill, run, and there was no creature of the night, no opossum or coon or copperhead snake, that faded as silently away.

When he reached the car, he slipped into the driver's side without a sound, turned over the engine and made his way up the neighbor's drive to the highway. He waited there a moment with his lights off till he saw the headlights of a single car approaching, and then he flicked on his lights and eased out onto the road in its wake, heading south.

What he dreamed that night, if he dreamed at all, he couldn't remember. There was a void, and he arose out of it to the sharp sudden stab of a column of sunlight that had worked its way up the rear panel of the car, through the back window and onto his face. For a moment, he didn't know where he was, and then it all locked in, the gray carpet and leather seats, the still life of the dash and the arc of the steering wheel, an intense, almost painfully articulated world of sharp-edged leaves pressed against the rolled-up windows. He was sprawled out in the back of a rental car—an SUV, gas hog, four-wheel drive—his throat dry, bladder full, a six-hundred-dollar Italian silk suit filthy in the knees and elbows and clinging damply to him as if it were made of Saran Wrap. There was a bad taste in his mouth. He had no toothbrush, no clothes, no house or fiancée or daughter. For a long while he just lay there, the sun on his face, considering his options, but then he heard voices, a dog barking, and sat up.

Outside the window, on the near side of the car, was vegetation, dense and Amazonian, and on the far side, just beyond a little white house set in the exact center of a square of lawn, was the river, right there, not a hundred feet away, driving down against the tide. The sun gave a shout. A bird shot past the window, folded its wings and plunged into the green. There were two people, a couple, the man in a sun-bleached shirt and the woman in an ankle-length hippie dress with bare shoulders, walking a black Lab down the dirt road and lifting their eyes periodically to throw a shy curious look at the car and then dropping them again to pat the dog and fling something over the charging wedge of its head and four scrambling paws—a stick, sailing out and coming back to them again in the wet grip of the animal's jaws.

He hadn't gone back to Beacon to hide himself along the back roads and he hadn't gone into Peterskill either, to cruise past his mother's house and snatch a quick glimpse of the place, just to see what it looked like, to see if the lights were on, to hope against reason that the sight of it would turn a key in the tumbler inside his head and let him know what was coming next. He hadn't done any of that, because when he left that driveway in the dark the full weight of the day suddenly hit him, a crushing glacial forbidding weight he couldn't begin to lift, and he'd gone no more than three or four miles and found himself winding through a dark turning that took him across the railroad tracks with a slow grinding bump and down this one-lane dirt road laid flat against the river and then on up the shoulder of it and into the bushes. Which was where he was now, dry-mouthed, needing to piss, watching these people and their dog watching him.

It took him a moment to come to his senses—he didn't need them calling the police on him, *Officer, I don't know, there's a drunk or something in a dirty suit crashed in his car out front of the house*—and then he was in the driver's seat and wheeling the SUV across the road in a broad pitching humping U-turn that took a bite out of the lawn and the people looked up at him out of unsmiling faces and he didn't wave. There was fast food in Peterskill, crap in a bag and crap in a waxed cup with a plastic top and flexible straw. He pulled into the drive-up lane because he really didn't want to show himself in public if he didn't have to, and he ate mechanically, without tasting it. Afterward he drove around without purpose, just to feel the wheels roll under him, and he worked his way to the outskirts of town and ducked into the bushes along Croton Reservoir to release the pressure on his bladder and move his bowels. Squatting there in the woods, with the mosquitoes at him, and using the paper napkins from the fast-food place in lieu of toilet paper, he couldn't stop punishing himself. The shit smell rose to his nostrils. There were burrs or seedpods flung like drift across both sleeves of his jacket. Mud on his shoes. The crystal of his watch was cracked. What was wrong with him? What had he come to? He gave himself a quick once-over in the rearview—the reddened ear, the thin crust of the scab, the black stubble coming in so that he looked like a cartoon bum—and before he could think the car was moving and he had the cell phone out, dialing information for Peterskill Hospital.

The road was narrow here, climbing now, and he was so focused on the phone he nearly ran a little Japanese car into the bushes, but then he had the number and for an extra charge they connected him and he was talking to the receptionist.

"Peterskill Hospital. How may I assist you?"

"You have visiting hours today?"

"All day till nine p.m., for all patients except intensive care."

"And can you tell me if someone's been admitted—if he's there. Or still there, I mean?"

"One moment, please." A pause, the sound of keys tapping. "And what was the name?"

"Martin," he said. "Bridger Martin."

He picked up a newspaper on the way and a cheap bouquet of flowers, the stems wrapped in tinfoil under a cone of plastic, just in case anybody should wonder what he was doing there parked in the lot amongst the sunstruck chassis and glinting windshields of a hundred other vehicles. It was hot, eternally hot. The radio gave him nothing, classical, talk, a garble of Sunday devotion, hallelujah and amen. Very slowly, with infinite patience, he read through the paper, section by section, keeping one eye cocked on the front entrance. And when he saw her there, finally, at half past two in the afternoon, her features working and her hands jumping in the face of the woman beside her as she came out the double doors and into the sun, it was no less than he'd expected. And when she ducked into a rust-streaked yellow Volvo with New York plates, the other woman at the wheel, there was nothing he could do but crank up his rented SUV, with all its ominous high-riding authority, and follow her out of the lot.

Four

SHE STOOD AT THE DOOR of Terri's car, the smell of the
exhaust running at her in the humid breeze that had come
up suddenly to agitate the branches of the trees and lift a
scrap of paper from the gutter and fling it down the street.
There was rain coming, yet more rain, one of the late-
afternoon thundershowers that blew up this time of year to
douse the streets for half an hour before the sheen of water
evaporated and the air grew dense and hot all over again.
"Thanks again, thanks for everything," she was saying for
the second or third time, leaning into the window frame as
Terri, her hair bound up in a black scrunchie to keep the
weight of it off her shoulders, said it was her pleasure and
that she hoped they'd keep in touch.

"Oh, definitely," Dana said. "I've got your phone and
e-mail, and you've got my cell—we want to have you down
for the day. I'll treat you to dinner. We can go shopping or
something."

"Or something?" Terri said, showing her teeth in a smile
that radiated up to her eyes and pulled the skin tight along
her cheekbones. This was a genuine smile, real and sponta-
neous, not like the pained contortion of the lips most
people gave her. And the term came to her then out of her
storehouse of odd bits of vocabulary—this was what phys-
iologists called a Duchenne smile, in which two different

facial muscles fired simultaneously, a smile that couldn't be faked.

Dana glanced up the street and back again. She was smiling too, feeling good, feeling liberated, the whole thing over now, out of her hands. "Shopping," she said. "Definitely shopping."

Okay then, Terri signed.

Yeah, okay.

She was turning away to cross the street to her own car, when she felt a tug at the back of her T-shirt and turned round again. "Here," Terri was saying, and she was holding something out to her—a scrunchie, lime green, with crimson polka dots. "So you can put your hair up for the ride home," pointing to the side of her own head in illustration. "For the heat."

"Are you trying to tell me something?" Dana said, and she felt so good suddenly she was clowning, making a show of raising her arms to sniff at the armpits of her T-shirt and then dropping them to smooth out the fabric as if she were trying on an evening gown. "I'm not reeking that much, am I?"

Terri laughed—the flash of her teeth, her head rocking and chin dipping, and here came the breeze again, an ice cream wrapper spinning out from under the car and cartwheeling down the street. "Not yet," she said, "but you're pushing it."

And then she was waving goodbye and working her hands through the thick mass of her hair to pin it back in a ponytail, the sweat cooling already on her neck and around the collar of her shirt. She stood there a moment, watching Terri's car—the hand-me-down Volvo she'd got from her parents after her teenage brother had put it through some rough use—as it moved off down the street, shedding light.

Then she looked both ways, crossed the street to her car, unlocked the door and slid into the driver's seat.

The station was no more than five minutes away, and though she got turned around and went down the wrong street—a dead end—she still got there with fifteen minutes to spare. As she pulled into the parking lot, the sun dimmed suddenly and she glanced up through the bug-flecked skin of the windshield to see a torn patch of cloud trailing past; beyond it, across the river, the thunderheads rose up out of the mountains in a dark unbroken band. There were flashes of lightning—no streaks or tendrils, just random swellings of light as if there were a bombardment going on in the next county over. The air through the open window smelled fecund and rich, as if it had been pumped up out of a deep well. Or a cavern. "Through caverns measureless to man / Down to a sunless sea," she chanted to herself, just to feel the words on her tongue, the small solace of the beat. Then she eased into a parking spot, shut down the car and began to sift through her purse for change for the meter.

She didn't know what she was going to do with her mother. She'd thought of treating her to lunch at the café at the depot, sitting outside under one of the umbrellas, off in a corner by themselves with the view and two glasses of chilled white wine and a grilled ahi sandwich or a salad, something to pick at—but the storm would ruin that. Her mother was going to want to go see Bridger before they drove back down to the city, but there was some part of her—a large and growing part—that resisted the notion. She didn't want to go back there. Not yet. She really didn't think she could take it, the whole symphony of her guilt building to a crescendo all over again, the look on the face of Bridger's mother, the smells, the nurses, the man with the feet, Bridger. Bridger lying there in his plaster and gauze, settling into his bruises, *having trouble breathing,* and who'd given him the trouble?

For a moment the picture of the two mothers squaring off rose up before her, but almost as soon as it came to her, she changed the channel. She wasn't ready for that. She wanted to be selfish now, purely selfish. She wanted to hook her arm through her mother's the minute she stepped off the train, lead her to the car and drive directly back to the city, the trees dwindling behind her and the road narrowing in the rearview mirror. She wanted to be in the cluttered room with the door shut behind her, her hair washed and wrapped up in a towel, the air conditioner breathing its mechanical breath as she settled into a corner of the bed and pulled the shades and let this new feeling bloom inside of her, the feeling of release, of letting go absolutely and completely and without regret, as if she were standing on the ledge outside the window on the nineteenth floor and letting go of every hand held out to her till she just floated up and away or dropped hurtling into the vacuum.

She got out of her car. Shut the door, clicked the remote to lock it. She was thinking she might walk a bit, stroll along the platform as far as it would take her in either direction and feel the wind on her face. There weren't many people around, Sunday afternoon, midsummer, the deep charcoal bank of clouds crowding closer and the boats on the river changing color as the light failed overhead. She walked past the café, the ticket office and waiting room, mounting the steps to the platform, and only then did she feel the seismic shift through the soles of her feet, the furious contained irruption of power, and there it was, her mother's train, pounding into the station five minutes early.

· · · · ·

Looking back on it, what remained most vivid in her mind wasn't the way the storm broke almost at the instant the train lurched to a stop, as if the weather were adhering to a timetable too, or how many people appeared out of nowhere with their tennis rackets and backpacks and fishing rods to swarm the platform, but the expression on her mother's face. At first, what with the sudden press of people, Dana didn't see her there in the crowd and wondered if she'd got the right train. The initial random drops of rain had surprised her, spattering her shoulders and running two cold fingers along the base of her neck where she'd put her hair up, and she'd moved in under the long narrow metal canopy that ran the length of the platform and everyone else moved in too. Then she felt the air concuss and glanced up to see the water falling in metallic sheets from both sides of the canopy. She felt something else too, a sudden chill, the sixth sense of the deaf, and she was about to turn around, to look over her shoulder and confront whatever it was, real or imaginary, when she spotted her mother. There she was, squeezing between two men with suitcases, coming toward her, overdressed in slacks and heels and a turquoise blouse cinched at the waist with a trailing scarf. And she had that expression on her face.

Her mother wasn't there to comfort her, not with that face, or at least not until she'd let her disapproval and disappointment and heartbreak be felt and acknowledged, because here was her daughter, her highly educated deaf daughter whom she'd taught to be responsible and independent, in trouble again, her clothes dirty, her knees bandaged like a child's and her fiancé—if he still was her fiancé—in the hospital. Beaten up—or no, beaten down—because of her. Because she wouldn't listen. That was the expression on her mother's face, that was what she saw in that sliver of a moment as her mother compacted her shoulders to move between the two men jockeying for position with their suitcases and the rain fell in sheets and the earth gave off its immemorial saturate smell. But then it all changed—her mother's mouth dropped open and her eyes leapt out at her—and Dana was hit from behind, hard, a shoulder digging into hers as if someone had stumbled into her, and she caught her balance and swung round and there he was.

For an instant, the rain sheeting down, her mother on the periphery, everyone on the platform arrested in midstride, she stared into his face, so close she could smell the raw ammoniac charge of his breath and the sweat bleeding through a lingering taint of aftershave. He was right there, right in her face, and there was nowhere to run now. A tremor coursed through her. She tried to swallow but couldn't. She saw the thin whip of the slash on his cheek, the unshaved stubble, the thrust of his chin and the two strips of muscle wadded in his clenched jaws. He didn't say a word. Didn't move. Just breathed his ammoniac breath and let his eyes burn into her.

He didn't know what he was doing, he really didn't. It was as if he'd been disconnected, as if someone had pulled the plug on him and the laptop of his brain was running on auxiliary power, the battery getting weaker and the connections ever harder to make. He hadn't been to prison, hadn't lived underground for the past three years, hadn't been tutored by Sandman or developed his street smarts or learned anything at all. She moved, he moved: that was all he knew. And when the yellow Volvo turned right out of the hospital lot and rolled down Route 202 into the heart of town and bore left on Division and headed for his mother's house, he followed.

They were two blocks away when the Volvo, without signaling, suddenly nosed in at the curb up ahead. He saw the black Jetta then, parked across the street in a line of cars, and he let the forward momentum of the SUV carry him on past to the corner and then back around the block. "No hurry," he told himself, and he realized he was talking aloud—and how pathetic was that? But he repeated himself, as if his voice were coming from the radio, as if everything he was thinking was being broadcast to the world and people were crowding into rooms and standing in doorways to hear him, "No hurry at all." When he came down the street a minute later she was standing there on the pavement, leaning into the driver's side window, her T-shirt hiked up in back so that he could see the smooth run of her lower back and the flare of her hips, and he flicked his signal and slid in behind a panel truck. He was blocking somebody's driveway, but that wouldn't matter because any minute now she was going to get in that Jetta—alone—and everything would fall into place. He backed up five feet and eased out just enough to be able to see round the truck. He left the car running, in gear.

They were talking, the two of them, back and forth, and now she was using her hands, parting words, goodbye, and he saw the other woman tug at her shirt and pull her back to slip her something. What was it: drugs? A cigarette? Some deaf thing? Maybe it was a hearing aid, maybe that was it. But no, she was putting her hair up in one of those flexible bands, snaring the mass of it in both hands and flicking back her head the way Natalia did, the way Natalia used to, the characteristic gesture, the dip and fall. And then another goodbye and she crossed the street and got into her car as the other woman pulled away. What he'd thought was that she'd be trapped there, that it would be nothing to pull up beside her and block her in and do what he had to do, but he didn't move. She was studying herself in the mirror, both her arms V-ed above her head, doing something with her hair, smoothing and adjusting it beneath the tight clench of the band, and he watched, transfixed, thinking of Natalia, of Gina, her slim pale arms moving in unison as the car gently rocked and she dug out her lipstick and her eyeliner and made herself up as if she were going out on a date. Which, in a way, she was.

That was a hard thought. And she was a bitch, never forget that. But there was something in the way she exposed herself so unconsciously—the way all women did—looking for beauty in a compact or a tube of lipstick, needing it, needing to be beautiful and admired for it and reaching always for grace, that hit him with the force of revelation and he let the car idle beneath him till she put the Jetta in gear and pulled out into the street and he had to duck down out of her line of sight as she wheeled past with her shining eyes and the drawn bow of her composed and glistening mouth. When she got to the end of the block, he swung a U-turn and followed in her wake.

It wasn't hard to catch up to her. She drove like somebody twice her age, utterly oblivious, crowding the middle of the street one minute and weaving toward the curb the next. Riding the brake. Going too fast round the curves and too slow on the straightaways. He put the sun visor down and kept four or five car lengths between them—he wouldn't want her to recognize him, not yet—but he could have been right on her bumper and she wouldn't have known the difference. She never glanced in the rearview, not once, except to adjust her makeup and watch herself compress her lips and run the tip of a finger along the fringe of her eyelashes. But where was she going? Back to the hospital?

The light was red up ahead and she drifted to a stop and flicked on her left-turn signal. He slowed, then pulled over to let the car behind him pass, and all the while he could feel that wire dangling loose inside him, that slow fade to nothing. The second car nosed in behind her at the light, father, mother, three kids in the back, the mother's hair wet and hanging thin as tinsel round her collar. There was a rumble of thunder. The sky closed in. Both his hands were on the wheel, but he couldn't feel a thing. When the light changed, he let the car carry him back out into traffic and he hit the left-turn signal and followed her down the hill toward the train station, wondering if that was where she was going and if it was, where he could trap her.

He was trying to visualize the place—café, depot, northbound platform and the overhead walkway to the southbound tracks, rails and crossties stapling the ground, the river, everything out in the open—when suddenly she veered left again, no signal, just a jerk of the wheel, and he had no choice but to keep going straight. Had she seen him, was that it? The thought made his blood surge and he was jerking at the wheel himself, cursing, the big hurtling front end of the SUV thumping so violently into the first driveway he spotted it nearly left the ground and for the briefest fraction of a moment he was staring into the eyes of a numb-faced little kid on a tricycle who was that close to being meat and then he was lurching back, jamming the thing into gear and whipping round the corner, down the street she'd taken.

It was a dead end. And that was perfect, or would have been, except that there were kids everywhere, shouting in Spanish and chasing a ball that ran from one foot to another so fast you couldn't follow it, and there she was, coming toward him, her eyes locked straight ahead, signaling left, left again. He could have run into her, could have slammed the SUV into the grille of that tinny little shitbox of a car and put an end to it right there, but he didn't, he couldn't, all the power leaching out of him and the world shifting in front of his eyes till he didn't know where he was or what he was doing or why. *Da-na,* that was what Natalia called him, and he heard her voice echoing in his ears, *Da-na, Da-na.* He cursed aloud and the curse brought him back. And as soon as the Jetta was past him he spun the wheel and veered for the opposite curb, abbreviating the soccer game even as the ball thumped against the back fender and skittered across the street as if all the air had gone out of it. "Hey, motherfucker!" some kid shouted. *"Pendejo!"* and he didn't give a shit if he ran them all down, every one of them and they had eyes, didn't they? And ears? He hit the horn. Wrestled the wheel. Up on the curb, back across the street—*"Puta! Puta!"*—and she was at the end of the block now, swinging out onto the main road and heading down the hill, for the station.

He watched her park. Watched her make a final appraisal of herself in the mirror and then slide out of the car and lift her face to gaze up at the sky and the bunched bruised clouds squeezing down the light. Very slowly, as if he weren't driving at all but floating up off the ground on some untappable current, he drove past her and swung into a parking spot two cars down and just sat there a moment, watching her shoulders and the way her hips rotated over the tight unhurried muscles of her legs and buttocks as she walked toward the station. She didn't have a clue. The bitch. The bitch didn't have a clue and he did, he had the whole puzzle worked out, the final piece in place, and he shut down the ignition and left the car where it was. He didn't bother to lock it. Didn't bother with the keys. And the meter—the meter was a joke.

The air seemed to boil around him suddenly, the heat exploding in his face, and then the breeze and the deadfall of the thunder and here was the train, punishing steel and crowding the scene, and when the rain hit he didn't try to duck it or quicken his pace, because he was focused now—focused on her, on her back and shoulders and the flash of color caught in her hair—and he was walking. With purpose. Up the steps and onto the platform, his face wet, his hair wet, the structure gone out of his jacket with the sudden assault of the rain, and he crowded in with the others, smelling the ferment of their bodies, colliding, shifting, touching. The thunder rolled out and shook the platform. Lightning broke the sky.

That was when he hit her. That was when he lowered his shoulder and struck her from behind, not hard enough to knock her down, not hard enough to do anything other than communicate the one inescapable truth that tore her face out of the crowd and gave it to him as if he were its maker and shaper. He had her. She was in his power. The two of them were face to face, occupying the same square foot of the universe, united, wedded, and he was the one, the only one, who could break the connection.

There was movement behind her, some woman crying out. Another peal of thunder. He watched her eyes, watched her lips, heard the flat toneless echo of her voice, no fear in her, not anymore. "What do you want?"

Everything beat down to that instant, to that question, to her lips moving and the scent of her breath, the heat of it in his face, the actual and the real: *What do you want?* The question took him by surprise. It froze him. Stopped him dead. Because he hadn't really thought beyond the moment and it was weakness and weakness only that had brought him here. He saw that now. Saw it clearly, as truth, the new truth of his life. And he saw that she wasn't afraid and that none of this mattered, not anymore. *Da-na,* Natalia had called him. He thought of Mill Valley, the condo there, the house in Garrison, the face of his daughter stranded on the porch. *Da-na. Da-na. Da-na.* People were jostling, staring at him, at the two of them, and he had the smallest fraction of a second to contemplate the question before the answer came to his lips, and the answer didn't involve her at all—it had nothing to do with her, but with him, Peck Wilson, a jerk, a clown, an imposter in a torn silk suit, worth nothing, worth less than nothing.

He shook his head. Dropped his eyes. "Nothing," he said, and he didn't know whether she could read that or not and he didn't care. Then he was moving, squaring his shoulders and tugging at the wet lapels of his jacket, pushing through the crowd, striding across the platform and up onto the train. He didn't bother to look back.

EPILOGUE

It was late, past nine by now, but Bridger wasn't going anywhere. He wasn't even hungry, though somewhere in the back of his mind the icon of the Campbell's Chunky Soup can glowed like the figure in a shrine. *Soup that eats like a meal* was the promo line the company had come up with, and he and Deet-Deet had bounced that one around, creating a digital can with stick limbs surmounted by Radko's squared-off head and glowering face—*The producer that eats like a special effect*—and how does a meal eat, anyway? Does it use utensils? Is it autophagic? Does it have a mouth? He was working late because he didn't have a whole lot else to do and he wanted to get on Radko's good side and stay there since Radko, against his better judgment, had brought him back on board. The young woman—girl—who'd replaced him hadn't worked out. Her name was Kate and she was just a tad bit self-obsessed, or so it went in Deet-Deet's recounting, coming in one Monday with a breast augmentation that took her from borderline flat to Graf Zeppelin overnight. She was a prima donna—or a diva, as she liked to call herself—but around Digital Dynasty she was known as Phisher because she was always phishing for compliments. At any rate, she was gone, and he was back. And he planned to keep his head down and make the most of it.

The only light in the long sweep of the burnished concrete room descended from the EMERGENCY EXIT sign

Radko had put up over the back door to mollify the building inspector when he put in the carrels and computer hookups and transformed what had been San Roque's last machine shop into a special effects studio. It was all right with Bridger. He had his iPod to keep him entertained and the soup was on the shelf by the coffeepot, awaiting the microwave. In the meanwhile, the screen gave him its solace, the solace of the proportionate world, edited, reduced, with the colors enhanced and the blemishes removed. At the moment he was working on a picture to be released for the Thanksgiving weekend, a remake of *The Wild One* starring The Kade in the Marlon Brando role and Lara Sikorsky as the sheriff's daughter, though the role of the daughter had been expanded and modified to reflect the post-feminist realities of the twenty-first century—she was now a motorcycle enthusiast herself, and there were any number of spectacular jumps and mid-air pas de deux that featured Lara and The Kade thumbing their noses at the clueless townsfolk and the smirking models and steroid freaks who'd been tricked up to represent the rival motorcyle club. It was all in good fun. Nothing more than a little reinvention of film history and an attempt to cash in on The Kade while the going was good. Bridger had no problem with that, no problem at all—he was just happy to be working again.

The cast had come off a week ago, but even with it on he'd been able to manipulate the mouse and run his programs pretty effectively—in fact, he'd got so used to propping the thing up on the edge of his desk he felt strange without it, as if his arm were levitating all on its own. There was no pain, though when he took a deep breath he could still feel a premonitory prickling in the place where the two ribs had sustained their hairline fractures, and his voice was huskier now. He hadn't noticed the change himself—you don't really listen to yourself unless you're singing, and he hadn't felt much like bursting into song lately—but when he'd first got back and called Deet-Deet to suss things out and then Radko to offer his services in the absence of the girl with the breast implants, neither of them had recognized his voice, and that told him something.

And his mother. Right from the outset his mother had wanted to know when and how and to what extent he would regain his voice, demanding facts, statistics, terminology, chasing nurses down the hallway and dialing every specialist in the phone book, starting with Ahmad and running down to Zierkofski. She'd swept into the hospital in a cyclone of flowers, putting on her adversarial face and grilling the doctor who'd operated on him (a soft-spoken Taiwanese woman with peeled-back eyes who looked as if she were awaiting the gun at the start of the hundred-meter dash) till the doctor had thrown up her hands and said, *Look, maybe what you need is an outside specialist,* and his mother had tightened her voice till it was like strung wire and said, *That's exactly what we need.* He hadn't known what to do. He was unfocused and tentative, adrift on a sea of medication. He was having trouble swallowing and it felt as if there were something stuck in his throat, some balled-up wad of cardboard that kept him on the verge of gagging all the time, and that concerned him. It scared him. It made him susceptible to his mother and her reductive fears in a way that brought him back to his childhood—she was his mother, and she was there for him, and he was glad of it—and when she told him she'd made an appointment for Thursday back in San Diego with the best otolaryngologist in Southern California, all he could do was nod. It wasn't his fault. He wasn't thinking beyond the moment. And he wasn't—forgive him, because he was the one who'd been hurt here, he was the one in the hospital—thinking of Dana.

She'd driven back down to New York, that was all he knew, and he messaged her on his cell that night, the second night in the hospital, but he couldn't find a way to say what he wanted to say, not without seeing her face to face.

Hi.

How you feeling?

Okay. Can't swallow too well.

What did the doctor say?

Not much.

When do you get out?

Tomorrow.

What time?

You don't need to come.

I do. I want to.

My mother's here.

So?

They released him the next morning, early, and he called from the train to tell her he was on his way, hoping to catch her before she left the apartment. It was awkward—the cast was on his forearm but they wanted him to wear a sling for the first two weeks, just to keep it stationary—yet he was already adapting, flashing on the summer he'd spent under the hoop out back of the house when he was in high school and trying, with mixed results, to train himself to take the three-point shot from either side. His mother sat beside him with the newspaper and a cardboard cup of coffee, making one-way conversation—his father was going to be happy to see him, and the dog too, and he was welcome to stay as long as he liked because nobody had been in the guest room since Junie and Al had been there in the spring and did he know they'd sold their business and had all the figures worked out for early retirement? Could he believe that? Junie and Al retired? As he listened to the phone ring he couldn't help picturing Dana in motion, sliding out of the cab at Grand Central with the light exploding round her and the pigeons blasting up off the sidewalk in living color or tapping her foot and doing the crossword as the northbound train hurtled past them at Tarrytown or Dobbs Ferry or some such place, the numb staring faces passing in instant review and hers shuffled in with all the rest. There was no answer. His mother, in high spirits, leaned in to read him choice bits from the newspaper and she sipped her coffee and worked one shoe off and on again with the toe of the other, and when he needed to respond, when she put a question to him—"So what's she like, Dana? Are you two serious? It must be, I don't know, *difficult* to communicate?"—he wrote out the reply in an awkward scrawl on one of the paper towels from the restroom (*Awesome; Yes; Not too bad*).

Then they were in the cab, the streets crushed by the weight of the light, monuments of light cut and formed and shaped by the buildings, everything held in stasis till the cab turned one corner and then the next and the weight came down all over again and he couldn't swallow and he had to have the driver pull over so he could scramble out and get a bright red super-sized container full to the plastic brim with Coke and ice and the straw to deliver it sip by soothing sip. And then they were at the apartment and the doorman was phoning up and he watched his mother's face as the elevator rose toward the meeting of the mothers, his mother and hers, and what that meant or could mean. Vera was waiting for them at the door. She'd combed her hair and put on lipstick. "You poor thing," she said, or something to that effect, and stepped forward to embrace him before he had a chance to introduce his mother, which he did a moment later with a shrug of the shoulders and a broad grimacing gesture that made the side of his face—the side that had hit the pavement—ache all over again.

He could see that his mother was tense, her smile automatic and her eyes panning away from Dana's mother to the open door and the dim interior beyond. She didn't know what to expect—she'd had no experience of the deaf and this was uncharted territory—but to her credit she held out her hand and Vera took it and then they were emerging from the hall into the living room in a scatter of small talk. "Would you like something to drink?" Vera wanted to know and he saw that she'd made an effort to push back the clutter so that the couch and easy chair presented their surfaces unencumbered and a good square foot of the coffee table was ready to receive the drinks and the blue can of Planters nuts. He watched his mother take it all in and he wanted to smooth things over, to make the off-hand comment that would put them at ease, but all he could do was hold out the Coke container and rattle the ice in response. His mother, looking doubtfully at the easy chair, momentarily lost her smile. "Water," she said. "Thank you."

Just as Dana's mother was about to turn away, thankful to have this little ritual of welcoming and graciousness to occupy her, he jerked his left arm into her line of vision, a sudden spastic gesture that must have made it seem as if he were fighting for balance, but it had the desired effect: he caught her attention. There was a suspended moment, both women staring at him, and then he signed, as best he could under the conditions, *Where is Dana?*

Vera looked to his mother and then turned back to him. "Sleeping," she said. "I let her sleep in. I mean, after all she's been through—yesterday, yesterday especially." She paused to draw in her breath. "Yesterday was a nightmare."

Yesterday?

"At the station. When he—I was scared to death. Literally scared to death." She saw his face then and caught herself. "You mean you don't know? Didn't she tell you?"

He could feel his heart going. The side of his face throbbed. The walls were closing in on him, the floor giving way, special effects, very special effects. *Tell me what?*

She started to say something—the words were right there on her lips—but she stopped herself. She was wearing a print dress in some shiny fabric, something she'd put on to impress his mother, and she was barefooted. He watched her shift her weight to her back foot as her toes flexed and rose on point for balance, and then she pushed a hand through her hair and gave him a sidelong look, a gesture he knew well, a Dana gesture. "Come on," she said, and she held out her hand even as a look passed between her and his mother, "maybe you ought to talk to her yourself."

They paused at the door to the guest bedroom, the light dim, books and newspapers stacked up against the walls, a chair there, strewn with dresses and undergarments, and then, all in one motion, Vera shoved the door open and jerked it shut again. She gave him a soft smile. "That's our knock at the door," she murmured, already turning away. "You can go in now. I'll sit with your mother—we have a lot to talk about."

As it turned out, Dana wasn't asleep. She was sitting at the desk she'd shoved up against the window, working on her laptop. Her face was turned to him as he stepped into the room, her hair shoved up away from her forehead and the faint white crescent of the scar that had bloomed there where she'd hit the windshield. She was dressed in T-shirt and panties, one bare leg folded under her, a Diet Coke at her elbow. "Hi," she mouthed, and she smiled, but didn't get up.

He crossed the room to her and leaned over to press his

lips to hers, instant communication, then took two steps back and eased himself down on the bed.

She was still smiling, though she was examining him as if she hadn't seen him in a week. "You look"—she paused—"better. Much better. How do you feel?"

There was something wrong here, something he didn't like. He needed more than this—he needed elaboration, needed acknowledgment. He was hors de combat, her soldier, her man. He just shrugged. Looked away. Almost without thinking, his hands said: *What happened yesterday?*

"I should have told you, but I didn't want to upset you. You were sleeping. That's what they said at the hospital—you were sleeping."

He just looked at her.

"He was there. At the train station. Peck Wilson."

His hands were like bricks. *What do you mean? How? Did they catch him?*

"He was just there—he must have followed me. He didn't do anything. He just . . . bumped me, that's all."

He wanted to repeat that, make a question of it, but he didn't know the verb. The muscles fired in his face. *What?*

"They didn't catch him," she said. "He just bumped me, to show he could do it, I guess—he could do anything—and then he just walked away and got on the train." She brought her leg out from under her and set both feet on the floor and leaned forward, her hair falling loose round her shoulders. "I don't know, it was strange, very strange, but I think he was saying it's over, like as if he was calling a truce."

Calling a truce? He couldn't believe what he was hearing. In a fury he pushed himself up from the bed and went to the desk, to the lined yellow pad there and the ballpoint—what was she doing, taking notes?—and started writing. Poorly. With his left hand. *You mean you didn't call the cops?*

She shook her head.

Or your mother? On the cell? They could have been at the next station—we could have nailed him.

She was still shaking her head, but more emphatically now. Her mouth was set, her eyes locked on his. "No," she said, "it's over. Let him go. It's not worth it. I mean, look at you. Just look at you."

The logic eluded him. He tried to pull the threads of it together, tried to see the beating he'd taken, down there on the sidewalk choking for air while Peck Wilson cracked his ribs and ground his face into the cement, as a link to the phrase she'd used: Not worth it to whom? Who was being sacrificed here? It all came up in him then and he slammed his fist down on the desk, even as he tried to gasp out the words that wouldn't come and she wouldn't have heard anyway, the hurtful words, the curses and recriminations.

"I don't want to talk about it," she said, and she snatched the pad away from him.

Clumsily, spelling it out, left hand only: *You never want to talk.*

She dropped her eyes to shut him out, and then, as if they'd been discussing the price of gasoline or where they were going for dinner or a movie neither of them wanted to see, she said, "But I do. I want to talk because I've got some good news, really good news—"

And as she told him, as he listened to her untethered voice ride the currents of her emotion, now cored-out and hollow, now muffled as if she were speaking through a gag, it became clear that the news was good for one of them only, for her. She'd e-mailed her former mentor at Gallaudet, Dr. Hauser—he remembered him, didn't he? The one who'd first introduced her to the Romantic poets and served as chair of her Ph.D. committee?—just to touch base and let him know what had happened at the San Roque School, and he'd e-mailed back to say that he might have something for her, two core classes in freshman writing—if she was interested, that is.

"So what I'm saying is maybe we should drive down to Washington, just to see?" She gave an elaborate shrug, and her face, the face that always told him so much, transformative, articulate, sad and beautiful and wrenchingly alive, told him nothing now. "I mean," she said, "we've come this far, anyway—"

Someone nailed a wall up in front of him. Bang, bang, bang, the hammer blows echoed in his head. And what was this wall made of? It wasn't stone, it wasn't brick—some temporary material, plywood, fiberboard, something you could construct and tear down in a day. The left hand, the awkward one, spoke for him, the index finger to the breast, then the jump, up and down: *I can't.*

It was past ten by the time he got up from the desk to shuffle back to the kitchenette by the soda machine, lift down the can of soup and peel back the easy-opening top to expose the contents. He licked the glutinous saffron-colored paste from the inside of the curled recyclable top before dropping it in the wastebasket, then upended the can over the coffee mug with *Sharper* stenciled along the rim, gave it a tap to facilitate the action of gravity and then shoved the mug in the microwave. It was quiet, preternaturally quiet, the long bare room held in equipoise between the absence of sound and the sudden startling mechanical beep of the microwave and the muted roar that succeeded it, cuisine in the making. And how would he have described the sound to someone who had never heard it? Like holding a seashell to your ear. For three minutes and thirty seconds. White noise. Static. And then there was the culminating beep, sharp as a gunshot.

He was back at his desk, working on a double head replacement—The Kade and Lara Sikorsky, suspended in mid-air on their motorcycles against a vibrant enhanced sky, a perfect crossing pattern, his face and hers, aloft—and spooning up soup when he heard the sound of a key in the lock at the front door. Radko, he was thinking, coming to check up, and he was thinking too that he wouldn't have heard him at all if he hadn't removed his earphones when he went up to fix the soup. Not that it mattered. He was hard at work, totally focused, and even if the boss had crept up on him he would have seen that. But now Radko was there, dropping his shoulders as he leaned back into the door and blinking as he came down the hall and peered into Bridger's cubicle.

"What, you are here?" he said, his face going through its permutations, running from surprise to suspicion—was Bridger in fact working or screwing around on company time?—to a kind of muted pleasure in the dawning awareness of his errant employee's dedication.

"Yeah," Bridger heard himself saying, "I was thinking I'd put in some extra time tonight just to push that deadline a little," and in the silence of the room he became aware of the faint lingering rasp in his voice. "Deet-Deet was here till seven. And Plum stayed late too."

Radko was silent a moment, squinting into the screen where The Kade's digital features were superimposed over the white helmet of the stuntman and Lara Sikorsky remained an opaque blur. "All right," he said finally. "But no overtime, only regular hour. Yes? You know that."

"Yeah," Bridger said, and he didn't want to tell him he had nothing better to do, "yeah, I know."

At some point Radko took his material presence and retreated back down the hall, footsteps echoing, to reverse the sequence of events that had brought him there in the first place, and the studio fell into a silence that seemed even deeper than before. Bridger was so intent on the screen he forgot about his iPod and before long it was so quiet he could hear the faint click of the mouse, and the keys—the keys rattled like thunder over a miniature world. He finished the frame he was working on and brought up the next, the figures frozen in position, the white nullity of their faces, his and hers. But then, instead of bringing up The Kade's head, he clicked on his own and implanted it there on The Kade's shoulders, and it took him a moment before he came up with the right expression, a smile, rueful and yet playful too, with all the promise of joy and fulfillment. And then, and he knew he was going to do it before his fingers crept to the mouse, he brought up Dana's face. He gave her a smile too and he put her there, right next to him, ascendant, with all the blue sky in the universe crowding in behind her.